Off the Edge

Enjoy!

Shirley Heaton

Aphrodite Publications

Copyright © Shirley Heaton 2014

The right of Shirley Heaton to be identified as author of this work asserted by her in accordance with the Copyright, Designs and Patents Act 1988

All rights reserved

No reproduction, copy or transmission of this publication may be made without written permission. No paragraph of this publication may be reproduced, copied or transmitted save with the written permission of the author.

Any person who commits any unauthorised act in relation to this publication may be liable to criminal prosecution and civil claims damages

This is a work of fiction. All characters, organisations and events portrayed in this novel are either products of the author's imagination or are used fictitiously.

ISBN: 1515293270
ISBN-13: 9781515293279

Other Titles by Shirley Heaton

(Medical Romance Series)
Love Will Find A Way
A Prescription for Love
A Private Consultation
The Turning Tide

(Contemporary Romance)
Chance Encounter
A Lesson in Love
A Break with The Past
Oceans Apart
Relative Strangers

(War and Romance)
Futile Glory (Writing as S L Heaton)

**Coming Soon
(Historical Romance)**
Till the End of Time

To my daughter, Alison and my son, Philip who

are always there for me

Prologue

Port Jackson, New South Wales, Australia
1788

Emily tried to steady herself and keep her balance through the quagmire beneath her feet. The heat was stifling, the atmosphere humid as the officer pushed her again, this time with excessive force. She stumbled forward into the official marquee, lifting her head slightly and casting a furtive glance towards the person reclining on a paillasse. It was the governor; his eyes closed. The officer quickly changed his approach from abusive to obsequious.

'May I speak with you, sir?'

The governor stirred. 'What is it, man?' he muttered with an air of reluctance.

'I have arrested this felon on a charge of assault.' He gripped Emily's arm forcefully and dug his nails into the flesh. 'She has attacked and wounded a member of the *Penrhyn* crew. The man is now unconscious. She may have killed him.'

The governor failed to open his eyes. 'Do not trouble me,' he replied, appearing to have neither the patience nor the inclination to deal with matters of assault. 'You know my orders.' He flicked his hand in dismissal. 'Deal with the woman. Place her in irons. She will be flogged on the morrow.' He shook his head and sighed. 'You are aware of the punishment for murder if the man dies. Death by hanging,' he added, his final three words clipped.

Thrown into stunned despair, Emily shuddered, unable to believe what she was hearing. The words had an ominous ring. How could an act of self-defence warrant being placed in irons and flogged? Even worse, how could the governor suggest she be hanged when she was merely defending herself and her child against the evil Rafton?

The officer, his face glowing like a furnace after the governor's apparent lack of interest, reverted to his abusive approach, tugging hard at Emily's sleeve with one hand and fisting the other viciously into her back.

'Out!' he commanded, dragging her from the marquee. He gestured to the sentry on duty and called out to him. 'You, lad! Bring me chains and leg irons for this felon.'

Startled, the young marine private looked up before scuttling away. Within minutes he was back.

'Yon tree,' the officer growled, pointing. 'That is where we shall place her.'

The lad looked up, his face masked in horror, his eyes wide and disbelieving.

'Get a move on, lad! You heard what I said,' the officer bellowed before turning to Emily and prodding her in the chest. 'You will be lucky to be alive by the morrow. God will repay you for your sins.' He loosened his grip and deliberately thrust her to the ground, kicking her in the stomach whilst she was down. 'Get up, you whore,' he ordered.

Emily, now badly dazed, struggled to her feet. If this was punishment for being innocent, for acting in self-defence, how would she ever exist in this hostile place?

'But my child?' she begged. 'I must go to her.'

'You will be lucky to see the child again,' he sneered. 'You heard the governor's words. You will be hanged if the man dies.' He dragged Emily's hands behind her back, shackled her wrists and passed a chain through before securing it around a nearby eucalypt.

He turned to the sentry. 'Fetter the ankles, lad.' The sentry crouched down and did as he was ordered whilst the officer stood back and pointed to the ground.

'Watch out for spiders, big as your hand.' He gestured crudely, cupping his hands together to demonstrate the size. 'And poisonous snakes,' he added, guffawing raucously as he strode away. The young sentry frowned and followed.

Alone now, Emily was filled with the warning light of truth. A heavy pounding hammered in her chest, slowly at first but then it became more rapid. Whatever happened, she was fated. If Rafton died, she would be hanged. If he lived, he would seek her out and she would be forever on her guard.

The ground was damp and slimy beneath her feet and the tree trunk felt like a block of iron on her back. Maybe she could drag the chain down the trunk with her wrists and slither to the ground. But that would be foolish. If the officer's warning about the snakes and spiders were true, her chances of survival would diminish. At least with her feet on the ground she could kick and stamp if she were attacked.

Time passed slowly. Her head began to ache and she felt a heavy weariness take over. It was more than twelve hours since she had taken a rest.

But now she must be on her guard. She could not afford to slacken her vigil when she had no idea what might be lurking beneath her feet.

Contemplating her future, she closed her eyes. But that fleeting moment was lost when an almighty clap of thunder rumbled through the heavens. Seconds later, the sky lit up to a blinding glow followed by a searing flash. Nearby trees were ignited; flames leapt into the air, licking viciously at the branches, some of them only yards away.

Terror struck within her. Her senses were bombarded with a cacophony of sounds as the heavy rumbling was augmented by a shrill squealing. And then her nostrils were filled with the smell of burning animal flesh.

The heat began to penetrate.

If she remained there for much longer she would surely meet her death – ironically at the stake as would have been her punishment had she remained in England. But there was no way of escape. The thick chain was too sturdy for anyone to break open. And by this time, she could barely see. The lightning was so bright it impaired her vision. She closed her eyes and sent up a silent prayer.

Dear God, please help me!

Chapter 1

Earlier in England
1786

'How's my birthday lass today?' Jacob Spence, an unmistakable look of adoration on his face, took his daughter, Emily, by the elbows and helped her on to the cart he had borrowed from the manor.

'I feel grand in my Sunday best,' she replied, her sparkling eyes alight with excitement. 'I believe I have the kindest mother and father in Ambledon.'

Jacob smiled, patted the horse's neck and sauntered to the other side of the cart before climbing up and sitting next to his wife.

'Though I say so meself, she's a bonny lass. See how grown up she is. Yesterday she was but a child.' He sighed. 'Today she's a young woman, and a beauty at that.'

'Stop your banter, Jacob.' Anna Spence gave Emily a sly wink and suppressed a coy smile as she lifted her hand to her face, a face showing the early signs of maturity but still radiating its beauty from under the straw bonnet.

'And why not, Anna Spence? Does she not take after you? She'll have suitors by the cartload. Pick of the bunch.' Jacob paused and rolled his eyes. 'Like when you snared me.' He laughed and dodged the tap of affection his wife was about to level.

'You do flatter me, Father.' Emily smiled and leant over, gently popping a kiss on his cheek, her glorious mass of rich chocolate brown hair cascading over her shoulders and shining under the touch of the sun's rays.

She turned to her mother and offered a kiss. 'Thank you for the gown,' she said, smoothing her hands over the soft, cream sateen. 'It is lovely Mother,' she added, the matching ribbons adorning her hair fluttering gently in the breeze. The gown was plain but beautifully stitched, one her mother had made after carefully unpicking the seams of a garment discarded by the mistress of the manor who felt it did nothing for her complexion.

'Glad you like it, Em.'

Emily pondered. Today every part of her body tingled with happiness. An only child, for her mother had been unable to conceive again after Emily's difficult birth, she received enough love for half a dozen children.

'Vicar's on his way.' Jacob pointed in the direction of the distant church where the Reverend Grayson, his surplice flapping in the breeze, battled to cross the field next to the church. 'He seems in a bit of a rush by the look of things. We need to put a spurt on Anna.' He squared himself on the seat and caught the horse's rump lightly with the whip.

Whilst Emily was relieved from duties at the manor on the third Sunday of the month, the mistress insisted her servants pay their respects to the Good Lord and Emily was expected to attend the morning church service with the others. Today was special because it was the sixteenth of April, Emily's fifteenth birthday. Her treat was a ride in the cart with her parents after the church service.

On reaching market square Jacob quickly tethered

the horse. As they hastened towards the heavy door, Anna murmured, 'I hope we're not late.'

The vicar had already started his service when they tip-toed inside. But no sooner had they slipped around the back and taken their pews than the huge doors burst open behind them, swinging back and groaning loudly on their hinges. They closed shut with an almighty bang and then came the sound of clipped footsteps echoing on the stone floor of the central aisle.

Heads turned en masse. The villagers were anxious to discover who was responsible for the unexpected noise shattering the peaceful gathering and, curious to see who would dare make such a display, the young ones strained to look.

It was the Honourable Richard Allenby who, despite his twenty-one years, was still known to most as Master Richard. His footsteps were intensely vigorous, unfaltering, and the proud, determined look on his face was an indication of his supreme confidence. Head held high and perfectly erect, he looked neither to one side nor the other but continued to the front of the church where he took his pew with his family. His father, a man of stern features, turned his head and glared. But his son merely lifted his chin in indignation and, as he did so, the clock began to strike ten. Turning to his mother he said, within earshot of the congregation, 'Just in time, Mother. Just in time. Ten o'clock.'

The nervous clearing of throats by some of the men developed into artificial coughing, betraying their embarrassment at the vicar's early start. The women, concerned with airing their disapproval towards the newcomer, huffed discontentedly. Did Master Richard always have to utter the last word?

The vicar, a look of disdain on his crimson face, appeared to ignore the comment and, as if hoping to quell further embarrassment, announced that the Lord's Prayer would be offered. The huge congregation sank to its knees and several of the younger members tittered uncontrollably.

At the end of the service the village folk drifted to the porch, each having a duty to shake hands with the vicar, whose head nodded in condescending acknowledgement, his sanctimonious smile fixed on an otherwise doleful face. Afterwards Emily stood aside whilst her parents mingled and discussed this and that with their neighbours.

Whilst she was waiting, Master Richard appeared from the side of the church. They reckoned he was the most handsome bachelor in the district, but there was something about his dark eyes, now focusing directly on Emily's, that unsettled her. It was a long moment before he smiled. It was a smile without warmth. Emily shuddered, quickly bobbed a curtsey and deliberately turned away. By this time her parents were moving towards her. She sighed with relief, eager to move away from the churchyard and the Honourable Richard Allenby.

It was five thirty in the morning and still dark when Emily took the back steps to the kitchen. Mondays were always busy at the manor and when housekeeper, Miss Rickerby, entered and said, 'These cupboards are in need of a good scrubbing,' Emily knew Cook was less than pleased.

'Mistress says the kitchen is my domain.' Cook folded her arms in protest. 'And it's only a month since they were scrubbed. I can't be doing with that carry-on today,' she insisted. 'I'm preparing luncheon. We have the guests to think about.' Her voice almost hit a crescendo. 'Twelve today.'

'Then I will get the girls to work around you, Cook. Don't worry,' Miss Rickerby replied in calm voice, ignoring Cook's comment about domain.

Emily slipped the heavy cotton pinafore over her head and shivered. There was a chill in the air but the hot water would warm her hands. According to Cook's regular instructions the fire was left to die down after dinner on Sunday nights and the grate given 'a good riddling' on Monday mornings. But Lily had 'riddled' the grate a mere half hour ago and, to Emily's disappointment, the fire was throwing out virtually no heat as yet. But as far as Cook was concerned it was not a priority at that moment in time. She was more irritated at Miss Rickerby's words and, always ready to disagree with the housekeeper on account of their dispute over seniority, she turned her nose up.

'Emmy get on with them potatoes and carrots lass. I don't want you getting involved with the scrubbing. You are here to help me,' she pouted.

'But Cook, that's Lily's job. She's the scullery maid. I thought I was supposed to help with the cooking, the kitchen maid's job.' Now that she was fifteen Emily resented taking on a job she had done when she was eleven.

'See here, Emmy, I am the one giving orders.' Cook was insistent. 'Yes, you are here to help with the cooking. And scrubbing's not cooking, do you hear? If she wants scrubbers she can have scrubbers. She can have Lily, but not you. Now get about your job,' she huffed. Cook turned away, opening the door of the bottom oven, slipping her hand inside and testing the temperature now that the fire was starting to glow. 'There's no heat in this wood. I do wish Tom would bring some good stuff.' She shook her head and frowned as she complained.

Emily began to tackle the vegetables. It was unreasonable of Cook to pick on her. She had promised to train Emily up. *You'll make a better cook than the rest of them put together,* Cook had told her. And here she was peeling vegetables in cold water! Fair enough, scrubbing floors was even more degrading, but Emily's hands were blue with cold and a little warmth was all she needed.

But by six o'clock sun up, Cook had relented and Emily had her way. Standing at the large wooden table, a broad smile on her face, she tipped flour into the stone crock, sprinkled on salt and began to mix the pastry. Just as she thought, Cook wanted to stand firm against Miss Rickerby, although why it was necessary Emily would never know.

Eventually Cook nodded towards the door at the disappearing housekeeper. 'Thank the Lord that's over and she's out of the way. Interfering ...' she didn't say the word but turned to Emily. 'Tell me, lass, enjoyed your birthday did you?'

'Very much, Cook. Mother made me a lovely gown. We went to church as usual and afterwards for a ride in the cart and a stroll through the fields. It was such an enjoyable day. The sun was shining, the birds singing...' she stopped mid-sentence and with a solemn look on her face gazed into space.

'Summat up?' Cook asked, taking her hands from the crock and dashing the flour from them.

Not wishing to pour out all her thoughts to Cook, Emily shook her head and began to laugh.

Cook sighed. 'Don't have me on. I thought summat had upset you. What's tickling you?' She folded her arms.

'I was thinking about what happened in church. It was Master Richard.' As she spoke the words, she attempted to blot out his image from her mind.

'When he arrived everyone thought he was late. And then the clock struck ten as he sat down. The vicar looked ever so embarrassed. He had already started the service. You should have heard the little ones laughing.'

'You didn't join in I hope.' Cook stifled a giggle.

'Not at all, Cook. I managed to keep my face straight.' Emily pulled her mouth down at the corners before bursting into laughter.

'I'm not surprised. Master Richard has a mind of his own, does as he likes. He's been coming down here giving me orders since he was a bairn.' She stared ahead ready to give of her valuable opinion. 'It's no different now. He rules the roost up there.' She pointed up to the kitchen ceiling. 'Her ladyship can't bear a wrong word about him. But his lordship argues the lad gets too much of his own way.' She fidgeted absently with her cuffs and rolled up her sleeves ready to continue mixing the dough. 'He wants pulling down a peg or two, so he does.' She shook her head as she turned to Emily who was now leaning on the table listening intently.

But Cook had had her say and focused on the task at hand. 'Come on, lass. Pastry won't make itself.'

By one o'clock, Emily had finished her kitchen duties. 'You've done a good job, Emmy. Take a couple of hours off but be back by four,' Cook insisted, giving the time off to compensate for the busy evening ahead of them when her ladyship had invited a party of fifteen guests to dinner.

Unlike most of the girls who had rooms in the attic, Emily lived with her parents nearby in one of the cottages belonging to the manor. Her father worked in the stables and her mother saw to the wardrobes, stitching and pressing the garments. The break gave Emily the chance to slip back home and make a little progress with her embroidery.

The field was damp with dew as she took to the footpath to the hamlet. But her feet were dry in the boots Nanny Coates had given her, having belonged to Lord Percy's daughter, Miss Anne, who was a year younger than Emily but a much bigger girl.

Emily swung open the gate, strode purposefully up the garden path and let herself into the cottage. The handkerchiefs she was embroidering for her mother's birthday were hidden in a drawer in her bedroom. They would be finished by the time November came around.

The clock ticked loudly as, contentedly, she sat in her father's chair by the fireside stitching away. It would be early evening before her mother returned to the cottage and by that time Emily would be back at the manor to continue her duties. Her father would return after Lord Percy and his son had completed their day's riding and her ladyship had finished with the carriage.

But Emily's concentration was broken by the noisy clatter of clogs on the garden path. Glancing up she saw a shadow pass by the window. That was strange. She was not expecting anyone. Surely it was neither of her parents. Hastily she stuffed the embroidery beneath the chair cushion and peered out of the window. Little Enoch Crossley stood at the door holding his chest, puffing and panting. 'Come quick Emmy. It's your pa.' He gulped in air. 'Been taken poorly. Cook says to look sharp.'

'Father, taken ill? But he was fine this morning,' she replied, anxiety clouding her deep hazel eyes. She snatched her shawl from a hook at the back of the door and set off behind the boy, her stomach churning violently. Surely it was nothing serious. 'What's happened to him Enoch?'

'Don't know Emmy. Cook just said to run as fast as I could and fetch you quick.'

The shortest way was to cross the field directly, and this time Emily decided to ignore the footpath.

Gathering up her skirts she raced towards the manor, slipping and sliding on the muddy patches where the horses had churned up the grass. By the time she reached the stile that led from the field to the manor's back garden she was breathless. She turned to look for Enoch but he was now a fair distance away, his little legs unable to move fast enough to keep up with her.

The image of Cook standing on the kitchen step, her apron covering her face as she sobbed, was ominous. Emily's heart began to beat faster and, as she approached, Cook held out her arms. 'Come here my petal.' She reached out for Emily and held her tight against the softness of her bosom.

'What is it Cook?' Emily was trembling slightly and dreading her reply.

'How can I tell you?' Cook moved her to arms' length and looked into her eyes. 'It's too late lass. Your pa's gone. Your ma's there with him in the stables. He'd just brought Miss Anne's pony, Gypsy, back to the stable when he collapsed. Lord Percy sent for the doctor. But by the time he came your pa had passed away.'

'Passed away? It cannot be true,' Emily gasped, a look of total disbelief on her face. Tears began to steal gently down her cheeks. 'I must see for myself.' Her heart echoed loudly in her chest as she shrugged her body from Cook's grasp.

She almost fell down the kitchen steps and headed for the stable. But when she reached the bottom path the truth confronted her. Through the open doorway she caught sight of her mother sitting on the stable floor cradling her father's head on her lap. Her eyes were red-rimmed as she lifted her head and looked up at Emily. 'I cannot believe it Em. Your pa's gone. What are we to do?'

The funeral of Jacob Spence took place a few days later, the scene charged with emotion, the weather as depressing as the occasion. A silent, diaphanous mist crept over the little churchyard in Ambledon where he was laid to rest. Emily stared at the coffin, her eyes full of sadness. It was over.

For days Emily and her mother tried to comfort

one another. And just when they thought things could not get worse, a devastating blow was delivered. Lord Percy's man called at the cottage.

'It is very sad that you have lost your husband, Mistress Spence.' He paused. 'But you know His Lordship's rules.' He swallowed hard. 'He insists this cottage be rented by the head stableman. Now that Jacob is no longer with us, I'm afraid you must move to alternative accommodation.'

Anna jumped to her feet in protest. 'But this is our home. We belong here. What difference does it make who rents the cottage when we both work at the manor? Surely we are entitled?'

'Decision's not mine as you well know, Anna lass.' His manner was more relaxed now that he had delivered the killing blow. 'Rules are rules. New stableman will need it.' Somewhat embarrassed by the scene before him the bailiff left.

Anna sat down heavily and began to weep. Emily held her close. How much more were they expected to take? It was so easy, so casual the way the bailiff had delivered such disturbing news on behalf of his master. Lord Percy's decision to oust them from their home had obviously been made without considering their plight. It was a thoughtless gesture and the master had much to answer to. Emily was aghast and, spurred on by the words of rejection, she threw her shawl around her shoulders.

'We shall not be thrown out Mother.' Her pretty face was veiled in determination. 'I will speak with Lord Percy himself.' Before Anna could stop her, Emily set out towards the manor. Rules might be rules but who was to say they could not be broken?

The heat of the kitchen met her as she opened the door. 'I didn't expect you this morning, lass.' Cook picked up a towel and wiped her hands. 'How's your ma? Feeling better is she?' She slipped an arm around Emily's shoulder.

'Worse, Cook. She's worse. Believe it or not we are being thrown out of the cottage. But we'll soon see about that.' Her boots clicked on the kitchen floor as she stormed towards the back hall.

'Where are you going lass?' There was a tinge of panic in Cook's voice. 'You can't go marching out there.' A look of unease veiled her face now at the very idea that Emily should even consider entering the sanctity of the private rooms.

'Oh yes I can Cook, and I will.' She threw open the door and aimed straight for the front of the manor and his lordship's study. There was no-one in sight as she knocked.

'Enter,' came the call.

Emily opened the door, her heart now throbbing violently in her chest. Lord Percy was seated at his desk writing. He looked up.

'What the...'

His words were cut short by Emily's interruption. 'I do beg pardon, sir, but it is urgent that I speak with you.' She sketched a curtsey.

He stared in obvious alarm at having been disturbed from his task by this whippersnapper of a girl, a girl it was clear he was unable to recognise.

'Who are you child?' His brow furrowed.

'My name is Emily Spence. I work in the kitchen. I do implore you to let me explain why I am here, Your Lordship.'

'What is there to explain?' His voice was gruff.

'It's about our situation at the cottage now that I have lost my father, Jacob Spence, your head stableman. You kindly sent for the doctor when Father was taken ill last week, but Father passed away.' Emily took a deep breath before continuing. 'And now your bailiff is about to throw us out of our cottage.' Her words were almost garbled.

'I see child.' He nodded his head, his frown becoming more pronounced. 'But what of my new stableman? Did you not think about him? I shall need the cottage. I am afraid my man is right.'

Emily felt the tears pricking, and she started to back away. 'It did not cross my mind, sir that you had already taken on a new stableman.'

Lord Percy looked up and smiled. 'But do not worry for there will be a room for you here at the manor. Did Pickard not mention that possibility?'

'No, sir.' Although a room in the attic at the manor was no consolation, it would have to suffice.

'I will speak to Her Ladyship. She will make the appropriate arrangements with Miss Rickerby.'

'Thank you, sir. I am most grateful for your kindness.' She bobbed a curtsey and turned.

Lord Percy picked up his quill from the desk ready to resume his task. But then he hesitated, his face revealing a softer, more benign expression.

'Do pass my condolences on to your mother. The death of your father was indeed a sad loss to us all here at the manor.'

Emily turned to face him once more. 'Thank you, sir. I am sure my mother will appreciate your kindness.' She let herself out of the room and quietly closed the door behind her. Now that Lord Percy had confirmed the cottage would have to be given up for the new stableman there was nothing more she could do. But at least they would have the shelter of the manor. She set off quickly towards the back hall. But she had taken no more than a few steps along the corridor when a figure loomed before her. She looked up. Master Richard was standing there facing her.

'What have we here?' he asked, reaching across and taking hold of her chin with his thumb and forefinger, lifting it abruptly and staring into her eyes with fixed intensity.

Momentarily stunned, a blush of embarrassment rose to her cheeks. But she took a deep breath, overcame her initial reaction and, feeling affronted, drew her face away from his clutches.

'A spirited little filly I see,' he continued, an arrogant smirk on his face. 'Have you permission to be lurking about near Lord Percy's room?'

'I have been speaking with His Lordship, sir,' she said, a blank look upon her face as she made every effort to rid her voice of the resentment she felt.

'Then run along and do not let me catch you here again,' he said, a brusqueness to his voice as he jerked his head towards his father's study. As she turned to leave he set his palm towards her and delivered a familiar pat on her behind. At first she flinched but then she held herself aloof as he gave a hoarse laugh and strode off down the corridor.

How dare the man take such liberties? She tried to steady herself before she entered the kitchen, for by now a trickle of fury began to bubble inside her. But she was determined to maintain control. The kitchen was her haven. She would be safe there. And it was an isolated incident, one she wished to forget. But if it recurred she would surely be forced to retaliate.

The kitchen door was slightly ajar as she approached, the voices coming from within rising and falling in agitation.

'How dare the girl? Her Ladyship will hear of this.' The caustic words came from Miss Rickerby.

'But you must understand. Emily was concerned for her ma. They're being evicted from the cottage next week. What d'you expect?' Cook asked, taking up the mantle of guardian on Emily's behalf.

'That is no concern of mine, Cook. I would like to speak to her when she returns.'

Indignant at hearing Miss Rickerby talking so behind her back, Emily entered the kitchen. 'Then speak to me Miss Rickerby,' she said, a somewhat rebellious edge to her voice.

Miss Rickerby looked across, startled. 'How dare you address me in that tone girl?' She stared hard, maintaining eye contact with Emily. 'If you dare to enter the private rooms again without my permission I shall dismiss you.' She huffed. 'Wandering through the house freely indeed!'

'I do beg your pardon, Miss Rickerby but the matter was urgent.' Emily paused. 'I have spoken with His Lordship. Now that our cottage is being taken from us he has promised that my mother and I are to live in the house.'

'Spoken with His Lordship?' she repeated, her gimlet eyes flashing a spiteful glare. 'And he did not turn you away?' Her voice almost reached a crescendo.

'No Miss Rickerby. He was quite kindly.'

'Then you have been fortunate on this occasion. But we warned!' she huffed. 'If you think you can take it upon yourself to knock on His Lordship's door again without my permission, you will have me to answer to.'

Before Emily could attempt to calm the situation and express her apologies once more, Cook intervened.

'I'm so relieved lass. You're not needed in the kitchen for an hour or so. Slip to the cottage and tell your ma the good news.'

But it was not such good news for Anna. Emily tried desperately to rally her into thinking in a more positive way about the move. 'Mother it is the only way out. We shall no longer have to clean the cottage. Our time off will be free. And our meals will be provided. Best of all we shall be sharing a room together. What do you think of that?' Her voice was filled with a false enthusiasm, for the thought of leaving the only home she had ever known troubled her greatly.

'I'll never get over losing your dear father, and now the cottage too. It's been my whole life,' she concluded with an air of despondency.

Despite her efforts being to no avail, Emily tried to maintain her optimism. 'But now it is time for change Mother. Do not fret so. We shall manage.'

Eyes misted with sadness, Emily turned and looked back at the cottage for the last time. The scene before her encompassed all her childhood memories and flooded her mind with reflections of those good times indelibly printed there.

But now that special part of her life had come to an end. Desperately trying to hide her anxiety, she fluttered her eyelids to stop the flow of tears and, steeling herself to remain strong, she took a deep breath and gazed at the clothes draped over her arm, the only garments she and her mother possessed. With a trembling hand she smoothed them, her mind questioning what the future held. Mother had lived at the cottage since she was sixteen after marrying Father, and Emily was aware of her anguish and suffering at leaving the place forever.

She pulled her thoughts together and offered an encouraging smile. 'We'll cope, Mother,' she promised. But Anna was already in a state of despair and in dire need of comfort. She clung to the bundles containing their remaining possessions, returned a weak smile and nodded.

Emily put an arm around her mother's shoulder and felt a frisson of warmth flooding her whole being. Maybe she could chivvy her along. She had lost Father and their home, but she still had Mother, and that was all that mattered now.

Her thoughts were interrupted when Tom Picton turned the corner and drew up with the flatcart. Obviously embarrassed by the plight of the two women, he averted his eyes from their gaze.

With the exception of a mirror and two small pictures her parents had received as wedding presents and one or two small personal effects, the contents of the little cottage belonged there and must remain. Without uttering a word, Tom jumped down from the cart and collected the items propped up against the gate. Emily took the bundles from her mother and placed them on the back of the cart, carefully draping their precious clothes over the top.

'Come along, Mother. We need to settle in at the manor now.'

Tom helped them to the wooden seat at the front and he climbed up beside them, clicking his tongue and cracking his whip as he did so. The horse set off at a steady pace. 'Better luck for the future, Anna lass,' he said, keeping his eyes fixed and his melancholy gaze ahead.

'Aye, Tom, we shall need that right enough,' Anna managed to utter.

There was a nip in the air but it was a bright, sunny morning and, as Tom picked his way with the horse and cart over the cobbles, they passed before the row of cottages.

Some of the doorways were open and, knowing their departure was imminent, the women were standing there waving, most with sorrowful looks upon their faces.

Emily, a vacant expression masking her face, stared absently at the little windows, spotting the twitching of curtains here and there. She took a deep breath and focused her mind once more. Their time at the cottage had come to an end. It was over and they must start afresh.

The room Beth had prepared for them was small. There was scarcely space to move between the double bed and the dresser, and they were forced to stack their possessions in the corner of the room.

It was perhaps Emily's fault that Miss Rickerby

had chosen a small room for them. She could only guess the visit to Lord Percy without the housekeeper's permission and her subsequent confrontation had affected the woman's choice.

But the room was adequate, the bed soft and the patchwork quilt and bedding beneath it clean. It was more than Emily could have hoped for when, days earlier, they had been faced with eviction from the cottage.

After their sad loss Emily had convinced herself, if only for her mother's sake, she must remain strong and take charge. It would be years before their grieving came to an end and, in the few weeks they had lived at the manor, her mother's confidence had dwindled and her appetite deteriorated.

Several weeks passed without incident and, despite Emily's desperate attempts to encourage Mother to take the air on brief outings away from the manor, her efforts were futile, for her mother was still unable to cope.

It was late October and winter was fast approaching but the weather had been settled for the past week, the days crisp and clear and the gardens flooded with sunshine. Determined not to give in, Emily approached her mother once more.

'Tomorrow is our afternoon off, Mother. Shall we put our sorrows to one side and visit the market? I know it will be difficult not to think about Father but we must make an effort,' Emily maintained, set on making the best of the situation at the manor. 'I have saved a little money now that we have no rent to pay. I should like to buy you a small vase for the room, one I saw the last time Lily and I went to the market. Do say you'll come and look,' she begged.

'As you wish. But my mind is on other things,' her mother confessed. 'I cannot take in what has happened. Your father was too young to die.'

'I know, Mother and I miss him too for I loved him dearly. But we cannot spend our lives grieving. He would not have wished for that.'

'I know my little Emily. But it is not easy.'

Emily kept to her word and gently held her mother's arm, leading her down the long drive towards the road. 'The walk will be good for us. We barely take the air now that we are living at the manor,' she stressed.

'I suppose you are right. But it takes some effort.'

When they reached the outskirts of the village they took a cobbled slope between whitewashed cottages and entered the market square. It was there the stalls were set out displaying all manner of goods, from dishcloths to coloured fabrics, from pails to door knockers.

'Mother, look at these lovely ornaments,' she said, pointing to a pirouetting dancer, but not picking it up for fear she dropped it. 'It's beautiful.' She turned and took her mother's arm. 'First we shall take a good look, and then we shall choose.' It was difficult maintaining her own enthusiasm whilst trying to keep her mother buoyant. But, having looked at every stall at least twice and checking the prices, Emily finally suggested they buy the little vase she had seen earlier when she had visited the market with Lily.

'I shall pick flowers from the field Mother and we

shall stand the new vase on the dresser. Would you like that?' she asked.

Anna gave a cursory nod of agreement and Emily was relieved that at least she had had some success.

Weary now, they trudged back along the road leading to the manor, Emily clutching the parcel containing the little vase. Darkness was already casting its gloom when they reached the outer door of the kitchen.

'You are looking tired, Mother,' she said, hoping her mother would sleep well after the fresh air. She needed a good night's rest for she had lain awake almost every night since Father had passed away.

'That I am Emmy, dear. Happen I will get off to bed a bit sooner tonight.'

It was nine o'clock by the time Emily finished her evening duties and, when she went back upstairs to the bedroom, Mother was fast asleep. Emily gazed at the small bundle no bigger than the size of a child. After all the fretting and lack of appetite, Emily feared her mother was wasting away.

Their walk to the market should have tired Emily too but her mind was still active, the jumble of thoughts inside her brain conflicting one with another. Her main concern was Mother's health. Cook had tried to encourage Anna to build up her strength by offering all manner of delicacies, but still there was nothing to entice her. And to complicate matters the mistress had complained that Anna's work was not up to its usual standard.

But there was nothing Emily could do and nothing to be gained by mulling these thoughts over and over in her mind. Knowing she must be up and about by five the following morning it was time she was asleep.

After a strange nightmare, sleep eluded her and it was after midnight when Emily slipped her legs out of bed and crept down the back stairs to the kitchen. The candle she held flickered in the cold air. There was no-one around. She pushed open the door and closed it quietly behind her.

Pouring milk into a pan and placing it on the coals she stared absently at the fire's burning embers as the flames licked the sides of the pan. Locked in her own world and mesmerised by the flickering image of her dead father smiling before her, she felt a stray tear trickle down her cheek. He was gone forever. She would never see him again.

The hiss of milk rising and spitting into the flames startled her, and she was suddenly brought back to reality. Snatching a cloth from the rail, she lifted the pan and poured its contents into a mug. After a deeply disturbing nightmare a hot drink might help to calm her troubled mind. She quickly washed the pan and replaced it in the rack.

With the candlestick held firmly in one hand, the mug in the other, she glanced around the kitchen. Nothing out of place. Feeling much calmer after taking a sip of the milk, Emily headed for the door to the back stairs.

But the silence was shattered by a scuffling sound followed by the click of a latch. Her heart began to beat rapidly in her chest as she fixed her eyes on the door. The knob began to turn slowly. Someone was there, but who could it be?

In the darkness, the candle cast shadows on the

kitchen wall and the figure of a man loomed before her. But then a loud crash almost deafened her, giving her more cause for alarm. She stared. Whoever it was had stumbled over a chair and fallen to the floor.

Within seconds Emily focused on a pair of familiar yet cold eyes glistening and penetrating the darkness. It was Master Richard. And, judging by the smell of alcohol pervading the kitchen, he was in a drunken state. He pulled himself up and, still swaying, held on to the table for support.

'Beth. Where ish she?' he slurred.

'She is in bed, sir. It is after midnight.' Emily backed away.

'I know the time, girl!' he snapped, his impatient frown barely visible in the gloom of the kitchen. 'Bring wood to my bedroom,' he ordered. 'The fire is almost out.'

'Yes, sir.' she replied and, although it was not her place to tend to the fires in the upstairs rooms, it was no use protesting.

He slammed the door shut and she listened to his heavy footsteps as he staggered down the hall. But she did not intend braving the cold night air for wood from the outside store. There was plenty beside the kitchen stove she could borrow and replace next morning before either Cook or Miss Rickerby appeared.

Picking out several sizeable logs she filled the scuttle and climbed the stairs to Master Richard's bedroom.

At first there was no reply when she tapped gently on his door. Was it the wrong door? She peered up above and there on the wall was a portrait of Lord Richard Allenby, Master Richard's paternal grandfather. Emily knew of that particular portrait outside the room. Her mother had mentioned the likeness between the now deceased Lord Richard and his grandson.

She knocked again. Hopefully he had fallen asleep. If so, he would not need the wood. But when she knocked a third time he called out, 'Enter!' and she opened the door gingerly.

Master Richard was sprawled out on the bed looking the imbecile, his mouth agape and his eyes almost closed. He snored loudly and Emily, realising he was well into his cups and seemingly on the verge of sleep, tried not to disturb him as she closed the door quietly and tip-toed to the fireplace.

She bent over and, with trembling hands, quickly placed logs on the fire. But when she heard a heavy thud behind her, she became anxious and she turned. He had slipped from the bed and was attempting to pick himself up from the floor. Stumbling and reeling in her direction he tried to feast his bleary eyes on her.

He mumbled, 'I thought I recognised you. You're the lively little thing I met outside Father's room.'

Emily tried to remain calm and pull herself to her feet, but a sudden panic came over her. Master Richard swayed and staggered forward, swinging an arm around her body and running his hand over her barely formed breasts.

'Too good to miss,' he muttered, now facing her with eyes far from calm and almost as dark as his hair. She shuddered when he tightened his grip and licked his lips in certain anticipation. 'Come here, little mouse. We shall have some sport.'

'But, sir, I am not that sort,' she replied, now horrified at his intentions.

'I am no fool.' He laughed and clutched at her bodice, his eyes bulging with curiosity. 'A little beauty too. And don't you know it. You came on to me like a doxy in the churchyard.'

'That is not true, sir. Leave me be,' Emily cried and in her desperation to defend herself she dug her fingernails in his face and screamed out loud.

But with one sharp movement he pulled her towards him and pressed his hand over her mouth. He stared hard, the emotions swirling within his eyes too complicated for her to decipher.

'It is no good screaming,' he stressed. 'You will not be heard. The rooms nearby are vacant.' He was unable to articulate clearly, but the very sound of his voice sparked terror within her. He stroked her cheek. 'Did I not say you're a spirited one? Let's see what you are made of.'

Despite her struggle to break free he overpowered her, throwing her on to the bed and tearing her clothes almost to shreds as he ripped them from her body. He mumbled unintelligibly and the spittle from the sides of his mouth ran down his chin. Emily was so terrified her heart began to drum loudly, her mouth became dry and she lost all strength for retaliation. It was then he ravaged her without remorse. Never had she known such terror. Sharp pain racked her body. Was she going to die?

When he sank back on the bed he gasped and mumbled breathy words.

'Life could be difficult little mouse if you breathe a word to anyone.' And then his eyes became vacant and rolled to the tops of their sockets, the whites prominent. Gradually the lids closed over them and finally his lips quivered as he let out a sigh of exhaustion.

Rigid with tension and fear, Emily slipped from the bed, crouched in the corner of the room and pulled down a sheet to cover her nakedness.

'You'll not get away with this,' she pledged in a whispered threat, a defiant edge to her voice.

But he caught her words and lifted his head, an inane smile etching his face.

'You think not?' he questioned. He sank back on to the bed and, within seconds, he was snoring loudly.

Swathed in the sheet, her body sore and bleeding, Emily crept silently along the corridor and up the back stairs to her room. The first thing she must do was scrub herself clean. And then what? There was no use trying to cause a commotion, for nobody would be awake at this hour. She must get into bed as though nothing had happened. Tomorrow she would decide what to do, for she knew in her mind he would not abuse her again. She would make sure of that. She would report the incident.

The water she poured from the heavy jug on the dresser into the bowl was icy cold as she bathed her sore and aching body. She patted herself dry with a towel before slipping on her nightgown and gently sliding her legs into the bed. Fortunately Mother was sound asleep and Emily clung to the edge of the mattress, remaining apart. She felt the warmth of her mother's body drifting towards her, but the last thing she wanted was to arouse suspicion, for if Mother awoke she would feel the coolness of Emily's body.

That night sleep never came for Emily. Her mind was filled with the horror of what had happened and thoughts of reprisal entered her mind. But it was unlikely that she would win. The world was an unfair place. The servants were the property of the rich to be used and abused as and how they wished. But Emily made a vow. She was determined that one day she too would belong to the favoured class.

Foremost on her mind was the disposal of the clothes she had worn, those Richard Allenby had torn from her body.

But what would she tell Mother? And to whom should she report the incident? More importantly would anyone believe her? Surely the scratches on Allenby's face would be proof enough that she had defended herself against the evil monster.

Chapter 2

Emily's questions were academic. After the carriage left to take Lord Percy on a week's visit to Northumberland, there was a high-pitched screeching coming from one of the upper corridors on the west wing. It was followed by loud sobs. Cook opened the door to investigate, and the noise flooded into the kitchen.

'Bless my soul that is Beth's voice,' she whispered. Taking hold of Emily's hand they stepped into the back hall to listen more closely.

'I have taken nothing from your room, Your Ladyship,' Beth insisted. 'I am no thief.'

'Then we shall search her room,' came the now familiar voice of Richard Allenby, the brisk sound of his footsteps resounding from above.

Cook dragged Emily back into the kitchen. 'Better not to be seen, lass,' she whispered.

It was some time later when the kitchen door swung open. Richard Allenby was standing there.

'You, girl – outside! The constable has need to question you,' he said, pointing to Emily.

'Me, sir?' she asked, a vacant look on her face, for she tried to curb her emotions towards the man she wished she could banish from existence.

'Yes you,' he said, avoiding direct eye contact. 'And be quick about it!'

The constable stepped inside, took hold of her shoulder and led her out into the hall.

'I have reason to believe you have stolen a gold bracelet from Her Ladyship's room.' The constable spun her around to face him and dangled a gold

bracelet in front of her. 'What have you to say, girl?
'Me?'
'Yes you. Who do you think I mean, girl?'
'Please, sir, I have stolen nothing. Why do you accuse me?'
'You must have taken it, unless it was your mother, for it was hidden within the bundles in the corner of your room.'
'Hidden in our room? That cannot be,' she replied, shaking her head in denial.
'But that is so, girl. The Honourable Richard here was with me when it was found. He tells me you have a habit of wandering about the manor at all times of the day.' The constable gripped Emily's arm tighter.
'But my mother and I moved in only a few weeks ago. I barely know my way around for I work in the kitchen with Cook.' She tried to shrug herself away from him.
'That we know, for we also have a statement from Miss Rickerby. She tells us she caught you trespassing in the house only recently.'
He paused. 'According to the good lady you sneaked into Lord Percy's room. And the Honourable Richard can corroborate her statement. Do you deny that?'
'Well no, sir but it was a matter of urgency, my father...' She was not allowed to complete her reply. The officer interjected.
'I am sure it was,' he sneered and gave Richard Allenby a knowing look.
Emily pointed her finger in Allenby's direction intending to complete her own statement to clarify

the matter. 'It is all his doing...' she started.

But again the officer intervened.

'And well we know that, girl, for it was he who stumbled across the truth.' He threw open the door and pulled her towards it.

'But I must see my mother,' she cried, attempting to drag herself away. 'She is not well. You cannot take me away. Who will take care of her?'

'Your mother will be told all in good time. I am sure she will manage without you,' the officer replied. 'You should have thought about her when you took the bracelet.'

Emily turned and focused her eyes on Richard Allenby once more. But he quickly escaped her gaze. Obviously worried on account of her retaliation the previous night, he had not waited for her accusation.

It was clever of him to start by accusing Beth and then to plant the gold bracelet, switching the blame on to Emily herself. But, confident she would be given the opportunity to speak up, Emily allowed the constable to take her away.

Despite her denial in front of the magistrates, Emily was given no chance to establish the truth and she was sent for trial to Leeds. Again the same question entered her mind. Why were the rich always right and the poor wrong? Her world was being demolished. First her father had died, then the cottage had been taken away, and now she was accused of theft. And what of her mother, left alone to fight her sadness and grief?

In the Leeds courtroom the judge, head bowed, contemplated his decision. That damning word, 'transportation' escaped his lips almost inaudibly and invaded Emily's mind. She swallowed noisily and, as she dwelt on his mumblings, she shuddered and sent up a silent plea. *Please God, not across the great Atlantic Ocean to the New World.*

The judge, now intent on making his verdict official, slowly lifted his head. His rheumy eyes glistened in the fading light of the courtroom and focused on Emily, penetrating her soul. He coughed and cleared his throat.

'It is the duty of the courts to punish severely any servant who robs his master.' He pointed his finger in Emily's direction. 'I indict you with stealing goods to the value of forty two shillings.' He paused for a long moment. 'The offence is double felony, a capital offence punishable by death.'

Emily began to tremble uncontrollably. The judge's words *'punishable by death'* cut through her like a dagger through her heart, completely numbing her senses. And yet she had distinctly heard him mumble, *'transportation'*. So why was he now serving the death sentence?

The old man glanced briefly at his documents before he continued.

'In view of your age and, since this is your first offence, I have sought permission to offer you the King's Pardon.' Emily's spirits lifted. Perhaps she would be freed.

He flicked over the page and ran his finger from top to bottom. 'The court has ruled a more lenient sentence. You will be transported to parts beyond the seas, to such place as his Majesty King George the Third shall think fit to direct you, for the natural term of your life.' The words rumbled from his thunderous tongue and reverberated like a timpani inside Emily's head. *For the natural term of your life!* Did that mean she would never return to be with her mother again?

Unable to assimilate his words fully, she cowered in the dock. And now cornered like the hunter's prey, her eyes became distended in horror and her breath caught in her throat.

'No, No,' she screamed. 'I did not do it, sir.'

But her pleas fell on deaf ears.

The screeching voice of a heckler came from the back of the courtroom.

'A slow death for women burnt at the stake, a quick death for men hanged by the rope.' The woman's voice faded into silence when she was muffled and hauled from the courtroom by a peace officer. He pushed her on to the street just as Emily was being dragged out. The woman struggled to her feet, brushed herself down and approached Emily. 'You are lucky, dearie. But a year ago my Alice was burnt at the stake for a crime she did not commit. Take heed. They are villains,' she shouted, pointing back towards the courtroom. 'They will abuse you.'

The peace officer pushed the old woman away shouting, 'Clear off you troublesome bitch.'

Emily felt his rough hand at the back of her tunic as she was pushed to the floor of a covered wagon waiting to take her away. She stared ahead as the wheels rumbled on uneven ground. All the while the words 'burnt at the stake' flooded her mind and thoughts of the young girl who had suffered that cruel fate refused to fade. It was a senseless act, nothing but a display for the gratification of the public.

By the time they reached Durham County Gaol it was late at night. The heavy doors to the prison opened and the warden appeared. The felons huddled together.

'What have we here?' The warden's voice boomed and he grabbed Emily by the shoulder, fixing his evil eyes on her and staring. She flinched and shrank away. Terror struck within her. He pushed her forward roughly and sneered.

Inside the prison the walls were thick and solid. Emily was led down a flight of stone steps and into its depths where in a dark, damp dungeon she picked out the gloomy faces of the felons crouched in an eerie light, their bodies cramped as they watched avidly for the slightest space in which to spread their limbs. The mood within was dour. And once in there, Emily fell to her knees and prayed to God for her release. *O Lord! Where are you now that I need you?*

But pessimism infected her mind. Although she beseeched the Good Lord she felt sure her prayers would not be answered.

'Over here, dear,' sang a voice from the corner of the cell. Emily looked up. The call came from a young woman she guessed to be maybe eighteen or nineteen years of age. 'Matilda Parkin's me name, but call me Tilly,' she added. 'And yours?'

Emily stared, tears trickling down her face.

'Emily Spence.'

'Sit yourself down, lass. There's room here.' She patted the floor beside her. 'Make sure you can move when you lie down.'

'Lie down? You mean we stay here all the time?' Horrified, Emily cast a glance around the cell.

'Indeed we do – until they decide our true fate, wherever they are taking us.'

Wiping away her tears with the backs of her hands, Emily crouched beside Tilly who turned to her.

'What is your crime?'

'I am innocent Mistress Parkin,' Emily insisted.

Tilly laughed. 'That's what they all say.'

'They accused me of stealing a gold bracelet.' Emily shook her head.

'Found it did they?' Tilly's husky cackle frightened her.

Emily frowned. 'I did not take it in the first place, Tilly.'

Tilly hollered again but Emily was too mortified at what confronted her to join in.

'Pardon me laughter. I know I'm a trifle noisy but it gets to you in here after a time.' She gazed into space. 'I worked as milkmaid at Greenwood Farm outside York. I lived alone in my cottage for I had been married only three months when my husband was killed at war,' she said, her eyes bright with tears. 'When my neighbour came back from the war they gave him my job and my cottage. They said he needed it more than me. I was thrown out on the streets with no money and no home.'

'That is dreadful, Tilly. What did you do?' Emily asked, wide-eyed with curiosity.

'I left the village and set out for York, thinking I would have a better chance of a job there in a shop or a manor house. But them jobs were taken too. I was desperate.' She gazed blankly ahead. 'I had to steal cloth from a draper to make a skirt. It was but a small piece,' she held her hands outstretched to demonstrate the meagre size. 'You see I had but a thin, worn-out dress to wear. The farmer's wife was sorry she had to dismiss me and she gave me a warm fleecy blouse. All I needed was the skirt. Thinking no-one had seen me I tucked the cloth beneath my apron. Winter was fast coming and it would be nothing to them.'

'What happened?' Emily stared in amazement at Tilly's confession.

'The assistant tumbled to my sleight of hand and sent for the peace officer. I ran through the streets as fast as I could, but the cloth dropped from beneath my apron and they caught me. I was summoned to appear before a judge. I thought I would be for the rope, or even worse, the stake, for he said it was a capital offence. I gave him the wink,' she said, her eyes twinkling in the gloom of the cell. 'He changed his mind. I am up for transportation. And you?'

'It was the same for me. Because of my age the judge did not apply the death sentence.' Not wishing to be doubted further, Emily said no more about the offence. 'I wish I could see my mother. But she cannot come. This place is too far away.' Emily dare not even contemplate how her mother would cope with the news. Perhaps Cook would keep an eye on her. But what if Mother had been dismissed? That thought had only occurred to Emily in that instant as she sat on the floor of the cell.

'There is nobody to visit me either. I have no husband and no family. But now I am lucky I have met you. We shall stay close together.' She linked her arm through Emily's.

'I would welcome that. But still I do not know how I will survive here.'

'You have no choice...' Tilly was stopped short when one of the men crouched before them, leering as he swigged from a flagon of ale.

'Who have we here? A nice little virgin by the looks.'

Tilly reached over and brought the palm of her hand heavily across his face. 'You filthy beast. Leave off. Into your cups again. I will be glad when your money is spent.'

'Why Tilly, I was only making comment,' he said hurtfully. He turned away and his shoulders shook as he cackled.

'Well keep your mouth shut in future Thomas Pike and your hands to yourself. You'll be up for the rope sooner than you think if you start anymore trouble,' she threatened.

Emily was puzzled and found it difficult to understand that that no account seemed to be taken of the crimes the inmates had committed. 'Why is he in here, Tilly?'

'He is up for murder – waiting his call for the rope. And the old man,' Tilly told her, pointing to the man slouched next to him. 'Don't be afraid of him. He won't touch you. He likes the little boys. But the lad next to him – he is a wily one,' she continued.

Emily focused her eyes on the boy, a ragamuffin

of maybe eleven or twelve. She had noticed that each time the old man tried to fondle him the boy dug his elbow viciously where he knew it would hurt.

'He knows how to fend for himself. He's in here for stealing a loaf of bread from the bakery. His father died during the war and his mother had no money to buy food for the bairns.'

Emily looked around. It came as a shock to her that there were men and women, the innocent and the bad, the simple and the clever. They were all crowded together in the labyrinth of cells, and hidden away from the public, out of sight, out of mind and rotting away.

And how many of them, like Emily herself, had faced death for offences they had not committed? But she supposed she was one of the lucky ones, the judge having ordered her sentence be commuted.

The next day she awoke to the stink of foul breath and when she opened her eyes Thomas Pike had his face close to hers, his mouth gaping open.

'I hear you are leaving,' he said, lifting her tunic. 'Going to the hulks.'

'Stop that you filthy man,' Emily yelled, knocking his hand away with as much strength as she could muster.

'Hoho!' he laughed. 'Another wildcat.'

Disturbed by the noise, Tilly awoke with a jolt, a heavy frown on her forehead. Obviously incensed that, despite her threats, Thomas Pike was up to his tricks again, she leant over from her place on the floor and swiped him viciously across the face, this time more heavily than before and scraping her fingernails down his cheek. 'Keep away you scum,' she screeched.

'Scum you say. And what are you? A harlot – that is what you are.'

Resentful of her insults, Pike began to argue more fiercely. And then Emily saw him slip his fingers down his stocking and produce a knife. Shocked by what she saw, her breath caught in her throat and, momentarily speechless, she crouched against the wall of the cell, now terrified of the consequences. But Tilly was a thin, bony woman with an amazing strength and she wrestled Pike to the floor.

'He has a knife,' Emily shrieked but Tilly failed to hear her above the noisy banter of the other inmates.

Biding his time until she was off her guard, Pike plunged the knife into her side and, in the dimness of the cell, Emily saw red blood oozing from Tilly's wound. She screamed out, 'Warden. Come quick.'

The warden sauntered towards the cell and peered inside. 'Who the hell is making such noise?'

'It is me,' Emily called out. 'Mistress Parkin has been stabbed.'

The warden entered the cell treading carelessly over the recumbent bodies. 'Who did this?' he roared, searching the faces of the inmates for an answer.

The young boy pointed to Thomas Pike.

'You'll swing for this, Pike. And not before time,' the warden bawled, dragging him to his feet and unfastening the irons from the wall.

'Out!' he ranted, and he lifted his boot giving Pike an almighty kick up the backside. A guard, who was making his way down the dim corridor, grabbed

Pike. 'Call help, Seth,' the warden continued. 'This woman is bleeding. We must get her to the infirmary before we have another death on our hands.' Two of the guards lifted Tilly from the floor and took her away.

Several minutes later the warden returned. 'Any more trouble and I shall have the lot of you flogged,' he promised, pointing to the felons who were now huddled in a corner of the cell. He turned to Emily. 'You will be leaving for London for the hulks in a day or two. Then across the seas,' he snarled, 'to the bottom of the world. You will be lucky if you get there. I say you will topple off the edge and plunge into hell.' He looked at the others, his face now grim. 'But no more than you lot deserve,' he concluded and, turning his head, he spat over his shoulder into their midst.

Saddened when she discovered that her only friend was not well enough to leave for the hulks, Emily was bundled into a covered wagon and fastened by the wrist to a chain which ran through a ring down the side of it. The floor was covered with rancid straw, but the felons were allowed to sit on benches down each side.

Although the day was chill the wagon was open to the rear and Emily was grateful for the fresh air and the clear views of the countryside as they travelled. The journey was long and was spread out over several hundred miles. Woolwich was their destination. And, once there, Emily was thrust with the others into a lighter and rowed down the Thames towards what appeared to be a fleet of ghost ships, nothing but worn-out shells, lingering in the murky waters. She soon realised the conditions on the hulks were no better than those she had left at Durham Gaol. How long would her ordeal continue?

Jimmy Ballantyne swerved to avoid the thrust of his father's punch. His mother shrank into the background.

'Please, Tom. Don't hurt him again,' she begged, her tiny voice strangled. On the verge of tears she was reluctant to meet her husband's gaze.

But Tom Ballantyne ignored her pleas, and her words fell into insignificance.

'Tha's not workin' hard enough, laddie,' he bawled, aiming a punch at his son's face. 'T'is time ye put ye back into it.' He tottered and, as Jimmy ducked out through the door, the older man's fist hit the wall.

It took only an instant for Jimmy to make a decision. *This is the end! No more.*

His drunken father took almost every penny they earned to pay for his ale and left just a meagre sum for his wife to buy food. Jimmy had begged his mother to leave, to take little Danny and Amy with her. But his words had been futile. He would never understand why she was so tightly bound in that love-hate relationship with her husband.

But Jimmy had suffered his father's threats far too long and he refused to bear the strain any longer. On more than one occasion he'd had in mind to lash out and retaliate. But he realised that if he dared to make an attempt, his mother would suffer. She would inevitably be bombarded with physical and verbal abuse. That had always held Jimmy back.

And now he felt a pinprick of anxiety clicking away inside his head and a knot of guilt forming in his chest. Now he had decided to leave home, Jimmy hoped his mother would not be made to take the blame and have to bear the brunt of his father's wrath yet again. It had passed through Jimmy's mind on many an occasion that there must be an alternative. History had repeated itself and now he must put an end to it.

When he was seven years old Jimmy was put to the dockyard where his father, then a proud man, had worked since he was that age. But no sooner had Jimmy joined him than, in celebration of his son's new capacity as joint breadwinner, his father had taken to the drink. As he matured and his wages increased his father made a transition to semi-retirement. He worked during the mornings until he could no longer cope with his desperate need for alcohol, and he spent the rest of the day swilling down ale.

It took only a short time for the bosses to discover Tom Ballantyne's vice. They dismissed him without remorse; his semi-retirement became full retirement. And then it was down to Jimmy. But it seemed that each time his face appeared in the doorway he felt the sharp end of his father's tongue, or the blunt end of his blows. Jimmy pulled his thoughts together. He had already made the move. It was time to leave for good.

His clogged feet resounded heavily on the cobbles as he turned the corner into the market square, his mind preoccupied with what lay ahead as he fought against the bitter frustration welling up inside him. But his thoughts were interrupted when he was distracted by the sound of a booming voice.

'Come on lads. Sign up for a life of adventure.'

Curious to investigate, Jimmy, now going on nineteen, shifted his tall, well-built frame in that direction.

Two marine officers, oozing confidence in their splendid scarlet uniforms, were strutting across the square, promoting the Marine Corps in a vigorous recruitment campaign and calling to the young men to join them. This could be his salvation! Jimmy was forced to admit how dashing they looked, and he had a sudden rush of eagerness to sign up, to get right away from that poverty-ridden place. The only doubt flickering through his mind was facing his mother with the news.

But there was no alternative. If he joined the Marine Corps he could save the money and pass it to her furtively when he was on leave. There would be no necessity for his father to find out.

He needed no time for subjective thoughts and within seconds his decision was made. He would not return to his home in Glasgow. He would write to his mother and let her know of his decision. There was nothing to be gained by facing his father; it would only cause more problems.

With a new zest, bright-eyed and confident, Jimmy approached the taller of the two men who flashed him a thin smile. 'I'd like to know more,' he said, his mop of fair hair feathering in the breeze, the expression on his face eagerly expectant.

The marine was a Sergeant MacVay, seemingly a

homely fellow who gave Jimmy such a rosy picture of life in the corps that there was no need for him to linger further.

'You'll be well clothed and fed, and travel to exciting places in the world. What more could you ask?'

Jimmy, convinced it was the best way out and now feeling strong and defiant, stated with an air of finality, 'Yes. I am willing.'

The sergeant dipped the quill into the ink and passed over the parchment. 'A cross if ye canna write, laddie.'

With a sense of pride Jimmy signed his name. He had paid attention when Maggie Kirk had taught him to write, and now it was to his advantage.

The barracks were sparse but the conditions there failed to deter him. At least he would be free from the clutches of his bullying father. And, once on parade, the sergeant inspected his men. He offered Jimmy a beaming smile, obviously taking in the strong, regular features of his face.

'Ye look just the part, laddie. Break the lassies' hearts ye will.' He chuckled thickly. 'Runnin' away from home are ye? That's the story behind many a recruit.'

'Not at all,' Jimmy told him, his body stiffening. The sergeant had guessed correctly but Jimmy was not about to admit it.

'I am tiring of the job in the dockyard. I would like to travel and discover new parts'

'Ye'll do that right enough,' the sergeant replied, his tight lips now holding a wry twist. 'We leave for Portsmouth in a month or two. Plenty in store for ye there.' He turned to the men. 'First ye will undertake a rigorous training. Before we depart ye must be capable of handling a musket and following the drill techniques.'

Once they reached the training camp in Greenock, Jimmy was billeted with a young, copper-haired recruit he regarded as a kindred spirit. Excitement built inside him.

'I'm Jimmy Ballantyne,' he said, holding out his hand.

'Sandy MacDonald,' the lad replied with a trace of relief in his voice. He shook Jimmy's hand.

'How old are you?' Jimmy asked for there was no doubt Sandy looked rather young to be a marine.

'If I tell you the truth will you swear to keep it a secret?' Sandy begged.

'I have no reason to tell anyone,' Jimmy replied.

'I am fourteen, going on fifteen,' he said. 'But I told them I was sixteen.'

Jimmy laughed. 'You have plenty of courage; I'll say that for you.' He was surprised the lad had been confident enough to lie about his age. He certainly didn't look sixteen.

The following day was the start of the discipline and the rituals. Up and away before sun up and back to the barracks by sun down was the daily regimen. The training was arduous, the discipline strict and the routine monotonous, but Jimmy was quick to learn the basic skills of marine drill and the safe handling of a musket. The sergeant appeared impressed.

'I have recommended you for promotion at some time in the future, Ballantyne. You are the sort we need to take charge. What do you say to that?'

'Thank you, Sergeant MacVay. If a promotion comes through I promise I will not let you down.'

It was still dark when they arose on the morning of their departure to Portsmouth. But that was no hardship to Jimmy for it was little different from his daily routine back at home. The relief that they were leaving Scotland served to put new spirit into him and within ten minutes he had managed a cold water splash and full dress uniform.

He stood to attention outside in the quadrangle. He felt proud.

The sergeant's voice echoed around them. 'Ye will be marching to the good ship *Caroline* anchored in yon harbour. She will take ye down the westerly coast of England and south eastwards towards Portsmouth. Our commanding officer there, Major Ross, has assigned ye to the *Lady Penrhyn* abound for Botany Bay.'

He paused. 'Our Marine Officer on board that ship will be Captain James Campbell. Ye will find him a most reasonable gentleman so long as you obey orders,' he announced, the corners of his mouth curling in a crooked smile.

'Where is this place Botany Bay? Do you know, Jimmy?' Sandy whispered.

'I have not heard of the place before. Perhaps the sergeant will explain. Portsmouth is a fair distance away, I believe on the south coast of England. Maybe this Botany Bay is further round the coast.'

When the time came for them to board the *Caroline* and leave Scotland, the rest of the men also appeared ignorant as to the whereabouts of this strange place, Botany Bay.

Contentedly they marched on and boarded the ship unaware of the thousands of miles they would be sailing to their final destination.

The passage through the Irish Sea and down the north coast of England was rough. Black rain clouds gathered and a heavy storm raged. The pitching and rolling seemed endless but Jimmy's gut feeling told him that anything was better than his father's physical and verbal abuse, the bitter edge and the heavy sarcasm of his words. He would soon harden to these conditions.

When they reached Portsmouth the weather had cleared and thin clouds streaked the pale blue sky as the crew dropped anchor at Mother Bank. Jimmy collected his few possessions before boarding the tug which transferred them to the *Lady Penrhyn*.

'Looks much bigger than the *Caroline*, newer too,' he commented to Sandy.

'Aye, it is, Jimmy. But there is not much space on the upper deck to bed down,' Sandy replied, his brow creased in a frown of disappointment.

Jimmy soon convinced himself the environment was something he could accept and, once on board, the men gathered eagerly on deck. He was ready for a challenge for during the voyage from Glasgow to Portsmouth he had turned nineteen and with a willing spirit he was keen to expend his excessive physical energy. His promotion had been confirmed. He was now Corporal Ballantyne.

But he was disappointed to discover that the tasks they would undertake would be light, merely to maintain sentry duty at the hatchways, guarding the cargo of convict women who were expected within the week.

With time to contemplate the situation, he realised that wherever this Botany Bay might be it was a long way from home. The memory of the last time he had seen his mother, his father's threats and her subsequent pleas, was a painfully vivid picture in his mind. He tried desperately to control his thoughts.

And now he must try to be strong, for there would be nothing to be gained by dwelling on the past. The future beckoned. It was time for new beginnings.

Chapter 3

Ashen-faced with the shame of her plight and the awful shock of it, Emily wrapped her arms around her chest as she tried to hide away at the corner of the bunk. Racked with the cold and damp of the orlop, the lowest cabin on the hulk, she shivered and fought hard to control her tears. By the nineteenth of November she had been imprisoned for a week in the bowels of the hulk, a rotting, floating hell of a wreck never to sail again and converted into a prison ship anchored on the Thames at Woolwich. Her only means of counting the days was by scratching a faint tally on the edge of her bunk with a scrap of granite she had hidden and smuggled into the orlop. She knew the wagon had arrived on the twelfth. The warden had checked the names of the felons, first calling out the date and ticking each one off on a slate.

The nineteenth stood out clearly in her mind. It was her mother's birthday. But there would be no gift for her. Emily had left the embroidered handkerchiefs behind along with her few precious possessions.

Anxiety filled her eyes and she tried to blink away the tears as the memory of her mother's face filled her mind. How she missed her and desperately so. Shoulders slumped, she felt numb, her senses somehow blunted as the silence of the cabin spread around her.

If only she could get away. But that would be impossible. Some of the women had tried to escape over the side. Two had managed it with help from their partners, but one of them had been re-captured and returned to the hulks. Her head had been shaved as punishment. The other fell to her death as she slipped from the bow into the filthy depths and, unable to swim, she had drowned.

Emily's tears began to flow profusely now. It was too much to bear.

'Irons digging in?' It was Mary Fletcher, her voice a whisper of a sound. She leant across and, avoiding the red, chafing skin on Emily's wrists, she gently ran her rough fingers over the dark, mottled bruises on her forearms. 'You must try to bear it Emmy. Johnny tells me we shall be away to Portsmouth soon. It will surely be better than this.'

Emily, one of the youngest and more naive inmates, was glad of Mary's protection in this hell-hole of a prison. She was a good-natured soul ten years older than Emily and, since Tilly was still in Durham, Emily had a new friend in Mary.

'It is not the chains. I am used to them now. It is a sickly feeling,' she said, pausing and swallowing noisily as though trying to fend off her nausea, 'a feeling that never goes away.' She lifted her hand to her chest, her face pale and strained.

'Not surprising with the filth around 'ere.' Mary nipped her nose and contorted her mouth as she spoke of the offensive odours pervading the ship. 'It comes from the bilges. Foul as a bucket of shit.' She stopped in contemplation. 'And it is the smell of fear too, Emily,' she said dolefully. 'Many of the inmates are frightened of dying. But not you and me! We will not be beaten.' Despite the gloom of the orlop Emily detected a flicker of light dancing in Mary's eyes as she draped her arm casually around Emily's shoulder and squeezed her. 'Do not worry. We shall be safe enough,' she whispered. 'Trust me. Mary will take care of you. A little bit o' mischief here and there and we will be out of this place and up aloft quick as a flash.' Mary rubbed her hands together gleefully, her bright eyes now sparkling even more and her generous mouth ripe with laughter.

'You stay cheerful, Mary.' Emily smiled weakly through her tears. 'What would I do without you?'

'What is the use in crying my little sweet? It doesn't change anything. Now dry your tears.'

Mary was right. Their fate was sealed. Not that Emily could help herself. But she nodded.

'I will try to overcome it, Mary.'

But Emily worried about Mary whose liaisons with the guards brought her one or two favours, a mug of porter to drown her sorrows so she said, and extra meat and bread which she shared with Emily.

But Emily strongly disapproved and, wary after Allenby's abuse, her reflections triggered a horrid thought in her mind. The very idea of being touched by a man repulsed her, and when she thought about Mary and what she may have to suffer in exchange for the rewards, her heart began to thump, the sound reverberating in her head. Almost thinking out loud, she gasped, 'Mary you surely don't let them do things to you, like touching?'

'Don't worry your little head, Emmy. Mary can surely handle it. I've been doing it since I was a girl of fifteen. I needed to make me living somehow.' She laughed. 'It is nothing but a little entertainment to keep the likes o' them happy. But I want you to promise me you'll keep away from them. Tell me if they call for you.'

'I surely will. But why are you here, Mary? I cannot believe you would do anything against the law.' Emily was puzzled. Surely keeping company with the men was not a crime.

'One night I had a customer, had his way and refused to pay. I needed food and shelter so I took his gold watch. Later, when he sobered up and tumbled to it, he sent for the constable. They found me at the flophouse, arrested me and here I am.'

Their conversation was suddenly cut short by the harsh voice of Johnny Gregson.

'Mary. Top gun deck,' he shouted. 'Warden wants you in 'is cabin.' He paused and lowered his voice. 'Shot me mouth off when I was well into me cups about you bein' a right rum 'un. And now look what's happened. He wants to check the goods for himself,' he said gloomily.

Mary smiled willingly into Johnny's face, struck a defiant gesture and, pouting prettily, she stretched out her arms provocatively. Johnny, a broad shouldered, heavy-muscled man with a chin covered in dark stubble, gave her a wicked grin. He watched her move, his eyes drawn to the swell of her rounded breasts, and he ran his fingers swiftly down her body.

Emily cringed at the sight of his fondling.

But, as he removed Mary's chains, his face became a mask of resentment, his eyes iced over and his mood changed suddenly.

'Stop your banter you flash piece. You're mine.'

It was clear Johnny had laid claim to Mary. His bitter tone revealed his anger at the warden's intentions to tamper with what he naturally felt was his rightful possession.

Perhaps he had overstated Mary's talents, bragged about her, and the warden felt he was now entitled to his share of entertainment.

Emily raked her fingers through her knotted hair now hanging limply and dulled through lack of washing. Dragging it back from her temples she tied it up with a dirty rag. A cold draught wrapped itself around her, and she felt the hard surface of the bunk.

But she curled up tight, hunching her knees to relieve the strain of the chains pulling on the iron rings fastened to the planking. Better keep quiet. What she dreaded more than anything was being hauled up to the gun deck and put on display like some of the other girls.

After Mary had disappeared Emily must have dozed. But she was disturbed when she felt the chains on her wrists being unfastened. Panic swept through her. There would be no way of avoiding the warden or one of the guards should they send for her. Maybe her time had come. The very thought terrified her.

She fluttered her eyelashes to shake off the sleep and tried to focus on the person standing before her. It was Johnny Gregson.

'Come on girl. My Mary's been on 'er back for you. Warden's ordered you out of 'ere and up above to the gun deck.' He jangled the chains.

'But I didn't ask Mary to do that.' Pale-faced and

close to tears she felt a sudden surge of guilt. 'And I do not want to go to the gun deck. That is where...' The remaining vestige of colour left her cheeks, and her voice trailed off, hot tears stinging her eyes.

'It is nothin' like you think. My Mary would challenge the king himself on your account. Treats you like her own child she does.'

Up above on the gun deck the port side had been scrubbed clean. Strewn here and there in some semblance of order were straw-filled paillasses. Light flooded in through the portholes and the stench of the bilges was diluted by the fresh air entering them. This was a good deal more comfortable than down below. But Emily was scared she might have to follow Mary's example and lie with the warden or one of his guards to keep her place on the deck. Maybe she was better off and safer down in the orlop.

Johnny leant forward, placed his strong forearms on the bulwark and whispered in her ear.

'Keep your hands still when there be guards 'ere. I'll slacken these chains later.'

Still shaken by the move, Emily was grateful for her new-found freedom, but she was ever vigilant and wary that she may be summoned at any time.

It was then a grey wisp of a woman sidled up to her. 'They want a penny for extra porter and bread.' Her voice was hoarse.

She sighed and continued. 'If you have no money I'll buy you some in exchange for your blanket. It is bitter cold up 'ere.'

'I don't drink porter, Nell and I would not take your money.' A sense of pity rasped her soul. 'If you are so cold I will lend you my blanket.'

'Nell will not forget you, dear,' she said, taking the blanket.

Emily smiled and stepped back, treading on someone's foot. On instinct she spun around.

'I do beg your pardon,' she offered.

Mary was standing in front of her, her dull hair tangled, a broad grin lighting her face.

'Oh, Mary. I am so glad you are here. I have been fretting.' There was a sense of urgency to Emily's voice on account of Mary's plight, especially if she had been forced to bear the same indignity and hurt Emily herself had suffered at the hands of Allenby.

'Worry gets you nowhere, Emmy. It will be more comfortable for you up here. I will be in with the warden – keeping him company so to speak. Johnny is vexed but orders are orders.'

The sleeve of her torn, shapeless tunic slipped from her shoulder revealing the dark red blotches patching her breast. She hastily dragged back the sleeve to cover them and pulled a thin shawl across her chest.

'Where is your blanket? Johnny promised to give you one.'

'I lent it to Nell. She was shivering, and she offered to buy me bread and porter. But I could not take anything from her.'

'You must learn to look after yourself Emmy. You are too kind. Now you need another blanket. I will make sure you get one for it is too cold at night when the wind sweeps through.'

'But it is fresh.' She gazed at Mary with affection. 'Will you stay here sometimes? I am frightened they will send for me.'

'There is no fear of that. Johnny has promised to look after you. I will come whenever I can, except when warden needs favours.' A frown replaced Mary's lively grin and her eyes glazed over. Emily's stomach churned. She had been right to feel uneasy for she was aware now that Mary despised what she did but it was in payment of comforts.

Mary kept her word. Emily was not disturbed whilst she remained on the gun deck. Just as he had promised Johnny slipped the irons from her hands and a fresh blanket arrived. It was much quieter up there. The only interruptions came from Nell, who was fine when she was sober, but she was downhearted on account of her friend, Billy when she was well into her cups. His plight became evident when one morning at the break of dawn they strained to look through the porthole.

'The men are on their way to the dockyard,' Nell told her.

A silent, grey mist swirled around the ship, and it was difficult to catch the vision. But Emily peered with greater concentration to get a closer look, focusing her eyes on the group of men.

'See. Over there. My Billy.' Nell pointed to an elderly man, his wispy grey hair ruffled by the breeze. Frail and bent, he struggled to walk with the weight of the heavy iron riveted around his right ankle, his chances of swimming to freedom handicapped by the shackles which would soon see him in a watery grave.

'He wouldn't get far Emmy. Not with them holding him back.'

'Poor Billy,' Emily concluded.

'Aye indeed, poor Billy.' Nell turned to her and whispered. 'He's here for forging the king's currency. Up for the rope but he escaped that.' She paused and then whispered, 'Nobody knows he has some squat,' she claimed, looking around furtively, 'same as me dearie, in me draws.'

Emily's eyes were wide in disbelief. 'But what if they search you?'

'I am too old for them to bother. They wouldn't want to poke about in my draws.' She started to laugh once more, and Emily joined her.

'Your secret is safe with me, Nell,' Emily promised and she clasped Nell's gnarled fingers and squeezed them gently.

'You are a kind lass,' Nell replied. Tears sprang to her eyes and she brushed them away with the back of her hand. 'Billy struggles to keep his strength going from dawn 'til dusk. And them what gawks at him in the dockyard don't help,' she said, shaking her head, 'pointing and telling the young 'uns to take heed and behave or they'll end up like my Billy.'

Their concentration was unexpectedly broken by the shouts of a bunch of new inmates mustered on the starboard side of the gun deck. They were being addressed by the warden.

'Stand where you are until I check your names.' He lifted a slate and started to call out before briefing the men. 'The stay here will short for you are to sail across the waters as soon as the fleet is ready. All valuables and money must be handed over for safe-keeping. Carrying them on your person causes stealing and will not be tolerated.'

The uproar continued and Emily turned to Nell. 'Surely the warden will take care of their valuables. It is better than some thief taking them.'

'You do not understand, Emmy. The warden is the thief.'

Emily shook her head, a naïve look on her face.

Nell continued. 'Looking after their valuables is but an excuse. The men will never see them again.'

She shook her head. 'Warden's safe-keeping means safe with him forever until he sells them to the second-hand merchants.'

'I see what you mean. Then it is not surprising they are making such a noise.'

Before long, pandemonium broke out. The men kicked, punched and shouted but they were restrained and searched. Some of them were flogged and, despite their protests, their valuables were removed by the warden before the men were taken down below.

It was on a crisp, clear night when there was a commotion on the upper gun deck. Two guards ran down the ladder to fetch their senior, Johnny Gregson.

'It is the warden. Collapsed. Too much whoring if you ask me.' They laughed raucously.

'Nobody's asking you, Blake. Shut your mouth,' Gregson roared, his face tight with anger as he set off at a stiff pace and called for the surgeon to be summoned from his bed.

Emily watched him disappear inside the captain's day cabin and, seconds later, Mary turned up at her side.

'I could not let Johnny see me in there.' She caught her breath. 'Warden collapsed on me. Proper scared I was. I think he's finished, Emmy,' she said slumping down on the paillasse.

There was a sudden hush in the conversation as they heard footsteps approaching. Johnny appeared.

'Lucky you wasn't there Mary,' he insisted as he addressed her smugly. 'You might have gotten the blame. I held the glass to his mouth, but it was too late.'

From that day onwards the captain's day cabin on the upper gun deck became the property of the new warden, Johnny Gregson. It seemed Mary had become his permanent property too. Emily saw little of her, except from time to time when she came down to check that nothing was needed. At least with Johnny as the new warden Emily was confident there would be no call on her from the guards and she was content knowing Mary was around somewhere. That was until she heard the staggering news.

Mary broke it gently.

'I don't know how to tell you, Emmy dear, but the wagons are coming tomorrow and are destined for Portsmouth. According to Johnny it will take ten days to reach the port. After that you'll be transported over the water to some strange place.'

'At least we shall be together Mary.' Emily searched Mary's face for confirmation.

Mary took a deep breath. 'I will not be leaving. You see Johnny told the magistrates of my good behaviour.' She averted her eyes.

Emily guessed 'good behaviour' meant those horrid things like bodily comforts and sexual favours, something the magistrates accepted as necessary. And now she grasped the awful truth. It was common knowledge that many felons had been sent across the Atlantic Ocean to the new world, but transportation to those parts had ceased since the revolution there. Rumour had it they would be taken on an expedition over the edge of the world, right to the bottom of the earth where there were savages. The journey would take more than a year and the voyage would be dangerous.

Emily realised her sentence had now become reality and she was concerned for her safety. But it was no good wallowing in self-pity. She must be strong and stop her selfish thoughts. It was time she considered Mary after the way she'd kept her from harm. She managed to hold back the tears as she dwelt on the prospect of leaving England, of leaving her mother whom she had not seen since that fateful day.

On the twenty-ninth of December, Mary appeared on the gun deck to say a tearful goodbye. 'Sorry my little sweet. I am lucky that Johnny has managed to save me, but I could not persuade him to keep you back too. I tried but he was afraid for his job. He said they would surely top him if they discovered his disloyalty to the crown.'

She lifted her hand and placed in on her chest. 'I will be thinking about you. You will always be here in my heart, little one.'

Menacing grey clouds filled the sky as the wagons,

pulled by teams of horses, rolled up in front of the hulks. Emily was quickly dragged away by the guards and together with the handful of females she was pushed to the wagon floor which was covered with filthy straw alive with cockroaches. The men, exhausted grey phantoms, drifted along behind. There were no seats and, despite the cold outside, the wagon was airless.

The convicts held out their hands to be shackled to the ring bolts down the sides of the wagon and, once the doors were slammed shut, the two guards climbed on top to join the driver under the shelter of the canopy. Soon the bodies of the convicts began to stink in the built-up heat as they struggled to balance on their haunches and avoid the vermin running freely beneath them.

Emily felt someone grip her canvas tunic and she looked down at the gnarled hand. It was Nell's. 'Please do not leave me, dear. I am too old for this.'

Emily turned to her and gently patted her arm. 'I will look after you, Nell,' she said. But tears welled up in Emily's eyes as, through the slats in the wagon, glimpses of the countryside flashed by.

Determined to stay strong, she fluttered her eyelids and shook the tears away.

Lizzie, one of the twins, grasped her hand.

'Will you look after me and Jess now that our Dot has gone to the Good Lord?' she begged.

'We will stay together, I promise.' Emily smiled bravely and squeezed Lizzie's hand.

'Thanks Emmy.' Lizzie sighed and struggled to wipe her wet face with the backs of her shackled hands, spreading the grime smeared there and emphasising the circles beneath her eyes. Almost identical twins they were fourteen when Emily met them on the hulk. They regarded her as more responsible and looked to her for support.

On the evening of the seventh of January 1787, they reached Mother Bank outside Portsmouth Harbour. Emily stared across the docks taking in the majesty of the fleet moored there. The ships were far superior to the hulks and, between them, spanned the length of the docks, their masts pointing high into the dismal grey sky.

The women were transferred by lighter towards one of the transport ships anchored there and, as they neared the fleet, Emily read out loud the name, '*Lady Penrhyn'*, which was marked on the stern. According to one of the guards, the ship was new, and to Emily's relief, only female convicts were being directed there. But they were pushed like cattle into the bowels of the ship where the headroom was limited. She thanked the Lord for her slight stature

She looked around. It was as dark as a grave and, pausing to allow herself a few seconds to become accustomed to the gloom, she noticed that twine and sail cloth were stored at one end. As she gazed towards the other end she focused her eyes on the women who were huddled together, clutching hold of one another like a bunch of frightened skeletons.

Her heart sank. Such a sorrowful sight! The women were afraid in the darkness of the orlop, which was below the waterline, only one deck above the hold and adjacent to the bilges. The bunks were assembled in banks of four and took the space of one large bed. Once the women were shackled there, they started to wail sorrowfully, for most were wet and shivering, some almost naked.

'How are we expected to stay warm when we've been robbed of our clothes?' one of them called out. 'The guards on the hulks promised to exchange mine for something better. But they sold them to the second-hand merchants. All I have now is these.' The woman stared down at the filthy rags she wore. 'Something better? Look here. They are not fit for a scarecrow.'

Emily's relief that none of the male convicts had been brought on board was premature. She had not accounted for the crew who could barely wait to check out the whoring talent.

They stole quietly down the ladder, the soft tread of their feet pressing towards the pool of light streaming down from the opening above. She sensed they were on some sort of mission, one in which she was determined not to become involved.

Sometime later there was the sound of footsteps descending the ladder and Emily looked up. A young marine confronted the sailors and, by the look on his face, he found the whole scene obnoxious

'Captain's orders. All crew back on deck.' He turned and looked around before smiling in Emily's direction. The light from up above shone down on him and she looked into his eyes. They were the most vivid blue she had ever seen, the colour of the bluebells growing in the woods near her home. Stunned, momentarily she held his gaze. But, realising she was staring, she pulled herself up sharp and smiled back before turning away, embarrassed. As he left the orlop Emily realised there was something about him she couldn't quite pinpoint, something that made her feel warm inside.

The crew members paid no attention to the order and Emily stared as anger bubbled inside her. 'They treat the women like pieces of cargo,' she whispered to Nell, her eyes bright with fury. 'And they think they are entitled to abuse us. I would die before giving in, Nell,' she vouched.

'They'd struggle, Em. I can fight like the rest of them even at my age, believe me,' Nell declared. 'But do not listen. Them whores are worse than a set of wild cats,' she insisted. 'Sell their bodies for ought. And the men are no better. Filthy beasts.'

Despite the captain's orders the bombardment continued with the screeching, fighting and obscene banter of the women, and the swearing, shouting and bawdy noise of the rutting crew who were rough in their handling of the women.

Disgusted, Emily covered her ears. And when it was over the women were rewarded from the sailors' rations of rum, fortifying their spirits and carrying them into oblivion. Those chosen by the more senior crew were given clothes from the slop chest too.

The company of red-coated marines, who had earlier directed the women down below, had remained on the upper deck except for the one young marine who had been sent down earlier. He was the one with the beautiful blue eyes, the one who had given her a friendly smile.

Later, when the women were summoned up

above, Emily realised why the marines had not dared to join in the orgy. Their commander was an awesome individual. Tall, yet slightly built, with a pinched, humourless face, he addressed the women in a distant and amazingly cold voice.

'My name is Major Robert Ross, commandant of the marines on this expedition. You prisoners of the crown on board the *Lady Penrhyn* shall be under the guard of Marine Captain James Campbell and his men here.' He pointed towards a more pleasant-looking officer. 'Once we set sail, you shall, by gracious permission of His Majesty King George the Third, be released from your shackles to exercise twice a day on the upper deck, allowing you fresh air to improve your health. Do not abuse that favour.'

Captain Sever, the ship's master, stood a distance away, his first mate at his side. Some of Sever's crew loitered behind him, grinning inanely when the mention of an expedition brought about an undercurrent of mumbling and a hiss of whispering from the women and the marines alike. What did this mean? Why were they so amused?

The major surveyed them through cold, grey eyes and continued his bark in stern voice, his mouth thin and mean. 'Stop your noise. Our destination will be Botany Bay where you will make new homes, God forbid.' He snorted derisively, turned on his heel and moved away.

'Botany Bay? And where might that be?' Nell asked.

'The other side of the world,' the first mate replied, showing little emotion. 'The voyage could take a year...if you survive that long.' He followed Captain Sever towards the poop deck.

On hearing the news, the smirks quickly disappeared from the faces of the crew to be replaced by frowns. It seemed they too had been unaware the ship was to sail such a distance. Perhaps they were afraid they would fall off the edge and plunge into hell, just as Emily had been warned in Durham County Gaol. Time would tell.

A storm appeared to be brewing after the women returned to the orlop, and the hatches were slammed down and battened.

Emily lay on her bunk and listened to the heavy waves crashing against the ship, knowing her destiny was sealed. But after a little while she became restless and carefully slid her legs into the narrow space between the bunks, trying not to disturb the others. She looked around her, taking a deep breath as she did so, now realising the nausea she had suffered on board the rotting hulk had suddenly disappeared. Perhaps the stench of the bilges was less prevalent on the newer *Lady Penrhyn*. Whatever the reason, the sickly feeling plagued her no more.

She stared down at Nell who was snoring lightly, a faint smile sketching her face. *God bless her.* Of all the women, Nell was the one who suffered the most and complained the least. And what was a little nausea compared with Nell's bone ache?

Emily's thoughts were disturbed when the hatch cover was flung back revealing the faces of two redcoats peering through the opening. The light spilled down as their heavy booted feet clattered on the rungs of the ladder. One of them approached.

'Come you lucky lot. Time for exercise,' he said removing the chains from her wrists.

Emily gently massaged her wrists and, reaching out, she took hold of Nell's hand. 'I'll help you up the ladder,' she said, knowing her friend, having been aroused so suddenly from her sleep, would be a little shaky on her feet.

'I'm fine, dear,' Nell said, rubbing her eyes roughly. 'Disturbed me dream he did. Me and Billy together. Happy times.' Her eyes were filled with sadness, and her voice wavered slightly as she struggled up the steps to the upper deck.

The gloom of the heavy grey clouds surrounded them masking the sun. Emily held out her hands to check the light drizzle in the air and wiped them on the front of her tunic, puzzled by the thickening of her waist and the swelling of her belly.

She turned to Nell. 'I do not understand why my belly is so swollen, Nell. They are not generous with the food aboard the ship.'

Nell turned sharply and placed her hand on Emily's belly. 'If I did not know better, dearie, I would swear you were with child.'

'But I do not understand, Nell,' Emily gasped, astounded by such a revelation.

'Have you lain with a man at any time?' Nell asked sharply. 'That's when babies are made.'

Emily's stomach lurched. 'I am aware of that Nell, but surely not after the once.'

'The once?' Nell queried. 'The once is all it takes, lass.'

Emily twisted the edge of her rough tunic in her

fingers. It was then the terrible realisation dawned and the image of Richard Allenby flashed before her. Perhaps she should have been stronger? But what more could she have done? She had fought back. But she had not been able to match Allenby's physical strength to free herself from his clutches.

The experience distressed her to such an extent that she had cast it from her mind until now but, wrapped in a cloud of unwarranted guilt, she began to reflect. As she explained the events of that night to Nell, her recollections sharpened her perception of the situation. Agonising over what had happened and still puzzled by what Nell had told her, she confessed her ignorance.

'I knew not what to expect. Allenby forced himself upon me. But I thought babies came when people loved one another. How has it happened?'

'How little you know, Emily,' Nell muttered, shaking her head. 'That is not how it works. Oh that it was.' She sighed. 'It is a cruel world and we must bear the burden,' Nell concluded.

Emily was stunned by Nell's words and, as a sudden glimmer of understanding registered within her, her legs lost all their strength. Her mouth felt dry and her heart began to thud heavily in her chest as she clung to the barricade. The ache inside her head throbbed rapidly and her stomach was tied up in knots. Holding back hot tears of frustration she looked to Nell for support and understanding.

'What am I to do?'

'You will not be the first to suffer, Emmy. The world is full of selfish, evil bastards,' she said, her voice heavy with disgust. She turned to face Emily, gripping her arms. Putting on a bright face, she continued. 'I've delivered many a baby in me time, my dear. We'll manage.'

Despite her headache and the fears she was trying to overcome, Emily felt a sense of relief that, at last, she had shared her shameful secret. In her heart she felt certain that Nell, who knew about these things, would help her through. She collected her thoughts. She had promised to look after Nell, yet here was Nell promising to look after her!

She turned and looked across the deck spotting the young marine who had descended the ladder earlier. He made eye contact and held her gaze before smiling once more. Emily returned the smile but then she thought about the incident with Allenby and Mary's activity on the hulks. Would she ever trust another man as long as she lived?

She turned away glancing up above. Storm clouds blackened the sky and the drizzle turned to rain. When it began to lash across the decks Emily took hold of Nell's arm, pulling her towards the hatch.

'Come along, Nell. It is no use getting drenched again. It will only make your bone ache worse.' Back in the orlop she gazed blankly ahead. Nell's words had been a shock, a bitter blow. But it was something Emily must come to terms with, for she knew the consequences were inevitable.

Chapter 4

1787

Emily still kept a count of the date. Her sixteenth birthday passed without mention and on the twelfth of May she was out exercising on deck when she gazed casually at the other ten ships mustered at anchor. Focusing her eyes on the *Sirius*, she saw one of the naval officers issuing orders through a speaking trumpet. She strained her ears to listen but the heavy wind whipped around the fleet and she was unable to catch his exact words. 'Who is that man?' she asked a red-coat. 'He looks important.'

'The Captain-General, Commander Phillip,' came a voice from the red-coated ranks.

'Commander Phillip,' she whispered, still straining to listen to his words.

When eventually the commander discarded the speaking trumpet and dismissed the men there was a flurry of activity and rowing boats were lowered. The dignitaries, the commander himself and Captain John Hunter, master of the *Sirius,* visited each transport in turn. Finally they arrived on board the *Lady Penrhyn* to inspect the crew members, the guards and the felons.

Emily noticed Commander Phillip was a slightly built yet important-looking man with a distinguished air about him. His nose was long and sharp, his bottom lip pendulous and she judged him to be in his late forties, about Nell's age, but much better preserved. He addressed the women.

'Once the fleet departs you will be freed of your

shackles. But be aware that the guards will be ever vigilant. The journey will be arduous but you will be expected to exercise at least twice a day to ensure you are fit and well. When we reach Botany Bay you will need to prepare the ground to build new homes. You will be given a chance to start life afresh. Let us hope you can make a success of it.'

Emily dwelt on his words. Unlike Major Ross who had spoken, the commander seemed a kindly fellow. And the positive way in which he referred to their voyage to Botany Bay gave her a feeling of optimism. She reckoned the rumours about falling off the edge of the world into hell were based on fear. Determined to be strong, she developed a resolve to make the best of the circumstances in which she was now inextricably bound.

But some days later her resolve began to waver. She was lying on her bunk, contemplating the future, when she heard the noisy footsteps of a guard descending the ladder. His voice boomed out.

'Emily Spence!' he paused and looked around the orlop. 'Speak up, woman! Captain Campbell wishes to address you up above.'

'I am Emily Spence,' she replied, puzzled by the order.

Nell took her hand. 'What is the problem?'

'It is no business of yours,' he sniped.

Emily was wary. Why had the captain called for her? She had done nothing wrong. Had he discovered she was with child and decided she was not fit to travel in that condition? But that could not be so, for several other women were in the same state.

The guard released her from the chains, and she was taken to Captain Campbell.

'You are Emily Spence, I gather?' He looked directly at her, and then he shifted his gaze to the ocean beyond.

'Yes, sir,' she replied, still wondering why she had been singled out.

'It is with regret I must inform you your mother, Anna Spence, passed away some weeks ago. I have no further details, but should I hear more, you will be informed forthwith,' he concluded in monotone, his words lacking any emotion.

At first, Emily was unable to take in the news. Her brain became numb and the captain's words were dispersed from her mind. But when she stared at the missive in his hand, a certain realisation came over her. Her legs buckled beneath her and she collapsed on to the deck, blackness crowding around her.

'You lad!' Captain Campbell bellowed, pointing to Corporal Ballantyne. 'See to yon woman. She has received news of the worst kind. Help her to her feet and see she takes in plenty of air before you take her down below.'

Jimmy turned as he heard the captain's words, his handsome face now creased with concern. The woman was no more than a girl of about fifteen or sixteen. She was the pretty one he had spotted down below earlier. He pulled his thoughts together.

'Yes, sir,' he replied, and he ran across the deck. She had passed out completely. The news must have been distressing. He knelt down and gently touched her cheek with the back of his hand.

'Wake up, lassie,' he whispered. 'Do not worry,

for I am here to take care of you.'

The girl moved slightly and opened her eyes.

Jimmy stared down at her and his heart began to pound in his chest. Despite the ragged clothes and the fact that her face was ashen, she was stunningly beautiful. She seemed to have some sort of aura about her, something special. But then he felt foolish for she was speaking to him and he was not taking in what she was saying.

'Who are you?' she asked, apparently for a second time.

'Corporal Ballantyne, miss. The captain asked me to tend to you. Let me help you to your feet.' Her shoulders began to heave and tears streamed from her big, luminous eyes, a rich hazel in colour. She allowed him to help her up and she stood before him, her face now resolute.

'I do apologise, Corporal Ballantyne. The Captain has given me very sad news. My mother passed away some weeks ago. I have only now been told.'

He felt a strong need to protect her and he slipped an arm around her shoulder to comfort her. 'I am sad to hear that. I understand how you feel, for I would have felt the same had it been my mother. I love her dearly...' Surprised he had made such an admission to the girl, his statement ended abruptly.

'Thank you for being so understanding,' she replied as he led her to the barricade. 'My name is Emily Spence.' She frowned. 'What worries me most is that I was not there for her funeral. She will be buried in a pauper's grave, I know it.' She sighed and the tears began again. 'And that means no coffin, nothing but a sheet to cover her.'

Jimmy placed his hands on her forearms, his blue eyes glistening as he listened to her plight. He looked into her face. 'When you left her behind was she with friends?'

'Yes, she was at the manor. There was Cook and the other servants. But how could they spare the money for anything other than to bury her in a pauper's grave? She should be with my father. He passed away not long ago.'

'Then I am sure her friends will have done everything they could. You must tell yourself she is now with your father. There is no use mulling it over in your mind, Emily.'

'You are very kind and perhaps you are right. But it is such a shock and so difficult for me to take in.'

'I understand,' he said, looking up and meeting the gaze of Sergeant Stockdale whose eyes were narrowing with disapproval. 'Maybe I shall see you again, Emily, once the ship departs for Botany Bay. But I must be wary of the sergeant,' he whispered. 'He is strict about discipline.' Jimmy dropped his hands from around her forearms. 'When you feel well enough, I will help you back down below.'

'Thank you. I will return now,' she said lowering her own voice almost to a whisper.

His mind was buzzing with the reality of the situation. How could such a pretty, fragile little thing have been involved in any sort of crime? It must have been something quite serious for her to be aboard the *Penrhyn*. No doubt he would find out eventually once he had a chance to talk with her.

Emily approached the ladder and he followed. She turned. 'I will be fine now, Corporal.'

'Please call me Jimmy,' he said as he watched her foot tread lightly on the ladder, his eyes following her as she descended. There was something special about her and he was determined to watch out for her in the future. But he was jerked back to reality by Sergeant Stockdale. 'Ballantyne, over here!'

Jimmy turned to follow the sergeant's orders but before he did so he reverted his gaze to the ladder. The girl had disappeared.

The ship gave a heavy shudder and Emily opened her eyes. Since there was no flicker of light, she was unsure of the time when the ship set sail but she was aware from her reckoning it was the thirteenth of May 1787.

The ship lurched forward, rolling and pitching slightly, its timbers creaking noisily, the sound of water slapping against its sides. There were moans from the women, many seasick at the movement. But the majority settled back into the orlop, lulled by the constant rhythm of the ship's momentum.

That morning they were allowed to exercise unfettered as the fleet, led by the flagship *Sirius,* in turn escorted by the frigate *Hyaena,* left Portsmouth for the south. The air was fresh. The smell of the wet canvas caught in the breeze and the fibrous tang of oakum pervaded the decks. Emily screwed up her eyes and peered ahead, half-blinded by the strong sunlight after the darkness below. The ship sailed clear of the estuary, the shoreline already fading from view. The sails flapped against the mast as Emily struggled to hold on to the strong barricade which ran across the deck from bulwark to bulwark.

'Can you manage?'

Recognising the Scottish accent, Emily gripped the barricade tightly and turned around. Her heart fluttered in her chest. It was Jimmy. 'Just about. The breeze is strong now that we have set sail.'

'That is true.' He noticed her bedding was strewn on the upper deck. 'Let me help you with that.' Between them they spread it out on the deck where the captain had allowed them to leave it to dry out.

Jimmy stood beside her and they stared out to sea as the ship, now in full sail, passed the Needles and the Isle of Wight, before entering the Channel. The frigate *Hyaena* loosened her ties with the heavy transport *Charlotte* and headed back to the estuary. At that point Jimmy touched her arm.

'I must leave you, Emily. I cannot linger. Perhaps when I am off duty we could talk but I will need to take care for the captain is adamant we must not fraternise with the women.'

'I understand, Jimmy.' Emily smiled as he squeezed her arm gently and left her there.

The bluster and the heavy winds persisted as the fleet entered the Bay of Biscay. Nell appeared on deck and turned to Emily. 'Storm clouds are brewing again, Em,' she whispered anxiously. 'Now that your term is drawing near, do not tire yourself dearie for it will harm the child.'

Emily gazed at the leaden skies. 'I am fine, Nell. I need to take in fresh air. It will be good for the poor soul too.' She placed her hand over her slightly swollen belly and rubbed. 'I will not tire myself, I promise. Once around the barricade, that is all.' But within minutes the cold wind had splattered raindrops into her face. 'Go quickly, Nell' she said, grabbing hold of their bedding and dashing towards the hatch.

During the long haul to their first port of call the *Lady Penrhyn* and the heavy *Charlotte* constantly lagged behind but, on the orders of Captain Phillip, the fleet remained together and none of them disappeared over the horizon and out of sight.

By this time a desperate need for food swept through the ship. And it was during the daily exercise that Emily discovered why. As she lingered on deck with Nell, she overheard a discussion between surgeon, Bowes-Smyth and Captain Campbell.

'The Captain-General complained vehemently before we set sail. The fleet is ill-equipped and poorly supplied. We shall all starve if we do not reach land soon,' the surgeon advised the captain. 'We need fresh food to prevent scurvy. We need medicines and extra clothing. It is a disgrace we have been neglected so.'

'I agree, Arthur. Those are my sentiments exactly. The commander should have insisted on the supplies being made available before we left England. Personally, I would have refused to leave without them,' Captain Campbell replied.

'And another observation. The crew are taking more than their share of food. The women are suffering. We need to have a word with Sever.'

Emily whispered to Nell. 'That is why we are going hungry.' But food was the least of Emily's troubles. For the past two months she had worried about the fate of her unborn child. And her new resolve to remain strong began to wane. She felt a combination of insecurity and fear at the prospect of becoming a mother.

Her thoughts were disturbed when Nell's arm slid around her shoulder. 'You are fretting again, Emmy. I can tell by the look on your face. The bastard, Allenby should have been caught for his crime. Some men charged with rape are hanged by the neck. But not the aristocracy.' she said. 'You are innocent and yet the victim, the one to suffer.'

'It is too late now, Nell.'

'You are right. I am venting my anger, nothing more,' she said, pausing to deliberate. 'Who is there to uphold the law for us? It is never on the side of the poor. It is there for the good of the rich who always get away with their crimes.' She sighed. 'But your time is drawing near, Emmy. You say it is eight months since that villain abused you?'

'It was October when it happened, for it was not long after Father died, and Mother and I had moved into the manor.' She blinked her eyes to prevent the flow of tears.

'Then it will not be long before the child is born.'

'I am worried. Rachael Cross lost her baby at birth, and what of Ruth Winder. When she died her child was left to be cared for by the other women.'

'You are strong, Emily. Some would have given up by now, but not you. And I am here to help.'

Emily's forehead puckered. She had told herself constantly she did not want her child, but she had difficulty quelling that maternal instinct, the need to hold the baby in her arms as soon as it was born. No matter how she tried to eradicate the feeling, it lingered. And now the child moved frantically inside her belly, wanting to escape. In a month's time, that would surely happen. But how would it get out? Would they have to cut her belly open? This was a constant source of worry to her.

By the end of May the fleet was in the North Atlantic Ocean well on the way to Tenerife. Another week or so and Captain Sever reckoned they would reach the island. Conditions were blustery up on deck and another storm appeared imminent. After their morning exercise, the women were mustered back down below.

Despite the straw mattress, the bunk pressed hard into Emily's spine, a suffering she would normally have borne without complaint, but in her condition the discomfiture was more pronounced. As she lay there in a pool of silence and slid her palm over her swollen belly her thoughts turned to Allenby. How she despised him. There was no future for his child, nothing to justify the little wretch's existence. She sent up a silent prayer, beseeching the Good Lord to prevent the unwanted soul from entering this world of poverty and injustice.

But how many times must she tell herself to stop the agony of this soul-searching? She would have to bide her time and face the future as it unfolded.

With a swoop of her hand she clamped down hard on the cockroach crawling across her thigh and knocked it to the floor. A cockroach was nothing unusual. It was the rats carrying disease from the filthy bilges full of excrement and debris that were dangerous. They were vile creatures. Nora Crowther had been bitten the previous week and her health had deteriorated rapidly. The surgeon was unable to save her and she had died a slow and horrible death.

The storm became worse and the hatches were securely battened down, enclosing around them the putrid smells of the bilges and the unclean bodies of the women who lay huddled together, shaking with fear. Many still suffered from seasickness, others from dysentery, and they cried out in pain. Some were with child, caught by the ship's rutting crew and guards, or earlier on the hulks. This was the inevitable consequence of selling their bodies, or of being raped and ravaged by the sex-starved men.

Her thoughts came to a standstill when, as she lay resting, the first twinges began. Nell, ever vigilant, heard her stifled cry and came to her immediately.

'It seems the baby has started, dearie.'

Emily felt a strange sensation, a sort of tightening across her belly just as Nell ran her hands over it.

'Hold strong, Emmy. You will feel it many times. But you must hold on. It is not time yet.'

Emily gripped the sides of the bunk and prayed the child would come quickly. Turning this way and that as the contractions intensified, she tried with immense effort to straighten her heavy body, only to be arrested by a much stronger spasm. Her voice, thin with urgency, brought an involuntary cry from her tightly compressed lips. 'Nell, please help me. Do something.'

'I am doing the best I can, Emmy. You must bear down now.'

Despite Nell's encouragement, Emily's agonising shrieks continued and after an hour or so she feared the baby would never be born. She was weary now.

'I am pushing as hard as I can, Nell. But it is no use.' Again and again she cried out in agony, but still the child failed to make its debut. And, as Emily struggled to give birth, there seemed to be nothing more Nell could do to relieve her pain.

'Jessie, go tell the guard we need the surgeon,' she urged. 'Something is amiss,' she whispered. She frowned and turned her attention back to Emily. 'Do not fret. It will be fine. I have sent Jessie for the surgeon.' Taking her hands, Nell pleaded. 'You must push as hard as you can.'

Emily, now too exhausted to scream, groaned, 'I cannot do it, Nell. I am spent.' She struggled with the heavy and frequent contractions. 'Please, God. Help me,' she cried. Now that Nell had sent for the surgeon did that mean he would need to cut her belly open? Eyes damp with perspiration Emily looked up at Nell whose frown deepened.

At that moment the hatch opened and light flooded in, shedding its beam on Emily. Her eyes flickered towards it as a shadow was cast and a boot appeared on the ladder. The ship's surgeon, Arthur Bowes-Smyth entered the orlop and climbed down, his lamp swaying with the roll of the ship, the pale beam now throwing its light on him. He was a man in his late thirties with a kind, sensitive face.

He covered his nose and mouth with his hand to avoid the pervading stink. 'My God,' he mumbled. 'The stench in here is repulsive.' His step quickened as Emily cried out again, and once he was beside her, she was aware of two bright eyes peering into her face. The surgeon's wide brow furrowed.

'The baby needs help if it is to survive,' he

insisted, turning to Nell. 'Hold the lamp,' he said, passing it to her.

Nell held it up before him and Emily felt the touch of the surgeon's hands on her belly. 'The infant is in the wrong position and must be turned. This may hurt, but you must bear with me whilst I apply a gentle manipulation,' he said. 'Take a deep breath. I will be as quick as I can,' he promised, and she felt his hands fingering the outline of the unborn child.

Swamped with pain, Emily's agonised, despairing shrieks could be heard throughout the orlop.

'Please stop, sir, for I cannot bear it.'

He stroked her forehead. 'There. It is done now. The child will come. Breathe very deeply and bear down as hard as you can.'

She tried to take deep breaths, her chest rasping with the effort. And by this time, the women, unable to disguise their curiosity, were gathering close. And the guards, wide-eyed and morbidly inquisitive, were breathing heavily behind them.

Bowes-Smyth called out to the sentries. 'Move these women right away, you gawping brutes. And bring more lamps. Dammit men, have you no sense? I need to see what I am doing.'

Emily was sure she was about to reach her end. The time had come to take the rightful punishment for her shame, punishment for Allenby's vile act. Now in a state of semi-consciousness she struggled for what seemed an eternity, but she managed to push when she was told to do so and she felt the child slip silently from her body. Completely exhausted she closed her eyes and began to float away, the only sensation being the dampness of the cloth on her face. She heard the faraway cry of the child as she tried to listen to the surgeon's words.

'It is a girl. But she is very small and frail.' He held the child above Emily and she gazed at the tiny infant, gently touching her cheek.

'Thank you, sir,' she managed to utter, but her strength disappeared and her head flopped to one side. She must sleep.

Rubbing Emily's cheeks with the back of her hand, Nell whispered with a sense of urgency, 'Do not leave me, dearie.'

'You need not worry,' the surgeon insisted. 'The girl is very tired. But it is not surprising. She has battled long and hard. She will be fine if only I can stem the bleeding.'

Nell dipped the rag into the cool water and wiped Emily's brow. 'And what of the child?' she asked.

'There are no guarantees. The child is small, and the conditions on board are not conducive to rearing an infant. The child will need to be succoured, fed with the breast.' His voice was heavy with sorrow. 'Whether the mother is capable or not, I could not say. We must wait until she is rested.'

Emily drifted into consciousness and heard the surgeon's words. Panic-stricken she realised her child might die and, although she had never wanted the baby, after seeing and touching the child she could not bear to lose her. She was determined to fight to save her child, for the infant deserved to be given a chance and desperately needed a mother.

The surgeon turned to Nell. 'The baby is very weak and may not live. This girl must be given extra food as sustenance to feed her child. I will speak with Captain Sever.' He turned to one of the guards. 'Go now. Fetch me my bag. Send some of the others down with plenty of water.'

The guard jumped to attention and left. The surgeon once again addressed Nell.

'I want no disturbance, for I must continue to stem the bleeding, otherwise we shall lose her.' He paused and stared down at Emily who was much calmer now. 'Rest. It is over. You will be fine.' He turned to Nell. 'She is a mere girl herself. Who is the father of her child?' he enquired, continuing to pack in gauze to stop the bleeding. 'She cannot have been willing.' Renowned for his lack of tolerance towards those who gave their bodies to the men, he regularly quoted from the bible, hoping that some of them might be 'saved'.

'It was the son of the lord of the manor where she worked, sir.'

'Always the same with the aristocracy,' mumbled the surgeon in an intended aside, an edge of anger to his voice. 'They think they are entitled to use those in their employ in any way they wish.' He sighed heavily. 'Anarchy and confusion prevails throughout our ships too. The men do not obey orders. They have their way with the women.' He shook his head. 'Some of the women are no better. The morals on board this ship are base.' He turned his attention back to Nell. 'Irrespective of that, this deed was carried out by someone who should have set an example.' He took a deep breath as though pulling his thoughts together. 'But why am I telling you something you already know?' He hunched his shoulders, picked up the infant and wrapped her in a piece of torn sheeting, nodding stiffly towards Nell. 'The child needs to be cleaned and kept warm. Take her whilst I attend to the mother.'

Nell took the child from him and wiped her clean with the torn rags they had put aside in readiness.

She returned to Emily's bunk where the surgeon was still battling to stem the haemorrhage. 'This child will live if I have to die for her.' Damp eyed, Nell gave her guarantee and gazed on Emily. 'Sleep now my dear. Your task is over.' She swallowed hard. 'Shall we call her Lucy? That was the name of my baby, the baby I lost to the fever.' She wiped her tear-stained face and cradled the infant.

Emily felt herself floating. Was she drifting to God in heaven where she would meet her mother and father? She tried to stop herself from slipping away, but it seemed impossible. With a flicker of regret in her gaze, she shuddered and struggled to speak, her words thin and frail. 'I fear I am leaving this earth. I am so tired, Nell. If that is to be my fate, I give Lucy to you. Please cherish her.'

Surgeon Bowes-Smyth was quick to respond, bringing Emily back to her senses. 'We will have none of that talk,' he insisted. 'Granted, you are exhausted but. after laudanum to numb the pain and a good sleep, you will be fine.' His voice wavered. 'The child is yours. You will live to rear it.'

The surgeon left the orlop but his concern for Emily was deep-seated. He felt in some way responsible for her safe-keeping, and it was with this in mind he approached Captain Campbell.

'One of the felons, a weak and frail child herself, has given birth down below. She must take in fresh air and light exercise to help her regain strength but she will need to be assisted to the upper deck until she has enough energy to cope for herself.' He paused to take in the captain's reaction.

'I see,' Campbell replied, showing no emotion.

'Have you a strong lad you can trust? I should be most grateful for your help, James. The girl has been abused at the hands of one of our own kind.'

'Most certainly, Arthur, one of my young marines could be of help. I will ask the sergeant to arrange it.' He turned and beckoned to the sergeant. 'But do not believe everything these women tell you. They are a set of vagabonds, thieves and whores. You seem to me most gullible, old boy.'

'Not so, James. You know quite well my views. These women are not whores by profession, and whoring is not a transportable offence. It is not the offence for which they were sentenced.' He frowned. 'Granted, some of them are willing to sell their bodies for anything they can lay their hands on. The Good Lord is aware of this and, unless they repent, He will punish them. They will go to hell.' He paused. 'But my grateful thanks for your generous offer.'

'But the women taunt both my men and the crew, Arthur. Captain Sever and I would have the greatest difficulty watching our men every minute of the day. What do you expect?'

'It is a minority of the women who encourage them. Most of the women did not choose crime. Poverty begets theft and other petty crimes. These women are desperate, thoroughly demoralised. I may even venture to say there was never a more abandoned set of wretches collected in one place at any period than are now on this ship.'

'Never was a truer word uttered,' Captain Campbell concurred.

'The male convicts are able to redeem themselves through work and penance. If they reform, they are admitted back into society. Not so the women. Their characters can never be retrieved. All they invite is contempt and rape rather than help from superiors.'

'Enough said, Arthur,' Captain Campbell replied, a look of boredom on his face. It was obvious he had heard the surgeon's words many times before. 'I appreciate your viewpoint but I do not entirely agree with it. I will have a word with Sergeant MacVay, a very shrewd individual. He has the measure of all his men. He will choose carefully.'

Spotting Jimmy, who apparently appeared at first glance to fit the bill, he turned to address MacVay who was standing nearby awaiting is orders.

'That corporal yonder, Sergeant MacVay, the tall lad,' he said pointing to Jimmy. 'He looks strapping enough. Is he of good nature?'

'He is indeed, sir. A very willing laddie.'

'Call him over, will you? There is a young girl, one of the felons who, according to the surgeon here, is very weak. We have been asked by the commander to preserve lives, to ensure these women arrive fit and well. I would ask you to set the lad on to help the girl. The surgeon wishes to speak with him, to give him instruction.'

The sergeant responded to the captain's request immediately.

'Corporal Ballantyne, over here, laddie. Ye are to

report to the surgeon. He needs help with one of the felons. Jump to it, Ballantyne, and no fraternising with the women.'

Jimmy drew himself up to his full height, saluted the sergeant and crossed the deck in the direction of the surgeon.

Aware that the child would surely die if a solution were not found quickly, Nell rocked the new-born infant in her arms to stop the hungry cries. Emily was too weak to provide suckle for Lucy, and there was a desperate need for Nell to find a wet nurse.

She gazed gloomily out to sea, her face pale and drawn, her bony hands shaking as she cradled the child. And then it came to her. She would approach Grace Luscombe who had given birth to a girl the previous week. A well-proportioned woman, her breasts were swollen with milk, despite the lack of good, nourishing food. She was a pretty girl with hair tumbling down over her face in thick auburn curls. Crew and marines alike were strongly attracted to her and she was easily flattered by their attentions. Perhaps with the right approach, a little cajolery, she could be persuaded to help. As soon as the opportunity arose, Nell approached her.

'Grace, dearie, my Emmy is too weak to feed this baby. If we muster up extra food for you, would you consider providing suckle for young Lucy?' A lump came into her throat. 'You're a fine, handsome woman with plenty for two.'

'Don't know about that, Nell,' she replied, a closed look on her face. 'I have my Jane to feed, poor little lamb. Don't know that I could manage two.' Her mouth was set, her tone and expression holding little emotion.

But Nell knew those looks were meant to hide her gentle disposition. 'I beg of you, Grace. Lucy will die if we cannot find help. You are such a kind soul, a wonderful, caring mother to that baby of yours. For Emily's sake, will you try?'

The barriers were broken. 'Suppose I could try. But if my Jane starts to cry because there aint enough milk, then I be forced to let Lucy go.' She frowned then hesitated. 'I know dear Emmy would help me if I needed her. Pass the child over, Nell.'

She pushed her hair away from her eyes and slipped the sleeve of her ragged dress over her shoulder, handing her own child, Jane, to Jessie Martin who smiled and rocked the infant. Nell held out the crying Lucy and Grace immediately placed her to the breast. Lucy gulped greedily and Grace smiled in satisfaction.

'I shall be ever grateful to you, dearest Grace,' Nell replied, knowing that once Grace had allowed Lucy to suckle she would not let her go without a fight. 'I will do anything you ask to help,' she stressed, as relief surged through her.

Despite Grace's reservations, Nell knew she would give of her best, and that something drastic would have to happen before she gave up on the poor little soul.

Chapter 5

It was the third of June 1787 when the ship approached the little port of Santa Cruz on the island of Tenerife. The mainsails slithered and flapped in the breeze as they were lowered. The ship's passage through the calmer waters of the harbour became much slower and the sound of the waves breaking against the hull became gentler. The enormous cable plunged into the water's depths and thundered down until the anchor struck the seabed. The hatches were removed and the women began to spill out on to the upper deck.

Jimmy had been shocked and disappointed when the surgeon told him of Emily's ordeal during childbirth. She was so young to be bearing a child. Surely it had not been through her own choice. And where was the father of the child? These thoughts bombarded his mind as, on the instructions of Bowes-Smyth, he descended the ladder to the orlop and approached Emily.

'The surgeon tells me you are in need of assistance now that your child has been delivered. I will help you up to the deck.'

Emily recognised Jimmy immediately and she detected a shyness tinged with some other emotion she could not detect. Whatever it was, she knew him to be honest and tender-hearted, not like some of the others who were fond of touching.

'It is very kind of you. I am sure I will soon be able to get about for myself.'

'It is no trouble, Emily. I am only too pleased to do whatever I can.' He helped her up the ladder and across the deck to take her morning dose of fresh air. He was extraordinarily strong and he lifted her as though she were a mere infant herself, gently placing her against the bulkhead from whence she could gain a panoramic view.

The sky was painted gold with layers of greys and blues, and the sun shone high above. Emily was enchanted by the vision of the little white cottages gleaming in the sunshine. The land surrounding the port rose steeply and there was a distinct lack of vegetation. In direct contrast to the sunny port, a layer of cloud hung over the sheer mountains and shrouded their peaks.

'What a wonderful view, Jimmy,' she gasped. 'Everything is so different from my village in Yorkshire. I have never seen anything like this,' she cried excitedly.

'Nor have I,' Jimmy told her as he glanced quickly at the scenery before gazing in Emily's direction. 'I have seen many mountains in Scotland, but not against such a colourful background. And, of course, this is the first time I have been away from my family.'

Emily sensed a tinge of regret in his voice. And she wanted to ask him why he had chosen such a life. But maybe he would think her too familiar, prying into his affairs. And she quickly decided against asking him.

'It is the same for me. But you know that I shall never see my mother and father again,' she continued, restraining herself from another tearful scene, for she was reluctant to reveal her sadness once again in Jimmy's presence. She smiled. 'But now I have my dear little Lucy. She is my family, and we must start life afresh.'

Jimmy's thoughts on Emily's plight returned. He was curious. She seemed so young to have borne a child. 'But what of Lucy's father? Will you not see him again, Emily?'

'I wish never to set eyes on him as long as I live,' she stressed, and it did not surprise her that Jimmy's forehead creased in perplexity. She took a deep breath. 'I realise you are puzzled by my words, and one day I will tell you my story. But not now, Jimmy, for I wish to remain strong, and rid my mind of all those hurtful images.'

Jimmy smiled. 'Of course, I understand, Emily. Forgive me for being thoughtless. I did not intend to bring back memories you are trying to forget.'

Not wishing to continue in this vein, Emily gazed across the water and pointed to Governor Phillip who, now that the full fleet was at anchor, appeared to be boarding each of the transports in turn. Drawing Jimmy's attention to the longboat approaching the *Lady Penrhyn*, she said, 'It seems the commander is about to visit our ship.'

At that very moment, Sergeant MacVay called Jimmy to muster on deck with the rest of his men. 'The lassie will be fine for a while, Ballantyne. Leave her there,' he ordered.

Jimmy turned to Emily. 'Will you manage if you stand against the bulkhead? I must join the men, for I do not wish to incur the sergeant's wrath.'

'I will be fine. Nell is here now with little Lucy. Go quickly, Jimmy.'

'I will be back as soon as the governor leaves.'

Now that the fleet was at anchor, Commander Phillip called to inspect crew, convicts and guard. Immediately he stepped on board, he addressed the gathering. 'It is my wish to avoid any possible trouble with the townspeople. Therefore, neither crew nor guard will be allowed ashore.' There was a groan from the body of men.

He continued. 'The women must be given the freedom of the deck whilst at anchor. They will neither be fettered nor confined below during our stay, do you hear?' Despite his slightness of stature, he was bold and emphatic in his statement, and he appeared to have the full respect of both crew and marines. He turned his attention to the women. 'A strict guard will be kept on you at all times, and the waters will be under constant patrol by longboats.' Turning to the men, he added, 'Anyone found disobeying my orders will be severely punished. Let that be understood. My first priority will be fresh food for everyone.' At that he left the ship, his entourage following close behind.

After returning to the bulkhead, Jimmy pointed to the boat heading for the port. It carried the commander and the senior officers, resplendent in full dress uniform.

'The dignitaries are to dine at the residence of the Spanish Governor of Tenerife,' he told Emily. 'According to the sergeant, who is very knowledgeable about these things, it is a tradition for officers of high rank to visit the governor or his deputy at each port of call.' He stared ahead then turned to Sandy who had joined the group. 'I wish we could visit the island, Sandy. We have not touched upon dry land for many weeks.'

'Maybe at our next stop,' Sandy replied.

The boats had been sent ashore for provisions and it appeared that rum was a priority to both crew and marines alike. No sooner had it reached the ship than a number of pannikins appeared and the stuff was quaffed freely. The effects of this consumption were rapid. Whilst, on the orders of the commander, a full guard was mounted during daylight hours, it was an unruly, pathetic mob, more often than not in a permanent state of inebriation, breath reeking of rum and eyes bleary and red-rimmed.

The provision boats sallied to and fro replenishing stocks on the three store ships, *Borrowdale, Fishburn* and *Golden Grove* with fresh fruit, vegetables and other vital provisions. The huge water tuns were lowered over the side of the ship into longboats and refilled with fresh water from the river which glistened in the sunlight as it flowed down from the mountains. Fresh goats' meat was available to convicts, crew and marines alike whilst they were at anchor in the bay at Santa Cruz, and Emily seized the chance to supplement Grace's milk with the fresh goats' milk issued to them.

'It is a relief to me that we are able to feed Lucy on the goats' milk, for it will ease Grace's struggle to keep both infants succoured,' she said.

'Grace has no problem feeding the two, Emmy, but I expect you feel beholden to her.'

'You are right, Nell. I do. I only wish I could repay her in some way.'

'You will, lass. There is plenty of time for that.'

Mr Bowes-Smyth made it in his way to visit

Emily each day to start, but less frequently as she regained her strength. Gradually her health improved but she would never be able to feed Lucy now that the little milk she had produced in the beginning had completely dried up.

After a week in Tenerife, the officers bade their farewells to the islanders and returned to the fleet. Emily was now strong enough to get about unaided but Jimmy chose to accompany her to the upper deck to watch the fleet departing the little port. Taking her hand, he led her to the barricade.

The weather was fine and sunny, and a gentle wind ruffled Emily's dark hair. Since the surgeon had taken her under his wing and supplied her with soap, her hair, now glossy and shining under the touch of the sun's rays, hung loosely in tendrils over her shoulders. She supposed it was favouritism, but it was so good to feel clean.

'See the people waving. They are like dots on the wharf, Jimmy,' she cried, her eyes alight with excitement and shining a rich mocha hue. Jimmy turned to her and studied her at arm's length, an admiring gaze on his face.

Emily was caught by the smile in his eyes which only moments ago shone a vibrant, rich azure, but now they radiated a softer, darker midnight hue revealing deep emotion. She felt the hair on the nape of her neck stand up and a pleasant tingle raced through her body. Her mouth felt dry. But seconds later, swept by a wave of discomfort, she quickly turned away.

This was something she had not experienced before, something she felt she could not reciprocate.

Whilst she knew Jimmy would never hurt her, she was afraid of any serious involvement. They stood in awkward silence for a moment or two before Jimmy spoke up.

'The crew reckon we will call at Cape Verde Islands, maybe a week away, to replenish the tuns with fresh water. Then we will head for Rio in South America which is not a direct route to Cape Town, but it is apparently the route chosen to avoid unfavourable currents.'

'But why do we need to take on more water?' Emily failed to understand why this was necessary. 'We watched the crew bringing back the full barrels before we left.'

'The water becomes salty in time,' Jimmy explained. 'It will need to be topped up again before we reach Rio. It is a long journey and there may not be enough water to go round,' he told her.

It was another week before they sailed through the imaginary line over the Tropic of Cancer, and the north-east trade winds gave them a gentle push, helping the ships on their south-westerly journey.

By the nineteenth of June, the Cape Verde Islands seemed ominously close, and the fleet advanced towards the south east to enter the harbour. But the high waves running ashore smashed against the reefs which circled the islands, and Captain Phillip ordered the fleet back to sea. It would not be possible to replenish the water tuns which meant that rationing at some point would be inevitable.

Emily leant against the barricade and gazed across the ocean, contemplating her future now that the journey to Botany Bay was well underway. But her thoughts were interrupted when she sensed someone behind her. She turned to find Nell standing there.

'I should have known it was you, Nell, for this is our favourite spot is it not?'

'It is so peaceful here,' Nell replied.

Grace came up behind them and intervened.

'Shall I feed Lucy now, Emmy dear?' she asked, taking the child from Emily and handing her own child, Jane, over to her.

'Goodness me, Grace, I was so engrossed and Lucy was so quiet, I was lost to the world.'

'It is good to let your mind drift, Em. There is nothing to be gained by thinking about our misfortunes. We must make the best of our lot.'

Emily confessed to herself that, apart from her anxiety at not being able to breast-feed Lucy, her spirits had brightened over the past weeks, and in her heart she knew the reason. It was Jimmy. But it was something she kept inside, something she was afraid to admit either to Grace or to Nell.

'You are right. I feel more at peace now that Lucy is making progress, and I have you to thank for that, dear Grace. I wish you to know how grateful I am for your kindness. My Lucy would surely have died had you not been willing to feed her.'

Grace smiled. 'You need not thank me, Em, for it helped me rid myself of the milk. There was too much for my little Jane.' She moved towards a quiet corner of the deck and sat upon a coil of rope. Calmly and gently, she put the child to her breast.

Once Lucy had been fed, Grace handed her back to Emily. Minutes later they were interrupted by the sound of a sentry standing behind them, bellowing down the ladder to the women in the orlop.

'All up top! Captain's orders.'

The women emerged on to the upper deck, some of them moaning for they were sick from the effects of the effluence.

Once assembled, all on board were addressed by Captain Campbell. 'There is a desperate shortage of water and Captain Sever informs me rationing will be inevitable. But we shall try to manage for as long as possible. Any of you caught washing either your person or your clothing with water from our tuns will be severely punished. Let that be understood.'

The crew made the best of the prevailing winds and currents carrying the ship forth, but the weather was hot and humid. The bilges became fouler with rotting food, dead rats and seawater, adding to the already putrid contents.

Emily, concerned about one of the twins, approached Jimmy on the upper deck. 'Lizzie has become feverish, Jimmy. Would you be kind enough to ask the surgeon if he would take a look at her? I am truly worried. Her body is burning up and she is saying all manner of strange things. I think she is losing her mind.'

On Emily's return to the orlop, Lizzie's delirium had intensified. She sat up, babbling incoherently and waving her arms in the air before falling back onto the mattress and becoming unconscious. Emily stared in shock, having minutes earlier talked to Lizzie and promised her all would be right. And now she was not responding. Jessie, the quieter of the twins, started to sob uncontrollably.

'Please, Emmy, make her talk.'

'I am trying Jess, but it is difficult. She seems to have fallen asleep.'

When Mr Bowes-Smyth arrived, he quickly examined Lizzie. Emily knew by his despairing countenance that there was something amiss. He turned to the huddle of women. 'I am afraid God has taken her from us. There is nothing I can do.'

Emily brought her hand to her mouth, her eyes betraying her disbelief. 'That cannot be. I promised I would care for her.' She took Lizzie's hands and bent over her, shaking them gently. 'Lizzie, Lizzie, talk to me.' But she was wasting her time.

The surgeon lifted Emily's hands and gently pulled her away from Lizzie. 'That will do no good, my dear. The child is lost to the typhus. There is an epidemic raging on board the transport *Alexander*. Let us hope, God willing, that this is not the start of the disease aboard the *Lady Penrhyn*.' He removed baby Lucy from Emily's bunk. 'Take all the children above. The bilges need to be pumped. I will have a word with Captain Sever. Purgatives are needed down below. The orlop must to be scrubbed clean and painted with oil of tar. If we are careful we can avoid an outbreak on board.'

It was the women themselves who dropped to their knees and scrubbed the orlop with such vigour that it would seem impossible for any lethal organism to survive there. The crew painted it with oil of tar, and it seemed that the purging had been successful, for no further cases were reported.

Now that Lizzie had passed away, Emily approached Mr Bowes Smyth about the burial, for there were rumours she might be buried at sea. Despite the women's pleas to bury her on dry land, Captain Sever refused to keep Lizzie's body on board. 'We have no means of embalming and it is impossible to keep her body here in the heat of the tropics,' the surgeon explained. 'Worse than that, Captain Sever insists there will be disquiet amongst his crew, even mutiny, if he does not abide by their sentiments. There is a superstition amongst the men. Keeping the dead on board is akin to keeping the devil harnessed. They reckon it can only bring evil.'

And so the inevitable happened. Tears stealing gently down her face, Emily strove to fight back her sadness at the indignity of it. There was no coffin, only a plank of wood resting on two barrels. Emily stared at the rough, canvas shroud covering Lizzie's now slight body which had been laid to rest on the plank ready to be cast into the sea. Captain Sever read from a small prayer book.

'In the name of the Almighty...' he sang out in monotone. He quoted from the bible, made a speech which had obviously been rehearsed and delivered many times before, and he ended the service with, 'We commit our sister's body to the deep...'

The process was a simple one. Emily's eyes were fixed on the small canvas bundle. Two of the crew members tipped the board, sending the body of Lizzie plunging into the murky depths. The women, now filled with sadness at the captain's solemn words, wept until their eyes were red-rimmed. Nell muttered, 'Here but for the grace of God go I.'

When Jessie began to scream, 'No, No,' she was restrained by Nell and Emily who took her arms and tried to console her. But to no avail. And Emily felt the glare of the sun beating against her face and the brisk swirl of the wind around her as she struggled to hold Jessie back. But Jessie was dragging her towards the barricade, her body wracking in spasms as Emily pulled her close and Nell clung desperately to Jessie's canvas tunic.

Two marines came to their aid, taking hold of Jessie and leading her down the ladder to the orlop. Emily followed and tried to pacify her. But the girl curled herself in foetal position on her bunk, shutting herself off completely, her only words, 'I want to be with dear Lizzie.'

After several attempts to throw herself into the sea during their daily exercise, the surgeon insisted Jessie be carefully supervised. It was then Emily took full responsibility for Jessie's safe-keeping.

In the middle of July the fleet reached the doldrums. The sails were constantly trimmed to catch the slightest puff of wind. The heat was intense, the humidity unbearable, everything damp. Emily felt weak and at night she was unable to sleep.

The ship neared the Equator and the breeze died down. Progress became slower. The tar between the planks on the top deck bubbled, preventing the women from treading there without some covering around their feet to protect them. Water from the tuns was rapidly depleting, and the crew fashioned huge awnings to collect the rain water. It was a long time coming. Only occasionally were there swirls of light baffling winds.

Emily, having surfaced to take the air, leant on the

barricade next to Nell and gazed into the depths of the sea at the huge animals frolicking there, porpoises and dolphins chasing each other and leaping through the waves. 'It is a relief to feel the wind in your face,' Nell declared.

'It is,' Emily replied, pointing at the waves. 'I never thought I would see the likes of these,' she whispered. 'If they were people, I would swear they were smiling at me, laughing even.'

Nell clapped her hands and laughed.

'They are the biggest fish I ever did see.'

Jimmy came alongside. 'Can you believe such a sight, Emily? They must surely be having fun.' He turned his beaming smile to her face and she took in the vision of him, tall, strongly built and so attractive. Encapsulated in the moment, she cherished an increasing affection for him. Hot blood rushed to her cheeks and she checked her thoughts in an effort to calm herself.

'Corporal Ballantyne. Away from the felons!' It was the harsh cry of the sergeant.

Without taking his eyes from her, Jimmy stood to attention. Emily became mesmerised. But on hearing the sergeant's second call, Jimmy moved abruptly and ducked beneath the rail on to the main deck. Emily turned and looked away.

Nell smiled wickedly. 'The lad has taken a fancy to you, Emmy. I can see it in his eyes.'

'Not at all Nell. He is doing only what Mr Bowes Smyth ordered, keeping an eye on me and making sure I can manage.' Embarrassed, she bowed her head but she caught Jimmy's lingering glance as he stood before the sergeant, and the sergeant's words.

'I said to check the orlop, make sure the women are taking their exercise. It is not a social outing!'

Nell nudged Emily and smiled. 'See what I mean. Even the sergeant knows the lad is attracted to you.'

Overnight the weather changed. The slight breeze died completely and it became very still. A flurry of rain started, light at first, followed by enormous, lashing spots which turned into a fierce, violent storm. Bright flashes forked across the dark, ominous skies, and the roar of the angry god, Thor, rumbled through the heavens.

The storm lasted only a short time, maybe an hour, and the sailors checked the water gathered in the large hammock above them. They struggled to fill their containers and left the awnings to gather more when the next storm arose. A period of calm descended, and the ocean became still once more.

Despite the collection of rain water, stocks gradually depleted. Rationing was inevitable and Captain Campbell addressed them.

'During this period of drought there will be two and a half pints of water a day for the women, and three for the men.'

This was much less than was vital for rehydration, but in the circumstances it would have to suffice. Emily gave Grace some of her allocation for, if Grace were to continue feeding both infants, she would need plenty of liquid, as well as the extra food Emily insisted she take.

It was two days later when the storm clouds gathered again and the fleet ran into heavy gales. The tropical rainstorms whipped the fleet. The ships rolled and pitched, and bobbed about like pieces of jetsam. Anything loose on deck was fastened securely, and all hatches were battened to ensure complete safety. Fortunately, after the storm there was more water to spare.

'That's a blessed relief,' Nell muttered as she watched the crew replenishing their containers.

But the relief she expected was not forthcoming, for the women were given none of the fresh supply, despite Captain Phillip's instruction that rationing be fair.

Chapter 6

On the fourth of August, the stunning vista of the South American mountain range came into view and the following day the fleet entered the harbour of Rio de Janeiro. The gun salute from the *Sirius* was echoed by that of Fort Santa Cruz. Emily gasped at the majestic South Sugarloaf, a tall, cone-shaped mass of rock in shades of rose and slate topped by a green bonnet of trees. The beaches of pale yellow sand stretched before them, and the sun struck down from a cloudless sky. The sight was magnificent. Emily gazed, transfixed by the sheer beauty.

'Be a cosy place to settle.' Nell gazed across the bay, her eyes shining brightly.

'Oh yes Nell. How I wish we could leave the ship and make a home here. My little Lucy would love to play by the sea and we would be warm and snug in one of those little white cottages. And you would have relief from the bone ache too with the hot sun casting its warmth.' She draped her arm around Nell's shoulder and pulled Lucy close.

'It is no use wishing. There is no chance,' Nell sighed, 'for our wishes are never granted,' she said sadly.

'You heard what Grace said about accepting our lot. Then you must pay heed too, Nell. What else can we do? Together, we shall make the best of it.'

'We shall, dearie and I thank the Good Lord for sending you to me, for I regard you as my own kin. You are the best friend I ever had.'

Without speaking, they continued to stare ahead.

'Weigh anchor,' came the call as a school of turtles clustered around the hull. But they dispersed rapidly when a host of Negro pedlars, their white teeth flashing as they smiled, flocked towards the fleet in their tiny boats. They swarmed up the sides of the ship offering their wares, only to be turned away and ushered towards the shore by the pilot, later by the longboats keeping a constant guard on the six transports. But they persisted and pedalled oranges, limes and lemons, and a plentiful supply of the local liquor. And by the time the fleet was fully assembled, a flurry of young boys in their tiny home-made boats raced over the water, competing with the Negro pedlars and offering slices of fruit.

'Look at the young ones!' Eyes agog with curiosity, Nell stared, pointing to those of mixed race, some with sallow skins, some nutmeg, and some as black as night, their individual features reflecting every racial type imaginable.

'They're such eager little things,' Emily replied, a smile beginning to form on her lips. 'They haven't a care in the world.' She clapped her hands and popped a smacking kiss on Lucy's cheek. 'That is how we shall be in the future my little one.'

All the while, the crewmen continued to reach over the side of the ship collecting new stores, fresh beef and a variety of different fruits and vegetables. Emily slipped a slice of orange into her mouth and relished it slowly.

'I hope we shall stay here for some time, Nell, for the food is fresh and wholesome.'

'They are fine, soft fruits, Emmy, such a relief for my aching gums. The bread and salt beef are often too hard to chew.'

Emily turned. Jimmy was standing alongside them. He pointed to the dignitaries in full dress uniform being rowed ashore to be met by the Portuguese governor.

'We could be here a while. Word has it that the governor regards Commander Phillip favourably. When he was a young man, the commander served in the Royal Portuguese Navy. Apparently he is able to speak the language without fault.'

'We would appreciate staying here a while,' Emily said.

Nell, taken up by the sights, nodded with enthusiasm. 'Aye, we would.'

Emily stared towards the port, surprised at the number of churches, their gold crosses glinting in the sunlight and illuminating the hillsides, coloured by their flower-decked shrines. It seemed services were held continually for the flicker of the candles competed with the bright sun and the church bells rang continually.

Most of the buildings in St. Sebastian town were painted white and were clearly defined against the circling bay. With its backdrop of mountains it presented a breath-taking vista. And the joy and happiness of the people of Rio milling around the port and moving up and down the steep, cobbled streets was reflected in their colourful dress.

Emily shook her head. 'It amazes me the way they carry on with their daily tasks despite the heat of the day,' she said to Jimmy.

'I agree, Emily. The sun's heat does not appear to deter them.' He slid an arm casually around her shoulder and turned to face her. 'They are used to it. I am not sure how we would manage.' He laughed and she joined in.

'If only we were given the chance, Jimmy.' She gave him a rueful smile.

'I understand how saddened you must be that this has happened to you. I cannot conceive that you would do anything so wicked as to be accused of any sort of crime. It surprises me that you are here on board with the felons.'

'The lord's son forced himself upon me and then set me up, accusing me of stealing from his mother.'

'So he is the father of your child?'

'Yes, he is and although I was mortified at what had happened, I would not be without my Lucy.' She stared into Jimmy's eyes. 'You do understand don't you, Jimmy.'

'Of course I understand, and I am glad you have told me.'

It was almost a month before the fleet prepared to depart, and by that time the women, the crew and the marines were all refreshed. The ships were well stocked with arms, for it was uncertain what might be encountered when they arrived in Botany Bay. The Commander ordered sacks of tapioca to be placed in stock, and he reckoned the empty sacks would be useful in providing material to make canvas tunics for the women.

On the day they left South America the crew offered a twenty-one gun salute and this was echoed by Fort Santa Cruz.

'I believe the salute to be an omen, Nell. Maybe our lives will take a different turn once we arrive at the colony. The past year has been the worst year of my life. Of course I would not be without my darling Lucy, but surely this is the end of our misfortunes.'

'Let us hope so, Emmy dear. You have been brave. And it can do no harm to look on the bright side. And I still treat you as my child even though you are maturing into a young woman.'

'But now that I have my own child, Nell, does that not make you a grandmamma?' They both laughed.

'That it does, and a proud one too.'

The fleet left Brazil and set out across the Mid Atlantic Ocean towards Africa. After leaving Rio de Janeiro there were gales for over a week. But by the fourteenth September there was a lull. Gigantic seabirds were spotted, including an albatross, a sign of death according to the superstitions of the crew. By the end of September, the gales had died down completely and the seas became a little easier.

On the thirteenth of October land was sighted and the ships dropped anchor in the bay beneath the Table Mountain. Emily went up on deck with Nell and Jessie.

'Cape Town seems more windswept than Rio, and look at the faces of the negroes,' Emily observed. 'They look sullen, unlike the ones who came along in their boats to welcome us in Brazil.'

Table Mountain was huge and flat-topped, covered in a layer of bush. The low cloud drifting above it gave the impression of a cloth covering the table. The bay was busy with private merchants and whalers of all nationalities. Emily watched as Captain Phillip was rowed ashore and met by the Dutch Governor, a more surly-looking individual than the previous two governors.

The Dutch appeared to be wary of foreigners and their ships, their companies and their convicts. When Jimmy returned from his time ashore he pointed to the sentries posted on the beach.

'The Dutch guard has been doubled. And there seems to be some problem in obtaining fresh supplies of food, I don't know why.'

It was more than a week before any supplies were brought aboard the ship. It was then that Captain Campbell addressed the assembled mass from the ship's deck.

'Commander Phillip has given instructions that every person on board this ship will build up strength for the final and most strenuous leg of the journey, for we shall likely encounter heavy storms and gales through the Southern Ocean. Here in Cape Town we shall obtain fresh beef and mutton. You must eat fruit and vegetables aplenty to prevent the scurvy.'

As they left for the orlop, Emily turned to Nell.

'It seems the commander is determined that we reach Botany Bay in good health,' she said. 'But it will not be difficult for me for I enjoy fresh fruit and green vegetables, unlike some who have never been used to eating them'

'Aye. The Commander is kind and caring,' Nell replied, but she refused to eat the green vegetables.

Emily found the food to be good, especially the Dutch bread which was most appetising. Both

Grace and Emily fed the infants on finely pulped fruit, for early weaning was essential.

During the third week of their stay in Cape Town, Captain Campbell called the women from the orlop to the deck. They were puzzled. It seemed he was about to impart bad news for his face became a mask of gravity. In stern voice, he addressed them.

'The Governor will require female convicts to vacate some of the space so generously allocated. Two mares and a colt will be brought aboard this ship. I shall leave Sergeant Stockdale to assist you in making available that space.'

'But there be little enough room already, sir.' It was Nell who dared to voice her opinion.

The captain, as reluctant to accept the animals as were the women, prickled at this remark.

'How dare you speak out of turn, you wizened old hag. Know your place.'

'It is unkind of you to speak to her so, sir,' Emily spoke up. 'She is getting old. It is difficult for her to bear the strain.'

'Another who dares speak out! Hold your tongue, girl, or you will be fettered and gagged.'

Emily caught Jimmy's eye as the irate captain turned swiftly around and left them. Jimmy winked and she managed a smile. Shortly afterwards they had a snatched conversation.

'I admire you for your bravery, Emily, for daring to speak up in front of the captain' Jimmy insisted. 'But be careful,' he whispered. 'I would be saddened if you were to be punished.'

'I have no regrets, Jimmy, for Nell is very dear to me.'

'But you must beware. The captain is a man of many moods, and he may turn on you if you continue to speak out.'

'Do not worry. I am not in the habit of causing trouble,' she said, laughing, and once more catching the look of adoration on Jimmy's face. She felt the heat surge through her body as she turned and descended the ladder to the orlop.

Later in the day, the horses were loaded and given sufficient space in which to stand, but no more.

'We cannot afford for any of them to fall for they would never be lifted upright and they would surely die,' Captain Campbell insisted. To the chagrin of the women, the horses were pampered and given plenty of water, as much as they needed.

Emily watched as a variety of animals were loaded onto the other transports, sheep, pigs, chickens, ducks, geese and turkeys.

'Look at them,' she said, pointing across the water to the remainder of the fleet. 'We must be grateful the space needed for the horses is not as much as we expected, and far less than will be needed for the other animals.'

But Emily had spoken too soon. It was shortly after the horses were settled that the peace and quiet aboard the *Lady Penrhyn* was shattered by the uproar of a group of women being brought aboard from the *Friendship,* where space was needed to house the abundance of livestock. Their places had been taken by sheep, described by their captain as being *much more agreeable shipmates than the felons!*

'Surely things cannot get worse,' Nell

complained, staring at the space between the bunks which was even smaller now they had been crammed more closely together. 'It is lucky Grace joined us when we lost poor Lizzie, God rest her soul, for now we are four.'

'And at least we are all of us quite small,' Emily added, placing her arm around Jessie who still needed to be coaxed into joining in the conversation.

'I was more thinking of the *Friendship* lot,' Nell continued as the rowdy women descended the ladder. 'There's no room here for one of them to join us, thank the Lord.'

'Perhaps you are being a little unkind for there must be civil ones amongst them.'

'Listen to the noise they're making. They're like a set of hell-cats.'

'But they have been disturbed and asked to move. That is why they are noisy.' Emily felt it wrong to pre-judge these women, many of whom, like her, must be innocent.

But no sooner had the *Friendship* women entered the orlop than an abrasive trouble-maker, Kate Bradley, picked a fight with Esther Wray, *Lady Penrhyn*'s self-appointed leader. There was no room for two leaders and the *Friendship* woman was bent on toppling Esther. But Kate soon discovered that Esther was an unknown force.

'You,' Kate demanded, pointing a finger at Esther and indicating the bunk she stood beside. 'Out. That is mine. I take the biggest.'

'The biggest, eh? Is that so?' replied Esther, hands on hips. 'You may have the biggest gob and the biggest arse but you'll not take the biggest bunk.' Her mouth curved into a cruel smirk. She threw out a challenge. 'And what d'you intend to do about it?'

'I'll show you,' Kate bragged, grabbing a handful of Esther's hair, clutching on tightly and dragging her forward.

Emily's senses became bombarded with the screams and shouts of abuse during the women's battle for supremacy. But, determined not to become embroiled in either their politics or their infighting, she cradled Lucy and remained in her bunk. All the while, the hatch to the orlop was open, and once the noise of the stormy exchange reached the upper deck, two marine officers, curious to know what the commotion was all about, descended the ladder to investigate.

'What sport,' one of them said, clapping his hands and sniggering. They stayed and watched, and it was not long before several of the other marines heard the noise and gathered there, cheering the women on, one of them passing a pannikin of rum to Kate from which she swigged noisily before handing it back.

'We'll soon see about that,' Esther said as she turned and noticed Kate had been distracted. It was then she delivered a hammer blow to the hand gripping her hair, pulling herself free. She spun around and clawed Kate's face viciously, causing a stream of blood to ooze down her cheek. 'You can whistle for yon bunk, filthy witch.'

'Filthy witch, am I? That's rich coming from you, you whoring bastard.'

Arms locked, they battled, but Esther forced her

Friendship rival to submit when she pinned her against the corner of the cabin and shoved her knee into Kate's stomach. Kate collapsed to the floor, her eyes protruding like marbles. 'You won't get away with this. Watch your back, slut.'

Incensed, Esther kicked out, her bare foot landing in Kate's chest. 'You want more? You'll get more.'

Kate rolled about in the filth of the orlop as Esther kicked her again and again. She had proved her supremacy and was rewarded by one of the marines who handed her a swig of rum. She quaffed it greedily.

Emily looked at Nell. 'I see what you mean. But I suppose it was inevitable,' she said. 'They must have resented being moved from their own ship. As for Esther, I know she can be abrasive but she does speak out for us.'

Nell paused and looked around at the other *Friendship* women, some of whom cowered in the background.

'Perhaps you are right. As you say, I suppose we should not judge them too harshly.'

It was clear that the rumpus between the women had entertained the marines, for they regarded Esther's victory as cause for celebration. Several more of the marines left their sentry posts and descended the ladder. Once down there, the rum flowed freely.

By the time the officers had realised the guards were missing and had spotted them fraternising with the women, there was pandemonium. The men were ordered up aloft. A period of calm developed and once more it was quiet down below. The women settled, having accepted their lot, for they knew they must conserve their energies if they were to survive the longest and most arduous leg of the journey.

On the twelfth of November, after thirty days in Cape Town, the fleet set sail on the most dangerous part of the voyage. The rumour was that only a few men had experienced the voyage before them, for close to the icy desolation of Antarctica the latitudes were notorious for bad weather.

The ships ventured towards unchartered mountain-high seas and the weather became dark, wet and gloomy as they advanced towards the south Australian coast. The women huddled down below, some of them once more sea-sick. Gales arose in tempestuous squalls, gusting so strongly that the waves were driven on to the decks, gushing down the stairways and the hawser holes deep down into the orlop and the hold. The ululation of the horses could be heard above the crashing of the waves, but in such a restricted area the storm had little effect on them. Gannets and terns circled the ship, whales were spotted, and an enormous albatross with a fourteen foot wingspan followed the fleet. It would be two more months before they reached unexplored country.

Grace, usually the optimistic one, voiced her concerns to Emily. 'I do not know how we will manage, Em, if things do not improve. There is not enough food for the babies.'

'I realise and I owe you a great deal, Grace for suckling my Lucy.' A flash of guilt swept through her. 'I feel desperate too, for there is little I can do. Perhaps if I ask Jimmy, he may be able to help.'

'I have said it before. You do not need to thank me. When the babies needed nothing but milk, I had plenty. And you have forced me to accept more than I should of your own food. Look at you! You are nothing but a bag of bones. But the little ones need something more than milk to fill their bellies now. And I will not allow you to starve, Em, for you cannot go on depriving yourself.'

'Going without food does not affect me,' she said, for her belly had become accustomed to the small amount remaining after making sure Grace was not left hungry. 'But it is not only the food. It is so cold down here and the little ones need to be kept warm.'

'They do and they will surely die if we cannot find something warm and dry for them.'

'Do not say that, Grace. We have struggled so far, surely we can manage a little further. I will talk to the others and see if they can help.'

The environment became more and more hostile and Emily became depressed as the situation worsened. But she tactfully called Esther and Kate to one side in the hope that they could persuade their own followers to give a little for the infants. And her heart was suddenly warmed by their generosity. Despite their rough and rowdy behaviour, when it came to the well-being of the infants on board, the women could not be faulted.

Once they realised the plight of the little ones and their struggle for survival, they stole and they sold their bodies to provide extra bread and meat for all those who suckled the young, and provided warm bedding for the infants' cradles.

'Here take this, wench. It is not much but I have

seen you feed them two babies.' It was Esther Wray who handed Grace the food she had 'acquired' from above. Kate Bradley, her *Friendship* opponent, took up the challenge too.

Impressed by their generosity, Emily was determined to cling on to the charity of these two women and keep it close to her heart. For at some time when her hopes were higher, she would snatch the first opportunity to repay them. She reflected on their circumstances. They were poor souls, never having been given a chance in life. Unlike Emily, they had probably never received love and comfort from their families. They were lacking morale, and had constantly been scoffed at.

They were totally demoralised by poverty and their ruin. And they had been pushed to the very rim of respectability, off the edge into petty crime, surviving by theft and prostitution. The more they tried to climb back, the more they slipped, never to be welcomed back. It was self-fulfilling.

Yet when all their bravado was over, these women were respected for their loyalties, and here they were, caring and generous-hearted.

At least Emily's parents had been kind and giving of comfort. How lucky she had been to have received their love. That was something she would never forget, something she would share with Lucy.

It was several weeks after the *Friendship* women had joined the ship and the battles between the groups had ended that the pecking order was sorted.

On a day when Lucy was particularly tetchy Emily had stayed below, her only companion Jessie who was now completely withdrawn. Since Lizzie had passed away, Jessie constantly clung to Emily's side.

They were disturbed by the clattering of heavy boots as someone descended the ladder. It was one of the crew, a foul-looking individual with a heavy squint in his eye. He made for her bunk, lifted her chin and thrust his ugly face close to hers. 'Spied you through the 'atch down 'ere alone. Pretty little thing. Waiting for a man?'

'Certainly not! Please leave me alone. I am not the sort you think I am.' She turned her face towards Lucy and started to rock the child.

'But you 'ave a babby. That is proof of your type.'

'It is no business of yours.' Resentful of his presence and, determined not to feel threatened, Emily returned his look with a long, hard stare as she continued to comfort her child.

'Playing the shy one,' he replied, now pulling Emily's tunic.

She began to struggle and Jessie ran to the upper deck crying, 'Nell, Nell come quickly.'

But Nell's pace was slow. By the time she arrived the seaman had torn Emily's tunic to tatters and was pushing Lucy away.

Incensed by his interference, Emily bent her knee and thrust it sharply into his groin.

He fell back, wincing with pain. 'You won't get away with this, you skinny little whore. I will have my revenge,' he hissed, his eyes bright with fury.

Nell appeared and rushed forward. 'What is it, Emmy?' She turned and spotted the seaman. 'You evil bastard,' she cried after him. 'Clear off you piece of filth.'

The seaman scuttled away, clutching his groin and trying to catch his breath. He turned and his angry glare flashed back at Emily. Momentarily fear swept through her and she hoped that was the last she would see of him.

'I swear I will swing for him,' Nell vouched as she took baby Lucy from the bunk and drew her close. 'Take heed, lass,' she continued. 'Do not stay down here alone again.'

Emily followed Nell's advice. If she were to avoid another incident with the seaman it was the only course open to her. But she resented having to make that decision.

The following day when Emily met up with Jimmy during her daily walk, she spotted the seaman climbing the rigging. The incident almost slipped out, but she decided to keep it to herself. Had Jimmy known the truth, she was sure he would have retaliated and threatened the seaman.

Although news of the incident filtered through down below, it went no further. The women were afraid of the evil-tempered Abel Rafton, renowned amongst the crew for his spiteful nature, his brawling and his vengeful attacks.

Emily kept a constant vigil. She never stayed down below without someone to keep her company, irrespective of Lucy's tetchiness. Perhaps Rafton was nothing but empty threats, a windbag. Perhaps when he was well into his cups, the incident would be forgotten. She could only hope.

Chapter 7

1787 – 1788

Over the final leg of the journey, the heavy transports, the *Charlotte* and the *Lady Penrhyn* became sluggish, and the lead vessels had to cut their speed. It became extremely cold, and many of the animals died as a result of this. Fortunately the commander's horses remained alive.

By this time, the women's clothes were thin and ragged. The water ration had been reduced again, and everyone was continually hungry, especially the babies who cried endlessly, for by now they were grossly undernourished. Despite their earlier efforts, there was little more the women could do.

The swell of the ocean became enormous once more, and the *Lady Penrhyn* pitched and rolled to such an extent that the gunwale was thrust heavily into the giant waves sending the stern crashing and the water spiralling through the ship.

'For God's sake, furl the mainsail!' came the order from Captain Sever, for the winds were so fierce that the sails were starting to rip apart.

Emily clung to Lucy as she watched the water flooding the ship.

The marines were forced to join the crew in baling the water out with buckets and pumps. After hours of struggling together they completed the task and they collapsed in exhaustion.

Down below, Nell wept when water seeped into the orlop on to the bunks. 'How can we carry on? I am weary. I wish the Good Lord would take me.'

Emily was alarmed at Nell's low spirits but she tried to remain optimistic. Nell's frail body was bent in despair and she constantly wrung her hands, but Emily tried to adopt a cheerful outlook and comfort her.

'Jimmy tells me we have not far to go now. Let us try to bear it. Here, take my mattress, Nell, for I am concerned that you might suffer more bone ache with the dampness. And I need you to be fit and well to help me with Lucy when we reach this Botany Bay,' she added lightly, ignoring Nell's disillusionment. 'How could I manage without you?' she continued, quickly exchanging her own thin but dry paillasse with the wet one on Nell's bunk. 'I will stand this on its side. The water will soon drain from it.'

By this time, there was virtually no food left on board the *Lady Penrhyn*. Grace was more fortunate than some of the other women for, although her milk had started to dry up through her own lack of nourishment, she could still manage a meagre amount for Jane and Lucy.

The surgeon became alarmed by the situation and contacted the other ships to ask if they could spare food for the children. The captain of the *Prince of Wales* sent over bread which was weevil-ridden, and fruit which was rotting. But the women coped. They cleaned and prepared the food as best they could and managed to keep themselves and the little ones from starving. But it could not last. Day by day they were becoming weaker.

Despite these adversities, Emily was determined

to take her daily exercise, knowing she must keep herself as fit as possible for the sake of Lucy. She climbed the ladder and when she appeared on deck Jimmy sought her out.

'I have not seen you for some time, Emmy.' He gazed into her open face. 'I think you have something to tell me,' he added, keeping his eyes fixed upon hers.

'Something to tell you? What do you mean?' Emily was puzzled.

'Why did you not tell me that Rafton had threatened you?'

'I do not wish to talk about it, Jimmy. It happened some time ago and I gave him more than he bargained for. I think I have seen the end of him,' she stressed, a false lightness to her voice.

Jimmy took her hands and pulled her once more to face him. 'I would say not. I hear he has been boasting to the others that you would not get away with it, that he would make you suffer in the end. They laughed at him, which made him worse. He is biding his time, Emmy. Don't you understand?'

'He is bragging,' she said, trying to muster up a little courage. 'But I promise I will not stay down there alone at any time. The women are aware of what has happened and they will protect me.'

'If he so much as lays a hand on you Emmy, I swear I will go after him.' Jimmy took a deep breath and released a heavy sigh, as though he were living that evil moment.

'Please, Jimmy do not become involved.'

'Except if I catch him harming you,' he replied gruffly. He left her standing there, his brow heavily furrowed, but his mask of severity did not conceal the love shining in his eyes.

Emily stayed on deck hoping there would be no further mention of the incident when next she met up with Jimmy, but her heart pained with fear that Rafton would eventually seek his revenge.

Sometime later, as the sky darkened she headed towards the hatchway and began to descend the ladder. The sky lit up and before the hatch was bolted down a deafening clap of thunder preceded the violent thunderstorm which flooded the decks and rampaged through the ship.

The women were terrified. 'Praise be to the Lord,' they muttered as they went down on their knees and prayed.

'God help us through this passage.'

'God save us from death.'

They heard later that the *Golden Grove's* topsails were badly split and the *Prince of Wales's* main yard had been carried away by the huge waves pressing down on the fleet. But the *Lady Penrhyn* remained intact.

The storm passed over.

After the heavy damage to his fleet, Commander Phillip realised the situation had become dire. With an important decision to make he confided in his good friend, Captain Collins.

'I realise it is against the principles I set out at the start of the journey that we keep the fleet together, but I must now separate my ships in order to expedite our voyage and reach Botany Bay as quickly as possible, otherwise we shall lose the felons. They are becoming despondent through lack of nourishment and the conditions brought about by the inclement weather. They may be felons but they are also human beings and can take only so much.'

'That is true, Commander. Perhaps if we left behind the cumbersome *Charlotte*, the *Lady Penrhyn* and the *Prince of Wales* together with the store-ships, we could make better progress.'

'My sentiments exactly. I have decided they will be headed by the *Sirius* and proceed at their own speed. We shall board the *Supply* and take an advance party to Botany Bay. I suggest the *Friendship, Alexander* and *Scarborough* accompany us for we shall need the men on board to prepare a site for the new settlement.'

On the seventh of January 1788 the leading party reached Van Dieman's Land, which was obscured by a thick, almost impenetrable mist. The ships made for the southern cape where the winds were light and fitful. They anchored and, knowing it was some eight hundred miles to Botany Bay, Commander Phillip was optimistic they would reach their destination within two weeks.

They made excellent progress and on the nineteenth of January, they sighted the mainland. The commander, a satisfied look on his face, turned to Collins. 'I believe I should feel amply satisfied to have travelled more than fifteen thousand miles in two hundred and fifty two days without the loss of a single ship. And only forty-eight dead.'

'It is indeed a wonderful feat, Commander,' replied David Collins, a strikingly handsome marine officer with a cheerful disposition.

The commander smiled at his colleague's enthusiasm, appreciating his positive manner, unlike Major Robert Ross, a pessimist if ever there was one. 'We shall anchor here, explore the area and decide where to set up camp.'

The *Supply* dropped anchor at Solander, the wide entrance to Botany Bay, named sixteen years earlier by Captain Cook. The commander took out his speaking trumpet. 'I permit no-one to land in this area until Captain Collins and I have first explored.'

But he was disappointed when they looked across the bay. 'This land appears to be barren. Look yonder,' he said, pointing. 'The sandy beach is fringed by a marshy shore.' He consulted his map. 'But this is surely the Botany Bay indicated by James Cook.' The commander surveyed the land once more. 'Where is the deep black soil and fine meadow he described? There seems to have been some confusion. Maybe it is the next bay, the one north of Botany.'

In the shadows of the bay an abundance of large stingrays were basking. The trees and scrubs were stunted, and the eucalypts, a grey-green colour, grew amongst them with spiny grass sprouting in tussocks amongst the rocks and sand dunes. Millions of insects filled the hot air and hundreds of brightly coloured birds, resembling small parrots, darted to and fro.

A slender canoe made from bark appeared as if from nowhere. It held two natives, dark-skinned and bearded, their naked bodies daubed with a greyish mud. Both men were armed with spears and clubs which they brandished. One of them stood in the canoe in a menacing pose whilst the other called out in an unintelligible tongue.

'According to Sir Joseph Banks, they are the native aboriginal tribe, the Eora,' explained the commander, ever the peace-maker. 'They are apparently not as hostile as they might appear. We must try to befriend them and communicate with them otherwise the inhabitants of our new settlement will constantly be at war with them.'

'Perhaps it would be pertinent if we set out to meet them, sir,' Collins suggested.

'A sound idea. Call for a longboat, Collins.'

They met with the natives in the bay, offering gifts of beads. Anxious to find fresh water, the commander gestured to them, hoping they would understand what he needed. In hostile manner, one of them called back to him, 'Warra, warra' which, by the man's tone, clearly meant 'go away.'

But Commander Phillip was not prepared to give in so easily. He and his men continued towards the beach and, after landing, they were confronted by one of the elders.

The commander offered a mirror to the elder. He took it and stared into it, screwing up his face and laughing out loud. He seemed to understand their needs and pointed to the fresh water stream nearby.

Eventually the governor, having decided that Botany Bay was not the best site on which to build a settlement, made another important decision.

'We shall explore the coast in a northerly direction. The next major inlet north of Botany Bay is Port Jackson. I fear the water here is too shallow and the bay is completely unprotected from invasion. It is exposed to the south east winds, and the heavy rollers will certainly cause violent and persistent swells.'

The governor shook his head and frowned. 'I am surprised that Cook's report does not truly reflect the conditions here. Rather than meadowland the extensive swamps are redolent of fever and will no doubt provide a breeding ground for flies and mosquitoes. And if our cattle are to survive, we must find more lush vegetation. The mosses and marsh grass are completely unsatisfactory.'

He set out with Collins and a small party of marines and, on leaving the harbour, he noticed two large French ships, La Boussole and L'Astrolabe, standing well off shore.

'Those names are familiar to me, Collins. I believe them to be on a voyage of discovery led by the Marquis de Laperouse. Fortunately they have made no claim on the land. But we must make haste for I wish to establish our claim before the French reach the next bay.'

'It appears to me that they have no interest in claiming the land, sir. I believe they are more interested in discovering the flora and fauna.'

The harbour at Port Jackson had a blue, tranquil expanse of water dotted with small islets. The shore was rocky with a ragged wall of sandstone fretted by incessant winds and covered by a thin soil and sparse shrubs. The sheltered coves had sandy beaches and were densely wooded with pink eucalypts, some with half-shed bark, smooth joints and hazy grey-green foliage. Water flowed in the gullies, beards of rusty algae clung to the sandstone lips and giant cabbage palms hung over ferns and mosses. The high-pitched noise of the birds was in contrast with the stillness of the ground, where there appeared to be no animals. But Captain Cook, during his earlier voyage, had reported sight of silver-coated marsupials with two short front legs and two long back ones on which they hopped. It was some time before the governor's pioneer party came across a small group in one of the clearings. The natives called them 'kangaroos'.

Filled with renewed optimism, the party returned to Botany Bay with the good news that Port Jackson was to be the site of the settlement.

On the twenty-sixth of January 1788 the Governor ordered the rest of the fleet to leave Botany Bay and head for Port Jackson. Once there, the Union flag was hoisted and Commander Phillip named it Sydney Cove in honour of Viscount Sydney.

When the *Lady Penrhyn* finally anchored outside Botany Bay the women, mesmerised by the sight of the natives, stared across the bay.

'I am mighty afraid of them savages, Emmy.' Nell scowled and pointed to the natives in the distance.

'I do hope they are not cannibals.' Emily frowned.

'Cannibals! What are cannibals?' Nell was puzzled.

'They are savages who eat people. I read about them in a book at the manor, after little Anne taught me to read. It was a book about the black people in Africa.'

'We must be careful to keep away from them.'

The first mate intervened. 'They are not

cannibals,' he told them. 'They live off fruit and fish.' He helped to allay their fears and Nell was able to rest more easily in her bunk that night, knowing that she would not be eaten by the natives of the land.

The *Lady Penrhyn* moved up the coast with the trailing party and glided smoothly through the entrance to Port Jackson harbour which was guarded by two majestic headlands with an opening a mile wide. The ship passed the dangerous reefs with their outlying rock formations and drifted towards the shore without incident. But it was decided that the women would not be allowed ashore until the men had prepared the ground and set up a basic camp.

'You serve no purpose standing there, waiting to disembark. The governor has not given Captain Sever permission to land you lot yet. You must remain patient,' Captain Campbell ordered gruffly.

The women and the few children and babies gazed towards the shore. Beside them was Surgeon, Bowes Smyth. 'It is my opinion that we are entering the finest harbour in the world,' he said, looking in awe at the dramatic picture before him.

'Prepare to weigh anchor,' came the call, and the crew rallied excitedly, awaiting their first experience on dry land for many months. 'Slow on the capstan.'

It was not until the following day that the women were allowed to disembark. But before they did so, they were allocated fresh clothing from the slop chests.

'That is an improvement if I might say so,

Mistress Spence,' the surgeon ventured, taking in the picture of Emily in her sailcloth tunic and ticking trousers.

'Thank you, sir,' she replied smiling to herself at the title, Mistress Spence, he had given her. 'I am most grateful for your help. You have been exceedingly generous to me and baby Lucy, and to my friends also. We shall not forget your kindness.'

'Think nothing of it, child. I was merely doing my duty.'

Before they were allowed to leave the ship, Captain Sever insisted a strict search be made in an effort to recover goods stolen on board during the voyage.

'They would believe us to be a set of bleedin' thieves,' said Esther Wray, obviously forgetting her original crime of stealing bedding from her employer.

Kate Bradley echoed her sentiments.

'They cannot trust a bloody soul round here, can they?'

Emily did not fail to notice the wry smile spreading across the surgeon's face as he listened to the women who, despite their criminal records, resented being accused. Someone had stolen the items from the ship, but who was to say the women were the culprits? Why not the crew or the marines?

Emily believed the surgeon had similar thoughts, but it would not be politic of him to put his opinion into words.

After a fruitless search the women were left on deck for two hours, Emily for most of the time holding Lucy. After a while, she became faint and when Nell offered to hold the child, Emily refused.

'You must look after yourself, Nell. Lucy is too heavy for you to hold out here in this heat.' The sun was coming up and Emily knew it would be difficult for Nell to withstand the rising temperature, especially in her newly acquired seaman's jersey, so generously given to her by one of the young sailors.

Three longboats drew alongside to collect the women who were finally allowed to gain their land legs. But Emily felt weak as she clutched hold of Lucy. Jessie clung on to Emily too, the tattered shawl, which had belonged to her deceased elder sister Dot, draped around her shoulders. Since the death of her twin, Lizzie, Jessie had become so vacant and withdrawn that she had closed herself off and was hiding behind the barrier she had built around herself.

As they stepped into the longboat, Emily felt optimistic that this new beginning was the opportunity she needed to start life afresh.

Chapter 8

Port Jackson, New South Wales
Australia
1788

'You lot. Pay attention!' a marine officer, his lip curled in venom, barked at the women and pointed to the fallen branches strewn over the ground. 'Follow the example of the men and start building huts.' He climbed onto a huge rock to supervise, a supercilious grin on his face as he issued his ultimatum. 'Else you'll be sleeping on the ground tonight with no shelter for protection.'

'It seems he is amused,' Emily muttered, feeling wearier now that the sun had reached its zenith and was beating unmercifully down upon her. It was not long since they had stumbled to the shore, and they needed to familiarise themselves with their surroundings. But that was not to be.

'There be no time for resting, I'll say that, Em,' Nell whispered, now taking Lucy from her. 'Better not answer back after last time.'

'I agree. And we must make an effort if we are to sleep under cover tonight,' she said, looking around at the men who were now attempting to erect primitive huts. 'Will you care for the little ones, Nell whilst Grace and I make a start? I will show Jess what to do. I am sure she can do her bit.'

'If you are sure. I would be grateful of the rest. My bone ache is bad today. Perhaps another storm is brewing,' Nell offered, looking up at the dark clouds amassing in the distance.

'I hope not,' Emily replied and she began to collect branches from the surrounding area.

Emily studied the four posts the men had erected. They were long and heavy, and far too cumbersome for Nell to contend with. The walls were built of branches, roughly interlaced and daubed crudely with mud to seal them. Emily showed Jessie what was needed and, once she had the hang of it, Jessie put herself wholeheartedly into the task.

'Well done,' Emily said, encouraging her to keep on searching for branches, whilst she and Grace battled to drive in the posts. Despite the officer's icy glare, no attempt had been made to direct Nell to the task. And by the evening they had built a hut of sorts. But the three women were exhausted.

Emily looked around her. Some of the others were bitter and disillusioned and found the place so foreign to them and the weather difficult to bear. But Emily remained optimistic, remembering Grace's words. *We must make the best of our lot.* And that was exactly what Emily intended to do.

They ate supper of stale, weevil-infested bread, salt meat and fruit collected by some of the marines. Even though clouds of mosquitoes and other flying insects were constantly on the attack, they remained out in the open.

'What do you make of this place, Em? It is very hot and humid. I do hope we are able to sleep.' Nell perched her weary bones on a small rock.

'Maybe after a night's rest we shall feel much better,' Emily ventured. 'And surely the warm climate will be soothing to your bones.'

'Indeed,' Nell replied, her face masked in a doleful expression. 'Give Lucy to me, and take some rest whilst she sleeps. You must be refreshed on the morrow if the work is to continue,' she added placing the child on the ground beside her. 'I will take Jane also, for Grace is weary too.'

But no more than an hour later, not long after dusk, brilliant forks flashed across the sky lighting up the heavens. A deafening rumble of thunder followed, the frequency gradually increasing until eventually there was an almighty crash. The rain lashed against the huts, washing away the mud and demolishing them and the tents the marines had pitched blew away too. The camp became a quagmire. The women feared for their lives.

'We have had nothing but storms since we left England, Emmy. When will it end?' Nell wailed as she crouched beside the fallen hut, her eyes misted with tears. And Emily wondered how much more her dear friend could take.

The marines offered the women protection, but it was a half-hearted commitment. Weary after the early start to the day, they were resentful of their commanding officers who had taken fright and hidden under cover.

Once the storm started to abate Emily struggled to re-assemble the hut. But then her ordeal began. With no guard to stop them, the crew of the *Lady Penrhyn,* who after fifteen thousand miles had seen nothing but huge oceans and empty horizons, seized extra rum from the stores and joined the male convicts, who were on the rampage and heading for the women's quarters.

They sang uproariously, they quarrelled and they swore, generally behaving in the bawdiest of manners. Emily saw what was happening, and her stomach lurched as she spotted Abel Rafton tottering towards her, his hair bedraggled by the lashing rain. Her first thoughts were for Lucy and she spun around, taking her from Nell's grasp. But Rafton paid little heed as he continued in her direction and knocked the child from her arms. Horrified, Emily bent to pick up her child from the boggy mass but Rafton dragged her away.

'Bitch! You'll not escape me this time,' he threatened, his speech slurred. He threw Emily to the ground and clung to her.

Emily screamed as she struggled, turning this way and that in an attempt to free herself. It was then she spotted, only inches away from her fingers, a thick branch which had fallen from the newly built hut during the height of the storm. It was well within her reach if only something would distract Rafton.

The thought had barely flashed through her mind when Jessie started to kick out at him. It was then in her state of desperation that Emily leant back, stretched out and managed to grasp the branch. Arms flailing dangerously, she hit out with the most powerful swing she could muster. The branch came down on Rafton making heavy impact on his face. He slumped and fell backwards. Without a second thought Emily jumped to her feet and rushed towards Nell who by this time had picked up the crying child from the ground.

'There, there. You are fine my cherub.' Nell gave comfort to the child.

Emily placed her arms around the two. 'Thank God she is not dead, Nell. That man has a sliver of ice in his heart.' Her dark hair clung damply to her cheeks. She lifted Lucy from Nell's arms and gently rocked her.

But within minutes she felt someone clutch hold of her shoulder. As she attempted to drag herself away she felt a sudden punch in her stomach and she slumped forward. When she looked up she was face to face with a red-coated marine officer who shouted at her in an outraged voice.

'Do not dare retaliate, woman! The crewman may have tried to seduce you, but now he is out cold. You may have killed him. You will be taken to the governor. Justice must be done.'

'Rafton did not try to seduce me.' She managed to answer back even though the officer had winded her. 'I was defending myself. The man threw my child to the ground, and dragged me away with the intent of raping me. Do I not have the right of self-defence? He could have killed my Lucy.'

'I am sure you are aware that some of these men are bluffing. According to the crew, he was well into his cups. He meant you no harm and he obviously did not realise the child had fallen.'

'My child did not fall. She was knocked to the ground by that evil man.'

The officer took hold of her arm and pushed her roughly towards the large marquee occupied by the Governor.

'Hold your tongue, girl. The governor must be told. The crew of the *Penrhyn* are dealing with Rafton,' he said, and he continued to shove her towards the governor's canvas marquee, gripping her arm tightly. Without removing his hand, he had a muffled conversation with the sentry who promptly disappeared inside. Within a few minutes the sentry returned, calling for them to follow him.

Emily tried to steady herself and keep her balance through the quagmire beneath her feet. The heat was stifling, the atmosphere humid as the officer pushed her again, this time with excessive force. She stumbled forward into the official marquee, lifting her head slightly and casting a furtive glance towards the person reclining on a paillasse. It was the governor; his eyes were closed. The officer quickly changed his approach from abusive to obsequious.

'May I speak with you, sir?'

The governor stirred. 'What is it, man?' he muttered with an air of reluctance.

'I have arrested this felon on a charge of assault.' He gripped Emily's arm forcefully and dug his nails into the flesh. 'She has attacked and wounded a member of the *Penrhyn* crew. The man is now unconscious. She may have killed him.'

The governor failed to open his eyes.

'Do not trouble me,' he replied, appearing to have neither the patience nor the inclination to deal with matters of assault. 'You know my orders.' He flicked his hand in dismissal. 'Deal with the woman. Place her in irons. She will be flogged on the morrow.' He shook his head and sighed. 'You are aware of the punishment for murder if the man should die. Death by hanging,' he added, his final three words clipped.

Emily shuddered. She was thrown into stunned despair and couldn't believe what she was hearing. The words had an ominous ring to them. How could an act of self-defence warrant being placed in irons and flogged? Even worse, how could the governor suggest she be hanged when she was merely defending herself against the evil Rafton?

The officer, his face now glowing like a furnace after the governor's apparent lack of interest, reverted to his abusive approach, tugging hard at Emily's sleeve with one hand and fisting the other one viciously into her back.

'Out!' he commanded, dragging her from the marquee. He gestured to the sentry on duty and called out to him. 'You, lad! Bring me chains and leg irons for this felon.'

Startled, the young marine private looked up before scuttling away. Within minutes he was back.

'Yon tree,' the officer growled, pointing. 'That is where we shall place her.'

The lad looked up, his face masked in horror, his eyes wide and disbelieving.

'Get a move on, lad! You heard what I said,' the officer bellowed before turning to Emily and prodding her in the chest. 'You will be lucky to be alive by the morrow. God will repay you for your sins.' He loosened his grip and deliberately thrust her to the ground, kicking her in the stomach whilst she was down. 'Get up, you whore,' he ordered.

Emily, now badly dazed, struggled to her feet. If this was punishment for being innocent, for acting in self-defence, how would she ever exist in this hostile place?

'But what about my child?' she begged. 'I must go to her.'

'You will be lucky to see the child again,' he sneered. 'You heard the governor's words. You will be hanged if the man dies.' He dragged Emily's hands behind her back, shackled her wrists and passed a chain through before securing it around a nearby eucalypt.

He turned to the sentry. 'Fetter the ankles, lad.' The sentry crouched down and did as he was ordered whilst the officer stood back and pointed to the ground. 'Watch out for spiders, big as your hand.' He gestured crudely, cupping his hands together to demonstrate the size. 'And poisonous snakes,' he added, guffawing raucously as he strode away casually. The young sentry frowned heavily before turning and following the officer.

Alone now, Emily was filled with the warning light of truth. A heavy pounding hammered in her chest, slowly at first but then it became more rapid. Whatever happened, she was fated. If Rafton died, she would be hanged. If he lived, he would seek her out and she would be forever on her guard.

The ground was damp and slimy beneath her feet and the tree trunk felt like a block of iron on her back. Maybe she could drag the chain down the trunk and slither to the ground. But that would be foolish. If the officer's warning about the snakes and spiders were true, her chances of survival would diminish. At least with her feet on the ground she could kick and stamp if she were attacked.

Time passed slowly. Her head began to ache and she felt a heavy weariness take over. It was more than twelve hours since she had taken a rest. But now she must be on her guard. She could not afford to slacken her vigil when she had no idea what might be lurking beneath her feet.

Contemplating her future, she closed her eyes. But that fleeting moment was lost when an almighty clap of thunder rumbled through the heavens. Seconds later, the sky lit up to a blinding glow followed by a searing flash. Nearby trees were ignited; flames leapt into the air, licking viciously at the branches, some of them only yards away.

Terror struck within her. Her senses were bombarded with a cacophony of sounds as the heavy rumbling was augmented by a shrill squealing. And then her nostrils were filled with the smell of burning animal flesh.

The heat began to penetrate.

If she remained there for much longer she would surely meet her death – ironically at the stake as would have been her punishment had she remained in England. But there was no way of escape. The thick chain was too sturdy for anyone to break open. And by this time, she could barely see. The lightning was so bright it impaired her vision. She closed her eyes and sent up a silent prayer.

Dear God, please help me!

Jimmy had heard from the other marines about the rumpus in the women's quarters. He put it down to the disgusting habits of the crew bent on drinking, making merry and taking the women to their beds. But, having been on duty since daybreak, he had not been called to assist in restraining them, not until later. After helping to pitch tents, he had been given time off to rest before the evening watch.

It was time once more to write to his mother for it was important he let her know what was happening. He had sent her letters from Portsmouth, Rio and the Cape but he had no idea if the letters had reached Scotland. The men relied on mail being taken home in returning ships. He did not expect to hear from his mother or anyone else. She was unable to write and there were no circumstances in which his father would contact him.

A feeling of sadness overwhelmed him. He knew his mother would be sent out to work, and soon little Danny would be put to the docks, just as he himself had been when he was just seven years old. But there had been nothing he could do to change the situation before he joined the marines. Now things were different. He was mature and far more physically fit and would easily overcome his father if the need arose. In time, when he returned to Glasgow, that was Jimmy's plan.

But there was nothing to be gained by dwelling on circumstances he knew nothing about. For all he knew his father may have reformed. But that was a most unlikely possibility.

Jimmy took out his quill and started to write:

My dearest mother
How I have mised you Mother and Amy and Danny too. I hope you are safe and well. It has been a long Jouney and now we have arrived at our Destinashon New South Wales. It is very hot here. We Pitchd a tent and will sleep there until we build

huts.

The Sargent is very kind and after my brithday, I was promoted to Corpral. There are indians here. We have to Take Heed. And are all maner of birds, very Colorful. We have Seen snakes too and very big Spiders. Some of them are poysenus.

I do not Know how long it will be Before you receve this letter. I will write agan soon.

God keep You safe.

Your Loving Son Jimmy

Setting the letter aside, he intended passing it over to one of the transports returning to England. Having been detailed by the sergeant to organise the guard for the governor's quarters he left the tent to start his evening duties. He placed two young marines at the entrance whilst he and Sandy made themselves available in case trouble of a serious kind arose near the huts.

As they set out to patrol the area they soon realised there was mayhem everywhere. The crew were shouting and singing, some of them rolling about in the mud. Most of it was harmless, and Jimmy decided only to intervene if the men were forcing their attentions on women who were reluctant to co-operate.

But before it continued much longer, the sergeant intervened. 'Get the bastards away from the women's camp,' he shouted. 'The governor has insisted those who remain will be punished.'

Jimmy engaged a party of marines and, together with Sandy they set off towards the riotous crew. But they knew in their hearts the task confronting them would be nigh on impossible.

Emily heard the words, 'Over here!' and felt sure the call came from nearby. Her greatest fear was that it was the officer back to taunt her or, even worse, accuse her of murder. Shaking now, she peered through streaming eyes. The words were repeated. Relief swept through her when she recognised the familiar voice of Sandy MacDonald.

'The lassie is moving. I think she is still alive.' He rushed forward and lifted her head, touching the heavy chains with which she was held to the stake. 'My God,' he called out. 'It is Emily and she is shackled.'

'Emily, my dearest Emily!' Jimmy stared, horrified, then slipped his arms gently around her. 'Do not worry. You will soon be free of these. Sandy, go quickly. Get the keys from Sergeant MacVay. Tell him it is a matter of life and death.'

Emily felt the warmth of Jimmy's body as he hugged her close. She felt safe and secure. But no sooner had Sandy left than the governor appeared beside them. Emily looked away. Her stomach began to churn. He was the one who had given instructions for her to be placed in shackles. He was not likely to react kindly to Jimmy's protective arm around her, nor of his intention to set her free.

'What the devil is going on here? It is the animals I came to check but, my God, I did not expect this. It is punishment unfit for an animal let alone a child. It is inhumane. Get her away from here!' He beckoned to MacVay who had appeared with the keys. 'Find out which brute did this and send him to me immediately'

Emily felt the release of the heavy chain as it fell to the ground, and then the shackles were removed. As the tension disappeared her body began to ache.

'Come with me, Sergeant, and bring the girl. I must investigate this disgraceful business,' the governor continued.

Emily struggled towards the marquee and Jimmy helped her along.

'Send for Bowes Smyth,' the governor ordered and he turned to Emily. 'Who placed you out there, child?' he asked.

'I do not know, sir, except that it was one of the officers.'

Minutes later the flap of the marquee was lifted and Bowes Smyth appeared.

'I have heard what happened, Arthur.' He turned to look at Emily. 'My God, it is you Mistress Spence.' He swung around and faced the governor again. 'It is a wonder the girl has not been blinded by the lightning. I am told that only yards away a pig and several of the sheep were struck and perished. It could have been this child.' He dabbed the blood from Emily's face where Rafton had scratched her and he examined the bruises inflicted by the officer.

The governor intervened. 'Sergeant MacVay will be making enquiries on my behalf. But,' he said, pausing in contemplation, 'I have a vague recollection. Last night one of my lieutenants brought someone in here. I was racked with severe pain in my head, and I was sorely in need of a rest. I left the officer to deal with the felon. Maybe it was this girl,' he said pointing to Emily. 'What do you recall?' he asked her.

'The lieutenant did bring me in here, sir.'

'It was Bridgewater.' The governor rose from his seat and called to the sentry. 'Ask Sergeant MacVay to bring the lieutenant to me immediately.'

It was several minutes before Bridgewater entered the marquee, a faint smile on his face as he eyed Emily. He stood before the governor.

'About this child.' The governor pointed to Emily. 'How dare you treat a human being in such a way, inflicting pain on her? I expected discretion when I instructed you last evening. You stepped beyond the bounds of humanity, Bridgewater.'

The smile disappeared from the lieutenant's face. 'But you...'

'I want no weak excuses,' the governor stressed. 'This girl is innocent. She was attacked by a crew member serving on board the *Lady Penrhyn*. Abel Rafton is his name. He threatened to rape her. She is but a child.' He turned to the sergeant. 'You tell me that Rafton is now fully conscious.'

'He is indeed, sir.'

He pointed a finger in Bridgewater's direction.

'I made it quite clear when I stressed that male prisoners attempting to enter the women's quarters should be fired at. That also applies to crew members. Had you acted lawfully in the first place, Rafton would have been caught in the act, before all this happened. But now it is too late to maintain such punishment. We shall both lose face at this late stage. Since I know that the ship *Lady Penrhyn* will soon be leaving for China, on this occasion the seaman will be given a severe warning.'

He turned to McVay. 'Send one of your men to the ship. I wish to speak with Captain Sever.'

Bridgewater flinched when the governor turned towards him.

'Mark my words, Bridgewater, if anything of this nature reoccurs, or the seaman Rafton tries to seek vengeance on this child before the ship sets sail, he will be shot. And the responsibility will be yours, you will be answerable to Major Ross to start, and then to me personally.' He turned to the sergeant. 'Take the girl away, MacVay. Bridgewater, you will remain behind.'

Jimmy was standing with the guard outside the marquee when Sergeant MacVay lifted the flap and brought Emily out. On impulse Jimmy took her hands and drew her towards him.

'I shall not forget what has happened, Emmy. I shall seek revenge.'

Emily replied. 'I want no trouble, Jimmy. The matter is over now. Please I beg you, leave it be.'

'Ballantyne, ye have been warned not to fraternise with the felons.' The sergeant spat out the words and dragged the two apart. 'The girl is right. Abide by my orders or ye will be punished. Take heed, lad or I may have to send ye with a forward party to reconnoitre ground some distance away.'

'I apologise most humbly, Sergeant MacVay. But Emily is innocent and I cannot but try to protect her.' By this time, he knew he must curb his wrath and control his urges, otherwise, if he were sent away, he would be in no position to help Emily. He took a deep breath and stood once more to attention.

'Ye canna take the law into yer own hands, laddie,' the sergeant offered kindly. 'Leave the matter be! The governor has taken control.'

But Jimmy knew that Rafton would soon be leaving when the *Lady Penrhyn* set out on her voyage to China to collect a cargo of tea and, as the sergeant had confirmed, the governor now had the matter in hand. As for the lieutenant, he had been unmercifully cruel to Emily, and there was no reason why Jimmy could not seek retribution, provided he was careful not to be caught. He knew that Sandy would be his ally. Since leaving Glasgow they had constantly looked out for each other.

The next day, back in the makeshift barracks, Jimmy sought him out. 'Sandy, please listen to what I have to say? I am determined to seek revenge on Bridgewater after the terrible way he treated Emily. Will you help me carry it through?'

'Have you not heard, Jimmy? Major Ross has placed the lieutenant under arrest. It is rumoured he will be taking an advance party through yon bushes on a pioneer exercise in a week or so.' He nudged Jimmy's elbow. 'It will be some time before he is back. Perhaps by that time your vengeful streak will have disappeared.' Slapping Jimmy on the back he added, 'And what will you gain by punishing the man except bring yourself down to his level?'

'Aye. Maybe you are right, Sandy. But I find the man most detestable.'

'Do you not believe that is why he is being sent away from the camp? The governor has enforced it.

And remember, the sergeant threatened to send you away too. There are surely two important reasons why you must control your anger. Firstly to be close to your dear little Emily,' he rolled his eyes, 'for I am most certain she has a special place in your heart, Jimmy Ballantyne.'

'She is but a friend, more like a sister to me,' Jimmy replied, averting his gaze.

Sandy laughed and continued.

'Secondly, if the lieutenant is leading the party, is he not the last person you could wish to spend time with? Let us wait a while and see what happens.' He smiled wickedly. 'But that does not mean we cannot make his life uncomfortable.'

Within the week, Bridgewater had been released and demoted to Second Lieutenant. That night in the officers' mess, Jimmy inadvertently spilled salt in the lieutenant's broth.

'Oh dear,' he said, passing it to Sandy who served it to him.

Bridgewater took a taste and frowned. Perhaps he had an idea it was a deliberate ploy. Perhaps he believed all the officers were eating salty broth. Who was to know? But after his reprimand by the governor, and his demotion, he would be reluctant to cause another skirmish in the camp, for that would surely isolate him as a troublemaker. He devoured the broth without complaint, and ordered a second flagon of water to be brought to the table.

The following day, it was the lieutenant's boots. It seemed a huge spider was lurking inside one of them. Unfortunately, the spider was one of the biting species and Bridgewater was witnessed by a young marine to slip his foot into the boot, wince loudly and withdraw it rather rapidly. He turned the boot upside down and the spider ran to safety. Luckily for Bridgewater it was not of the poisonous variety. Both Jimmy and Sandy sniggered when they were told the news. The spider was the biggest they could find.

After the previous night's orgy the governor sent for a party of marines to search the women's camp and flush out any miscreants who had spent the night with the women.

'I will not tolerate this sort of behaviour,' he announced.

The guilty ones had been called upon to march in files, enforcing the drunkards, both sailors and convicts, through their midst. Confronted by the marines, the men tottered out, buttoning trousers, pulling on shirts as they appeared from the makeshift huts and tents.

Jimmy looked away and from a distance, he spotted Emily and her friends re-building the huts. He dearly wished he could go over and help her. She was such a slight little thing and should not have been made to carry out such a physical task. But he knew if he disobeyed the sergeant once more, he may be sent away with Bridgewater to reconnoitre the area up river.

Chapter 9

Governor Phillip decided it was time he addressed the assembled masses after witnessing the havoc caused by some of the crew and felons alike.

'I require you to instruct your men to round up all convicts and bring them before me,' he instructed Major Ross. 'There are few things more pleasing than the contemplation of law and order, and this satisfaction cannot anywhere be more fully enjoyed than where a group of civilised people is about to settle upon a newly discovered, yet savage coast.'

Major Ross ordered his men to line up the convicts and march them towards the governor's marquee. Once assembled, they were made to sit on the ground in a circle before the governor. The marines formed an outer circle to guard them.

The governor appeared from the marquee to issue the rules about punishment.

'There will be no repetition of last night's orgy. I have issued orders that any male prisoner caught attempting to enter the women's quarters at night will be fired upon. Do I make myself clear?' The convicts nodded absently. 'That also applies to the rest of you,' he added harshly. 'Anyone attempting to steal cattle or chickens will be hanged. If you do not work, you will surely not eat. Discipline will be maintained.' His voice softened. 'For good behaviour I shall grant rewards. Ticket-of-leave status will be offered to those who consistently prove themselves to be honest and hard-working.'

Major Ross, who was described by many as the most disagreeable commanding officer ever, looked to his sergeant in disapproval.

'What is the justification for rewards?' he whispered out of earshot of the governor. 'In my eyes no man or woman is entitled to a pardon. The convicts are guilty and they are here to be punished not rewarded.' It would certainly not have been his policy to sanction the measures of democracy and diplomacy offered by his superior.

The governor continued his address.

'My intention is for the land to be cleared and for the building of the officers' quarters to start immediately, followed by the marine barracks. Finally you will build for yourselves which is surely something to aim for.' He surveyed the gathering. Many of the convicts appeared apathetic, but still he persisted in outlining his plans. 'Furthermore, since there is a lack of fresh vegetables, the kind we are familiar with in England, you will be allocated plots of land, and there will be incentives for those who are successful in producing food for the colony.'

One by one he introduced the dignitaries. 'Major Ross is my Lieutenant-Governor, Captain Collins my Judge Advocate, Mr White my Chief Surgeon, and the Reverend Johnson the Colony Chaplain.'

The newly appointed Judge Advocate ceremoniously opened two red leather cases, each holding the seal of King George III and containing the royal instructions. He stepped forward and read out the lengthy contents of the documents, which indicated that complete power and authority had been bestowed upon Governor Phillip.

The convicts, now unable to hear clearly or understand the contents of his speech, became restless. Lucy began to cry and Emily tried to hush her by rocking her gently, wishing it would all end.

Eventually the women returned to the huts they had newly built after the storm. They were almost complete and were made from the cabbage tree palm. They measured nine by twelve feet and comprised two windows, a door opening and a hipped roof thatched from reed. Although they harboured spiders and other such bugs, and they leaked each time it rained, Emily was relieved that they offered some privacy away from the men.

Having been together since the days of the hulks, Emily had always promised she would share a home with Nell. But things did not go smoothly for she had not bargained for Jessie's reaction.

'I cannot leave you, Emmy. You promised to look after me. I am afraid to leave.'

'But you will be next door and Grace will look after you. What will poor little Jane do without you?' she said, trying to humour her friend.

'And what of Lucy? I love them both, but I wish to stay with you.'

Emily had no alternative.

Nell reluctantly agreed to move in with Grace.

'I had set my mind on staying with you, Emmy,' she whispered, 'for you know I treasure you as my own kin. But I shall enjoy Grace's company, and I will be nearby should you need me.'

It was several days before the storms abated and all was tranquil. The governor's message to male convicts and crew had stopped their little jaunts to the female quarters. But the ruling seemed not to apply to everyone. One dark night Emily was standing outside, talking quietly to Nell and taking in the cool night air when she spotted a most unwelcome guest making a stealthy approach to Grace's door. Her breath caught in her throat when she realised it was Bridgewater. She stepped back into the hut dragging Nell with her. They stood inside the doorway listening.

'Grace, Grace,' whispered Bridgewater. 'Let me in. It is me, Bridgewater.'

They heard the door open and close. Emily and Nell turned to each other. 'Grace must have allowed him in.' Nell was astounded. 'I am surprised that she should betray us so?'

'Perhaps she is afraid. If she refuses, he may issue some punishment. Remember what happened to me, Nell. He is an evil man and I think it will be for the best if you keep the matter to yourself.' She sat down next to Nell and added, 'According to Jimmy, Bridgewater will be leaving the camp soon.'

'But I am not happy the way Grace is prepared to put up with this. I know the rations are meagre, but we can manage without the extra she provides.'

'It is obviously her way. Do keep this our secret, Nell, I beg you. I would not wish Jimmy to find out, for if he became involved he could be seeking trouble himself.'

'But the governor said that the convicts, the crew and soldiers would not be allowed to visit the women's quarters. Why should his orders exclude Bridgewater?'

'I am sure they do not. Judging by his furtive approach, he did not wish to be seen. Forget it. If you wish to beg the question with Grace, so be it.

But if you let spill that she has taken Bridgewater in, then she will surely face punishment.'

'Do not worry. I understand. But I shall speak with Grace. I do not approve of her entertaining the men, especially Bridgewater. It is my home too.'

It was more than an hour later when Bridgewater slipped from the hut, checking the immediate vicinity as he did so. Nell, her face scarlet with anger, hurried next door and Emily followed close behind.

'I am indeed surprised, Grace that you have allowed that man into our abode. No doubt you are aware who he is.'

'I am well aware, Nell. But, as I have said before, I have the right to choose for myself,' she replied. 'And it is not what you think.'

'But when he is here I am forced to stay with Emily, at least until he returns to the barracks. Is that fair?'

'He had not arranged to call, Nell. I was as surprised as you. But trust me. It will not continue.'

It was three days later when the news reached them. 'According to Surgeon White, Bridgewater is ill with stomach cramps. They say it could be dysentery,' Jimmy told them.

'Is that so? I do hope he does not suffer too much,' Grace offered, a curious tone to her voice.

But before the week was out Nell came back with more news. 'Poor Bridgewater is getting worse, Em. They fear for his life. How sad that is,' she said, her eyes revealing no emotion.

'Indeed and he will be greatly missed,' Grace added and, as she turned away, her face was touched with a knowing look.

Emily suspected Grace had played some part in Bridgewater's fate but, whatever had happened, it was not her business to enquire. After all, Grace had insisted to Nell that she had the right to make her own decisions. Emily could only agree and she felt relief on one score. The authorities were unaware Bridgewater had visited Grace, which placed Grace in the clear. And that was how it would remain.

Bridgewater's recovery was a slow process. Surgeon White, unable to pinpoint exactly what had caused this condition, was of the opinion the lieutenant would always have a weakness and, much to Major Ross's chagrin, White insisted it would be some time before Bridgewater was well enough to resume his duties.

Major Ross became even more annoyed when he was summoned to talk with the governor.

'As you are aware, I have sent Lieutenant King to investigate an island in the great ocean to the east of the colony. But I am disappointed that my plans to reconnoitre the area up river, beyond Sydney Cove, have not been carried out. Is there some valid reason why this is so?'

'There is indeed, Arthur. I have been obliged to change my own plans, for it was Bridgewater I had detailed to send. You remember some time ago you recommended that he would be the ideal choice,' Ross insisted.

'I do indeed, Robert. That is why I mention it.'

'The lieutenant has not yet recovered from his illness.'

'But the colony cannot be dependent upon one soldier. Why have you not chosen another officer?'

'I was as determined as you that Bridgewater be punished, especially after the way he brought disrepute to the corps. I was awaiting his recovery. Had the land been suitable, I would have left him there to supervise the convicts as they set about building and working the land. But it seems the sickness has brought him down completely. I have decided he must return to England on the next available ship. In his present condition, he is no use to the corps,' he said, sighing and trying to control his anger at being taken to task by the governor. 'But I have another man in mind to lead the party.'

'And who might that be?' the governor asked.

'Captain O'Donnell.'

'Captain O'Donnell is a good friend of mine. I would not wish him to remain up river for long. His wife, Martha, and their children are here in Sydney Cove. Martha has developed a plan to help with the women and children of the colony.' The governor stood to his feet and pushed back his chair, an indication that it was time for the major to leave. 'I assume you will bear that in mind and make the requisite arrangements immediately. We must make advances and look for more resources,' the governor insisted impatiently.

Shortly after his reprimand the begrudging Major Ross sent Captain O'Donnell to survey the area and, as a result, recommended that a party of felons be sent there to grow wheat and maize and to build homes. In recognition of patron Sir George Rose, the governor named the area Rose Hill. As for the island to the east of the mainland, Lieutenant Gidley King and twenty-two men left in the *Supply* to carry out a reconnoitre. Despite the rocky coast and the heavy surf, they came across a good landing place to the south west. The island was found to be thickly wooded, the trees tall and straight, and the soil rich, black loam.

It was to be called Norfolk Island and King remained as Commandant. It would be a good place for animals to eat well. Fish there was plentiful too. Once the enormous red gums were felled, the first corn could be sown. Delighted with the news, Governor Phillip made a decision. He would prepare to send another small party to the island.

Once the huts were complete, the governor allocated the women a patch of land on which to grow vegetables. But the land was hard, full of roots and contained many rocks and stones. 'I know nothing about growing crops,' Emily confessed, staring down at the red earth beneath her feet.

'If the soil is good enough, they will grow,' Grace said. 'When I was a young girl, I worked on the nearby farm with my mother, and we came to know about crops and the like. My father was a gardener at the manor, and he taught us many things. We had our own little patch at the back of our cottage. I used to watch father tending the plants.' She gazed ahead of her and kicked at the stones beneath her feet, most likely adrift in her memories.

'If you would show us how, we could start to cultivate the land.'

'It is a challenge but I am sure we shall manage.

First we must clear the land of rocks and stones.'

Emily realised the ground was difficult to prepare for cultivation without the right implements to dig or hoe, except for a few hatchets brought from the ship. But the women managed to penetrate the ground, painstakingly poking, prodding and riddling until their little patch was clear. But when they asked at the government store for seed they were disappointed.

'The seed we brought from the Cape has already germinated as a result of the damp aboard ship and the heat of the colony. It is completely useless. Of the remainder you shall have whatever we can spare, mainly barley and a few vegetables.'

Grace tended the ground with loving care, and the others followed her instruction. She nurtured and watered the young plants and soon they began to yield a light crop of scraggy, yet edible vegetables and a small amount of barley. The women were delighted. But no sooner had the results of their toils come to fruition than a sergeant from the marines paid a visit.

'Your crop is meagre but you have had some success. When it is harvested you must bring it to the government store.'

'But we have spent many hours tending the plants, keeping them safe from the natives. Surely we are entitled to some small amount?' Grace replied.

'It is the property of the government of this colony. Did you not obtain the seeds from the government store?'

Grace was angry and frustrated but when she enquired at the store, she was told they would have their share when the total crop was harvested. Emily tried to appease her knowing she must motivate Grace otherwise she may be reluctant to continue.

'It is a wonderful feat to have succeeded in this alien land,' she stressed. 'We must not give in, Grace. We shall continue, and soon we shall be allowed some food for ourselves. Perhaps the governor will allocate a bigger patch. I will make enquiries.'

Emily's request to the governor's man was successful and their plot was considerably extended. The four women tended the patch, attempting to grow wheat, maize and fruit saplings. But they had no help from the men, some of whom were lazy and completely ignorant of any aspects of farming or growing. Many of them came from the slums of London and they had no intention of learning. Others were too feeble through old age or through incurable illness to become involved.

Within a short space of time Emily realised they would need to set up a rota.

'Now that Lucy and Jane are walking, one of us must stay back for we cannot care for them properly when we are tending the garden.'

'It was on my mind too, Emmy, for you know the problem with my Jane. As soon as my back is turned she wanders off, bless her.' Grace smiled and Emily nodded in understanding.

'Then we shall take turns, say half a day at a time. What do you say, Nell?'

'That is fine by me, Emmy,' Nell replied, a look of relief upon her face. Emily had earlier suggested that she took time off; all the bending and heavy work affected her bones. But whilst Nell was adamant she should share the load with the others, now she was in agreement.

Emily was hugely satisfied. The little team worked happily together, the quality and quantity of their produce improving greatly. And they were the envy of many of the other women in the camp, some of whom were slothful and whiled away their time doing nothing useful at all. By the end of the growing season, the night air was cooler. There was a light frost in the mornings and winter was drawing near. When the day's work was ended Emily decided to walk down to the harbour.

'Come with me, Jess, for Grace is stitching and Nell is resting. Shall we take a look at the governor's new mansion?'

Jessie nodded, picked up her shawl and they set out towards the wharf where Emily was curious to look at the newly manufactured bricks.

'I have heard they are made from the lime remaining from burnt oyster shells. The natives are partial to oysters and they have left lots of shells along the beaches.' Emily gazed across at Government House. 'It looks very sturdy, Jess. The new bricks seem to have proved successful. The governor will have lovely views across the harbour,' she said pointing towards the huge heads leading from Sydney Cove out to sea. 'And he will see the ships as they enter the bay.'

They lingered at the water's edge, taking the air and searching the sea for ships. When Emily looked back at the mansion, she spotted two small children playing on the grass outside the governor's house.

'I was not aware the governor had young children,' she said to the still silent Jessie who followed her gaze. One of the children was running ahead, the other, a smaller child followed more slowly. But Emily became agitated when the first child tripped and fell, rolling down the grassy bank towards the sea. Sensing the danger, Emily set off at a rapid pace towards the child, panic and urgency spurring her on. 'Come quick, Jess,' she called.

But by the time Emily reached the sea the child, a boy of about four, had fallen in and, losing his balance, was submerged by a huge wave and drawn back by the heavy tide.

All Emily could hear were his muffled screams when he came to the surface. Almost breathless, Emily waded into the water until it was waist-high. Unable to swim, she dragged herself on to a huge rock and, reaching forward she caught hold of the boy's waistcoat and hauled him towards her with enormous effort. 'Jess, please take him,' she begged, breathing heavily and trying to keep her balance.

Jessie quickly paddled into the surf, grabbed the boy and placed him over her shoulder, patting his back. The other child, a little girl, stood on the bank, tears streaming down her face. Emily, now emerging from the waves, was aware that a man was running towards them. She brushed her eyes with her finger tips to clear away the salt water and peered in his direction. It was the governor.

The boy, now turning blue in the face appeared to be on the verge of choking, but Governor Phillip took him in his arms, tipped him over his knee and patted his back soundly with the palm of his hand.

'That's the way,' he said as the child, coughing and spluttering, spewed out water. Despite his ashen appearance, a little colour returned to the boy's cheeks. 'I think he will survive.' The governor smiled and tucked the boy under his arm. He turned to Emily. 'That was remarkable, young woman! We have you to thank for the life of young Joshua here. I was taking a walk to inspect my property when I spotted you. These two must have given the nursemaid the slip. It was lucky you saw them.'

He beckoned Emily and Jessie to follow as he set out towards the house. 'This part of the house is complete,' he said. 'Come, follow me. We must obtain dry clothes for you both.'

He took them through into the kitchen where a woman was busy preparing food. 'Sarah, call Mistress O'Donnell immediately,' he said, gently placing the child on a wooden chair. 'This lad needs attention.'

'Oh, my good lord,' the woman muttered as she stood rigid, gaping in astonishment.

'Sarah, the matter is urgent,' the governor insisted. 'Do as I ask.'

'I do beg pardon, sir,' she muttered and darted quickly out of the kitchen.

Joshua started to cry and his sister joined in.

'You are safe now child. You have no cause to bawl in that way,' the governor stressed, patting the lad on the back. But the boy obviously anticipated his mother's wrath.

Minutes later, Mistress O'Donnell, an elegant woman dressed in a fine gown of emerald green silk, entered the kitchen. 'The children are causing problems I presume,' she said, smiling.

The governor spoke up immediately. 'I am afraid Joshua here has had a little accident, Martha,' he announced, now lifting the dripping child from the chair and handing him over to Sarah.

Mistress O'Donnell let out a gasp. 'Oh my goodness, Arthur,' she cried as she stared at the child who was now clinging desperately to Sarah. But she swept the boy into her own arms. 'What am I to do with you, son?' She shook him gently and turned to Sarah. 'Do ask one of the girls to bathe and change him, Sarah dear,' she added, dashing the water from her gown.

The governor then turned his attention to her.

'Mistress O'Donnell, allow me to introduce this brave young woman who rescued Joshua from the sea. She was out walking with her friend here when she saw him running towards the water. She tells me he rolled down the bank and fell in.'

'He fell in? She rescued him from the sea?' she said, taking Emily's hands. 'I shall be eternally grateful to you.' She turned to the governor. 'And my nursemaid, poor Kitty, is in such a state. She told me they had hidden when they were playing a game together and she couldn't find them.'

'But you are too soft-hearted, Martha. You must reprimand her, for it is her job to keep a watch on the children.'

The woman smiled. 'That I will, Arthur, but only when she has calmed down.'

By this time, Emily and Jessie were left standing there, dripping wet and shivering from the cold.

'My goodness,' the governor said, jumping to his feet. 'What am I thinking? We must see to you two. Sarah will find you dry clothes. When you have changed, come to my study. I wish to speak with you. Perhaps you would come along too, Martha.'

Sarah soon returned.

'Mona will bathe the little one,' she said to Mistress O'Donnell and then she turned to Emily and Jessie. 'Come. I will see to your needs. Follow me.'

They followed her to a small room where Sarah gave them fresh water to wash away the salt from their skin. The clothes she handed them smelled fresh and clean.

'You need not return them,' she said when they were ready.

'But we cannot take them. They do not belong to us,' Emily insisted.

'Mistress O'Donnell wishes you to keep them,' Sarah added. 'Come now. I will take you to the governor's study.'

She led them along a corridor where Emily was surprised to see one of the native aborigines leaving the governor's room as they entered.

The study was large but sparsely furnished and the governor was sitting at his desk, smiling amiably as they entered. 'Do sit down.' He turned to Emily. 'What is your name?'

'Emily Spence, sir.'

'I believe I have seen you before.' He closed his eyes and sat in silence. 'Let me think. It was some time ago I believe, not long after we arrived at the colony.' He nodded his head. 'I have it. You were shackled by that scoundrel, Bridgewater. Yes that was it. I assume you are well after such an ordeal.'

'Indeed I am, sir.'

'And have you taken on any duties since you arrived? Caring for the sick perhaps or providing food for the colony?'

'We have set up a large garden, sir, and we are very pleased with the harvest.'

'Well done. You have proved to be a fine citizen.' He paused. 'The child you rescued is the son of a friend of mine, Captain O'Donnell. His wife, whom you met earlier, is visiting. I have asked her to come along for she is indebted to you for your courage.'

'I do not wish anyone to be in my debt, sir. For I did what any mother would do. I was concerned for the child. And my friend, Jessie, helped too.'

'But you thought not of yourself, my dear.' His brow furrowed. 'Do I take it you are a mother too?'

'I am, sir. My child, Lucy was born on board the *Lady Penrhyn* and, but for the kindly surgeon, neither of us would have survived.'

'Bowes Smyth,' he nodded his head, 'a caring gentleman. But you are very young to be a mother. Was it one of the men on board the ship?'

'No it was not, sir. It happened in England.' Emily was reluctant to continue further, but by this time the governor was curious to know the exact story.

'I am saddened to hear what happened. I will write to Sir William Brice and ask him to look into the matter, for he is a lawyer of renown and a philanthropist. He has taken up the cause of others wrongly convicted. Maybe he will help.'

The door opened and Mistress O'Donnell entered.

'Come in, Martha dear. Do sit down. There is something I wish to discuss in the presence of Emily Spence here.' The governor turned to Emily. 'Mistress O'Donnell is about to embark upon something that will make life easier for the women of this colony,' he began. 'What she has proposed will allow them to proceed with important work, stitching, laundering, caring for the sick, and so on, unencumbered by their children. If the children were to be taken care of whilst the women continue with their work, productivity would improve. Mistress O'Donnell is anxious to set up a nursery where the children can be brought together to play, and I have made arrangements for a suitable place to be built.'

He paused and smiled, turning to Mistress O'Donnell. 'You said you needed help, Martha. Have you someone in mind?'

'In view of what has happened, I know Emily to be a caring young woman, and I have not yet come across any other suitable person to help.'

'You have echoed my thoughts exactly, Martha. That is what I was hoping. What I propose is that you take on Emily to help you.'

'That is an excellent idea and it makes good sense.' She turned to Emily. 'Judging by your actions today, you do indeed have the protective instinct. I would be delighted to take you on.'

'I do not wish to sound ungrateful Mistress O'Donnell but what of the garden? My friends will still need help.'

'If they are unable to find help, I am sure we can find a suitable worker for the plot,' the governor insisted, 'someone reliable.'

'That is indeed very kind of you, sir. I am sure the others will be pleased.'

Mistress O'Donnell turned to Jessie who was sitting quietly in the background.

'You helped your friend to rescue my dear little Joshua and I don't even know your name.'

'My name is Jessie,' was her timid reply.

'Thank you, Jessie for your kindness towards my Joshua. Perhaps you would like to help too.'

'I am sure she would,' Emily replied tentatively, anxious for Jessie to help. 'Jessie is very willing. She cares for my child and that of my friend whilst we are busy working in the garden.'

'What do you think, Jessie?' Mistress O'Donnell asked her directly.

To Emily's amazement, a smile started to develop on Jessie's face. 'Yes, I would like to help you, Mistress O'Donnell,' she replied.

Emily gasped at Jessie's clear and forthright answer, and with a look of pure delight on her face, she made a firm promise.

'We shall make every endeavour to help you Mistress O'Donnell. Do you not agree, Jessie?'

'Indeed I do, Emily.' Jessie's smile widened.

The governor spoke up. 'Until now, other matters have been more pressing. But it is time to act. The building will begin immediately.'

'I will send a message when we are ready to start.' Mistress O'Donnell nodded in appreciation. 'Thank you for agreeing to help. Now I must go and see to my darling Joshua,' she added and left the room.

'Do let me know if your friend is unable to find

help for the garden,' the governor said. 'And with regard to the other matter, I will contact Brice and ask him to investigate. But do not place too much hope on his finding out the truth, for these things are difficult to prove.'

'I understand, sir. But I would like to extend my grateful thanks for your offer of help.'

'Should there be some tangible proof that your story is true,' he hesitated, 'not that I have any doubts in my mind, then I shall recommend that the gentleman involved be punished severely. You must leave it with me.'

It was with that in mind, Emily and Jessie went back to their little hut.

Nell and Grace were astounded when they saw the two approaching in unfamiliar gowns. But Nell's face was veiled in anxiety.

'How did you come by those gowns?' she asked, a suspicious edge to her voice.

Emily started to laugh. 'It is not what you think, Nell. Give us the chance and we will explain.'

Nell and Grace were truly delighted when Emily told them the news.

'I shall take both Jane and Lucy to the nursery with me each day,' Emily said.

'That would be very useful. Now that we have organised the plot and the governor has allocated more land, I am keen to proceed with the project. But first I shall need to find help,' Grace said.

'The governor has promised to help find a suitable replacement,' Emily told her.

'There is someone I know who would be interested, and then perhaps Nell could take some rest, for the two of us will manage fine without the children to care for.'

'And, Nell. How do you feel about that?' Emily asked.

'I think my duties lie here with the huts. Someone will need to clean them and prepare food for your return. Would you agree to that?'

'I think it is a very suitable arrangement.' Emily placed her arm around Nell's shoulder. 'I am so excited,' she added. 'I hope it will not be long before the governor provides the accommodation and then we can start. What do you say, Jess?'

'We will look after the children really good, like Dot looked after me and Lizzie.' Jessie dwelt on her words for several seconds. 'But poor Dot and poor Lizzie have gone to heaven now and we must get on with the job the Lord has given us.'

'Well said, Jess. I knew Mistress O'Donnell had chosen well when she suggested your help.'

Such a breakthrough! Emily was aware that since Lizzie's death, Jessie had mourned her loss but had never mentioned Lizzie's name. But now something had re-awakened within her. Perhaps this would be the making of Jess. Emily certainly hoped so.

Chapter 10

1788 - 1789

On the few occasions Jimmy had a chance to slip away from the barracks he visited Emily, taking food and whatever else he could acquire. After Sergeant MacVay's warning about fraternising with the felons, he was careful not to over-extend his visits, although he knew the sergeant had sympathetic tendencies. When Emily told him of the governor's plans to set up a nursery and her future involvement in caring for the children, his face lit up in adoration.

Some weeks later he asked if there had been any news from Mistress O'Donnell.

'Why, yes, she sent for me yesterday. The building will be ready by next week,' she confirmed, her eyes bright with enthusiasm.

'I cannot help but feel proud of you. It was brave of you to rescue Captain O'Donnell's child from the sea. News of the incident has spread throughout the camp and the officers hold you in high esteem.'

'It is kind of you to tell me.' She paused. 'Do sit down, Jimmy and take some tea. There is something I wish to tell you.' The tone of her voice suggested she was about to reveal something serious.

A flash of anxiety dulled Jimmy's blue eyes, veiling their usual vibrancy as he watched Emily take the pot from the fire and pour the boiling water over the leaves. The 'tea' was not akin to that his mother made, for it was sweet and brewed from a type of spinach leaf and a liquorice-flavoured creeper she picked from the bush. But it was hot and it was palatable.

Emily, seemingly aware of his concern, smiled. Jimmy relaxed and sat down on a stool before reaching for the tea. Perhaps he had misinterpreted her tone, and picked up the wrong message.

'It is good news, Jimmy. The governor has promised to contact Sir William Brice and request that he examine the details surrounding my prosecution. I would be most gratified if my name were to be cleared, if I were to receive a pardon.'

'That's wonderful, Em! I will pray for it to happen. But do not build up your hopes for, although there is no doubt in my mind that you are innocent, you will not be in England to influence the judges. Another tissue of lies could be presented in your absence.'

'I understand what you are saying. But still I can hope.'

Jimmy reached over, taking her hand in his. 'You must know how much you mean to me, Emily, here in my heart,' he said, lifting his other hand to his chest. 'That is why I am so concerned.'

Abashed that Jimmy should confess to such sentiments, a bright crimson flush touched her cheeks, and her whole being was filled with warmth. Did he feel the same way too? It was difficult for her to decipher the myriad sensations flooding her body.

'Thank you for being so kind. I know you feel warmth towards me and I realise that is why you protect me.'

'It is more than warmth, Emily. And some day

you will understand.' He took her hands once more, pulled her to him and kissed her gently on the lips.

Emily's heart seemed to flip and she turned her head, pressing her face against his jacket and relishing the comfort. Not since her parents had passed away had she felt such closeness, such protection.

When Jimmy departed, she was left pondering. In normal circumstances, things would have been different. But she was determined not to allow her feelings to develop. How could she? No good would come of it. He was a marine and she was a convict.

The governor's plan to set up a nursery came to fruition at the end of September. Knowing Grace would struggle to cope alone in the garden, Emily broached the subject.

'The governor promised to find someone to help but he is obviously too busy. It is important that we look for someone suitable now that Jessie and I are no longer available.'

'Do not worry. For some time now I have had my eye on someone I think would be a willing helper.'

'And who might that be?' Emily was puzzled. Grace had intimated earlier that she knew someone who might be interested, but no mention had been made of the name of the woman.

Grace smiled warmly, her eyes conveying some secret message Emily was unable to detect.

'I have spoken with Ned Wilks and he has agreed to share the work with me.'

Emily laughed. 'So it is not a woman as I believed. But I am sure you have chosen well. Ned has always tried to keep a watchful eye on us especially before the crew departed. I have always thought him to be caring and reliable.'

'You are right. He is reliable, I am sure of that, and a hard worker. Do you remember the way he built the huts?' She did not wait for Emily's confirmation. 'He has agreed to start tomorrow.'

Contented that Grace had solved the problem, Emily was adamant the nursery project would prove successful. A large hut had been erected next to the hospital, both buildings made from wattle and daub.

Some of the male convicts who had fathered the children set about making all manner of toys, whittling away and shaping most of them from scraps of wood. The women worked with string and bits of fabric to make the crudest of soft toys. Emily was impressed.

Warmth shimmered through her as she became fully immersed in the new venture, having earned the respect of the other women who trusted her implicitly with their offspring.

By now both Esther Wray and Kate Bradley, the two forceful characters on board the *Lady Penrhyn*, each with a child of her own, appeared to have seen sense. Esther, now contented with life, had a furtive yet stable relationship with the marine she had partnered on board ship, and Kate was living happily with one of the convicts who had travelled on board the *Prince of Wales*.

'Fancy that scrap of a girl looking after the bairns,' Esther commented to Kate as they entered the nursery. 'Who would have thought it?'

Emily smiled to herself. A scrap of a girl they had

called her but she hadn't been a girl since the incident at the manor.

Kate handed her child over to Emily. 'Bless your heart for you have made life easier for us.'

'I am pleased I can pay you both back for what you did for me and Grace and our little ones on the *Penrhyn*. Think nothing of it.'

Emily became so involved that only occasionally did she think about the place she had left back in England, excepting when she was alone at night and when Lucy was fast asleep.

It was then she dwelt upon the circumstances she had faced before being sent to the hulks. It was then she dreamed of her ultimate goal. Her freedom.

By October of 1788, the governor decided to send a party of convicts to Norfolk Island. The *Golden Grove* was preparing to leave Sydney Harbour in the coming days. Grace and her new husband, Ned, were to be in that number. Their progress together had proved to be so successful that the governor felt they would be an asset in the new camp.

Emily's reactions to the news were mixed, for although she was sad that Grace and Ned were leaving, she was happy Grace had, at last, settled down. Their courtship had started almost immediately they began working together, and it was not long afterwards they were married by the Reverend Johnson.

Grace and Jane moved in with Ned, leaving Nell alone in the little hut. Jessie spent much of her time helping Nell whose bone ache had progressed since they had arrived at the colony.

'I worry so much about Nell. Sometimes she can barely lift herself from her bed to get up and clean the house. The sunshine helps but the damp and steamy atmosphere get to her bones.' Jessie paused in thought. 'What say if I move in with her? It will leave you and Lucy plenty of space. And you are just next door.'

'What a good idea, Jess. It would mean you could keep an eye on Nell and I am sure she will appreciate your company.'

Jessie's confidence had soared since Mistress O'Donnell had invited her to help at the nursery, and now here she was taking responsibility for Nell. She collected her few belongings and went next door. Emily heard Nell's cries as Jessie entered the hut. 'Bless my soul. I was never so pleased to see anyone in my life, excepting my poor Billy of course, God rest his soul.'

Nell's condition had worsened since they reached the colony and, when Billy was taken ill during a storm, she became depressed. Billy never recovered and when he passed away during August Nell was filled with sadness and she seemed to lose all hope, her spirit having dwindled.

Emily collected her thoughts when she heard a knock on the door. She crossed the room and opened it. Jimmy was standing there.

'Sorry to call on you at such a late hour, Em, but there is something I must tell you.' He entered the hut, swallowing hard and taking a deep breath. 'I am to leave for Norfolk Island tomorrow night on the *Golden Grove*. I am heart-broken to be leaving you but I am sure the stay will not be too extended.'

He took her hands in his and kissed them gently.

Emily's stomach began to churn. She felt her heart start to beat more rapidly in her chest. What would she do without him? She had come to rely on him, not for any physical needs but for his comfort and support. Her eyes filled with tears.

'I shall miss you, Jimmy.' She squeezed his hands. 'I hope it will not be too long before you return.'

'Those are my sentiments exactly, my sweet. I shall think about you every day. And I will write whenever I can.'

'God speed,' Emily said as Jimmy reached out and took her hands once more. This time he leant forward and gently pressed his lips on hers. He lifted his head and their eyes met. 'I love you with all my heart, Emily. Please wait for me.'

'But Jimmy. It will never work for you are a marine and I am a felon. I would never wish to bring you down to my level.'

'You are no felon, Emily. Please wait for me,' he begged. He reached over and kissed her more deeply this time.

She relaxed and relished the comfort of his strong arms around her and his mouth on hers, responding to his kiss knowing she loved him too. When he released her he held her at arms' length.

'I must leave you now but please do not forget what I said, Em. I will never stop loving you.' Without giving her the chance to respond he left.

Emily touched her lips. The feeling that raced through her body was something new. The tingling sensation was unlike anything she had ever felt before. She stood there as if in a trance, all manner of thoughts passing through her mind. But as baby Lucy started to advance towards the door, Emily pulled herself up sharply.

'Oh no you don't my precious,' she said, scooping up the child from the floor and squeezing the little mite. Filled with that wonderful sensation, she sat upon a stool and rocked her child. But the feeling did not last for suddenly she realised it would be a long time before she saw Jimmy again. And her heart sank.

It was the following night when the *Golden Grove* left the harbour bound for Norfolk Island. Grace, her husband Ned and her baby daughter were on deck. Emily waved and her eyes searched for Jimmy. She spotted him some distance away. He raised his hand, pressed it to his lips and waved.

Maybe it was a good thing he was leaving for she now knew for certain her feelings went far deeper than friendship alone.

The recent spell of optimism around the camp did not last. Spring turned to summer and the corn Grace and Ned had planted before they left for Norfolk Island was starting to grow. But by the summer, the harvest turned out to be poor, despite the efforts of the new gardener, Will Hopwood, with a little help from Emily and Jessie. It was a meagre yield. And similar results were widespread.

The governor was bitterly disappointed at the situation now developing in the colony.

'The drought is responsible for the poor harvest, David, but the soil is not fertile,' he told Judge

Collins. 'We need manure to maintain the natural fertility here. But there are few animals excepting the kangaroos and they are too timid to venture into the camp.'

'I believe the animals are wary of our presence. They will breathe in the scent of death if they come too close. Their meat is tender and the soldiers would have no hesitation in shooting them.'

The governor nodded. 'I agree but it seems the supplies I requested will never arrive. I am becoming impatient waiting for farm implements.'

Pointing to the garden area, he continued. 'The women struggle. They are making an effort to produce food, but do not even have the resources with which to tend the land. And, God forbid, I am blessed with a wretched set of city dwellers, most of them completely ignorant of any aspects of farming.' He sighed loudly. 'I must contact London once more and impress on them that we need settlers, men and women with farming expertise, otherwise our crops will neither increase, nor improve in quality.'

'We need domestic animals for food too, Arthur. It was a great pity so many of them died during transportation, and the lightning storm took more. I know some escaped to the bush, but not a single one has been seen since that fateful day. Perhaps they have been slaughtered by the natives.' He shook his head. 'So much for our breeding plans. Let us hope our fortunes change with the next transports.'

'We have so many problems! Where are the tradesmen we were promised, the carpenters and the builders? It is impossible to start a new colony without their expertise. Emphasis has been placed on ridding the country of the lowest of the low, the dregs of society, with complete disregard for the government's original plans.'

'That is so, for many of them are nothing but a drain on our colony.'

'How much longer can we struggle? We are completely dependent on supplies from England otherwise the threat of starvation will hang over us. And that will be the case for many years to come unless we establish our own means of producing food. I find the situation most depressing, Collins.'

Several days later the governor's anxiety continued when the stores were overrun with rats. There was insufficient food to keep the colony from starvation and he was forced to cut the flour rations.

In desperation, he sent the *Sirius* to Cape Town with Captain Hunter at the helm to collect supplies. He was surprised at the captain's expertise. Hunter cut the time of the trip from five to three months by taking a longer but quicker route. But many in the colony were already weak and unable to withstand the wait. Before the *Sirius* returned, many had died.

Within weeks the situation became dire. Some of the soldiers were discovered stealing from the public stores. They were arrested and the entire community was ordered to assemble outside the building. The governor arrived to address them.

'I am saddened to learn that food has been stolen from the public stores. No individual, including myself and my officers, has the right or the privilege to take extra rations,' he stressed.

'Here at the colony we are all equal and will

receive equal shares of the food. I shall impose the maximum penalty on anyone found stealing food.' He paused. 'Death by hanging.'

He beckoned to the marine sergeant. There was an almighty groan from the crowd when the soldiers were hanged from a tall tree outside the store, whilst two of their corps gave a final drum roll.

Thoroughly dejected, Emily still had the incident on her mind as she made her way in the early morning to the nursery. She was distraught that the assembled masses had been forced to witness the act. If the men were so hungry that they were forced to steal food, was it fair that they should be hanged? How could the governor be so callous? But deep down Emily realised that the hangings were intended to act as a deterrent to those who thought they would follow the soldiers' example. Thoughts of the approaching famine were on her mind too.

'I fear we shall run out of food completely and the lives of our little ones will be in danger. It seems they are given little at home. We need food for the nursery. Mistress O'Donnell has spoken with the governor. He is optimistic there will be a better crop from Rose Hill where the soil is deeper and richer than that in Sydney Cove. And it is a mere fifteen miles away,' he said pointing in that direction.

'The plots run down to the river the natives call the Parramatta and the harvest can be collected and brought down here in boats. We can but hope.'

'Will has heard there are wild dogs out there. They ravage the chickens and hens. The people are afraid to tend their gardens,' Jessie added.

'Without food the sick will become even sicker and, if things worsen, there will not be enough room in the hospital; it is so small,' she said, pointing to the building beside the nursery. 'The governor has asked the men to build one of brick, but progress is slow. They do not have the energy to work for a full day. They are too hungry.'

Still dwelling on the famine and the fate of the colony, Emily heard a rustling noise coming from the bushes. Thinking it was a snake or some other animal she stepped back and looked carefully around her, anxiety causing her stomach to churn.

Jessie gripped her arm. 'What was that?'

Emily stared hard and brought into focus a pair of black eyes looking at her through the lower branches of a tree. She started to laugh.

'Come on out, you little scamps.'

Two native children, maybe three and five years old, emerged from the bushes, their white teeth glinting as they smiled. Emily knew they could not understand her language but they knew her gestures and facial expressions. It was the second week they had appeared.

'Let us take them with us,' Emily said, smiling. She looked ahead and saw a young woman who nodded her head and smiled back.

'Are you sure we should? We want no trouble with the soldiers.' Jessie turned towards the nursery.

'The natives know what is happening. They have no doubt seen the women bringing their children here. Why should their children not be included? Governor Phillip wishes to encourage them to visit the camp,' Emily replied. 'He has made one or two native friends himself. One of them is Bennelong, a favourite of the governor's, who often stays at the mansion. I do believe he was there when we visited, after young Joshua's escapade,' she said. 'And Mistress O'Donnell told me that some of the natives look up to the governor and treat him as someone special. They call him Beeana.'

'Beeana? What does that mean?'

'Apparently it means 'father'. The governor is much revered. It has some connection with the gap in his front teeth. It is a custom of the natives, a ritual if you like, to knock out one of their own front teeth with a stone. They believe the governor to be a chosen one.'

'How strange.'

'It is no stranger than some of our own traditions.' She smiled but seconds later she became serious. 'The governor has given strict instructions to the marines not to fire on the natives. Until now they have fired mercilessly and with little provocation.'

'But it is not only the red-coats. Some of the convicts have made matters worse. Remember the two who tried to steal our first crops?'

'I do indeed, Jess. What of them?'

'They tried to steal the natives' canoes and spears two nights ago, so Will tells me. One of the red coats found them last evening down by the bay, speared to death.'

'Oh my goodness. But the natives cannot always be blamed. They have the right to defend themselves.' Emily sighed as she took the hands of the two native children and led them inside the hut. Jessie followed.

One of the convict mothers mumbled her disagreement at the sight of the two unclothed native children.

'This place is for our children not for them,' she stressed, the sour expression on her face matching her cutting voice.

'They are mere children just like the others, Dorothy,' Emily replied calmly.

'They are nothing like my children. My children are white. We may be poor but my children have clothes on their backs.'

'Please try to understand. It is their custom. It is perfectly natural for them.'

'I tell you my bairns will not come back here until you rid this place of them blacks.'

'The decision is yours, Dorothy,' Emily said calmly. 'Both Mistress O'Donnell and the governor have expressed a desire for us to befriend and tolerate the natives in any way we can. I agree with them wholeheartedly and I cannot deny them that request. I have no intention of sending these children away.'

'Then be it your own doing for it is no place for our bairns if the natives are allowed here too. You must make a choice.'

'It is you who must choose. If you wish to stay away then there is nothing more we can do.'

She watched the other women in somewhat of a dilemma. Should they follow Dorothy or remain true to Emily?

Dorothy turned to leave, staring back at the others, her brow drawn in a heavy frown. 'A set of cowards you are. Dare you not speak yer minds?' She picked up her child and opened the door. Two more women followed her.

Emily stood firm, resolute. 'You are not obliged to stay if you feel the same as Dorothy. You have your rights, too. You are free to leave.' She looked around at the women. 'But who will look after your children whilst you work? Children are children whatever their background, whatever their colour.'

The women looked to one another. Emily continued. 'They did not choose to be born black, just as we did not choose to be born poor, convicted and brought all this way to the colony. Do not forget had we been born into the aristocracy we could have bought our freedom.' She hesitated. 'And this is their land, not ours,' she added, pointing to the two natives. 'They were here before us. From now on, life must be what we make it. I, for one, will never deny these children.'

There was a low murmur amongst the women. Kate Bradley spoke up. 'Emily is right. Bairns are bairns. They are innocent little things. Maybe Dorothy is aggrieved on account of her Frederick. He was with the two who stole from the natives but he managed to escape. There is bound to be bitterness there. But as Governor Phillip has said many times we are here to make new lives for ourselves. How can we do that if we continue to steal?' She addressed Esther Wray. 'What do you say, lass?'

'I am bound to agree. My Richard is a red-coat, and a good man. He is here to keep the peace. I say we should try, if only the others will allow it.'

It was as the women were handing over their

children to Emily and Jessie that Mistress O'Donnell arrived.

'Has there been trouble, Emily? I passed three of the women leaving the nursery and dragging their children along with them. Why have they left?'

Emily told her of the two native children she had brought to the nursery and of the complaints from Dorothy. 'But Esther and Kate believe there is some connection with the killing of the two thieves by the natives.' Emily was not prepared to divulge the reason why. 'Apart from those three women the others have remained. Whether they were in agreement with Esther and Kate or whether they realise that if they rebelled life would be more difficult for them, I cannot say.'

'You were right to stand firm. Your principles have remained intact and that is the way we intend to continue.'

Contrary to the initial doubts in Emily's mind, the young aborigines were not left in isolation. The other children invited them to join in. And despite the language difference, they seemed to understand one another.

At the end of the day Mistress O'Donnell's gaze drifted towards the doorway where Esther and Kate were leaving. 'I must say,' she whispered, 'those two are certainly reformed characters.'

'I think they are settling well. And there is no call for crime if, as the governor says, we are all equal.'

Emily and Jessie prepared to leave.

'All the children have left,' Emily said, now ready to return to the garden to help Will finish the day's work. But then she spotted the two aborigines standing by the door. 'Excepting you two little ones,' she said, a smile on her face. Taking the children by the hands she set out towards an opening in the trees where they had appeared from the bush. When she looked through at the clearing she was surprised to see the young woman waiting there. Assuming she was the mother of the two children, Emily smiled and turned to Jessie. 'Stay there, Jessie. The native woman is waiting. I believe she is the children's mother.'

'No, Emily. For you do not know what she will do.'

'Do not worry so. She will do us no harm,' Emily told her and she set out towards the woman, a steady and direct look in her eyes. Before handing the children back to her, she kissed them gently on the cheek. 'Farewell, Tuba. Farewell, Tagaran.'

The children started to giggle and their mother joined in as she turned to leave with them. But then she looked back at Emily, and speaking softly, she said, 'Patye,' pointing the tip of her forefinger to her chest. Emily was puzzled. Again the young woman repeated the word. By this time, Jessie had moved closer.

'Maybe that is her name, Emily.'

'But of course. I think you are right.' Emily repeated the word. 'Patye.'

The woman nodded. It was then Emily and Jessie went through the motions of indicating their own names and Patye repeated them.

'Emmlee,' she said, 'Jessee,' she added as she hurried away.

Emily was delighted with the progress they had

made and that they had managed to communicate with the children's mother. She was all the more determined she would hold on to the friendship of the aborigines. They were the ones whose lives had been disturbed by the influx of the British, and they should be allowed to live in peace in this land.

'I think we have made steps towards befriending Patye.' Emily turned to Jessie. 'What do you think?'

'I am sure the governor will be pleased when he finds out.'

'He will be overjoyed. Other than telling the governor, perhaps we should keep this to ourselves for a while until the animosity has faded. If Dorothy and her friends find out about Patye, they may cause more trouble.'

'Maybe you are right. We would not wish for Patye to be attacked.'

'Some of those women can be vicious, as we well know from our experiences on the *Penrhyn*. For now, we must not breathe a word, Jess.'

They took the track from the Cove back towards the hut, and Emily was surprised to see Nell waiting for her at the door.

'See, Emmy. There is a letter for you. It came with the *Supply* yesterday. I believe it is from Norfolk Island.' Nell's eyes shone brightly as she watched Emily unfold the letter.

Emily recognised the handwriting, knowing it was from Jimmy. Her heart fluttered in her chest as she ripped open the envelope. She read:

Dearest Emily
It is now many months since I left the Cove and I

have mised ye Dearly. I am Looking forwad to the day when I can retrun. It was nigt wen we arived at this Iland and in the morning I stood on the deck and Wachd the sun rise as we anckord away from the reef. It was a Wunderful sigt. I have never in my life seen anythig So Stunning. I looked across at the Beatiful lagoon with its bright yellow beaches. And I thought of you Emily and wished ye could be here with me.

Close to Norfolk are two smaler ilands Phillip the biggest named after our governor and the smalest Nepean named after a minister of the crown. They say the Current can be dangerus betwixt Nepean and the reef. We were lucky to land without issue. Life is not as hard here as at the cove and there is more food for us. At the begining of summer I found plums and bananas which were delishus.

I mist you at Cristmas Emily and my mother too. After the new year the wether was Foul it raind day after day and the winds were high. Hundreds of tall pine tress fell down in the gales. Leftenant King calld it a herricane for it causd a lot of damage.

I see your face before me when I go to bed at nigt and think of you every day. Lucy too. God keep You Safe and I send you my love. Jimmy

Tears filled Emily's eyes for she had missed Jimmy, and she had thought about him every day. Until now she had been able to control her feelings.

'Come inside, dearie,' Nell said, taking her hand. 'We shall have some tea. Sit down and tell Nell all about it.'

'I have been afraid to tell anyone how much I

missed him, Nell, for we cannot be meant for each other. It is difficult to hold it to myself. How am I to bear it when he comes back here? He has asked me to wait for him. But I shall never be able to marry him. The governor will never allow that. We all know the rules. And how can I expect Jimmy to take on my darling Lucy when she is a bastard child.'

'Jimmy would not ask you to wait if he did not accept Lucy too. And things may change, my dear. You must remain in good spirits. Who knows what the future holds?'

Chapter 11

1789 – 1790

The food shortage accelerated and the attacks on the aborigines continued. The convicts, now desperate for food, resented them especially for their survival techniques and the fact that the waters, which were full of fish, provided the main diet the natives needed to survive.

'Why do our men stand idle and complain about the lack of food when fish is such an excellent source of nourishment?' the governor asked his colleague, David Collins.

'Despite their animosity towards the aborigines, most of the city-dwelling felons despise fish and are not prepared to eat it. They are not accustomed to such fresh food, and the appearance of the fish from the cove is foreign to them. The ones who fish are those who realise their survival may depend on it.'

'If the felons do not want the fish, what causes them to dislike the natives?'

'It is something deeper,' Collins replied.

'You are referring to a matter of class I take it.'

'Exactly! Until now the convicts have been the dregs of society, but desperately want to believe there is a group inferior to them.' Collins explained. 'When they arrived here they assumed the bottom level would be filled by the natives. Unfortunately the problem is a conflict of status.'

'I understand. But that does not help us feed the masses. If they will not eat the fish which is in abundance in these waters, what can be done?'

'If the crops continue to fail they will have no alternative. They will eat the fish or die.'

'Exactly. And for the colony to build and develop successfully, harmony with the natives is absolutely essential. The convicts could learn from them.' He pondered. 'In view of the desperate shortage of food, I shall send the *Supply* together with the *Sirius* and one third of the convicts, the most wretched and rebellious, and half the marines to Norfolk Island. They will have a better chance of survival there.'

But there was another reason for his orders to send half the red-coat population. 'I am afraid my decision may be a selfish one but it is the only way I can rid the Cove of Major Ross,' he told the judge. 'I have suffered his negative comments and sarcasm long enough and I am determined to tolerate him no longer. He has little intention of helping to make a success of this colony. He is waiting for failure.'

'I agree, Arthur. His own men dislike him. He shows no understanding of their needs and regards the felons as dirt beneath his feet, the scum of the earth. In his eyes, they can never claw back the respect they have lost. They are damned forever.' The judge paused as though deep in thought. 'He resents my position as Judge Advocate too. His solution to crimes is either corporal or capital punishment according to the severity of the offence. He believes in neither fairness nor true justice.'

The governor smiled. 'Then my decision is justified. I will ask him to assemble his men and the chosen group of convicts to prepare them for the journey in two days' time. He will take the place of Philip Gidley King as Commandant there.'

The ships departed and the governor sighed with relief. 'Thanks be to God that I have managed to rid the colony of my bête noire. I am a happy man now that he has gone.'

But his happiness was fleeting for, sometime later, the sight of the *Supply* returning alone from Norfolk Island and entering Sydney Cove at the South Head presented an ominous picture. Where was the *Sirius*? As the officers disembarked, Philip Gidley King proceeded to Government House.

'The ships reached Norfolk Island without problem and the *Sirius* was left standing off outside the bay waiting to unload her cargo when the time was right. As I explained to you Arthur the island is bounded by cliffs and surrounded in part by dangerous reefs close to the shores.'

The governor nodded.

'The day appeared to be still and the crew prepared to off-load the cargo on to longboats. But the light breeze developed into a gale, the ship drifted and was flung broadside on to a reef. There was no hope of saving her.' King sighed heavily.

'What damnable bad luck!' the governor exclaimed and he remained silent for a long moment. Then he continued. 'And Hunter? Could he not have saved the ship?'

'Unfortunately Hunter deigned not to seek advice from those on the island. Had he done so, especially with regard to the two outer islands, and their effects on the winds and the currents, then the *Sirius* could have been saved.' He shook his head. 'Of course, Hunter's case of negligence was further corroborated by Major Ross who, as you must be well aware, detests his fellow Scotsman.'

'True. Hunter was probably stubborn on account of Ross's presence. But he will never live it down.' The governor's words had a bitter tone to them. 'It is a blow and it seems we shall wait forever for store ships to arrive. I have lost a valuable ship which was destined to go to China after her return from Norfolk Island. The situation is getting worse.'

'The *Sirius* was still intact but she lay at an angle on the reef, her back broken. The crew emptied the holds and threw the animals and the cargo overboard. Those who could swim herded the animals towards the beaches, left them to fend for themselves and delivered the cargo ashore. '

'A blessing, Philip, a blessing,' the governor concurred. 'But we must acknowledge that since the ship was lost, John Hunter will have to stand trial in London.'

'A most unfortunate business.'

The governor stood up and stared at some fixed point across the room. He sighed and sat down again. 'Now that you are back we can discuss your forthcoming trip to London as my envoy.' The governor was well aware of King's eloquent powers of persuasion and his guaranteed diplomacy. 'I have every confidence in you, and require you to explain to those in power that the great potential here in New South Wales can never be realised unless substantial capital is invested.'

'It will be a pleasure for me to represent you, Arthur. Rest assured I shall do my best.'

'We are expecting supplies from England soon. But I have two theories as to why they have not yet arrived. Either the ships have been lost at sea, or we have been abandoned.' The governor sighed wearily. 'This state of affairs cannot last. The whole of the convict population has become devoid of morale through fear, hunger and exhaustion. The marines have become sullen and discontented since I ordered equal rations for the convicts. The situation is dire, Collins. What are we to do?'

Two months later the governor, whilst walking along the cliffs, gazed towards the two mighty headlands which acted as bastions guarding the Sydney Cove. Something moved and attracted his attention. He peered more closely. It was a flag. His heart began to race. The colony was surely saved. A crowd gathered at Dawes Point, a prominent place on the cliffs. The ship entering the bay was the *Lady Juliana,* the word *London* plain to see on her stern. The crowd quickly dispersed and fled towards the huts, elated and rejoicing at the news, weeping with relief and embracing one another.

On board the *Lady Juliana* Captain Aitken apparently unaware of the colony's impending famine, was taken aback. He stared aghast at the sight of the colony's marines climbing aboard his ship in ragged, threadbare uniforms. It seemed they were interested only in the food and the cattle on board. The cargo of female felons went unnoticed.

The governor was disillusioned when he finally realised the summation of the cargo. 'I expected a store ship with ample supplies to feed the colony, and the arrival of the skilled men I had requested.' Faced with more than two hundred women and their children, he looked with disbelief More hungry mouths to feed. He sighed. 'The provisions should have brought relief to the colony. But now with another two hundred convicts and their children to feed, it is an impossible task. There is not enough to feed our increased population.'

The new arrivals were disappointed and their expectations dashed. They had dreamt of a South Sea welcome, golden beaches and palm trees in a warm and sunny climate. What met them was the coolness of the rain and in the distance they saw the flickering lights of the fires built by the natives.

But their dejection went deeper. They had hoped they would be highly sought after by the males of the colony. They had dressed in the best clothes they possessed and made themselves presentable. But it seemed they came second to the provisions and the animals on board the *Lady Juliana*.

When Captain Aitken met with the governor the reason for the lack of provisions became apparent. 'We set sail from England in July last year. The store ship *Guardian*, loaded with a full cargo of provisions, sufficient to last a further two years took a more direct route with Lieutenant Riou at the helm. When we arrived in Cape Town the Dutch officials brought us the sorrowful news of two British ships in distress. One was the *Guardian*. She limped back into port, a massive hole in her hull. They had sailed dangerously close to the Antarctic regions when the ship struck an iceberg in the Southern Ocean and became impaled. The only stores remaining were a small number of livestock, including two stallions, some flour, and casks of wine. We took them on board and brought them with us. Fortunately, some of the missives and admiralty dispatches were saved.' Aitken handed over the bundles to the governor.

'At least that is some explanation. I had begun to think we had been forgotten.' He placed the letters on his desk. 'And what of the other ship?'

'It was *The Bounty*, Bligh's vessel, on its way through the Endeavour Straits when a rebellion led by his second in command, Fletcher Christian, occurred. The mutineers demanded to stay with the women they had met in Tahiti, thinking what an idyllic life they would have. Christian forced Bligh and eighteen of his men into a longboat. Bligh managed to reach Timor before they were picked up and brought to Cape Town.'

'Lieutenant Bligh? I know the fellow well. It is difficult to believe his men would set up mutiny.'

The governor pondered. 'As for the women on board your ship, I am afraid I shall be obliged to send the majority to Norfolk Island and the only ship I have at my disposal is the *Lady Juliana*.'

'My ship will require considerable repairs before any further undertakings are arranged.'

'I see, but we shall need to find accommodation for them until such time as the vessel is ready.'

When the women were eventually brought to shore, the whole of the community was out there watching. Emily advanced towards the wharf.

'I think I should volunteer to take someone in, Jessie. Lucy and I have the place to ourselves now.'

'But consider who you might be getting, Emily. Do not make a hasty decision,' Jessie begged.

Emily ignored Jessie's comment and watched the dejected mob, some with children, dragging their blankets and other belongings towards the huts. It was then she saw a familiar figure, a tall, skinny woman with hair the colour of ebony. She could scarcely believe her eyes.

'Tilly,' she called, running towards the woman. Lucy was bobbing up and down in her arms and laughing almost hysterically. 'I did not expect to see you again.' She grabbed the woman's sleeve.

'Gracious me, Em! I am saved. What a joy to see you.' She took Emily's hands, looking into her face. 'You have surely grown, girl. You were just a child when I last saw you. Now you are a woman.'

'You have not changed, Tilly. I would have known you anywhere. Come let us go to my hut.'

'We have been told we shall be moved shortly to another island. Norfolk, I believe it was said. Although our ship has brought provisions here from England, they say there is not enough food for us.'

'It is difficult for the governor. He has been awaiting a store ship for months. The people here are almost on the point of starvation.'

'Then the rumours are true. I suppose you have not sufficient room for me to stay with you, Emmy, just until we are moved once more.'

'If I had no room at all I would give you my own bed. I owe you that much after the way you protected me when we were in Durham. What happened after I left?'

'I stayed in the dormitory for some time,' she laughed, 'that was after I had put on a little performance, the pain you know. And then I returned to the others. Pike had gone by then. He went up the step – sentenced to the rope.'

'They said that it would happen.' Emily looked ahead and remembered Jessie. 'Jess, sorry I neglected you. Tilly is a good friend of mine, just as you are. Come and meet her. Bring Nell, and we shall all have tea together and talk.'

Jessie ran ahead.

'I see you have a child, Emily. A happy little thing. Is she yours?'

'She is. Her name is Lucy. She was born on board the *Lady Penrhyn*. She is almost three years old.'

'My, my. You kept that little secret hidden.' Tilly smiled.

'I knew nothing about it when I was with you. But I will tell you later.'

They reached the hut and Emily ushered her inside. 'Do sit down.' She placed the pot on the fire.

When Emily handed her the tea Tilly took a sip and frowned. 'What is this? It is hot and sweet but not like the tea back in England.'

'You will soon become used to it. It is all we have,' Emily told her, smiling.

'I am grateful for it, believe me, but the taste is different.'

'English tea is something we have not had since we arrived.'

'Is that so? But at least you have comfort here,' Tilly added as she surveyed the contents of the hut.

'Do tell me about your voyage, Tilly.'

'The journey was much better than I thought it would be. By the time we reached Rio, I had taken up with one of the seamen, George Potter, God Rest his Soul.' Tilly's head drooped and she sighed. 'He was a good man, and when we reached Santa Cruz the captain allowed those of us who were with a respectable crew member to leave the ship with them. It was good to stretch our legs on dry land.'

'We were never given chance to leave the ship. We felt ourselves fortunate that we were allowed on deck unfettered.' Emily sipped her tea.

'The next port was Cape Town. George was allowed shore leave but not us women.' Her eyes became misty.' That was the last time I saw him. He was robbed by a native and stabbed. He never returned to the ship.' Tilly lifted her skirt and dabbed her eyes. 'He had promised to marry me and take me home when I gained my ticket-of-leave.'

'I am so sorry, Tilly. You deserve to have a good man.' Emily placed an arm around Tilly's shoulder and squeezed her. 'You will be comfortable here with us. And if we can find you work, perhaps you will be allowed to stay at the Cove instead of moving to Norfolk Island.' Emily smiled, hoping she was right in her assumption.

'I would be most grateful to stay.'

'You worked as a dairy maid at the farm. Are you able to care for poultry, and tend to the garden for us? We have a man in charge, Will Hopwood.'

Jess intervened. 'Emily and I work at the nursery and have very little time to help Will.'

'Exactly. But the colony is desperate for food; we need to produce as much as we can. Nell cleans the huts and cooks. But sometimes, Jess and I help Will, for it is too much for him to complete all the gardening and look after the animals without help.'

'I can do all that! But who will tell the governor? Surely he does not know everyone in the colony?'

It was Jessie who answered her question. 'He does try to get to know as many of his people as he can, even the natives. But Emily is the one to pass on the information. She helped set up the nursery with Mistress O'Donnell and she is in charge there when the lady herself is not available.'

'Is that so, little Em? I am indeed proud of you.' She clapped her hands. 'And I have been lucky to meet up with you again, and your kind friends too. I will do my best for you all and hope you can manage to convince the governor that I am needed to work here.'

Chapter 12

1790

Governor Phillip's dream was about to become reality when a month later sails were sighted. The *Justinian* had made a speedy journey from London without calling at either Rio or Cape Town.

'What wonderful news, David. At last we have been remembered,' the governor announced with a sigh of relief. 'Her provisions will keep the colony away from starvation for some months before the *Supply* returns from Batavia.'

'But what of the *Lady Juliana* women, Arthur? Do you still intend sending the entire group to Norfolk Island?'

'I may reverse my decision and allow some of the women to stay here in Sydney Cove. My request to London for women to redress the balance between males and females has been satisfied. The women will provide for the needs of the men,' he lowered his voice and mumbled, 'in bodily comforts, so to speak, and in breeding.' He coughed and cleared his throat. 'Children are the colony's future.'

'But surely some of the rowdier element would be better sent to Norfolk. We do not wish to set up the sort of situation prevalent in London, the brothels and the prostitutes.'

'That was never my intention, David. Hopefully, when ticket-of-leave candidates are considered, those women with serious intentions will marry the new settlers.' The governor smiled to himself. His judge advocate's puritanical viewpoint seemed ironical, since Collins sought his own bodily comforts from convict, Nancy Yates.

The *Lady Juliana* was being careened up river and the governor realised there would be time to make a decision once it was ready to sail. But his joy at the earlier arrival of the *Justinian* was soon quashed.

By the end of the month, the flag at the South Head was raised to signify the pending arrival of the second fleet. The population surged forward at Dawes Point, looking towards the Heads and searching. The *Surprize*, the *Neptune* and the *Scarborough* entered the harbour, but it was night time and the ships stood out in one of the coves. Next day, once it was daylight, the ships were warped into Sydney Cove.

The governor was horrified when he later discovered that the ships' crews had spent most of the night at anchor off-loading the bodies of convicts who had died at sea and left to rot. They were washed up on the beaches, their hands still fettered.

'This is a disgrace,' he barked at the ship's agents as he watched more sick and dying being dragged from the ships and piled into longboats.

'You gave passage to one thousand convicts and more than a quarter have died. Some of those carelessly off-loaded by your men have drowned on the shores of Sydney Cove. Do you have any human feelings at all?' He pointed to the water. 'Look at the poor devils crawling and staggering ashore from whence your oarsmen have dumped them. Half the felons will be lost by the time we make our final count.' He turned to the marine sergeant. 'Bring the soldiers and a blacksmith to rid them of their irons and anyone you think can assist these poor unfortunates. This is a matter of urgency.' He shook his head angrily and sighed loudly. 'London will certainly hear of this. The animals on board my fleet were given better treatment.'

The convicts had not been allowed to exercise and when their shackles were removed they were too weak to walk, their muscles completely wasted. Some of the convicts had died of neglect or from the brutality of the ship's masters who regarded them akin to the slaves they had transported in those very same ships.

There was uproar amongst the population, especially those who searched for loved ones and friends. They ran along the shores, turning over bodies to check the convicts' identities.

The governor was in a quandary. He had no alternative but to oust the *Lady Juliana* women from the hospital where they were housed, and replace them with the sick.

'I cannot send these women away,' he announced to his officers, 'for they are serving a purpose by caring for the sick. When the crisis is over I will review the situation.'

A timber-framed portable hospital, which had arrived on board the *Justinian*, was assembled next to the small brick one recently built. The convicts were washed and the rags they were wearing burnt.

The women ran up clothes from bolts of cloth newly arrived with the fleet, and some of the men were sent to the bush to collect myrtle said to be both prevention and cure for the outbreak of dysentery which was once more raging throughout the camp.

When Emily received another letter from Jimmy she read it with interest but she was puzzled by the inferences towards the end.

Dearest Emily

I cannot withhold my exitment without telling ye. The Sergant believes it will not be long before we leave the Island, for When we are replaced by another marine cor, we shall Return to Sydney Cove. I cannot wait to see ye once more for I have missed ye Dearly.

The Conditons here are not too bad and we are still eating well. There is plenty of fish if only ye can Manage to catch it in the pownding surf. We call it red Snapper and the reef is swarming with it. Sandy caught one yesterday and we lit a fire outside and cooked it. It was Delishus.

We also have a Flock of big birds which landed on Mount Pitt high above us in March. They are firm and fat and make fine eating. We call them mutton birds, but the officers call them the bird of providense for, without Suplies from ether London or the colony, they have made up for the lack of food and saved our lives.

The wreck of the Sirius is still lying here, stuck upon the reef. I Know food is still scarce there and I Hope that by the time ye receve this letter, more food will have arrived for ye.

When I return I have a Plan to discuss with ye. I hope ye will give me a fair hearing before ye make any Dicisions.

I am ever thinking about ye my Sweet one and I look forward to coming back when the new guards arrive.

I send you all my love
Jimmy

What did he mean by a plan? Emily was adamant she would not enter into any commitment until she was a free woman. With Jimmy's words still prominent in her mind, Emily set out for the nursery. It was shortly after her arrival that the governor and the Reverend Johnson appeared.

'Good morning, Emily. I have brought along the chaplain to see your good work.'

'That is very kind of you, sir,' she said sketching a curtsey.'

'I see you have three more native children,' the governor continued as he glanced around and counted them. 'I am pleased you are persevering. As you know I would like to build up our relationship with the aborigines.'

The chaplain frowned and intervened. 'But surely it causes trouble taking in the blacks,' he remarked, addressing his comment directly to the governor.

Emily replied. 'At first there was resentment by some of our women, but now even those who left earlier have swallowed their pride and returned.'

The chaplain who considered himself superior to everyone, especially the convicts, glowered at Emily. She knew of his reputation. But unless she and the other women gained confidence to communicate rationally, they would always be downtrodden.

The governor was supportive.

'I am delighted. Keep it up.' His smile was a kindly one.

The chaplain looked on disdainfully.

'I cannot see the likes of the New South Wales Corps tolerating the blacks.'

'That is a dilemma. Once again London has failed to respond to my requests. These men are not marines. They have most likely been press-ganged to keep the peace amongst the felons here. But they are an insolent lot. They can barely keep the peace amongst themselves, let alone the convicts. The officers are of a low intellect, few of them with more common sense or mental capacity than their men.'

'But I hear the marine officers are ready to leave.'

'I shall have a mutiny on my hands if I do not recall the Marine Corps from Norfolk Island and allow them to leave when the ships depart.' He shook his head and turned to Emily. 'Now, Emily, let us see what the children have learnt.'

Emily hushed the children and when she started to sing, they joined in.

One, two, buckle my shoe
Three, four, knock at the door
Five, six, pick up sticks
Seven, eight, lay them straight

As they did so, Emily held up her fingers as the numbers increased. She was delighted that even the aboriginal children, who did not understand what they were singing, had learnt the song by rote and joined in.

The governor clapped his hands. 'Wonderful!'

But the chaplain, hands gripped tightly behind his back, sniffed and commented, 'A hymn would have been more appropriate.'

'But the hymns are too difficult for them, sir, and they would not understand the words. At least with the simple songs they will learn their numbers.'

'You are right. I am indeed impressed,' the governor concluded.

But as the sour-faced chaplain glared once more, she watched the two men walk away and disappear towards the gardens. She was deep in thought. After listening to their conversation she realised that, if the Marine Corps were to leave and be replaced by the New South Wales Corps, Jimmy would soon be gone from the colony and, knowing she would have to refuse his proposal, it would be the end of their relationship. She would never see him again.

The situation at the hospital was easing and although those still suffering remained there, others were placed in the tents provided and, for those who were able to carry out light tasks, more huts were hastily built to house them.

The governor made a decision to send one hundred and fifty *Lady Juliana* women to Norfolk Island and leave fifty back in Sydney Cove. Tilly held her breath. To her relief she was chosen to stay behind and she looked forward to Emily's return from the nursery, eager to give her the good news.

It was dropping dark outside when she entered the

hut. The fire was low and, whilst she could barely see, she wanted to prepare tea for her friend. She filled the pot with water intending to collect sticks from the garden area to bring the fire to life.

No sooner had she hung the pot over the fire than she was startled by a scuffling sound coming from behind her. Could it be the sound of an animal in search of food? Her heartbeat quickened. But why should she feel nervous? She was capable of defending herself against anyone or anything. She had surely proved that during her battles with Thomas Pike at the prison, even though she had come off the worst on the last occasion.

Believing it to be Emily, she called, 'Is that you, Em?' But there was no reply. Her pulse began to race even faster. The fire had dropped even lower and when she turned away she was unable to see anything at all. But still she sensed there was someone in there with her. She felt her way over towards the doorway to collect the wood from outside but suddenly she felt a hand snatch hold of huge handful of her hair. She screamed.

'You will not get away this time.' the voice came from behind her.

Although she was unable to see the culprit she knew by the gruffness of the voice it was a man. He began to shake her violently, pulling viciously at her hair, swinging his other arm around her and gripping hold of her body, pinning her arms down by her sides. When she screamed again she felt his hand release her hair and clamp it over her mouth to muffle the sound. He started to punch her in the stomach and it was more than she could bear. She felt nauseous and she knew she would lose all consciousness if he continued.

On instinct she dragged her arm away and slipped her hand to the table where she knew she had left a knife. She fingered it, avoiding the blade and clutching hold of the handle. In an act of panic and fighting for her life, she lifted the knife and plunged it into his chest. He slumped before her and fell with a heavy thud to the floor. She stared in horror at the outline of the body lying there, her hands wet and sticky with his blood. In desperation she wiped them down the front of her tunic.

The silhouette of Nell appeared in the doorway, a lighted candle in her hand. She let out a piercing scream and stared down at the body. But she took a deep breath and seemed to pull herself together.

'I saw what happened, Tilly. It was self defence.' Nell's voice was calm now and she crossed over to where the man was lying, shone the candle before her and bent down to examine him more closely.

'I fear he is dead.'

Tilly took hold of the candle, leaning over the man and checking his breathing. 'You are right, Nell. What are we to do?' The rapid thudding of her heart began to resound in her ears. Panic-stricken, she dashed to the door searching the area for Emily and Jessie. 'I cannot understand where they are.' She was weeping now. 'They are usually back before nightfall.'

She hovered about outside and when she heard them approaching, she ran towards them. 'Emily, come quick! Something terrible has happened,' she cried, the words falling from her lips in quick succession. 'I have killed a man. He came into the hut and attacked me. What shall I do?'

'Slow down, Tilly. What do you mean, you have killed a man? Who? Where is he?'

'He is in the hut, Em. He attacked me.'

Emily handed Lucy over to Jessie. 'Please take her into your hut, Jess.' Grasping the candle from Tilly's hand, she dashed inside. Aghast, she stared down at the man before turning to Nell. 'Do you realise who this man is, Nell?'

'No, I do not,' Nell confessed.

'It is Rafton. Remember him?' She paused and placed her hand in front of his open mouth. 'And you are right. He is dead.'

Tilly started to sob again more loudly this time.

'Please calm yourself, Tilly. We must decide what to do,' Emily said as she took her friend's arm and led her towards the door. Taking both hands in hers she turned to face her. 'I apologise for being so late. Jessie and I would have been back earlier but we met with Patye after leaving the nursery, otherwise Rafton would have attacked me not you. Had I been alone, he would probably have killed me. You are strong, Tilly, and I believe you have saved my life.'

'I am glad it was not you, Em, for you have Lucy to care for. But what I have done will surely be punishable by the rope.'

'We will plead on your behalf. Nell is certain you killed him in self-defence. Had you not done so, he would have killed you. We must go to the judge immediately and tell him what has happened. There is nothing to be gained by hiding the matter.'

'I cannot do that, Em. I am afraid I will be in for

the drop.'

'Trust me, Tilly. I know you will suffer punishment, but I am sure when we plead your case you will not be hanged. Please believe me.'

Tilly was reluctant but she knew they must move quickly.

'Otherwise conclusions might be drawn that do not truly reflect what has happened,' Emily added. She called for Jessie. 'Please take care of Lucy whilst we go to Government House to tell Judge Collins what has happened.'

Tilly panicked. 'But Jessie cannot stay alone. Not after what has happened.'

Jessie interceded. 'Do not worry, Tilly. Nell must go with you. She is your only witness. I will feel safe if little Lucy is with me. Go quickly and may God be with you,' she stressed.

Judge Collins was not available when they reached Government House, but one of his young deputies met them and listened to what they had to say.

'Why did you not report this to the guards? The man may still have been alive had you done so. Are you professing to be surgeons, making a decision on the mortality of the victim? It seems strange that you killed the man and then walked here freely as though nothing at all had happened.' The deputy, obviously relishing the importance of the occasion, paused for effect. 'And the body of this man, Abel Rafton, has been left in the hut?' He shook his head. 'You have been extremely negligent.'

Nell spoke up. 'He was dead. I have seen the likes often enough.'

'And who are you to interrupt?'

'My name is Nell Walton. I was there when the man attacked Mistress Parkin. She had to use the knife to defend herself otherwise he would have killed her. He was an evil, vicious man.'

'So you knew Rafton? You had met him before?'

'Indeed, sir. He attacked my friend here, Emily Spence, when the first fleet arrived at the colony.'

'The picture is becoming clearer in my mind. It is obvious it was an act of revenge. Perhaps the good judge has placed the incident on record.' He walked across the room and turned. 'It appears to me there has been some sort of conspiracy. I am not satisfied.' He pointed towards Tilly. 'You will be placed in irons and sent to Pinchgut until the judge has had the opportunity to decide whether or not you are to be hanged. I cannot allow a dangerous woman to remain here on the mainland.' He turned to Emily. 'The guards will visit your hut and check on the dead man.' He opened the door and called out. 'Guard!'

The guard appeared at the door and the deputy gave him instructions.

'This woman here,' he said, poking Tilly in the back and pushing her. 'To Pinchgut!'

Emily shuddered, aware that Pinchgut was the most severe punishment given to any felon.

Four miles from the settlement, it was no more than a natural rock stack in the middle of the harbour fully exposed to the shark-infested waters. Felons were shackled to a narrow ledge and left there to starve and dehydrate in all kinds of weather. The daily ration was a chunk of stale bread and a small stone jar of water.

The young guard looked on in dismay and swallowed noisily. It was obvious he knew the place and had taken felons there before.

'Did you hear me, lad? Pinchgut. I take it you understand,' the deputy stressed.

The guard nodded and when he took hold of Tilly's arm she turned to face him.

'Do not worry. I will go peacefully, wherever this Pinchgut might be.'

Emily confronted the deputy.

'May God forgive you. This is a punishment worse than death.' She turned to Tilly. 'Pinchgut is amid the islands in the harbour. I cannot bear to think of you there alone.'

The deputy looked on, solemn-faced. 'Hold your tongue, girl. There is no call for me to be forgiven. You must save your prayers for your friend for it appears to me that she has carried out a premeditated and heinous crime in cold blood. And I do believe the two of you are involved as conspirators,' he added pointing to Emily and Nell.

Ignoring the deputy's comments, Emily addressed Tilly once more. 'I will see the governor tomorrow. I would take your place if they would allow it. Please put your trust in me.'

But the next day Emily realised her visit to see the governor was without success.

'I asked to speak to the governor this morning, but he has left for Rose Hill and will be staying there for two days.' She wrung her hands and stared into space. 'Nell. What am I to do?'

'You must be patient, Emmy. It is no use

returning to Government House. You may be confronted with the deputy again and he already has his suspicions. And the guards were sympathetic when they took Rafton away, for they know of his kind, but they cannot close their eyes to everything.'

'I need to see Patye. If she or her husband could take me to Pinchgut in one of their canoes, I could speak to Tilly and take food for her.'

'They will think you a mad woman. D'you wish to be shot? You will never get past the guards. They stand lookout. And Tilly will be shackled. She will not be able to escape.'

'I do not intend for her to escape, Nell. It is through me she has been placed at Pinchgut. I wish to make it more bearable for her until I have seen the governor.'

'It is no fault of yours. It is the fault of the wicked Rafton. But we can do nothing about that now. I tell you Emily if you attempt the impossible you too will be caught by the guard.'

Nell's words were empty ones for the following morning before daybreak Emily left Lucy in Jessie's charge, and she set out towards the clearing where she knew Patye and her family could be found. The sun was coming up, and she followed the track where Patye had taken them earlier. The undergrowth became thicker and she heard a hissing sound nearby. Her heart began to pound. She knew that some of the snakes were harmless but others were venomous and she was not able to recognise the difference. But it was no snake. It was one of the aborigines confronting her, spear at the ready.

She put up her hand. 'Patye,' she said loudly and

clearly. The man advanced towards her, a hostile look on his face.

'Patye,' she repeated, shaking with fear now, but trying to appear bold by taking a step towards him. As she did so, a small child ran from the bushes towards her. 'Emmlee, Emmlee,' she called. Emily opened her arms and the child ran to her. It was Tuba who was followed by Tagaran and Patye.

Emily gestured to Patye that she needed help, and they turned towards the native camp. When they came to a clearing, Emily picked up a stick and poked it into the dust, drawing the bay and the island of Pinchgut, indicating as best she could that her friend had been banished there.

She drew a boat with an arrow directed towards Pinchgut. Patye nodded but Emily was not sure if she fully understood the meaning of the drawings and the gestures. Patye beckoned to her to follow. No doubt the natives knew exactly what was happening. If there was someone on Pinchgut, they would know about it.

She struggled to keep up with Patye through the bush, but eventually they reached a small cove where several canoes were tied to the rocks. Patye freed one of them and climbed inside, balancing Tuba on her shoulders. She beckoned to Emily to lie flat on the bottom of the boat, and then she set out across the harbour towards Pinchgut. It was damp on the floor and she felt nauseous with the constant movement. But that was because Patye kept stopping to fish on her way across. Emily watched her. All the time Patye's dark eyes searched the bay to make sure none of the guards appeared suspicious.

Once she reached the point where Tilly could be seen clinging to the rock, she drifted nearby, making sure her fishing trip appeared casual.

As they closed in, Emily called, 'It is me, Tilly,' her voice little more than a whisper. Tilly looked up startled, her face bathed in worry and fear. 'It is me, Tilly.' Emily repeated and she raised herself slightly from the floor of the canoe.

'Oh Emily, I cannot believe it,' Tilly replied, her voice wavering. 'I beg you to beware of the guard for they circle the rock all the time.'

'I had to come for I feel responsible that you have been placed here.'

'That is foolish, Em. I will be fine,' Tilly replied, drawing a flimsy shawl about her body. 'Last night it was cold when the water splashed over the rock and wet my clothes. But now I am dry. It is when the sun comes up I shall need protection. I shall try to move into the shadiest spot if only I can manage to drag the chains.'

Emily was aware that once the sun's rays touched Tilly's skin it would concentrate on the parts of her body covered with fine salt from the sea water and she would be burnt.

'You will need something to cover your head. I have brought Jessie's shawl. Place it around your shoulders and cover your head with your own shawl. That way the guards will not recognise it.'

'You worry so, Em,' she stressed. 'Who is your friend?'

'Patye,' she whispered. 'She is a very brave woman. She will drift close and leave the things I have brought. There is fish Nell cooked before I set off at dawn. Throw the bones into the sea when you have finished. There is bread too. Patye will try to balance the fresh water so that it is within reach. Try not to spill it, for it will be very hot later in the day,' she explained.

'I have visited Government House,' she continued, 'but the governor will not be back from Rose Hill until the morrow. I know you are suffering my dear Tilly, but I will do my best.'

'I know you will.' Tilly blinked away her tears. 'Please take care. Do not come again, Emily,' she begged, 'for you will be caught. I will survive.' She smiled bravely, but her sad eyes betrayed her words. 'I am determined I will be freed.'

'We are ever thinking about you. God protect you,' Emily said, her voice wavering with emotion.

Despite her fate since she left the manor, Emily could not have been more fortunate in the friends she had made. There was Nell, and there was Jessie, also Grace who had left for Norfolk Island and now Tilly. And of course on the hulks there had been Mary. These women were supposedly the scum of the earth. But not to Emily. They were the salt of the earth. If it meant that she had to put her own life in jeopardy, Emily was determined that Tilly would be saved. Nothing could be more certain.

The journey to the shore was more hazardous than the outward one, for the guards appeared to have their suspicions. One of the longboats came dangerously close to the canoe as Patye calmly fished with her rod and line, Tuba still balanced on her shoulders, and now laughing at something her mother was saying in their native language.

Emily was aware this was a deliberate ploy to throw the guards off scent, and she sighed with relief as she heard the voices of the red-coats fade away into the distance. She had silently thanked the Good Lord for her English friends but what of Patye? She had risked her own life. Emily felt blessed. The Lord had looked favourably upon her. And when they reached the shore Emily wept with relief, hugged Patye and kissed the child.

'Thank you,' she said as she trod the undergrowth back to the clearing aware that, by this time, the sun was fully up. Tilly would be feeling the heat but hopefully she would have a cool, refreshing drink to slake her thirst.

Emily slipped back unobtrusively. Nell, who was standing in the doorway, opened her mouth as though to speak, a trace of incredulity sketching her face as Emily reached the hut. She stood mesmerised by Emily's appearance and then she spoke. 'My word! I do not believe it. You are back. Trouble was there?'

'Not at all, Nell. Patye took me there. I handed over the food and water to Tilly and here I am.' Emily smiled as she entered the hut.

'You had no trouble from the guards?' Nell's brow furrowed.

'Not at all, Nell. Patye is a wily character. She duped them right enough. As I lay in the bottom of the canoe to prevent myself from being seen by the guards Patye fished in the harbour.'

Nell stared in amazement and Emily continued, smiling. 'It was only when we reached Pinchgut that I lifted myself sufficiently to see that Tilly was safe. Patye is a very brave woman.'

'She is indeed.' Nell sat down. After a few minutes she continued her words. 'Not long after you had left to meet your friends, two seamen from the *Lady Juliana* called and asked to see you. They will be back some time before you leave for the nursery.'

Emily felt a gnawing in her stomach. She hoped they had not come to make more trouble. Did they know Rafton? Were they here to take their revenge, to support Rafton? Surely not!

It was a mystery to Emily but she must wait until they returned to hear the reason for their visit.

Chapter 13

1790

Judge Advocate, David Collins returned to his house during the early hours of the morning after a successful liaison with Nancy Yates. She had been more than ever possessive that night and was reluctant for him to leave.

'Nancy, my sweet, I must return to my office,' he told her. 'I have been absent since sundown and there may be urgent matters I need to attend to.'

'But do you not wish to spend the night with me? I thought you loved me.'

'Of course I do. But I have my duties to attend to.'

Nancy clung to him.

'I must leave you now,' he insisted as he kissed her and promised to see her again very soon.

He hurried back to his house and no sooner had he entered than there was a loud knocking on his door. He was confronted by his deputy.

'What now at this hour, Jarvis?'

'One of the felons, a woman called Matilda Parkin has killed a crewman. She was brought here last evening to see you but you were unfortunately away on business, sir,' the deputy informed him, an ingratiating smile on his face. 'She was accompanied by two female convicts, a young woman named Emily Spence and a crone named Nell Walton. Do you recall any of these women?'

'Not immediately. But you are right. I have had business to attend to, and now I am tired,' the judge replied, knowing his colleagues were secretly aware of his liaisons. 'Was it not something you could attend to in my absence?'

'It was indeed, judge, except that the story was rather confusing.'

'In what respect, Jarvis?'

The judge listened to the details of the story, including the previous encounter between Emily Spence and Abel Rafton.

'Do you recall the incident?' Jarvis asked him.

'I have a faint recollection,' Collins replied. 'But I must refer to my papers. I believe it is some two years since that particular incident and I am not certain of the details or of the outcome.'

'I have sent the woman to Pinchgut, sir. I take it you approve,' he boasted, the contempt on his face plain to see.

Collins disliked this haughtiness. Who did the young fellow think he was?

'It is not your place to make such decisions. You should have waited until I returned.' He frowned. 'Leave the matter until the morrow when I have the opportunity to check out my records. Maybe then I can give you a better indication of the requisite procedure. If the woman is guilty then, according to the governor's ruling, she will be hanged.'

Appparently satisfied he had made some sort of impression, Jarvis left and the judge sighed with relief. After an evening's entertainment with the talented Nancy, who possessed a world of experience in knowing how to pleasure a gentleman, the judge was reluctant to direct his mind to such mundane tasks as exercising his judgement over the misdeeds of the felons. At that late hour he wished more to lie in his bed and concentrate his thoughts on the wonderful bodily skills of his woman.

The following day Collins searched his files for details of the case between Spence and Rafton, which he recalled had occurred with the arrival of the first fleet early in 1788. But his search was interrupted when, in the absence of the governor, he was called to intervene in a dispute between the captain of the *Scarborough*, bitter on account of the killing of Rafton, and Captain Aitken of the *Lady Juliana,* who claimed two of his men were missing, also in connection with Rafton's death. His ship was ready to leave for Norfolk Island but until the two men were found he was not prepared to sail.

'What is the trouble?' The judge sighed, reluctant to become involved. It was important he continued his search.

'Two of my men are missing on account of the death of Rafton, the rogue this man here took on as crew,' Aitken complained.

'My men are not rogues,' the *Scarborough* captain maintained. He turned to the judge. 'I hear you have arrested a woman on the charge of killing Rafton. I am here to see justice is done. The woman must be hanged by the rope,' he insisted.

'Nobody hangs until proved guilty.' Judge Collins was adamant.

'There seems to be no doubt about her guilt. Aitken is whining over the disappearance of two of his men. It would appear they have some involvement with both Rafton and the woman, Matilda Parkin who was transported aboard

Aitken's ship. When his men are found, they will no doubt reveal truth about her.'

'You misunderstand,' Captain Aitken stressed. 'I wish to discover why my men have become involved when we all know that the *Scarborough's* crewmen are no more than a set of brutes. If you ask me, you are better off without the deceased.' He turned to the judge. 'I know little about the evidence my men have available but I do know the character, Matilda Parkin. She is a decent woman.'

'A decent woman?' *Scarborough's* captain shook his head. 'She is but a convict. Why are these felons allowed to get away with such crimes? Rafton was not the most popular crewman, but he worked hard. My men are threatening to stay with the convict women in the colony and are disappearing from my ship. If Parkin is not hanged for Rafton's murder, others will use it as excuse to leave in protest. I shall be left without crew to man my ship.'

Collins stepped in at this point. 'You have lost one member of your crew, possibly through the woman's self-defence. I have yet to investigate. As for the rest of your crew, they are not my problem. And why cause such an issue with Aitken here? What is your complaint?'

'He is casting the blame on me because two of his men are missing.'

Captain Aitken intervened. 'Unlike this man,' he said, pointing to the captain of the *Scarborough*, 'I have kept a good and caring crew and, now that we are leaving Sydney Cove, I have no intention of losing them. With a complete cargo of female convicts, many couplings were formed aboard my ship. Does he believe he is the only one whose men wish to remain here? I too am having problems.'

'I resent your insinuations. My crew did what they were ordered to do.'

'Can these accusations be justified, Captain Aitken?' Judge Collins asked.

'They can indeed, sir. I assume the captain gives the orders. The evidence lies in the state the felons were in when they arrived after being fettered and left in the orlop to die as though they were slaves.'

The captain of the *Scarborough* became more irate. He interjected. 'What do you expect? If the felons cannot act in a civil manner I have no alternative but to keep them down below.'

Judge Collins intervened. 'Enough! I must search my files. Somewhere I have previous evidence of the man, Rafton. I will speak with the governor when he returns from his duties at Rose Hill, for I recollect he had some personal involvement in the Rafton case two years ago.'

'But what of my men? I cannot leave Sydney Cove until they return,' Aitken insisted.

'I will ask the marine captain to send guards in search of them. Please go back to your ship. I will summon you as soon as I have news.'

The men left the judge's office and Collins returned to his files. If the Parkin woman had been placed on the rock at Pinchgut, she would be suffering in the heat of the day. And he was not in the habit of enjoying the hardships inflicted on the convicts, although he realised his decisions must be fair, and they must reflect the wishes of the governor.

He must take up the case immediately, and have in place details of the previous incident between Spence and Rafton before the governor returned. Only then would he be in a position to make a decision about the future of Matilda Parkin.

The seamen returned to the hut before Emily left for the nursery. 'Emily Spence?' one of them asked.

'That is right,' she replied, maintaining a steady tone to her voice.

'It is Rafton we are here about,' the man continued. 'I take it you knew him.'

'I did, indeed.' Emily's tone was now defiant. 'What is it to you?'

'We are friends of Matilda Parkin who is apparently accused of murdering Rafton. We have heard through some of the *Scarborough* crew that, when he was well into his cups, he boasted that he would kill you, Mistress Spence. But we know it was not you he attacked. It was Matilda Parkin because he must have thought her to be you? What recollection do you have of the man?'

'The man was an animal. Had Tilly not defended herself with the knife, she would have been dead. It is also true to say that, had I been left alone in the hut, I would surely not have survived his attack, for I could not have defended myself as successfully as Tilly did. She is much stronger than I am.'

The second crew member continued the story. 'Matilda was transported aboard the *Lady Juliana*. She is a good woman wrongly accused. She sought friendship with one of our crew members, George Potter. It was unfortunate that, when he went ashore at Cape Town, he was robbed and stabbed to death. Matilda was most aggrieved at her loss, but she managed to overcome her sorrow, and we were indeed delighted when she found respite with you, Mistress Spence.'

His colleague continued once more.

'It is against Matilda's nature to have killed anyone deliberately. I sincerely believe whatever she did was in self-defence. The fellow Jarvis is so bent on impressing the judge, he will do anything.'

'Then let us go to the governor when he returns. I know he will understand for he showed me kindness when Rafton attacked me. I have always been grateful for I believe the governor saved me from certain death when I was left to struggle in a lightning storm.'

'We will return, Mistress Spence,' one of them said as he turned to his shipmate. 'It will...'

His departing words were cut short when four red-coated marines appeared. Two of them grabbed the men whilst the officer spat out his words.

'In the name of the governor, I arrest you.' The two men turned to fight off the marines but, after a scuffle they were overpowered and marched away towards Government House.

Now in a dilemma, Emily went back inside.

'What are we to do, Nell, now that the only men who could have helped us have been arrested?'

'There is nothing more we can do until the governor returns. It is our misfortune that we did not see Judge Collins for we know him to be a fair and kindly man. I agree the young Jarvis is trying to impress the governor.' Nell sighed and placed the pot over the fire. 'Let us have tea and then you must leave with Jessie for the nursery. Allow the day to proceed as normal. Try not to think about Tilly. She will survive, I am certain of it.'

But it was difficult for Emily not to dwell on the fate of her dear friend. Each time the picture of Tilly chained to the rock at Pinchgut entered her mind she tried to replace it with happier times, of memories when they shared their home together.

The governor returned during the late afternoon of the following day. No sooner had he retired to his room than there was a knock on the door.

'Come,' he called and the judge entered.

'I do apologise profusely for interrupting when you have only now returned from Rose Hill, but I have a particularly difficult case on my hands.'

'Tell me, David, are you not able to make a judgement for yourself?'

'In part, it concerns you, Arthur. Do you recall the young girl, Emily Spence being attacked by a crewman, Rafton, from the transport *Lady Penrhyn*? It happened when we arrived at the colony.'

'I recall the incident most vividly,' he said, lifting himself abruptly from his chair. 'What of it?'

'The man, Rafton, returned two days ago and visited Spence's hut as darkness was falling. He set about the person he thought to be Emily Spence. But it was one of the *Lady Juliana* women, a Matilda Parkin, a woman we chose to stay at the colony because she had made such good progress with the garden plot run by Spence and her friends. When Rafton attacked, thinking her to be Spence,

Parkin retaliated and took a knife to him. She told my deputy she had killed him in self-defence.'

The judge looked away. 'It was most unfortunate that I was not in attendance when the three women, Parkin, Spence and Walton arrived. Jarvis did what he thought best. He sent the woman to Pinchgut, pending investigations into the death of Rafton.' Collins shook his head. 'I was grossly unhappy at his actions, but the man is new to the post and I did not wish to criticise him too heavily, for he seems conscientious in his approach.'

'What is the problem? The woman killed him in self-defence. Set her free.'

'It is the captain of the *Scarborough* who is insisting the woman be hanged for murder. He tells me the character, Rafton was not an evil man.'

There was a loud knock on the door and the governor called, 'Enter.'

The guard pushed open the door and a young woman was standing there. 'Sir, this woman is insisting she sees you on a matter of life and death.'

The governor looked up in both surprise and recognition. 'Ah, Emily Spence,' he said. 'Do come in. I have received some most disturbing news regarding Rafton.'

'That is why I am here, sir. Two of the *Lady Juliana* crewmen came to see me yesterday to tell me that Rafton had boasted he would kill me. When they heard about Matilda Parkin's actions, they came immediately to add their own evidence, for they know her to be a good woman who would not harm a soul, other than in self-defence.'

'Where are these men now?'

'They were arrested by the guards and taken away. They were not given the opportunity to report to you, sir.'

The governor turned to Judge Collins.

'Do you know anything about this?'

'I do indeed. I had the men arrested for I was worried they would cause more trouble. And more to the point, the captain of the *Lady Juliana* is waiting to take some of the women to Norfolk Island. He cannot leave without these men, for already there are several others who are threatening to remain at the colony.'

The governor went to the door and opened it.

'Guard, bring over the two seamen arrested last evening. The judge tells me they are crew members of the *Lady Juliana*.'

It was no more than ten minutes later when the two men were pushed into the room by the guard.

'Now let us hear what you have to say,' the governor said.

The two men confirmed Emily's story informing the governor of Rafton's boastful intentions to attack Emily.

'I believe these men to be telling the truth, Judge Collins. The character reference on the woman, Parkin equates with that given to me by Emily Spence. I would like you to release them.'

The men bowed slightly and left the room. The governor turned to Emily. 'Do not worry about Matilda Parkin. All will be dealt with fairly.'

As Emily closed the door, the governor turned to the judge. 'The man Rafton was evil right enough. What the captain of the *Scarborough* told you is nonsense, David, and if he wishes to take further issue, I will see him. But he seems to forget I have a report to send to London. The state of the felons when they arrived at the colony was an absolute disgrace to humanity. Send him to me if he complains.' He walked towards the door. 'Now I must rest, for I have spent an anxious time at Rose Hill. We must send out the guards to free Matilda Parkin immediately. However, the decision is yours. Perhaps you would speak with Nell Walton in order to confirm that Matilda Parkin did indeed kill Rafton in self-defence. '

'Most definitely, Arthur. Thank the lord you had information about Rafton. In view of the conflicting evidence I was certainly in a quandary.' He turned to leave. 'The report Jarvis wrote includes evidence given by Nell Walton who insists she witnessed the deed. But I would like to speak with the woman myself to confirm Jarvis was wrong in his assumption that there was a conspiracy between the women to carry out the killing as an act of revenge.'

'Indeed, David, I understand, and I am grateful you awaited my return before committing the woman to trial. I am determined to maintain civility in the colony through our system of justice.'

Emily was standing at the harbour awaiting Tilly's return from Pinchgut when she came across the two seamen from the *Lady Juliana*. They had been released by the guard the minute the governor had made his decision. Captain Aitken, in an act of goodwill, had allowed them to wait and see Matilda before the ship left Sydney Cove.

'What excellent news, Mistress Spence,' one of them declared. 'I hear Deputy Jarvis has been severely reprimanded by the judge for his decision to send Matilda to Pinchgut. Maybe he has learnt his lesson. It would do no harm if he followed the ways of his superior, the good Judge Collins.'

'I agree but it was the governor who was instrumental in making sure Tilly was released from Pinchgut. I believe he was the one who reprimanded Jarvis,' Emily was determined to stress.

'Aye, God bless the governor for he too is a fair man,' he continued as they both searched the harbour for the longboat. Emily followed their gaze and saw the vessel appear from out of the heat mist that was hanging low over the harbour.

She lifted her hand to wave and, turning towards the men, she smiled warmly. It was not surprising their captain was concerned to have them back on board, for they were not like some crew members who cared only to satisfy their own selfish needs.

The longboat drew closer and in her excitement, Emily waved her arms to catch Tilly's attention. 'Tilly, I am here,' she called. It was such a relief to see her again.

The boat reached the wharf and was securely tied to the mooring. Tilly, assisted by one of the guards, stepped out and Emily suppressed a cry of horror as her dear friend came into view for her face, touched heavily by the sun's rays, resembled a glowing fireball. What agony she must have suffered. But despite her appearance, Emily detected a weak smile beneath the swollen surface of Tilly's face.

'Thanks be to God for my good friends,' she said

turning to the two seamen. 'The guards told me what happened. George would have been proud of you for standing by me.' She wiped a stray tear from her eye.

'We did what was fair, Matilda. We were anxious to see you before we left for we needed to make sure you had not been abused,' one of them told her.

'I am fine now and I am grateful you waited.'

The other seaman interposed. 'We must leave you now. Our ship sails for Norfolk Island this evening, provided the captain can round up the crew. Certain of them wish to remain here in the colony with the women they took as wives during the voyage.'

'I understand completely. It would have been the same had George still been alive, God bless his soul. He would not have left me willingly.'

'But Captain Aitken runs a good ship and he is not prepared to release his men, otherwise he will not have enough hands to man it. He has told them that if they wish to live with their women here in the colony, then they must return as free settlers and set up some sort of occupation here.'

'I suppose that is the only way,' Tilly said. 'Maybe I will see you both again.' She paused. 'But perhaps not, for it is a long journey for you to endure. God be with you.'

The two men left the wharf and headed for the *Lady Juliana*.

'Nell has prepared food for your return, Tilly, for you must be hungry.' Emily took her hand.

'There is something I must tell you.' Tilly drew her close and continued in hushed tones. 'I did not tell you within earshot of the guards, but your friend, Patye, came to see me again this morning with fresh fruit and water. I was indeed grateful for her kindness. Maybe in a day or two you would take me to see her. I would like to thank her and take her something of mine. Will you do that for me?'

'That is the least I can do. It is a pity the inhabitants of this colony do not give the aborigines a chance to prove their kindness and friendship.'

'I agree, Emily. But there is little we can do until their fears are quelled, for I do believe their dislike of the natives is based on fear, of their strange appearance and their strange ways.'

As they reached the hut, Nell hobbled towards them, her uneven gait having become more pronounced over the past few months. Jessie followed closely behind and Lucy, eyes sparkling, ran beside her.

Nell took hold of Tilly's hands and squeezed them. 'Oh Tilly! It is good to see you once more.' She lifted her apron and wiped her face, now damp with tears. 'Thank the Lord you are back with us.'

Tilly held out her arms and Lucy ran towards her. 'My little sweet,' she said, swinging her around and smacking kisses on her cheek. Lucy giggled.

'She has been asking for you, Tilly. Last night she cried because you were not there to kiss her goodnight.' Emily reached over and took Lucy's hands and, looking into her eyes she asked, 'Are you happy now, my little treasure?'

'Yes, yes,' Lucy answered, clapping her hands, her dark curls bobbing as she did so.

'We have all missed you,' Jessie said, slipping her arm around Tilly's shoulder. 'I feel privileged to have you as a friend. You are a brave woman contending with the evil Rafton, defending yourself, and saving Emily too. We are proud of you.'

'It was nothing, Jess. I was never desperate for food or water at Pinchgut for the day after Emily visited me Patye came along on another fishing trip, so to speak.' She laughed and then became serious once more. 'Now, there you have a brave woman.'

'A brave woman, indeed,' Nell concurred. 'It is a pity I have not met Patye. But I suppose I cannot expect her to come here to our home.'

'You are right. Many of the natives are still reluctant to mix with us out in the open. They would prefer that we visit them. And it would be difficult for you to walk through the bush to their camp, Nell.' Emily smiled. 'But maybe someday Patye will come and visit us here. We can but hope.' She turned to Tilly. 'Thank the good Lord it is over now. Maybe we have seen the last of our worries and can start our lives afresh.'

The governor's plan for the *Lady Juliana* to transport the women to Norfolk Island before setting sail for China was scuppered. The crewmen who had formed strong relationships with the women during the voyage from England, some of whom had fathered their offspring, were reluctant to be separated. But when they were told they would be sailing direct to China, furtive plans were made to stow their women away until they had reached a point too far north to return to the colony. Aitken, aware of this, sought the help of the marines.

The women on board lashed out viciously, but the

guards passed them down to longboats to be taken ashore. Broken-hearted, the women cursed, screamed and sobbed, and their babies, now terrified by all the noise, bawled uncontrollably. The crew, desperate and resentful at the guards' intervention, fought with them, shouting and swearing as they tried to follow the women ashore. But their protests were to no avail, for more guards were sent to quell the affray. The *Lady Juliana* left the harbour bound for China without the women.

The one hundred and fifty women were pushed aboard the *Surprize*. Many of them tried to rebel, and they struggled with the crew and the guards, but they were soon restrained, some still weeping as they watched the *Lady Juliana* sailing through The Gap and out to sea. The *Surprize* followed with the *Justinian* in her wake carrying extra stores for Norfolk Island.

Jimmy, desperate to leave the tiny island after more than a year away from the mainland, was disappointed when the *Lady Juliana* sailed past Norfolk Island, its sails visible at first but quickly disappearing over the horizon. He left the shore, entered the barracks and lay on his bunk. He soon became drowsy but his rest was disturbed when he heard voices. He opened his eyes and realised one of the officers and a sergeant were talking in confidence, obviously unaware Jimmy was there.

'The governor has accused the government of abandoning the colony. But I do so believe we here on the island have been abandoned by the governor.' The officer's voice was raised. 'I shall complain to Major Ross. He informed us that when the women arrived, we would be sent back to the mainland. But the ship has passed us by.'

'Surely the major will keep his promise. There will be other ships,' the sergeant replied but his attempts to maintain an optimistic approach were misconstrued.

'That cantankerous ass, Ross, is a madman. I cannot abide him. He places his men under arrest over trivial matters. His actions could prove treacherous. He is too busy insulting certain members of the Royal Navy, no names mentioned,' he muttered, 'to think about his own men. He is conceited and cares only for himself. He sits in his office, Commandant of Norfolk Island, governing under Law Martial, and he thinks he is God.' He spat the words out, his face a scarlet glow.

Jimmy held back a grin as he watched the sergeant's crooked smile.

'Aye, sir. Maybe you are right. He is not a popular choice, I am bound to agree. The men seem to have a dislike for him,' he said, the comment obviously intended to appease the officer.

'A popular choice? He is not disliked by his men, he is despised by them, and by the governor too, so I hear. Not to mention Captain Hunter whose reputation goes before him.'

Enough, thought Jimmy as he pulled himself up. He must leave. The two men had their backs to him as he edged his way silently towards the door, setting out towards the square close to the barracks. Drawn to a small group of guards, he listened to their animated conversation as one of them pointed towards a distant hill where a small lookout station was established. 'Sails have been sighted to the far south. Maybe she is the one we are waiting for,' came the expectant cry of one of the guards.

'Aye, that may be so but the Commandant does not always keep to his word. We must await instructions before raising our hopes.'

Jimmy's heart began to beat rapidly. This could be his salvation. He could return to the colony and be reunited with his darling Emily.

But were his feelings reciprocated? On account of her position in the social structure of the colony, her views were biased, and he feared she did not love him in the same way he loved her. But he could do nothing to change things, not from the faraway Norfolk Island.

He decided to climb the hill and see for himself what was happening. As he reached the summit he stared out across the vast ocean. There were two ships approaching, but their progress was slow, for their sails were billowing vigorously and they appeared to be fighting against the wind.

Suddenly a slight movement caught the corner of his eye. A cutter was heading from the harbour out towards the ships. Once it arrived alongside them there was little further movement from the two ships. The vicious winds continued and it was apparent a lesson had been learnt when, months earlier, Captain Hunter's ship, the *Sirius*, had been flung broadside against the reef. Supplies from the store ship, *Justinian* were successfully transferred to the longboats and taken ashore, but the women remained on board *The Surprize*. And it was three days later before they disembarked to the north east of the island at the calmer Cascade Bay.

Major Ross assembled the total population of the island and referred to the newcomers.

'These women will need to be housed with those of you already living here.' This caused a stir amongst the island's inhabitants. But when the major addressed the marines the news was depressing. 'You will not be leaving the island until the *Supply* returns from Batavia, and that will not be for some considerable time.'

Jimmy's hopes were dashed.

Chapter 14

1790 – 1792

Nell had not stirred from her bed when Jessie was ready to leave for the nursery.

'Nell,' she called. 'We are leaving.'

But there was no response. Jessie frowned.

'What should I do, Em? Should I wake her?' she said to Emily. 'She is usually awake by sun up.'

'We are early this morning, and the sun is not yet up. Leave her resting,' Emily suggested. 'She was tired after yesterday, for she cleaned the huts, cooked the meals and helped Tilly and Will in the garden too. The rest will be good for her.'

When they reached the nursery, Tuba and Tagaran were waiting in the bushes with a boy of about four they had brought along. Emily bent down and took his hands. 'And what is your name, little one?' she asked. The child, obviously nervous to hear a foreign tongue, and not able to understand, stared back, his lip quivering slightly as though he were about to cry.

Tagaran, the elder of the two girls smiled. 'Caruey,' she said and took hold of his hand as she followed Emily.

Once all the children had arrived and the mothers had left, Emily started to chant a nursery rhyme and the children joined in. But minutes later the door burst open and Tilly, her jet black hair dishevelled, rushed across the room to Emily. The children stopped chanting and stared open-mouthed

Emily was startled too. 'What is it, Tilly?'

'You must come quickly, Em. It is Nell,' she said, trying to catch her breath. 'I fear she is ill,' she paused, 'or worse.'

'Worse? How do you mean worse?' But Emily did not wait for Tilly's explanation. Worried by the words, she turned to Jess. 'I must go immediately,' she added. 'Take care of the children until Mistress O'Donnell arrives. I will come back as quickly as I can and let you know what has happened.'

'But Emily...'

'Sorry, Jess. You will be fine with the children.'

The sun was blazing down upon them as they ran back to the hut. Will was standing near the door, a fearful look upon his face.

'How is she, Will?' Emily, panting now after the exertion, put her hand to her chest.

Will shuffled his feet and began to stutter, 'I... I... I think...'

'You think what, Will?' Emily brushed past him and ran towards Nell's bed. 'Nell, Nell. Speak to me.' But there was silence. She took hold of Nell's hand and lifted it but her arm was limp. She turned to Tilly. 'How long has she been like this?'

'After you left I went to the garden but I had a strange feeling when Nell did not appear. I became worried. She is usually around by sun up. I told Will I would go back to the hut and check on her.'

'It was almost sun up when we left,' Emily told her. 'We must call the surgeon quickly. I fear it must be the bone ache which has caused her to pass out. But we do not have smelling salts to revive her.' She scribbled a note and turned to Will. 'Quickly, Will. Run to the hospital. Ask if one of the surgeons will come and attend to Nell.'

Emily went inside and talked to Nell.

'I am here Nell. Rest a while. We have sent for the doctor. You will soon be fine.' But she knew Nell's condition was critical, for her face was becoming more and more ashen and there was no response from her. Suddenly she remembered Jessie. 'Tilly, would you please go to the nursery and tell Jess what is happening. If Mistress O'Donnell has not arrived would you stay a while and allow Jess to come and see Nell, for I fear her condition is now becoming serious?'

'But I am no good with children, Em, and I cannot read.'

'You can sing,' she said. 'Sing to them. Play with them. That is all they need.' Tilly had a lively personality and Emily knew she would be capable of keeping the children entertained.

After Tilly had left for the nursery, Will came running back to the hut. But he was alone. His face resembled a bright red beacon and his cheeks were damp as he panted for breath.

'He is too busy to come. He told me you must take Nell down there.'

'Take her down there? How can we do that? The two of us will be unable to carry her, and Tilly has gone to the nursery for Jess.'

'I can carry her, Emily. I will do it,' Will replied, following Emily into the hut. 'Please let me help,' he offered. 'Nell is only slight, not much heavier than a child.'

'Are you sure, Will? I will help you all I can.' She paused. 'Maybe we could borrow the small hand-cart from Josh on our way down there.'

Will slid one arm under Nell's back and the other under her knees.

'Leave me to lift her. I am sure I can manage.' But he struggled as they set out to the hospital, and by the time they were nearing the nursery, Jessie was coming towards them.

'Oh poor Nell! I hope she will recover. And poor Will, too. See, let me help you.'

'I am fine, Jess.'

Emily spotted Josh tending his plot. She called out to him and he rushed over to see what was happening. 'Josh, would you lend us your cart please?' Emily asked him. 'We will return it as soon as we arrive at the hospital.'

Josh looked to Will and pulled the cart towards him. 'Here, Will. Let me help you.' Between them they gently slid Nell's body onto the cart. 'Rest your arms now,' he added before turning to Emily. 'And do not rush to bring it back.'

Still panting from his exertions, Will pushed the cart to the hospital. Emily hurried along beside him, her heart thumping in her chest. *Please God, let her live. She is my dearest friend.* By now Nell's stark white face had turned grey with a blue tinge to her lips which indicated to Emily that her condition was now critical.

The door banged behind him as Will struggled to place Nell on a table indicated by the man they assumed to be the new surgeon. It was a pity that Surgeon Bowes Smyth was no longer with them for the young surgeon, who had apparently arrived with the second fleet, stared as though he had a foul stench beneath his nose.

'You took your time, lad,' he said to Will, lifting Nell's wrist and holding it. He felt the skin around her neck and face. 'I told you to be quick. It is too late. This woman has passed away. Rigor mortis is already setting in,' he told them, a casual tone to his voice. 'Move her for I have others to attend to.'

'You mean Nell is dead?' Emily couldn't believe his words.

'That is exactly what I mean, girl.'

'Maybe Nell would have died whatever happened, but you did not consider coming out to visit the hut, even though it is only minutes away from the hospital. And now that Will has struggled to bring her here you cannot even be civil. Maybe to you we are not worth saving, but if that is the case, why are you here?' Tears began to trickle down her face.

'How dare you speak to me in that manner? You are nothing but a felon. Do you realise who I am?'

'No, but I realise what you are,' she sobbed.

Full of his own importance, he ignored her insults.

'I am The Honourable Oliver Reece Withers, a highly qualified surgeon. I make the decisions here,' he boasted.

'I realise that,' Emily concurred, a hint of sarcasm in her voice. 'And a fine decision you made on this occasion.' She turned to Will. 'I know you are weary from carrying Nell here Will but let us take her back home where she belongs. We shall bury her nearby.'

'You will do no such thing, girl. The governor has issued instructions as to the disposal of the dead. Move her from this table, but do not take her away.'

'I would like to take her back and prepare her for the coffin. I take it a coffin will be made available for her. I will not allow her a pauper's burial with nothing but a sheet wrapped about her against the earth. She was a very dear friend of ours and we must ensure she leaves this world with dignity.'

The surgeon turned to a younger man who was hovering behind him. 'Take details of this felon. After they have prepared the woman, you must make sure she is dealt with through the proper authorities.' He turned to Emily. 'The coffin is your own responsibility.'

Will intervened. 'I will make the coffin, Em. Do not worry.'

'I am grateful to you Will Hopwood for you are a caring young man, not like many round here,' she said, looking pointedly at the hospital staff.

Hot blood flushed Will's face for he was not used to compliments and as Emily was about to leave, the surgeon sidled up close to her.

'Plenty of mettle, I will say that for you, something I do so admire in a woman.'

Her stomach lurched. She cringed inwardly as she felt his warm breath on her face and saw the leering look in his eyes, a look she'd seen before. He laughed and turned to the others.

'On this occasion, I will allow it. Take the body away.'

Two days later, the Reverend Johnson carried out the burial service and Nell was laid to rest. For many a day, the three women wept at their loss, for Nell had been the one they had turned to when problems arose, the one they had talked to about their feelings, their thoughts and their fears. But it soon became apparent that Jessie, living alone now that Nell had gone, was falling into the same depressed state as when Lizzie had passed away on board the *Lady Penrhyn.*

Emily approached Tilly. 'What are we to do about Jess? If we do not try to carry her through this ordeal, I fear she will forever suffer this terrible depression.'

'I will move in with her. It is company she misses. I know I can never take the place of dear Nell, but I can talk to Jess.'

Emily smiled.

'I know what you are thinking,' Tilly continued. 'You know me well, Emily, at least I can keep her spirits up. She will have no time to feel sorry for herself.'

Emily began to laugh. She respected Tilly's spirited, garrulous nature. She recalled the days when they were at Durham together, when Tilly had carried her through her own ordeal.

Tilly moved in with Jessie and once more Emily and Lucy were left alone. And it was in her lonelier moments that her thoughts turned to Jimmy.

It was more than two years since she had last seen him. But that did not change her feelings towards him for, on the day they had parted, she knew her love for him would never wane.

Many things had happened since his departure. Their huts were greatly improved. They were now much stronger, and there was a plan for brick houses to be built. The garden surrounding the two homes had increased to an acre. But still there was something she would have cherished more than anything, her freedom. The pardon she had been hoping for had not been forthcoming. The governor had mentioned nothing since his communication to Sir William Brice. Whether the missive had found its way there and been acknowledged, Emily had no idea. But she knew it was not her place to enquire.

With no news of the pardon she was certain that, if Jimmy's feelings towards her remained the same, and if he approached her with a proposal of marriage, she would be obliged to refuse. Until she was a free woman, she could not become bound in any legal commitment with Jimmy. But would he be prepared to wait?

By mid-November the temperature had soared. Emily fingered the rough hessian fabric of her tunic. The one given to her by Mistress O'Donnell had become threadbare. Although the hessian tunic was hard wearing it labelled her a convict. But she was not a convict, she never had been a convict and she never would be. It was time to put the situation to rights. But first she needed money.

Nell had left a substantial amount of the counterfeit money given to her by Billy but, wanting nothing to do with illegal currency, Emily had hastily burnt it whilst the others were out. Nell had never tried to use it. It was merely of comfort to her knowing she had something of Billy's.

Suddenly Emily remembered the small amount of Portuguese currency Jimmy had given her before leaving for Norfolk Island. It was change from a crown he had spent in Rio when he had bought fruit from the pedlars there. Emily had been reluctant to accept it but Jimmy had insisted it may be useful to buy necessary items from a ships' agent, whom he knew would accept 'sliding' coinage which he explained was currency other than sterling.

The time had come to take his advice, for she regarded cloth for new garments to be a necessity. And she was sure he would have agreed. She approached the others.

'Now that the *Lady Juliana* is back from China, I shall ask the agent if there is cloth available, for we cannot continue to wear these coarse tunics throughout another summer. I can sew a little. We could make new tunics for ourselves.'

'That is a wonderful idea, Emily, but I have no money. I would not be able to pay for cloth.' It was Jessie who made a response.

Tilly was quick to intervene. 'I have English currency the crew obtained for me from the kindly Captain Aitken in payment of wages due to George after he passed away, God rest his soul.'

'But Tilly I cannot take your money. It would not be fair.'

'And d'ye think Emily and I would buy new clothes and leave you in sacking?'

Emily interjected. 'Let us not argue. I think I may have enough money to buy the cloth for all three of us, and Lucy besides. Let us spend the Portuguese money first,' she said, 'for the English money will be of more value later.'

'I have experience as a seamstress. Lizzie and I helped our mother to stitch the gowns and capes for the ladies at the manor,' Jessie was quick to offer.

'Then that will be your payment for the clothes,' Emily stressed.

'Yes, indeed, Jess. And you are not to dispute it.' Tilly smiled warmly but her look failed to mask her determination not to debate the issue further.

The following day after their daily chores were complete, Emily decided it was time they sought out the agent to buy the cloth they needed. 'Would you mind staying back with Lucy whilst Tilly and I walk down to the wharf to seek out the *Lady Juliana's* agent? There are all manner of men down there and I think we are more able to contend with their banter than you Jess, for you are so gentle.'

'That is fine by me for I do not wish to become involved with those men,' she confessed.

The light of day had faded and the sky was painted the palest of silver when they reached the wharf. A longboat was tied up and one of its oarsmen was seated on the edge of the wharf swinging his legs and idling his time away obviously waiting for someone. Emily approached him. 'We are anxious to speak to the agent. Do you know his whereabouts?'

'He is not on the *Lady Juliana* but he will no doubt return from an evening with the officers when their business is complete.' He gave them a knowing look. 'Perhaps you are here to do business?' he suggested, his eyes betraying his anticipation of whatever he had in mind. Emily could guess what that would be, but it was not what she had in mind.

'We are indeed,' Tilly replied, 'but not the sort of

business you are referring to.' A look of disdain mantled her face and she turned her back on him.

The two women waited, and it was late by the time the agent returned to the longboat. He was most unsteady on his feet and obviously well into his cups. 'What have we here my pretties?' his words slurring one into another.

'We require good, soft fabric for the purpose of making garments. What do you have?'

The agent laughed at Emily's request.

'I have a little silk cloth from China. I was keeping it to take back to England but if you are willing to offer the right price I may let it go.'

'And what do you call the right price, for our currency is Portuguese?'

'For silk? No. I could not let the cloth go for Portuguese currency unless there was something more you are willing to offer.' In the darkness of the night, Emily detected a look of speculation in his eyes as he swayed backwards and forwards.

It was Tilly who answered him. 'Nay, good sir, if you saw us in the daylight you would not be suggesting such a thing.' The nudge she gave to Emily went unnoticed by the agent. 'If the silk is not for sale, do you have anything less expensive?'

He stumbled forward to peer even closer, but his eyes were now half-closed. He almost fell into the water and, obviously believing the two women to be ugly, as Tilly had inferred, took the arm of the oarsman and stepped into the longboat. The boat wobbled dangerously.

'Wait for me tomorrow when I come ashore at sun down. I will see what I have available.'

They made their purchase the following evening when the agent offered remnants he had obviously been unable to dispose of elsewhere, and these suited their purpose exactly.

During daylight hours when her time was her own Jessie set about the task of stitching the garments, and Emily assisted her whilst Tilly continued with the chores. There was sufficient fabric for all four of them, and finally the garments were complete. Delighted, Emily slipped on her new tunic.

'How soft it is on my skin. Thank you, Jess,' she said, smoothing it down.

'Thank you for the cloth, Emily. I, too, am delighted.'

'Now we must prepare to leave for the nursery. Remember Tagaran is bringing the new boy with her today,' she continued. 'We shall need to set out early for I would not wish for the children to be waylaid. Remember what happened last week.'

Emily was referring to an incident when the three children arrived early at the nursery. It was apparent they had been chastised by someone for they quickly fled back to their camp. Eventually Patye took them back but it was well after sun up.

'Someone is resentful of the native children's visits to the nursery. There will be four of them with the new child and this could trigger even more animosity.' Emily's mind was constantly filled with the children's safety.

When they reached the clearing the children emerged from the bush. Emily pointed to the small furry bears nestling snugly in the tangy-scented eucalypts and munching away at the delicate leaves which fluttered in the breeze. The Aborigines called them koalas.

'See the little bears.' She pointed up above. 'They must be hungry this morning. The leaves are nearly gone.' She laughed and they joined in.

The children looked up as Tagaran translated Emily's words into her own language and the little boy, whom she had introduced as Mongana, looked up too. Lucy took his hand and they walked ahead.

'See, Jess. The children don't regard the natives as being any different from themselves, so why should the mothers resent their presence?' She pointed to Lucy who was busy chatting to Mongana and laughing. And although it was obvious the little boy did not understand a word she was saying he was laughing along with her. 'But I am determined to uphold the governor's wishes. For as long as I attend this nursery I will continue to encourage the native children to join us.'

The *Supply* was sighted off the south coast of Norfolk Island at the beginning of February and Jimmy's spirits were raised. But his return to the mainland was not to be, for Major Ross informed them the only men to return on the *Supply* were the crew of the doomed flagship *Sirius* and their captain John Hunter. Once more Jimmy suffered a depressed state of mind. It seemed he would remain on Norfolk Island for the rest of his life, for he felt he had suffered so many setbacks.

But by mid-April the *Supply* had returned once more with the replacement guards in the form of the unruly New South Wales Corps.

Major Ross addressed the marines.

'Those who wish to make a home here may elect to join the new guard on Norfolk Island. If you choose to board the ship and return to the mainland, your duties there will be complete. You will sail for England shortly after you arrive at Sydney Cove. The choice is yours.'

As soon as the major had dismissed them, Jimmy turned to Sandy. 'Staying here is not an option. I have dreamt of returning to Sydney Cove for so long I can scarcely believe my luck that at last we are to leave Norfolk Island.'

'And who is there in Sydney Cove you wish to see so urgently?' Sandy teased.

'You know the answer to that, my friend,' Jimmy replied, having confessed to Sandy that his feelings for Emily were more powerful than mere friendship.

At the beginning of May they finally set foot on the sloop *Supply* which, in comparison with the other ships, was very small. It was not intended for transportation, and conditions were cramped. But seeing Emily again was all Jimmy dreamt of, and it was no hardship for him. The passage back to the mainland was rough and the ocean stretching before them was a mass of violent agitation. During the squalls, the ship swayed up and down like a see-saw, rolling and pitching through the heavy swells, the very extremities of the yards dipping into the sea. But despite this, over a hundred feet above the main deck with no footholds to aid them, the topmen tended the upper sails, furling them to prevent further excessive movement.

Once the gusty winds had ceased and the ocean

calmed, their passage became slower and they encountered dolphins, sharks and barracuda. Some of the men threw out lines and obtained constant supplies of fresh fish from the wide open ocean.

Then came a perfect wind and they were once more under full sail, the crew having spread the topsails and mainsails, enabling the ship to ride through the water at twenty knots.

Some of the marines went down below to rest but Jimmy, keen to improve his learning, preferred to be up on deck. He spent most of his time watching with interest as the captain and the first mate stood on the quarter-deck, checking the position of the sun on the horizon and studying their charts and tables. He noticed how, once they believed they were nearing land, they swung the lead to check the depth of the water and took soundings whilst watching the sea change from blue to green as land was neared. Jimmy was intrigued.

The sloop entered The Gap at Port Jackson and anchored in the harbour at Sydney Cove. Jimmy gazed ahead, a tingle of pleasure stirring within him, for now he was back at the mainland where, once again, he could be re-united with Emily.

The longboats began to transport the marines ashore and, once there, Jimmy searched the wharf for Emily. 'She must be here somewhere for surely the whole population know of our return to the Cove.' But search as he might amongst the people crowded there, Emily was nowhere to be seen. Perhaps she had obtained her pardon from the governor and returned home. Jimmy's heart fluttered in his chest. If that were the case, he would never see her again for he had no idea where she lived. But he was being foolish.

'She will be at her work still, Jimmy,' Sandy suggested, 'for she cannot leave the children.'

'You are right. That is where I will go.'

He was about to move from the spot, when the commanding officer called to them. 'Attention you men! You are to report to the barracks immediately. I will address you there.' He crossed the deck and climbed into a longboat.

Jimmy sighed and his stomach churned aggressively. Just as he had anticipated searching for Emily, he must report for duty. When would he ever be re-united with her? Perhaps he could slip along to the nursery on his way back to the barracks. But his plan was foiled when the sergeant took command of the men and marched them back.

Sergeant MacVay informed the men they would be returning to England in two weeks' time upon the transport *Surprize* which had returned from China. The men cheered. They were going home. But for Jimmy, the news was bad; home for him was with Emily. They belonged together.

Later that evening the marines were given their freedom for now that the New South Wales Corps had arrived they took over the responsibilities previously held by the marines. Jimmy headed for Emily's hut and was amazed to see the transformation.

The surrounding land was neatly cultivated and the hut itself had been extended. He knocked at the door, his heart almost bursting. The door opened.

Emily stared, open-mouthed, Lucy beside her.

'I do not believe it.' She lifted her hands to her mouth but Jimmy pulled her close and kissed her tenderly. When he held her at arms' length he noticed her eyes were glistening but then she seemed to overcome her emotion. 'I thought I would never see you again, Jimmy. Come in, come in,' she said, taking his hand and leading him inside. She turned to Lucy. 'You will not remember Jimmy. He is a dear friend of ours.'

Lucy gave him a shy smile, ran to the other side of the room and picked up a rag doll.

'You have grown, Lucy and you look very pretty,' Jimmy told her. Lucy ran to the door and disappeared.

Emily turned and placed a pot over the fire. 'We shall have tea Jimmy, and then you can tell me all about the island.'

Jimmy gazed at her slender figure draped in the soft blue fabric. Gone was the rough, shapeless tunic. Emily the girl was now Emily the woman and, he hoped, *his* woman. He took a deep breath and sighed.

'Emily, you look wonderful. You are more beautiful than ever.'

She turned and he took her hands once more and, as he gazed into her eyes, he realised they were full of love, and he knew it was for him.

'Thank you, Jimmy. It is kind of you to say so.'

Jimmy drew her towards him again.

'I cannot resist my darling,' and gently pressed his lips to hers. Emily's lips were firm and she gave a sigh in helpless surrender as his warmth enfolded her. But he became aware of a slight trace of resistance and he released her.

'I have missed you, my love.' He swallowed hard. 'Please say you will be mine, for I must leave the colony in a few weeks' time and return to England. But it is my intention to come back here as a free settler after I have seen my mother once more.'

'Jimmy, you agreed not to press me on this matter. You know that until I am a free woman, I cannot promise myself to you. Unless I hear from the governor that I have been pardoned, it will be another three years before there is any possibility of freedom.'

'Emily, I will wait forever for I love you more than anything in the world.'

'But I have my Lucy and she is not your child.'

'I would take Lucy as my own, for I love her too. Please agree to marry me.'

'Then we must hope that soon I shall hear from the governor.'

Emily took his hands and gazed into his eyes. 'You must know how I feel, Jimmy, for I cannot hide it from you. Your love is returned but you must agree to wait. It may be that when you return I still do not have my freedom.'

'My darling Emily,' he said drawing her close and whispering through her hair. 'At last you have agreed.' He kissed her once more and they held each other tight.

When she drew him to arms' length her eyes lit up to a wonderful glow. 'I do believe we are a perfect fit both in heart and in mind.'

Jimmy responded by pressing his lips to hers again, relishing her kisses. Her body was warm and inviting and he took in the sweet intoxicating smell of her skin. His yearning to hold her close had built up during the time they were apart.

But he must control his feelings. He must take things slowly.

Emily felt the comfort of his arms around her. She had never felt like this before and the stirrings inside developed gradually. But this was neither the time nor the place to allow herself to give in to those feelings.

She felt him release her from his grip.

'I must go now. I hope to see you each day until I leave.'

He paused. 'I do not know how I shall survive the journey back to England without you. But now that you have given me a promise, I have something to strive for.'

Chapter 15

England
1792

The man listened intently to the other two, their voices raised in disagreement. But he was not about to stay and listen to more. He had heard enough to be convinced that his best move was to get away as quickly as possible, right away from this place.

Collecting the few pieces of baggage he had earlier packed, he left and headed for town. There he took a coach destined for London. It was with great relief that he settled down into the seat, a sly smile lighting his face. He had beaten them. Now they would never find him.

The coach rattled along on uneven ground and, after a time, he felt some discomfort for the seat was hard and the journey was long, but it was no use complaining. He needed to get there, and fast.

Their first stop was Nottingham where the coach discharged the passengers for an overnight stay at an inn on the outskirts of the city. He ordered a flagon of ale and a meal of mutton stew, not exactly what he was used to but this was a new life. He must try to save as much money as he could for there would be no more once it was gone, not unless he went back home. And that was not an option.

The innkeeper's wife presented the tray of food, and it seemed she was taking in the fine cut of him and thinking she might make a little extra money extending the inn's hospitality.

'A little comfort for the night, sir? Would that suit?' she whispered.

Would that suit? he asked himself. *Would that bloody suit?* He could feel the stirring in his groin. *By God it would.* His wife and child were back at home, and he had appeased his wife by promising to send for them once he was out of the way and settled. But that situation would never arise. Why resume that responsibility?

He took his time before he answered.

'Only if she is comely and experienced,' he offered, not wishing to sound too eager.

'Her's that right enough, sir. She's sixteen and in 'er prime. I'll get 'er to follow when I see you on the stairs.'

He swigged the ale and hurriedly devoured the food. It had been some time since he had taken a woman to his bed and he could hardly wait. Arabella had not allowed him near since she had heard the accusations. She had refused to take to the bed with him.

Now he was about to get what he deserved, a pretty little wench who, according to the innkeeper's wife, was well worth the money. He set off upstairs, entered the room closing the door behind him, the sensation in his groin heightening with every thought of the wench..

He slipped off his shirt and poured water from the heavy jug into the basin. As he did so, there was a gentle tapping on the door. He jumped and in his haste to open it, he dropped the jug. It went crashing to the floor.

'Damn.' The wench would think he was over-eager. He kicked the broken porcelain to one side and waited a few minutes until she knocked again. He opened the door. The wench slipped inside and he closed it quickly behind her. She was comely right enough! Her dress revealed lovely creamy breasts, and she was such a tease, such a temptation to touch!

She smiled.

'Betsy's me name, sir. You wanted comfort for the night?'

Before he had the chance to answer, she smiled agreeably, lifted her arms and slid them around his neck, pressing her body against him. To his delight, she started to brush her lips gently and seductively upon his. His hands explored the curves of her body, soft and rounded. He knew he must have her immediately.

Aware of the urgency she started to take off her clothes keeping eye contact as she did so, but her movements were slow and it was all too much. How could he be expected to wait? He clutched at her petticoat, lifted it over her head and pushed her to the bed.

She giggled loudly, but he glared at her. This was not the time to jest. In a rough movement, he spread her legs and drove into her. Within seconds he had had his way.

Minutes later, she pushed herself up from the bed. 'That was quick, sir,' she said. 'Maybe you'd like more a little later,' she offered, a knowing smile on her face which puckered the dimples in her cheeks.

She was right there. But without any further acknowledgement he pulled the blanket over the top of them. He turned her on her side, pressed himself against her back, sliding an arm around her and clutching at her breast. Ten minutes and he would have her again. But his breathing became deeper and he dropped off to sleep eight minutes before his intentions could be met.

By the next morning Betsy had disappeared, having attended to his needs several times throughout the night. He prepared to leave and went down for breakfast. The innkeeper's wife fussed around him, a fatuous look upon her face. He supposed he must pay up for last night's service but he was determined to offer no more than he was forced. The woman bent down and whispered, 'Good night's sleep, sir?'

He nodded and slipped his hand into his pocket and took out the money he had put on one side. The coachman stood at the door, shifting from one foot to the other, waiting impatiently.

'Thank you kindly,' she offered. 'Do call again sometime.'

But he knew he would not be around to call at the inn again. Not that another night with the girl would go amiss. But knowing it was an impossibility he wiped his mouth on the napkin and left the inn.

On the crack of the whip, the coach left Nottingham. The only remaining passenger, an elderly woman, was bound for Northampton. When she disembarked and he had the carriage to himself he decided to count his sovereigns and he took from his portmanteau the maroon velvet bag, untied the string and poured the coinage carefully on to the seat beside him. He counted it once. He counted it twice. He was two sovereigns short. That was strange. He knew exactly how much he had when he set out. What at first appeared to be a mystery was no mystery once he turned the matter over in his mind and thought about it seriously. It was that little bitch, Betsy. She must have taken it whilst he was asleep. Thieves, liars and cheats. Was there nobody you could trust these days?

Eventually the coach reached London, its final destination. He booked in at the Globe Inn a place he would not normally frequent, but he needed to maintain his anonymity. And he needed somewhere out of the way with time to think and, most important of all, no questions to answer.

He must remember no gambling houses, for he needed to hold on to his sovereigns, no visits to the club since he wished not to meet up with friends and no whorehouses for it was important he remained in good health when left the country. One never knew what these women carried. And after the escapade back in Nottingham, he had no intention of giving those whores the chance to rob him again.

The food at the inn was wholesome enough he supposed but too stodgy for his taste. The people frequenting the place were boring too and far beneath him. Perhaps he could go to a little eating house tucked away on the outskirts of the city and have a decent meal later, one the likes of his class was accustomed to. If he shaved off his beard and brushed his hair slightly differently maybe no-one would recognise him.

He strode through the streets feeling confident, as

though his face were masked against intruders and, eventually, he came upon Clarissa Bizet's place. His mouth watered. The food there was indeed delicious, the likes of which he had not tasted for many a month. He would take the chance. The light was fast fading as he entered. An unfamiliar figure with his newly disguised appearance, he was shown to a table. He could hardly make up his mind on the choice of food but eventually he did.

'Over here, wench!' he called, snapping his fingers.

Before anyone had the chance to approach him, he felt a heavy slap on his back.

'Dickon, my boy. I do not believe it. A change of image, you old rascal?' came a booming call from behind. 'But you cannot fool me. I would know that voice anywhere.'

My God, he thought as he spun around. *Not Ralphie de Mille*. But he knew it was. It could hardly be anyone other than that larger-than-life character breaking the silence of the room. And the idiot, calling him Dickon, the name his friends had used when they were at school together. It was all too familiar. If Ralphie met up with any of the others, he would be sure to tell them, and then everyone would know he was in London.

'Ralphie. It must be months since I last saw you.'

'Months? More like years. It was eighty nine if you recall. Monty's wedding.' Ralphie sat down beside him.

'You are right,' he said, now squirming inside, and wondering how to get rid of this buffoon.

'Down here alone or is the good lady with you?'

'I am down on business,' he said, winking. 'It is foolish to let the ladies know everything.'

Ralphie's asinine guffaw caught the attention of the other people in the restaurant. They turned and glared across at the table, and the young lady who was sitting alone, a very pretty lady too, looked away. Ralphie lowered his voice. 'You're right there,' he said and guffawed once more.

The word 'ladies' had obviously triggered Ralphie's thoughts, for he pointed to the delightful young lady and added, 'Let me introduce you to dear Elizabeth.' He walked across to her table. 'Elizabeth, there's someone I would like you to meet,' he said, pulling her gently from the chair and bringing her across to meet him.

In different circumstances it would have been admirable passing his time in their company. But his main aim now was to get away. The question was, how? It would be difficult keeping up the front about his business trip without divulging the real reason why he was in London. But he had covered his actions and his tracks so far, and there was no reason why he could not continue to do so.

They joined him for dinner and despite his fears that he might let something slip, he remained calm. But once out of the restaurant, having given Ralphie the name of a much larger, more expensive hotel in the centre of the city, he took a cab and returned to the Globe Inn.

There was no doubt it would be foolish to remain in London any longer. It was far too dangerous. He packed his bags and ordered a cab to take him to the London coach station. He would take another coach and head for Portsmouth. Surely once he reached the port, there would be a ship to take him away from here. Even to the new country, America. Anywhere – provided it was far enough away for no-one to get at him.

Throughout that night the coach travelled at speed towards Portsmouth. By arrangement with the driver and his co-driver the journey was broken only when food was required. There were no overnight stops; he slept in the coach. The last thing he wanted was for news of his whereabouts to get back from his so-called friends to the justices, especially after that babbler Ralphie de Mille had spread the news that Dickon was in the city. They would no longer be friends once news of the accusations against him filtered through to them, at which time they would more likely be his enemies. For did not the women folk always take the side of their own kind, never considering the needs of the men. And that would be the start.

But that was not his main reason for his journey from the north to London. After many unsuccessful bouts of gambling at several clubs up there, he had lost all the money he possessed and, despite the many promissory notes he had left hither and thither, he had neither the assets nor the property to cover them. He had no alternative but to get away.

The coach rattled on and they reached Portsmouth during early morning. He paid the driver and set about looking for a small boarding house. Before he approached anyone about a sea voyage, he was desperate to clean himself up. He had several days' growth of beard which needed to be trimmed, and a hot tub would certainly freshen him.

He booked in at a small place not far from the harbour and when his ablutions were complete and he had partaken of a hearty meal hastily prepared by the woman, he left the house and set about checking the ships in the harbour, enquiring as to their destinations. There were voyages to India and to China but he had no desire to travel to a country where the language spoken was not English.

Eventually he came across the *Gorgon,* said by one of the seamen to be destined for the new country. America had been in his mind since he had left the capital and fled to Portsmouth and now here was his chance.

'I am interested in booking a passage aboard this vessel. What is the cost of a decent cabin?'

'Depends what you call a decent cabin,' the ship's master replied. 'Perhaps if you came below with me and gave me some indication then I could tell you more clearly.'

They went below, inspected a number of cabins and he decided he would like an outer one with a porthole.

'The cabin you have indicated is that of the first mate,' the captain told him. 'He will expect to be rewarded handsomely for giving up his cabin.'

After a certain amount of haggling the deal was done and he was told the *Gorgon* was to sail in three days' time.

'How long will this voyage take?' he enquired.

'Five or six months. Depends on the weather,' the captain informed him.

'Five or six months? I was given to understand it

would only take a matter of weeks.'

'Half way around the world in a matter of weeks? Surely you realise that is impossible. The quickest route takes five and a half months.'

The man was puzzled. 'To cross the Atlantic?'

'The Atlantic? We do not cross the Atlantic these days. The early ships took the route across to Rio to avoid the doldrums but I shall be going direct to Cape Town.'

'Cape Town? I was under the impression you were travelling to the new country. I have no desire to travel to the African continent.'

'My voyage is to the new country, New South Wales, sir. Cape Town is one of our ports of call.'

Disappointment flashed through him. He may have to wait several more days before there was a ship to cross the Atlantic.

'Can you tell me of a ship crossing the Atlantic in the next few days?'

'There are none at the present time. You will be lucky to find a passage. All felons are now being taken to New South Wales. That is the voyage most of the masters are taking, especially now that there are free settlers moving to the colony.'

'I suppose I could try the place, as a settler,' he said in desperation, for since he had met Ralphie de Mille and thoughts of a possible chase to find him tormented his mind, he must make a hasty decision and leave England behind. 'I have heard there are land allocations for the aristocracy.'

'I believe you are right there, sir. If you are of the aristocracy it would be a fine place for you to settle.' He realised the master's only interest was to make money from the deal. He probably knew little about the conditions at this place, New South Wales, but he was prepared to give it a rosy picture. It took a mere five minutes to make a decision.

He must get right away, especially now that he had made the same mistake twice. The first was under the sod, he could vouch for that.

But what of Arabella? That was his biggest mistake. He had no intention of either returning to see her or of sending for her once he was settled. He had not wanted the ugly wench in the first place. She had made a play for him and, of course, he had taken up the challenge as a sporting man would. As for the boy, he would want for nothing. Arabella doted on him.

With nothing on his conscience, he smiled to himself. He would leave for New South Wales but he would make sure he changed his identity and his title too. Lord Samuel Clarendon had died some months earlier and had left no heir. That was the solution. He would inherit the title.

'Count me in, will you? I would like to take my cabin tomorrow if I might. I have several matters to attend to today, and after that I shall need the peace and quiet of my cabin to draw up documents I wish to dispatch before we leave.'

'You are at liberty to take the cabin on the morrow, sir. And your name?'

'Lord Clarendon,' he said hurriedly. 'Samuel Clarendon.' He smiled. 'I shall report to the ship on the morrow.'

Chapter 16

New South Wales
1792

It had come as a shock to Jimmy when the sergeant announced the marines had been detailed to leave the colony within the next two weeks. But now that The New South Wales Corps had taken over, Jimmy had a little free time to be with Emily. And each evening when she returned from the nursery, he was waiting at the hut for her.

But one particular day, Jessie beckoned to him and they sat on the step outside whilst Emily prepared tea. 'I intend leaving the nursery early with Lucy and taking her down to the wharf tomorrow to see the new ship, *Tranquillity*. I shall not be here when you arrive, Jimmy,' she said, and he knew her plan was to give him the opportunity to spend time alone with Emily.

'Perhaps if that is the case I should go along and meet Emily. We could walk back together from the nursery.'

'I am sure she would like that.'

When he set out next day, all manner of thoughts flitted through his mind. Since his return from Norfolk Island, his moods had vacillated between elation now that Emily had agreed to wait for him and depression at the very notion of leaving her.

Still deep in thought, he was brought back to reality by what he could only describe as a faint moaning sound. When he tried to listen more carefully he realised it was coming from nearby. He concentrated hard. It was either a woman or a child. Perhaps someone was injured? Tentatively he stepped forward into the bush but there was no-one to be seen. As he advanced towards the nursery, the sound became louder and the voice he could hear was familiar. It was Emily's.

He set off running and, when he reached the nursery, he tried to push open the door. But it was jammed. Placing his shoulder firmly against it, he gave a hefty thrust and it flew back crashing against the wall. Almost losing his balance he pulled himself upright and his eyes focused on the image before him. To his horror, Emily was sitting on the floor, blindfolded and gagged, her wrists tied behind her back.

'Emily, my precious,' he cried as he bent down, quickly removing the ties and freeing her wrists. She snatched the blindfold from her eyes and clutched at the rag gagging her mouth, pulling it free. Her face was bruised and damp with tears.

Jimmy was incensed. 'Who attacked you, Em?' He placed the rags on the desk and soothed her wrists with his hands before taking her in his arms.

Emily clung to him sobbing and breathless, unable to speak. After a few seconds she muttered, 'I do not know. Whoever it was came from behind. I struggled but he overcame me then disappeared.'

Jimmy looked around, checking for clues and his gaze fell on the window. The shutter was broken.

'The culprit escaped through the window,' he said, pointing. 'And he did not expect you to leave the place tonight. The door was wedged shut.' His stomach began to churn violently. The only thought in his mind at that moment was revenge. 'Whoever he is, I will see him in gaol.'

'Jimmy, please,' Emily interrupted his threats. 'Do not seek trouble on my account,' she pleaded.

But Jimmy was adamant. 'You must allow me to protect you,' he urged, and his feelings soared. 'You are my responsibility now that you have promised to marry me.'

It was then a sudden thought struck him. What would happen when he left the colony? Who would be there to protect her then?

'What sort of man would do such a thing?' he asked as he held her close. But then he became aware of an acrid smell drifting in from outside. Something was burning. He looked up and his gaze fell on the open window where a thin film of smoke was rising up outside.

He grabbed Emily around the waist, lifted her bodily and dashed towards the door.

'What on earth are you doing, Jimmy,' she cried.

'Stay there,' he said and, placing her firmly on the ground, he ran to the side of the hut. He was amazed to see that sticks had been placed beneath it and already tiny plumes of flame were shooting into the air, extending higher and higher by the second. The deed had obviously been done hurriedly, for the flames were just out of reach of the hut.

'Whoever carried out this evil deed tried to set fire to the nursery. But I disturbed him,' he called out before stamping out the fire.

He took Emily's hand in his and pulled her close. 'I am worried Emily. Had the hut set on fire, you would have been burnt alive.'

'How many times am I to be threatened? It seems someone has an earnest desire to see me burnt at the stake. It almost happened the night of the storm if you remember.' She shivered. 'When will this nightmare end?'

'I will ask Sergeant MacVay to make discrete enquiries. I am sure he will try to help. He knows that we are promised to each other.'

'I was not aware you had mentioned the matter to him. Was that wise? He knows I have not yet been given ticket-of-leave status.'

'The sergeant is sympathetic, Emily. He is aware of your innocence.' Jimmy took off his jacket and placed it around her shoulders. 'The evening is becoming cool. Let us go back to the hut. Lean on me, my dear Emily, for you must be feeling weak.'

'I would prefer neither Jess nor Tilly to be told of this. Jess worries so, and Tilly would surely try to retaliate. You must promise me, Jimmy. As you suggest it will be better if you ask the sergeant to make enquiries.'

'I will do that. I suspect it is either one of the convicts who is anxious to rid the nursery of the aborigines and is bitter, or one of the Aborigines, for it is their way to burn the bush.'

Emily shook her head.

'It cannot be the natives, Jimmy. When they set fire to the bush they are careful and accurate. It is an act of nature. They burn only what is necessary. The fire at the nursery was the work of a novice.'

'Maybe so. We shall see.'

Jimmy put on a calm front but inside he felt the

strain. But his decision to return to Scotland had Emily's full support. Knowing how precious her parents had been to her, she agreed Jimmy must return to see his mother again. Most of all Jimmy wanted to deal with his father now that he had both the confidence and the physical strength to exert control over the bully.

He intended working at the docks in Glasgow, saving the money to provide both for his mother and for his return to the colony as a settler with capital to start a new life together with Emily.

He collected his thoughts. Who could be responsible for that vile deed at the nursery? He began to dwell once more on the circumstances.

'Before I leave for England, I will do whatever I can to seek out whoever made this attempt on your life.'

When they reached Emily's hut they went inside.

'Rest awhile Em and I will make tea for you.'

'I can see you are worried, Jimmy but we will be fine until you return. We have coped with adverse conditions since our arrival here at the colony. I feel sure nothing else can go wrong. Please come and sit next to me.'

Jimmy did as she asked and, slipping an arm around her, he kissed her. Her response was submissive and a great surge of love filled his soul.

Cherishing the moment, Emily welcomed the warmth of his body next to hers. If only it could be like this forever. She felt herself sinking more and more into the comfort of his arms and her senses seemed to come alive. When he bent his head and kissed her again on the lips his love washed over her in giant waves.

The sound of Lucy laughing startled them and Jimmy knew it was almost time for him to leave.

'I cannot wait for the time when we'll be together forever, Em.'

'It is something we must look forward to and keep in our hearts, Jimmy. The time will pass.'

Jimmy left the hut knowing he wanted her, and badly. He had used every shred of willpower not to make love to her as they clung together. But he must rid his mind of such an idea. He would have to wait until they married. He must take things slowly, especially in view of Emily's ordeal with Allenby.

Emily arrived at the nursery the following day, realising that the blindfold and the tie which had been used to bind and gag her were still on the desk. She scooped them up and hurriedly pushed them into her canvas bag before Jessie had the chance to see them. Jimmy had agreed to abide by her request. Neither Jessie nor Tilly was aware of the incident.

After leaving Jessie to organise the children, she went outside to make sure the remnants of the fire started the previous evening were out. She kicked the evidence away from the hut into the grass but, as she was about to enter the nursery once more, she was aware that Dorothy had been watching her.

'Was that the remains of a fire you were disposing of?'

'It was indeed Dorothy for someone must have been playing tricks on us. I thought it better out of the way so as not to give the little ones any ideas.'

'You are right. I imagine it to be one of the blacks

for I am sure they will try to get their revenge after the recent trouble.' Her smile was wreathed in malicious pleasure.

'What trouble was that?'

'Did you not hear? One of our men was killed by a black,' Dorothy gloated, intent on blaming the natives after her earlier refusal to allow her child to attend the nursery and mingle with the aboriginal children.

'Indeed I heard about that, but it was in self-defence.'

'Self-defence? It was our men who were forced to defend themselves. The blacks can be vicious. I would not be surprised if the fire had not been started by one of their number.'

'I think not. The Aborigines light fires only for the benefit of nature, to control the growth of the bush. You have it wrong. And you must know it was the convicts who started the attack. It was the natives who were merely defending themselves.'

Unable to justify her own accusations Dorothy failed to respond directly. But she threw out a challenge to Emily.

'Then who is the culprit?

'I have no idea,' Emily replied, suspecting Dorothy knew more than she was intimating. 'But it is of so little importance, it matters not to me.' Determined not to be drawn into any speculation by Dorothy, Emily pushed open the door of the nursery and went inside. Fortunately the conversation had not been heard by Jessie who had started to take out the slates and chalks ready for the children to draw.

'Who can draw me a house?' she asked.

Emily smiled for the only houses the children knew were the huts they lived in. But she was surprised when one of them, a boy who was particularly talented, drew a larger building.

'What a lovely big house, Isaac,' she said. 'Who lives there?'

'The governor,' he replied.

'Well done,' she told the child. 'And why did you draw the governor's house?'

'One day I shall have a house like that one,' he replied, continuing to embellish his picture, not even lifting his eyes from the slate. Emily gave Jessie a knowing look. The child had high ambitions and she smiled to herself. That was the spirit. Inside she wished him well.

But the incident of the previous evening was still on her mind. More than anything she was relieved Jessie knew nothing about it despite Dorothy's tactless attempts to stir up more trouble.

It was time for the children to take a break outside and Jessie left the hut to be with them. Emily sat down inside and, as she did so, she felt her canvas bag beneath her feet. She slid her hand down to pick it up and felt the bundle of rags used as the blindfold and the tie. They must have slipped from her bag. She quickly grasped them and placed them on her knee before she picked up the bag.

It was then she had the first indication as to the culprit's identity. The blindfold, the gag and the tie were made from muslin. They were bandages.

Jimmy ran his finger inside the collar of his jacket. The sun was blazing down and the heat was building up inside his heavy, red tunic. He approached the wharf, and stared out to sea. The good ship *Surprize* leered ominously at him from the harbour. The journey home would be long, but it was one he must endure before his eventual return to the colony. He must return to England to fulfil the promises he had made in his letters to his mother, and to realise his eventual hopes and ambitions for a new life with Emily. He stared ahead. There was no going back on his decision.

But then he stopped suddenly, a look of surprise etching his face. Emily was there before him, her eyes brimming with love and adoration. He opened his arms and she ran to him. He felt the softness of her skin as she nestled into his embrace. It was a painful experience leaving her. But he remained strong. 'Emily, my precious, I did not expect you, for did we not say our farewells last night?'

'I had to see you once more before you depart for I find it hard to bear, Jimmy.'

'Time will pass. Once I have visited my mother in Scotland, I will make haste to return to you.'

'Believe me, I understand, Jimmy. How I wish I could come with you for it would please me greatly to visit my friends too. But I am not free and it is not to be.'

Jimmy produced a slip of paper from his pocket.

'I have the information you gave me. I promise I will search for the whereabouts of your good friends at the manor, especially the cook, Jemima Broadhead, and let her know we are to marry.'

'She will be delighted, I know that for sure,' she said, 'but I will miss you, Jimmy.'

Jimmy took her face in his hands, kissing her gently. 'God bless you and keep you safe,' he said, wanting to hold her close forever, to protect her.

But he knew common sense must prevail, and he climbed into the longboat. And now on board the *Surprize*, he leant against the barricade and focused his eyes on the wharf. Emily was still there, a speck in the distance.

More than ever determined to succeed, he was adamant he would return as a settler and make life easier for himself and his darling Emily.

Emily made her way back to the hut, the bright sunshine casting its glow on her face. But she had no feeling of warmth inside, not now that Jimmy was gone. She had missed him when he was away on Norfolk Island but since he had returned and they had agreed to wait for each other her feelings had intensified. She told herself there was nothing to be gained by becoming depressed. She must concentrate her thoughts on the positive aspects of her life, Lucy, her friends Jessie and Tilly, and her work at the nursery.

It was Sunday, their day of rest, and she set out with the others to the service to be delivered by the Reverend Johnson, for she must give thanks to the Lord for his mercies.

Tilly turned to her. 'It is sad that Jimmy has left, but you must remain hopeful, Emily, for he has promised to return. Many of the men on board the *Lady Juliana* made promises but the women are still waiting. I feel sure Jimmy will keep his promise.'

'I think you are right, Tilly, but that does not stop

me from fretting and thinking about him.'

'I know but I lost my George forever. You are the lucky one,' she said, her bright eyes moist. 'And Jessie and me are here to help you through.'

'I am grateful to you both. But I wish Nell could have been with us. She often made comments about Jimmy's affections towards me. And, as ever, I denied them. But she would have been proud to know that Jimmy and I are promised to each other.'

The Reverend Johnson, accompanied by his wife, arrived at the little church. Sober and sedate, Mistress Johnson sat at the front of the church clutching a prayer book in her hands, her plain, scrubbed face reflecting severity. Emily's gaze reverted to the reverend who took to the pulpit. She recalled his condescending attitude and his rancorous comments the last time he visited the nursery. What a lacklustre pair. But she checked herself, for it was unkind to judge them so.

The Honourable Reece Withers, the new surgeon, sat near the front with his back to her. He remained perfectly still and his head never turned despite the tedious sermon. Somehow Emily had the feeling he was embarrassed to face her. And in her mind one thing led to another. The bandages were the clue to the idea that now entered her mind.

She wanted to challenge the surgeon for she suspected he could have been the one who had bound and gagged her, but she controlled her urge and remained silent. What puzzled her most was the attempt to set fire to the nursery. Maybe he had wanted to punish her for the way she reacted towards him at the hospital, for he thought himself superior. But the fire did not seem like the work of an educated man. Surely it must have been someone with a lower mentality. What satisfaction would the surgeon derive from burning down the nursery?

It was several days later when a further clue emerged as to the identity of the arsonist, and this contradicted Emily's flimsy suspicion that the surgeon was the culprit. Jessie had been talking to some of the women at the door of the nursery when Emily joined her to greet the children. As she did so Dorothy came towards them limping. The other women turned to look at her.

'Been in the wars again,' Esther said. 'You want rid of that man of yours. Treats you bad, he does.'

'Shut your mouth. What is it to you? And who are you to talk? Your man's a coward.'

'You may think so,' Esther said, obviously not allowing the slur on her man to have any impact. 'You mean he would not hit a defenceless woman?'

Emily interjected. 'I beg of you. Do not argue in front of the children.'

Without a further word, Dorothy handed her child to Jessie and left the nursery. Esther turned to Kate.

'Works at the mortuary her man does, he looks after the dead,' she grimaced. 'That'll be where she will end up the way he abuses her,' she continued, pointing to the departing Dorothy. 'He is a bully and a thief. Steals blankets from the hospital and sells them on.' She turned to leave. 'Dorothy was fired up right enough about you taking in the blacks. She would have returned straight away with the bairn once she realised the nursery was her salvation. But he stopped her. He hates the blacks.'

She gave a heavy sigh and shook her head. 'You wouldn't catch me with a brute like him.' Her words faded away as she left the nursery.

When the women had departed, Emily was left pondering. If Dorothy's man worked at the mortuary, which was a part of the hospital, and he stole blankets, it would be just as easy for him to steal bandages too. And now she recollected whoever had come up behind her had an acrid smell about him. That was something she had forgotten. Had she thought it through sensibly she would have realised it was not the surgeon for he appeared to be scrupulously clean.

She had misjudged the situation. It was not Reece Withers after all. But, whilst she had no proof that Dorothy's man was the culprit, she was highly suspicious. If, as Esther had said, he was bitter about the blacks attending the nursery, it could have been his doing. She decided to take the matter no further. But in the future both Dorothy and her man needed to be watched.

Chapter 17

England and Scotland
1792

Clarendon did anything but settle once he boarded the ship. Although the cabin he had booked for the passage was supposedly superior to the rest, it was so small he felt claustrophobic each time he closed the door. Perhaps the captain had fooled him, telling him it was the first mate's cabin. Those fellows would do anything to get their hands on a few sovereigns. It was difficult trying to eke out his money. He was forced to pay the cook for extra food, for there was insufficient to meet his appetite.

But he had his priorities. He was not prepared to spend six months of his life journeying to the other side of the world without a woman in his bed. But that came relatively cheaply in the form of the willing little maid travelling with the Honourable Catherine Stewart. He would have liked to bed Catherine herself, of course, but he couldn't afford to become embroiled in another piece of scandal.

The main cargo was made up of stinking convicts. He could not abide their thieving and dishonesty and it was right they should be punished for such despicable behaviour. Clarendon was aware that, although the captain and crew, wherever and whenever they felt the urge, availed themselves of the services of the women, he would not degrade himself, especially after having been robbed of his sovereigns in Nottingham.

Clarendon sought more respectable company and he befriended Catherine Stewart. 'It surprises me that you are travelling alone,' he said, 'with only your maid as companion.'

'My father, Colonel Stewart, will meet me when we arrive in New South Wales,' she told him. 'He travelled to the colony with the first fleet, intending to return with the marines. But he decided to stay on and he promised to send for Mother and me as soon as he had a place for us. Unfortunately, Mother died of the fever six months ago,' she added, taking a lace handkerchief from her reticule and dabbing her eyes. 'That is why I am travelling alone.'

'I am saddened to hear that, my dear,' Clarendon said. 'But you need not feel alone, for I am here if you are in need of solace.' He smiled, knowing he could supply more than a little comfort, given the chance.

Once in Cape Town they disembarked and Clarendon escorted Catherine on a sight-seeing tour. 'You asked me why I was travelling to the colony, Lord Clarendon. But you did not mention the purpose of your journey.'

Clarendon was taken aback. He had told himself to take care, not to be too familiar with the lady for fear he became embroiled in personal matters.

But what he had not considered was that her father, Lord Stewart, may have known Samuel Clarendon. To be recognised as an imposter once he arrived at the colony was the last thing he wanted.

'My wife died some two years ago, and I found I could not get over my loss. We were devoted to each other. Everything I did, everywhere I went reminded me of her. I had to get away and I decided to start a new life out there in the colony.'

'You must indeed be sad, Lord Clarendon, but I am sure you have chosen the right path, despite the fact that you will never overcome your loss.'

Clarendon bowed his head as if his thoughts were with his dear wife, but unbeknown to the Honourable Catherine, he was laughing to himself. He had been smart enough to leave the lot of them behind and all he could think was 'good riddance!'.

His lesson had been learnt when he had met up with Ralphie de Mille. That must not happen again. He would continue his liaisons with Mary, for Catherine was unaware of the actions of her maid. But in the future he would cool his relationship with Catherine, for it was crucial that when he left the ship in New South Wales he should avoid a meeting with Lord Stewart.

It was less than two weeks after Jimmy had left for England when Emily was summoned to appear before the governor. With a strong feeling of unease inside on account of this request she set out for Government House. When she arrived she realised she was one of several who had been asked to attend, for the garden was buzzing with another twenty or so men and women who had gathered outside. She joined them. *Dear God*, she thought. *Please tell me I have done nothing wrong.*

Eventually, the governor appeared at the door, stepped outside and addressed them.

'You may be wondering why I have asked you to attend. Before I begin I wish you to understand you are not here to be reprimanded. The news is good.'

The little group sighed in unison, and Emily's anxiety quickly faded. Recognising most of the others for they had arrived with the first fleet she turned and smiled.

The governor continued. 'Some months ago I wrote to the Lord Justice in London advising him of my intention to offer ticket-of-leave status to those men and women who had proved to be good and honest citizens of this colony.'

He paused. 'Yesterday I received a missive from the justice department advising me of their full agreement to my proposal.'

He clasped his hands together and smiled. 'I am delighted to inform you that you good people gathered here today are amongst that number.'

There was a loud cheer from the little crowd and a clapping of hands. Emily held her breath. She could scarcely believe what the governor had said. And as his words penetrated her mind, her eyes shone with joy and a huge smile lit her face. At last she was free! Not through the pardon she had hoped for, but through good behaviour.

Oh, that she could have told Jimmy this wonderful news for now they could be married.

The governor raised his hands and the mumbling undercurrent ceased. 'Judge Collins is in attendance to ensure that everything within our plans is carried out within the letter of the law. I would ask you to wait outside and you will be called when we are ready to see you.'

Emily sat with the others on the grass awaiting the guard's instructions for her to enter the house. One of the governor's servants collected bunches of grapes from the governor's small vineyard and handed them out. The vines had been brought from the Cape with the first fleet and had grown successfully. Emily's mouth watered. Perhaps someday she would grow grapes in her own garden.

Some of the chosen few were summoned in groups, others individually. Amidst the hubbub of those milling around her, she looked up at the excited faces of those who had been called and were now leaving. But none passed on the governor's plans, for they dashed away immediately, obviously heading towards their loved ones.

It must have been an hour before her name was called. As she entered the governor's office, he looked up from his desk. 'Ah. Emily Spence. Do come in,' he said and he stood before her. 'In view of your good behaviour, it gives me great pleasure to offer you ticket-of-leave status.' He held out his hand to shake hers.

Emily stretched forward and tried to steady her hand which trembled slightly when she offered it to the governor. 'Thank you, sir,' she replied, releasing her hand.

He sat down at his desk and picked up a document to which he referred.

'I am truly delighted with your work at the nursery, as is Mistress O'Donnell. It has indeed been an asset your helping the good lady. Production in the gardens and in the workshops has increased since the women were able to leave their children in your capable hands.' He referred once more to the document. 'It is also pleasing that you and your group have had considerable success with the crops you have grown. You have proved to me that you have a caring spirit towards your fellows, and that you are capable of pursuing a business venture the likes of the garden plots. You are indeed the sort I wish to encourage here in New South Wales.'

He paused. 'Unfortunately, I have heard nothing from Sir William Brice. But do not give up hope. These things take time. Notwithstanding the absence of a pardon, I am sure you will appreciate your freedom.' He replaced the document on his desk.

Beside him, Judge Collins selected a manuscript in the form of a booklet from another pile. He turned over the page. The smile disappeared from his face, and his voice took on a serious note.

'In pursuance of the power and authority vested in the governor he does give and grant you and your heirs ten acres of land, to hold forever in one lot, free from all taxes, fees and rents for a term of ten years. Thereafter you shall pay an annual quit-rent of one shilling. All produce will be yours and you will be at liberty to sell to the government store, with the exception of such timber which may now be growing or may grow hereafter on the land and which may be deemed fit for naval purposes to be reserved for use of the Crown.' He looked up and replaced the manuscript on the desk.

The governor spoke up once more. 'I take it you still have workers tending the land.'

'Yes indeed, sir, two of them, Mistress Parkin and young Will Hopwood.'

'It may be that you will need extra workers. If that is the case, you are free to choose, provided you negotiate with the requisite authority before doing so. On the other hand, you may wish to use the land for some other purpose. Whatever you choose, you must inform one of my assistants accordingly.' He smiled. 'The land will be allocated within the next few days. I assume you will take up the offer.'

The shock of the news rendered Emily speechless and in the absence of a reaction the governor must have thought her slow-witted or ungrateful, for his smile changed to a look of gravity.

But, sensing he was about to comment further, she pulled herself up sharply and managed to speak. 'I do beg your pardon, sir, but I was so taken aback, I could not find the words to thank you and tell you what wonderful news this is. My dear friends and I will make every effort to continue our success.'

'Do not forget the land is yours. The others will have their reward when they have proved themselves model citizens of this colony as you have,' he said, standing up as an indication that he had finished the interview. 'Take with you my best wishes. We look forward to your plans for the land.'

Her eyes were bright with the tears of joy as she was leaving and she turned and said, 'I will cherish the land forever for it is all I have dreamt of, my own property, a place for my dear child Lucy and me.'

She left Government House to the sound of rejoicing. How could she ever thank the governor for his kindness?

She set off running towards the huts, her feet

skidding on the grass. But suddenly she stopped. What of the others? They had not received ticket-of-leave status. How could she celebrate when they had been ignored? Her eyes clouded over as she slowly advanced towards the open door of Jessie's hut. Jessie spotted her.

'What is it Emmy?' she asked, searching Emily's face, for her forehead was now crumpled into a heavy frown.

Emily held her breath. They must be told, but in a kind and gentle way.

'I do not know why I have been chosen but the governor has issued me with ticket-of-leave status, Jess. I am free.'

'How marvellous,' Jessie cried. 'You deserve it, Em. We would not have survived here without you.'

'Of course you would. We have worked together. But it is surely a stroke of luck.'

As they reached the door of the hut, Tilly came into view.

'And what may I ask is this stroke of luck?'

'Emmy has been sent for by the governor. She is a free woman, Tilly.'

'But that is no stroke of good luck,' Tilly stressed. 'There is no-one who has worked harder and been more loyal to the Crown that you, Em. Jess is right. You surely deserve it.'

'But why me and not you?' Emily asked.

'Our time will come. Jess is already making her mark at the nursery and I have not been at the colony long enough to establish myself yet. It will happen, I am sure of it.'

Their words of acceptance without question sent a

tingle of relief down Emily's spine.

'But that is not all. I am to be allocated ten acres of land which shall be mine for the rest of my life. And the land will pass on to Lucy as my successor.'

'That is something to be proud of, your own land,' Tilly said, and Emily detected a tinge of envy in her voice. But she knew there was no malice to it.

'It is indeed something to be proud of, Tilly. And the profit from the sale of the produce will be ours. The governor is aware that you and Will tend the land, and he has suggested we take on more workers.'

'He is right. We shall need extra help for I cannot see Will and me tending ten acres.'

'Do not worry for I have other plans which I would like to share with you. We shall use just part of the land to start. And what say we take on just one more worker to help with the produce? Hopefully, in time we shall make a profit. On the rest of the land I would like to introduce chickens and hens and eventually horses, that is when we have the means to buy them. What do you think?'

'Why horses, Em?'

'I would like to continue the family tradition in memory of my father. He worked all his life with horses, God bless his soul, and I would like Lucy to follow on at such time when I am unable to continue.'

'I understand, Em, and I hope you realise your wishes.' Tilly's eyes shone with excitement. 'If we bought hens it would mean we would have our own fresh eggs. We could buy a goat, too, Em. She would be of great use in clearing away some of the scrub before we start to cultivate another plot. A goat is just the animal to do that, and we would have our own fresh milk, too.'

'A splendid idea, Tilly. But first we need to know the cost of the stock and decide how much we shall need to save each time we sell to the government store.' She turned to Jessie. 'You are quiet, Jess. What do you think? Are you in agreement?'

'I am indeed. It is so exciting, and it is all because of you, Em.'

'Not so. The land will belong to me, but I would like us to have equal shares of the profit from our produce. We all work hard Jess and we all deserve to benefit.'

Within the week a surveyor arrived to check out the measurements, defining the extent of Emily's land. The thoughts of running her own business spurred her on and her enthusiasm was infectious for the little group worked harder than ever. The extra land they had plotted as an extension to the garden needed to be cleared of stones and stubble, but Emily was convinced they could easily achieve that for now they had the benefit of the newly acquired garden tools which had arrived on board the *Justinian*.

But they would not benefit from the goat Tilly had suggested they buy. That idea would have to wait. Emily had made enquiries and discovered a milk goat would cost eight pounds eight shillings. Laying hens were ten shillings each and chickens one shilling and sixpence.

'At ten shillings we could only afford to buy one hen and that would not be much use when there are four of us here, five including Will. Maybe we should wait until we can buy six. Perhaps we should buy six chickens to start. They will cost us nine shillings, cheaper than one laying hen. They will grow quickly and provided we can keep the wild dogs away we should soon have laying hens. What do you say?'

'I am disappointed at the cost of a milk goat. I was so looking forward to having our own supply of milk. But yes I agree we should invest in the chickens first, for as you say, one egg a day is not much use. And the goat will come later.' Tilly took the kettle from the hob and mashed the tea. 'It is all so exciting, Emily, I can barely wait for us to get started.'

'So it is,' Emily replied. 'It will be a challenge for us all. But I am sorry to say that it will be some considerable time before we have fresh milk from our own goat,' Emily told them, 'for eight pounds and eight shillings is not easily come by.'

'But at least it is something we can all look forward to for the future,' Tilly offered, 'And if we all work hard it shouldn't be long before we can invest in more.'

The passage to England seemed to last forever, even though it was a much shorter journey than Jimmy had encountered with the first fleet. But he was impetuous.

The sooner he reached Glasgow, saw his mother and dealt with his father, the sooner he could get down to some hard work at the docks. After that he had other business to attend to before he booked his ticket back to New South Wales. But that would not be for some considerable time for he needed to make sure he had enough money to pay for his passage and a decent amount to set up home with Emily. He was determined she would not live in poverty as she had since she left England. He would make her proud of him.

Sergeant MacVay bade them farewell as they stepped ashore at the docks in Glasgow. Obviously disappointed that Jimmy would not be joining them on their next expedition the sergeant shook his head and turned to leave. But then he made his final plea.

'We are to leave for India in two months' time. Think on. You might change your mind by that time, laddie. I hope to see you back again, Jimmy.'

But that would never be. Jimmy was determined. He had promised himself. And he must get on with the business at hand if he was to achieve his eventual goal.

The market square was empty as they approached and Jimmy slapped Sandy on the back as they went about their final farewells.

'Keep your nose clean, Sandy and who knows you may be promoted to corporal if you stick by Sergeant MacVay.'

'I hear what you say, Jimmy. Do you reckon you might come to India then? That would please me.'

'No, it is not possible. And you know why.'

'But I do hope to see you again sometime,' Sandy said, indicating his reluctance to leave his friend. 'If that is not possible I wish you Godspeed on your return.'

'Thank you Sandy. You have been a good friend

to me. Perhaps our paths will cross in the future. I do hope so.'

Feeling a similar loss but steeling himself to avoid a sentimental parting, Jimmy turned and once he reached the far corner of the market square he waved before setting off down the narrow streets beyond. He thought about what Sandy might encounter when he arrived home. How would his mother and father react? After all, like Jimmy, Sandy had run away to sea but he was a boy of only fourteen at the time. Now the lad was nineteen.

But here he was thinking about Sandy's predicament when he had his own parents to face, his mother at least. But he would no longer suffer the disgraceful behaviour of his father. Any trouble and he would oust the man, for Jimmy must be strong now for his mother's sake.

He reached Petyt Street and the familiar sight of his house. As he neared the front door he realised it was not so familiar after all. The door had been changed. Previously there were huge dents in the panels where his father had kicked it after returning home in a drunken state.

Perhaps his mother had moved? The only way he could find out was by turning the door knob and going in. He reached out to grasp it and the knob turned but the door was locked. Maybe his mother was out. Maybe as he had guessed, his father had forced her out to work. He turned to leave and was met by Flora Graham, a close neighbour.

'Jimmy lad, grand to see you back home again. Is your ma not in? I saw her only a few minutes ago in the back yard sweeping it clean. Go round. You'll catch her there.'

'Pa not about then?' he asked.

'Did you not know, laddie?' Flora folded her arms and stared as in disbelief. 'Your pa passed away more than two years ago. Better go round and see your ma. She'll surely have plenty to tell you.'

Passed away? Jimmy's first thought was 'good riddance'. But he must be careful not to convey that thought to his mother for he knew that, despite his father's temper and his abuse of her, she had loved him. He strode through the passage and round to the back yard, his heart thumping inside his chest as he gently pushed open the high gate. But there was no-one in the yard. He approached the back door, knocked, opened it and called out.

'Ma! It's me, Ma!' His voice seemed to echo through the whole of the house.

He heard heavy footsteps approaching. That was certainly not his ma. A giant of a man appeared in the doorway.

'And who might you be?' he asked, his tone surprisingly gentle for the size of the man.

'More to the point, who might you be? This is my house. It's me ma, Mary Ballantyne, I am looking for.' A feeling of resentment enveloped him.

The man held out his hand, grasped Jimmy's and shook it soundly.

'You must be Jimmy,' he said. 'Welcome home. Come let your ma have a look at you.'

Still Jimmy had no idea who the stranger was. But he was obviously a friend of hers. He followed the man into the living room and there she was, his lovely ma. He could not believe the transformation.

He had never thought of his ma as a young woman for she seemed always to be crying. And that was the image he had taken with him to New South Wales. But now she had changed so much.

'Jimmy, my boy Jimmy,' she cried, jumping up from her chair, tears springing to her eyes. 'I thought I would never see you again.' She pulled him close, hugged him and then she released him, studying him at arm's length. 'How you have grown!' She paused for a long moment. 'Your pa passed away, Jimmy, 1789. His heart, you know.'

There was no time for Jimmy to react for the stranger cleared his throat loudly, drawing attention to himself. Jimmy's mother turned and continued.

'Henry, my dear. I do beg your pardon. As you have guessed, this is my son, Jimmy.' She gestured to the stranger. 'Jimmy, meet your step-father, Henry Colvill. And before you say anything, he is very good to me,' she added taking the hand of her new husband. 'We were wed almost a year ago. Amy and Danny think the world of him.'

A sigh of relief issued from Jimmy's lips. His father gone and his mother happily settled with this kind man. That was how his mother had described Henry.

But Jimmy was determined to check that for himself. He wanted no more of the kind of abuse his father had given her. She looked happy enough though, and most of all young and beautiful, her rich auburn hair fastened into a topknot, her cheeks aglow.

His thoughts were disturbed when Amy and Danny ran through from the kitchen.

'My, my, Amy. How you have grown. Look at you, almost as big as Ma,' he said, catching the girl in his arms and laughing.

'Jimmy. Are you staying with us?' she asked jumping up and down excitedly. 'I hope so. Please say he can, Pa,' she added, directing her question to Henry.

Pa! That was an affectionate plea. It seemed his mother was right. The children did hold Henry in good light.

Henry smiled and nodded.

'It is Jimmy's house as well as ours my sweet. Of course he will be staying.'

Jimmy turned to Danny and grasped his hand.

'Looks as though I'd better watch my step,' he said, shaking the lad's hand vigorously.

'I am the one who needs to do that, Jimmy.' Danny laughed and released his hand, shaking it loosely and pulling a face as he did so. 'I only hope you haven't crushed me bones.'

Jimmy grinned and Amy joined in, obviously delighted to have Jimmy back home. But he must be very careful. His intentions to return to the colony to marry Emily would have to be broken gently. And he must decide how he would relate his story, for he was determined not to cast a bad light on Emily. She was not a convict and never had been. But still there would be a stigma attached to anyone out there. He would need to think it over and tell them when the time was right.

But that would have to wait until another day. For now he was home with his family and the new stepfather he was already beginning to like. At least he could return to the colony in the knowledge that his mother had found happiness at last.

'Hope you're more reliable than your pa, laddie. Killed hisself he did with the drink.' The manager at the dockyard stepped back.

'You should know, sir, I am nothing like my father,' Jimmy told the manager, an indignant edge to his voice. 'Did I not work here until I was sixteen?'

'Folks change when they get older. How am I to know how you are going to turn out? Your pa was a good 'un 'til the vice took him.'

'I have been half way around the world holding a responsible post with the Marine Corps. Is that not proof enough?'

'Then I'll take your word for it, Ballantyne. Tomorrow morning, five o'clock. Can you manage that?' The manager gave a sly grin and looked up at Jimmy who stood proudly, the full six feet four of him towering over him.

'I can manage anything you ask.'

The day Jimmy started at the docks brought back vivid memories, some amusing, like when the men played tricks on one another, others of the times when his father bullied him. But those latter memories made Jimmy feel sad and they were better forgotten. He remembered the hard graft, especially when he was a young lad and had to fetch and carry whatever the other men required. But now it was much easier. Jimmy towered above the majority of them and he could carry greater loads than most.

Gradually, after paying his mother a reasonable amount for his board and lodgings, he was able to build up his capital. He spent nothing on ale or any other vice but stayed at home with his mother and Henry for most of the time when he was not at work. And still he had not mentioned his return to the colony or his forthcoming marriage to Emily. Perhaps it would be better left until nearer the time of his departure, for his mother would only fret and try to persuade him not to leave her again, although the difference now was that she had Henry to give her comfort.

It was about two months after his return to Glasgow that he saw a familiar figure approaching him down at the docks. It was Sergeant MacVay.

Coming to try his luck again, no doubt, thought Jimmy. But he had no intention of changing his mind. He had put his plan into action now, and that was the end of it.

'Good morning to you, Corporal Ballantyne,' the good sergeant called out. 'I came to tell you that MacDonald has returned and he wondered if you might join us.' That was a cunning way to put it. More likely the sergeant had mentioned him to Sandy and put the words into his mouth.

'It is kind of you to come here and ask me again, Sergeant MacVay but my mind is made up. I shall definitely return to the colony for I have promised to marry Emily.'

'I can but ask, laddie. Good luck for the future. You will need it,' he said and strode away.

Now what did he mean by that? The passage was quite safe now that many more voyages had been made. The colony had appeared to be making progress when he left. Indeed there was no longer a struggle for survival. But then he remembered the New South Wales Corps, a set of lazy, undisciplined men who had little more experience in dealing with convicts than the convicts themselves. If that was all the sergeant was referring to he was sure the colony would survive, despite the reputation of the new guard.

When Jimmy arrived home that evening his mother was waiting for him, dabbing her red-rimmed eyes with a lace handkerchief.

'What is it, Ma?' Jimmy was full of concern, for the last time he had seen her cry was when his father had been around. 'Is it Henry? I hope he has not harmed you.'

'It is not about Henry, it is you, Jimmy.' Her shoulders began to shake once more.

'Me? But what have I done?'

'Why did you not tell me you were planning to go back to that hell-hole at the other side of the world? And who is this Emily? One of the convicts I presume.' The tears started to flow.

'Mother, please do not upset yourself so. I intended to tell you. But not yet, for here you are fretting already. It will be some time before I have enough money to buy my passage and provide for my dear Emily.' He knelt down beside his mother. 'You would like her very much, Mother, and when we are married I intend booking a passage back here and you shall meet her then.' He took a deep breath. 'Mother you are right. She was taken there as a convict. But she is no convict. She was set up.'

He decided not to mention the details surrounding Emily's past for his mother would be even more upset if she thought Emily had a child already. 'The governor has written to Sir William Brice and asked him to investigate the case. He is hoping she will be sent a pardon.'

'I shall never live it down, Jimmy. Marrying a convict. I would have thought you were worth more than that.'

'Mother you have not listened to a word I have said...' Jimmy was interrupted when Henry entered the room.

'Is there trouble, Mary? Why are you crying?' he asked, slipping his arm around Mary's shoulder and giving Jimmy a questioning look.

'It is nothing like you think, Henry. It is merely that Mother has been told of my plans for the future by someone from the docks. I cannot think who.'

'Flora Graham! Her lad told her last night.'

'Well I suppose I cannot blame the lad. Sergeant MacVay came to the docks to try and persuade me to leave for India with the Marine Corps, and I refused. I told him of my intentions to return to the colony. The lads must have been listening.'

Henry listened with interest.

'Jimmy is of age, Mary dear. He must be allowed to live his life. Now you see why he did not mention it to you. And he is not about to leave us yet. Come along, dearest, listen to what he tells you and help him realise his hopes and dreams.'

'Thank you, Henry for speaking up on my behalf. It is only because I know you are both happy together that I can return to the colony with some peace of mind. It was with dread that I returned, thinking that my father would still be abusing my mother. But now I have no worries. And I did promise Emily I would return for I love her so.'

'Then continue with your work at the docks for it is the only way you will make enough for your ticket. Your mother and I have a little put by from my business. It is a meagre amount for I do not make a large profit cobbling shoes but you are welcome to half of that, provided your mother agrees.'

'Henry, I would not take your money. You will need it when the time comes for you to retire. I am satisfied with the way I am saving. My wages are higher than most of the men for I can carry heavier loads.'

'Henry is right,' his mother interjected obviously now accepting the inevitable that Jimmy would be leaving once more. 'We can afford to give a little of our savings. I do not want you straining yourself carrying too much. If, as you say, you intend bringing the lassie back to see me, then take the money with our good wishes.'

'You worry too much, Ma. I am capable of carrying heavy loads. Leave me to it. And my savings are mounting nicely. I am determined to work until I have enough. But it may be some time yet.'

'Could you not work your ticket, Jimmy, and save the bulk of your savings for the little house you and Emily will share when you return?' Henry asked.

'That possibility had not crossed my mind. But you are right, Henry. Perhaps I could work my passage for I have had experience of two long voyages on board ship and I have done my share of work. When I returned from Norfolk Island I spent time watching the captain and the first mate making decisions and giving orders to the sailors. The idea is sound, if only I can manage to secure a berth and work my way back to the colony.'

Chapter 18

New South Wales
1792 – 1793

The year was almost at an end. It was November and Emily had heard that the governor would be leaving in December. This was disappointing news, and she was anxious to know who would replace a man so compassionate and just, always willing to help those in the colony who were prepared to work and live an honest, frugal life. It seemed to Emily he would be difficult to replace.

And now that she had been allocated the ten acre plot she was faced with a dilemma. It would not be viable to work a full day at the nursery when she was needed to work in the gardens and be there to negotiate prices when the man from the government store came to inspect the produce they had to offer.

The gardens were developing into the business she had hoped for and already they had bought chickens, hens and the goat Tilly had hankered after. Having scrimped together enough to buy two mares and a stallion, not of course of the highest pedigree, Emily reckoned it was a good start for she knew horses would be in great demand as the colony developed and free settlers began to arrive. Already one of the mares was in foal and the women were excitedly awaiting the delivery.

In line with Emily's suggestion Mistress O'Donnell had agreed that Jessie should take charge of the nursery in the mornings with the help of a young girl, Alice who was the daughter of one of the female convicts. Alice was coming up fifteen and Emily felt she had a caring nature. This meant that Emily could start her daily routine working in the garden until midday when the sun reached its zenith and attend the nursery in the afternoons when the weather was too hot for any of them to work outside.

That left Tilly, Will and the new boy, Alfred, to tend the garden. Most things had gone smoothly except that at the start they had problems with the wild dogs digging beneath the fences and squeezing under them to get at the chickens. Four of the chickens had already been killed and Will had been forced to lock up the coop at night.

'Should we dig deeper, Will? Surely the dogs will not try to tunnel underground,' Emily suggested.

'I am told they're not like the foxes back in England. Tunnelling is not in their nature and they do not climb fences to get at the animals. But they are much stronger than the foxes and they could break down fences if they were running in a pack. But I have put a stop to that by raising the height of all the fences and reinforcing them, the coops too.'

'You certainly know how to deal with the animals, Will. I'm proud of the way you've taken on the responsibility.'

Life was slowly improving for Emily, but only when she and Jimmy were together would it be perfect. He was constantly on her mind, and she had every faith that he would return to be with her.

She collected her thoughts. It was midday and time to finish her work in the garden. She wiped her damp brow with the back of her hand, took off her apron and set out for the house which was now a stouter, more stable structure built from timber. With a smile of satisfaction she looked ahead and had almost reached the house when the familiar figure of the governor appeared at the far side of the garden. It was not often he visited the gardens these days for so many things were happening elsewhere including the new barracks at Rose Hill, and the new storehouse. Emily knew it must be important for him to come personally.

'I thought I might find you here, Emily. I have good news.' He smiled. 'I have received a missive from Sir William Brice. You remember I asked you to be patient.'

Emily nodded and her stomach gave an almighty lurch. Good news from Sir William? Surely that could only mean one thing.

'You will be delighted to know that he has been successful in obtaining the King's pardon on your behalf. The others for whom I put in similar requests have not as yet been so fortunate. They are still awaiting a response.'

Emily thought she must be dreaming. She stood there stunned to silence. The governor laughed.

'I see you are lost for words, Emily. It is becoming a habit.'

'I cannot believe it, sir and I do not know how to thank you,' she cried. 'You have been so kind to me and I shall sorely miss you when you leave the colony. I hope you are replaced by some other kind and fair gentleman.'

'I do not know about that, my dear,' he said, and it

appeared to Emily there must be some dilemma in choosing his successor for surely the governor himself would have been informed. But he quickly steered the conversation to the purpose of his visit. 'I must leave you now. I realise you have many questions you wish to ask but they must wait until this afternoon for I have several visits to carry out this morning. I would like you to come to Government House before you attend the nursery. Mistress O'Donnell is aware that I am calling upon you – she knows not the purpose of my visit for I wanted you to be the first to know. There are things we need to discuss and it is important that we speak together. But I must now be on my way.'

He turned to leave, inspecting the crops as he passed by and nodding his head in satisfaction as he exchanged a few words with Tilly.

Emily couldn't believe it. Everything was happening at once. It was not long since the governor had given her ticket-of-leave status, and now this. But she felt she could never celebrate fully, not whilst Jessie and Tilly were still complying with the convicts' rules and hours of labour. It was yet another predicament. She had mentioned the possibility of ticket-of-leave status to both Tilly and Jessie, hoping it would not be long before they became free citizens and now here she was with yet more good news for herself in the form of a full pardon.

Tilly approached her before she left for Government House.

'The governor has such kind words for us. I dread to think who might replace him.'

'It is a problem, Tilly for we have no indication as to who will be the next governor. Governor Phillip appears not to know himself. It is said that those on Norfolk Island have complained vigorously about the disagreeable Commandant Ross who replaced the kindly Lieutenant King. Let us hope we are blessed with someone like him rather than the unpleasant Ross.'

'I agree, Em,' she said as she turned to pick up her spade. 'But why did the governor come here this morning? He rarely visits these days. Was it something important?'

Emily swallowed hard. She may as well get the news over with.

'It was indeed, Tilly. I have something to tell you and it has made me exceedingly happy. The governor has heard from Sir William. I am to be given a full pardon.'

'What wonderful news, Em. Has the governor told you how it came about?'

'He has asked me to go to Government House this afternoon before I attend the nursery. I shall find out then.' Emily saw a look of delight in Tilly's eyes.

'There is nothing you deserve more, Emily. Remember when we were in Durham and you told me you were innocent?'

'I do indeed, Tilly.'

'At first I thought you were like the rest of us, denying your crime, but I soon realised I was wrong in my assumption.'

'Thank you my dear friend. Let us hope your time will come soon, Jessie's too.'

The governor was waiting for Emily when she arrived. 'Do come in Emily and sit down. I would like you to listen carefully.' He pointed to a chair at the other side of his desk.

'Sir William has surpassed himself in checking your story. He obtained many statements from the servants working at the manor, and indeed from Lord Percy himself, who at first refuted the allegation. But eventually, after listening to all the evidence, he accepted his son's guilt.'

He paused and sighed, shaking his head. 'But you will realise the aristocracy are not likely to be flung into gaol on the whim of the justice, not if they can establish a means, be it honest or otherwise, by which they can be vindicated.' The governor glanced at the document before him, and then he continued. 'It is believed Lord Percy paid the constables for their silence. He agreed to deal with the matter in his own way, whatever that might be. There were no further proceedings.'

'I am not vindictive, sir. If Lord Percy has accepted my story and I am now free, that will suffice. It matters not to me whether Allenby is punished further or not. Perhaps he has a conscience.'

'I realise you have no wish to punish him further, Emily for you are such a kind-hearted girl. But the way Sir William described Lord Percy's son, the brute possesses no conscience and would not stoop to acknowledge the shame of his deeds.' He folded his arms on the desk. 'But that is not the end of it for included with the missive from Sir William is a document for you.'

He passed the document over to Emily. 'Please do read it, my dear.'

'It is for me?' she said, staring at the document, her wide eyes almost in disbelief. She opened the folded sheet and read aloud.

To Emily Spence

I was indeed sad to hear of your misfortune. I have been advised of the birth of your daughter and it is my desire that her future be secure. With that in mind, I enclose a promissory note for two thousand guineas which I hope and pray will provide for the child. I do sincerely hope that this matter is now at an end, and I wish you and your daughter every success for the future.

Signed and sealed this fifteenth of May 1792 Lord Percy Allenby

'But this is acknowledgement that the child is his granddaughter and, as for the money, he must keep it. I want nothing of it.' Hot blood surged to her face. How dare the man patronise her?

'Read it again more carefully,' the governor urged, 'for you will note that there is no admission of his son's guilt or of any parentage within the letter. And if I may say so you are being exceedingly foolish. What have you to lose by accepting the money? Your pride maybe? But what have you to gain?'

The governor rested his elbows on his desk.

'The way you have set out to make plans for your future with the small plot I granted is a great achievement. With the money from Lord Percy you could set up whatever business you wished to secure a prosperous and happy future for your child. Think of the child, Emily. She is the one Lord Percy wishes to protect.'

'I do not accept charity, sir. We have worked hard for the small success we have made at our little farm. Why could not Lucy be happy there?'

'Of course she would be happy there. But what of the future? If you agree to accept the money I will grant you a substantial amount of land alongside the Hawkesbury River. You deserve that to compensate for the ordeal you have encountered. It would be an even greater challenge. I realise you have friends at the farm working with you but there is no reason why you cannot place tenants on the new plot until you have decided how you will proceed.'

'I will think it over and let you know on the morrow. I am grateful for your help and kindness, sir, but you will appreciate I need to discuss the matter with my friends.'

'That is a fair comment Emily and one I would have expected you to make. But there is something else I wish you to know before you leave. I am telling you this in the greatest of confidence. I would not wish it to go further, not even to the people it concerns.'

Emily was puzzled.

'I can keep a confidence, Governor Phillip. You have my word I will not repeat whatever you tell me to a single soul.'

'You are aware I shall be leaving the colony next month. It is not clear who will take my place and I am sorely disappointed the name of my successor has not been forthcoming. In view of this I shall announce a second group of men and women to be issued with ticket-of-leave status. Two of your friends, those currently working at your farm, are amongst that number, for they too must be rewarded for their industry and their honesty.'

The governor pondered. 'Hopefully, I shall receive the justice department's agreement when the next ship arrives in the harbour, which will give me very little time before I depart from the colony on that same ship. Should the agreement not be to hand at that time, I shall nevertheless go ahead and make an announcement. It is for certain the confirmation will be received in the very near future.'

Emily became a little alarmed. Was she hearing it right? 'Who exactly are you meaning, Governor Phillip, for the two who work on the farm are William Hopwood and Matilda Parkin? I would have thought Jessica Martin would have been more deserving than William for she has done wonderful work at the nursery.'

'Those are the two I was meaning, Parkin and Martin, for the young boy still needs guidance and more experience before he is ready to be left to his own devices.'

'I beg you, sir, not to misinterpret my words for I am indeed proud of the way Will has handled responsibility. But as you say, he is still rather young to fend for himself.'

'I am pleased you agree. I shall send for the women before I leave for England but until such time I trust you to uphold the promise you made.'

'This is marvellous news. And I promise I shall

not tell a soul. My lips are sealed.'

Emily's heart throbbed in her chest for now all three of them would be free. Oh, that Nell could have witnessed this for she would surely have been freed too.

When the governor made the announcement and the news finally reached the two, Tilly's face was etched in smiles.

'I cannot believe it, Em. I thought Jess may have been lucky, but me too!'

'You have both worked hard, and I see no reason why you should not both be rewarded.' Emily sat down and folded her arms. 'We must plan for the future now that I have acquired the land near the Hawkesbury River. I have decided to take Governor Phillips' advice and set up business there.'

Emily smiled and continued. 'We have had unexpected success with the horses and I have it in mind to build a stable on the land for the purpose of breeding. Lucy has grown very fond of the horses – I think she must take after my father,' she said, laughing, 'and now that she is getting older, it is time to consider her future.'

'But what of us if you move to the Hawkesbury district?' Jessie asked, frowning.

'I would like to leave both you and Tilly in charge of the farm here at Sydney Cove,' Emily replied. 'You, Jess have built up a splendid reputation at the nursery and Mistress O'Donnell is indeed very fond of you. I suggest you continue there and help Tilly here at the farm whenever you can spare the time. Now that you are working as a free citizen, you will be allowed to make your own decisions and be paid a reasonable wage for your labours.'

Emily turned to Tilly. 'What say you take care of the land for me, rent free, and run the farm as you have been doing? You have the experience now. The profit will be yours to do with whatever you think fit. You will need to pay Will and young Alfred, and share some of the profit with Jess to make her wages from the nursery equal with yours'

Tilly was quick to interject. 'We are grateful for your kindness but we could not take up your offer, Em.'

'Tilly is right in what she says.' Jessie agreed.

'What say we do as you say with half the profit and pay you the other half? I am sure Jess will agree with me.' Tilly looked to Jessie for her agreement.

'Yes, I am in favour of your suggestion, Tilly.' Jess turned to Emily. 'Please take into consideration Emily that now we are free citizens we have a huge challenge ahead of us. Whilst I am grateful for your offer, I would like to continue my efforts and be responsible for my own future.' She leant across and took Emily's hands in hers. 'We shall miss you but we realise you must plan for Lucy's future.'

'I understand your reasoning. Being independent is very important to us and I will abide by your wishes. But let us not be hasty. We shall see how it goes. I must say that since so many free settlers have arrived and there are obviously many to follow, the demand for produce will increase. Perhaps you would wish to take on more workers, Tilly. The decision is yours.'

'That may be necessary for since we bought the pigs and cows and increased the number of chickens, much of our time is taken up tending them.'

'Then I will leave you to work out your own strategy.'

When confirmation arrived from England Jessie and Tilly were issued with official ticket-of-leave status. They were awarded ten acres of land each at the Cove adjoining that belonging to Emily which meant they would need to take on even more workers to cover the extra twenty acres.

But Emily left them to make their own plans for she needed to concentrate on the new plot of land near the Hawkesbury River and the building of a new homestead. She was excited at the prospect and had decided to call it Ambledon Farm after the name of her village in Yorkshire, but her only regret was that Jimmy was not there to share this new experience. Although it was now coming up to two years since he had left the colony, Emily had never stopped thinking about him.

When she finally left Sydney Cove, she stressed to both Jessie and Tilly that should Jimmy return they must inform him immediately of her new farm up the Hawkesbury River. And she never gave up hope that someday they would be together.

By the middle of 1793 Emily walked proudly through the doorway of her new house which had been built of brick and tiles. It was sparsely furnished, not through lack of money but through the shortage of supplies. Each time ships entered the harbour at Sydney Cove the goods were quickly snapped up. There appeared to be some sort of monopoly by those who purchased the supplies.

Emily suspected the monopoly had its roots in the New South Wales Corps. But she had her own plans. There was a skilled carpenter now living at Rose Hill. He had been given ticket-of-leave status at the same time as Jessie and Tilly. Emily had invited him to the house to design the furniture she needed. And now she was awaiting delivery.

Before buying in stock for the stables, she needed to make sure everything was in place. The stables were spacious and built of wood with brick at the base. And there was enough money from Lucy's inheritance to buy well-pedigreed horses. Emily chose carefully, remembering what her father had told her when he worked at the manor.

Once the stock was delivered she realised she could not run the venture alone. She would need a strong and willing helper, someone reliable and trustworthy. It was Will Hopwood she chose.

'How dare you steal our good friend Will,' Tilly ventured sharply, but she was smiling all the while.

'I cannot allow you keep everything. There are plenty of men around for you to hire. Surely you can find another,' Emily replied, joining in the banter.

'But not of Will's class,' Jessie added, winking in Will's direction.

Will's face was now flushed with embarrassment. He sidled out of the door for he could take no more. The women laughed as they saw him disappear.

'He is so proud Tilly, and yet he is so humble. I am sure he will enjoy working at the farm with me.'

'I believe you are right for he has handled the horses well and is surely the best man for the task,'

Jessie said. 'But you will need more than one helper.'

'I have been thinking, Jess. Will is to be in charge of the stables and hopefully Governor Phillip's successor, Governor Grose, will recognise his efforts. I will take maybe two or three more convicts, men I can rely on. I am also considering hiring two of the natives to help.'

'Natives? You need to be careful. For if some of the hardened men find out, you may have trouble.'

'I realise that, but it is a chance I am willing to take.'

By the end of the year Emily was running a thriving business. And she had chosen well for Lucy loved the horses and she visited them each day with her mother. *Oh that Jimmy could be here*, Emily kept on thinking but it seemed either he would not or could not return. There must surely be something amiss for Emily had not received news of him since he had left the colony two years earlier.

Her decision to hire Aborigine labour proved to be a sound measure. Whilst horses were not native to the colony, having been introduced to New South Wales only when the first fleet arrived, the natives seemed somehow to understand the animals. The two boys Emily chose were about fifteen or sixteen years old and they were strong and helpful especially in assisting Will and Emily deliver the foals, for the two were quick to learn and Emily was delighted she had set them on.

But despite her constant optimism her spell of contentment was broken when one night three men came to the stables, attacked the native boys who slept outside, and set free some of the horses. One of the natives had a bad gash to his arm inflicted by an assailant as he was trying to fend the man off, and the other native had been bound and gagged with bandages. Emily's heart sank when she saw them. *Not Dorothy's husband, Frederick Bell yet again*, she thought. The assailants appeared to have no purpose other than to cause disruption to the farm, and according to the boys, the last man to leave had been kicked by a horse and had limped away leaving behind one of his shoes.

Emily was called from her bed by Will and together they rounded up the horses.

'Tomorrow at sun up I shall head for Sydney Cove, Will. You will take care of the farm whilst I am away. I am determined to confront the culprits. I have a fair idea who one of them might be.'

'But Emily, would it not be best if I went down to the Cove? You may be taking on a dangerous gang for according to the Aborigines there were three of them.'

'Do not worry for I know what I am about, and I shall take care.'

The next morning she set out on one of the mares and headed for the Cove, the shoe in her backpack. After the arson attack at the nursery more than two years earlier she had decided not to report Dorothy's husband, Frederick. But after yesterday's incident the bandages seemed to confirm her suspicions and she felt sure he must have been one of the assailants, and all because he had a grudge against the natives, and probably against Emily too since she had befriended them.

As she neared Sydney Cove she ignored the stares and the open mouths of the passers-by and she headed for the hospital. A woman riding astride a horse was certainly out of the ordinary and a sight with which they were not familiar.

The hospital loomed before her and she tethered the horse before boldly entering the building. The door to the corridor was open and there she saw the familiar figure of Surgeon Reece Withers attending one of his patients. He looked up and, spotting her standing there, he advanced towards her.

'Ah Mistress Spence, to what do we owe this pleasure?' he asked, a sarcastic edge to his voice. At least he had not resorted to insults.

'I wish to speak with Frederick Bell who works in the mortuary.'

'The mortuary? What do you want with the mortuary?'

'It is Bell I wish to speak with,' she repeated.

'But that is not possible my dear for he is sedated. I am about to apply surgery to his badly wounded leg. He has apparently been attacked by the natives.'

'By my horses more like,' Emily stressed, her words deliberate and clipped.

'Your horses?' The surgeon looked puzzled. He stroked his chin in contemplation and then he continued. 'Now it all makes sense and it explains the wounds. I thought it an unlikely story that he had been attacked by unprovoked natives. And the wounds appear not to be in keeping with those inflicted by the thrusting motion of a native spear.'

'I am sure they are not Mr Reece Withers,' she said, hoping to keep him sweet now that the true story was unfolding. 'He attacked my stable boys during the night. Unfortunately for him as he opened the stable doors in a malicious act to set free the horses one of them kicked him.' She slipped the shoe from her bag. 'I do believe this shoe belongs to him. It was left behind when my men took chase.'

'I will check his other one. If as you suspect it belongs to him I shall have the fellow reprimanded, you can rely on that. For I cannot abide liars.'

'That is very fair of you and I would be much obliged. I knew it was he who attacked for as with the fire at the nursery some years ago he left behind evidence. On each occasion he used bandages to bind and gag.'

'Bandages?' Reece Withers spun around and looked down the corridor at the man lying on the table. 'That is a disgrace, for bandages are always in short supply. I was aware that the stocks were depleted but I never suspected Frederick for why would he need bandages when he works in the mortuary?'

'Perhaps you should check the rest of your stock, sir. Maybe bandages are not the only items missing.'

'I will indeed. Thank you for bringing this matter to my notice. You can rest assured, the fellow will be punished.'

Some weeks later, after his wounds had healed, Emily heard that Frederick had been thrown into prison for the theft of goods from the hospital. As far as she was aware he had no knowledge that she had given evidence leading to his arrest.

It was on her next visit to Sydney Cove to buy feed for the horses that Emily came across Dorothy Bell wandering aimlessly about the streets.

'Dorothy,' she called. 'Are you all right?' She crossed the road and took the woman's arm. 'You look rather pale.'

'Emily,' Dorothy replied, her dull eyes now beginning to shine. 'It is good to see you. We have missed you at the nursery.'

'I have missed all the children too. But I am so busy with the farm and there is no time left for visiting.' Emily took in the sorrowful sight of Dorothy. 'You look sad, Dorothy. Why are you here? I thought you had work, sewing in one of the workshops.'

'So I have but I have been sickly for another child is due in a few months' time. It is unwanted too.' She bowed her head and mumbled. 'Frederick forced himself upon me and now he is back in prison for stealing blankets from the hospital.'

'And you are left to fend for yourself no doubt.' Emily felt the anger build up inside tinged with a spear of guilt that she had been responsible for Bell's arrest.

Tears sprang to Dorothy's eyes. 'That is true. It worries me so for when Frederick is released I want no more to do with him. He is nothing but trouble. But I do not know how I will manage?'

Emily paused. An idea came into her mind, one she felt sure would interest Dorothy.

'Are you able to cook and clean, Dorothy?'

'Indeed I am.'

'Then I will have a word with the trusty at the workshop and ask him to free you. How would you feel about working at my place? Now that my farm is growing, I am in need of help. There is a room you can share with your bairns and you will have no worries about Frederick when he is released. I will see to that.'

Dorothy took hold of Emily's hands. 'I cannot believe you are willing to take me in. There is nothing I would like more.' She wiped her eyes. 'Please forgive me for being spiteful when you were at the nursery.'

'That is in the past. Forget it. But there is one more thing you must promise me before I take you on, Dorothy. There are native Aborigines working at the farm. You must accept them as equals, otherwise I cannot employ you.'

'What happened before was Frederick's doing, Emily, believe me. I had nothing against the children or their parents for that matter.'

'Then leave it with me. I will arrange for your things to be moved to the farm, and I will send Will Hopwood to collect you on the morrow.'

Chapter 19

1793 – 1796

The *Gorgon* master's estimation turned out to be accurate for it was exactly five months and twenty five days before the ship sailed through the heads at Sydney Cove and into the harbour. Clarendon knew he would need to make representation to the acting governor if he were to secure a land grant. He had heard that Governor Phillip had left and had been replaced on a temporary basis by the Commandant of the New South Wales Corps, Francis Grose.

He said his farewell to Catherine before he reached the upper deck and he took great care to avoid her before he stepped ashore. An introduction to her father, Lord Stewart, could prove difficult if the fellow knew Samuel Clarendon personally.

He staggered ashore for he was unused to carrying his own baggage. But he must put on a display of strength and confidence if he were to request a land grant from this tough, military man now acting governor of the colony.

It was much easier than Clarendon had ever expected for it seemed Grose kept no records of the men to whom land grants were allocated.

He had given out twenty-five acres apiece to the guards of the New South Wales Corps for the asking, and one hundred acres apiece to the officers.

Clarendon soon discovered too that Grose had replaced the magistrates with corps officers. That was good news for as far as Clarendon could gather those appointed as magistrates appeared to be a set of novices. If he were recognised by anyone in authority or rumours spread about his true identity the magistrates could either be duped or bought off.

He entered the governor's office. Grose looked up from his desk.

'I take it from my sergeant you have a request for land at the colony.'

'I have indeed, sir,' Clarendon replied, an obsequious tone to his voice.

'And what are your credentials?'

'My name is Clarendon, Lord Samuel Clarendon.' He stretched out his hand in invitation.

Grose stood up, reached out and shook it.

'Just the kind we need here in the colony,' he said, and after a little polite conversation, it was obvious Grose had never been acquainted with the real Lord Clarendon for there was no sign of suspicion.

'Tell me, what use will the land be put to? Do you favour arable land or pasture land?'

'I had in mind pasture, for it is my wish to set up a farm and rear domestic animals, mainly sheep. I have no interest in growing crops of any description.'

'Sheep you say? A good choice, Lord Clarendon. I think I know the ideal location. I could grant you five hundred acres of land that will convert to excellent pasture. If you would like to inspect it and you find it suitable I will draw up an agreement.'

The excitement grew inside him. Apart from the voyage which had rendered him sea-sick for most of the five and a half months, things were going well. Five hundred acres of land without so much as confirmation of his title, his reason for travelling to the colony or any promise of repayment was excellent news. Grose could not be faulted. And now he was offering four convicts to work for him provided he paid them fairly of course. It seemed Grose had taken him at face value. He acted the gentleman and he was a gentleman.

And of course what does a gentleman need? He needs a housekeeper. He laughed to himself as he thought of all those women lined up in their Sunday best ready and willing to serve. And service is exactly what he needed. But why choose any slovenly wench when he had his pick of the bunch.

He spotted her immediately. Kitty O'Brien was her name, a spirited minx if ever he saw one, with huge blue eyes and jet black hair streaming loosely down her back. What a brilliant spark of luck meeting Francis Grose.

His fellow Officer William Paterson who followed in Grose's shoes turned out to be even more pliable than Clarendon could have wished. It was probably on account of the fact that they truly believed him to be Lord Samuel Clarendon. Whatever happened he must keep up the pretence. There was no going back.

Clarendon became involved in their devious practices too. And why not? The good old New South Wales Corps, now nicknamed The Rum Corps on account of what some may called their dishonest dealings, had enforced the monopoly on many of the consumer goods arriving in Sydney Harbour on supply ships, the main one being rum which was the true currency. Clarendon wormed his way in, collaborating closely with the officers of the Corps. To his joy he was allowed to participate and he invested most of his profits from the rum he sold in more land and more stock.

He surveyed his land. He now possessed a thousand acres and five thousand head of sheep. He rubbed his hands together. This allowed him to maintain exclusive control over prices, and he was criticised for putting at risk the fate of the emancipist farmers who possessed only a small acreage of land and virtually no power.

But why should they have power? After all they were mere convicts and should know their place.

When Governor Paterson left, Governor Hunter, who was not of their ilk, took up office. Clarendon realised more care would be needed in his dealings, although it was clear that the new governor had little control over the Rum Corps.

Life was still good, better than he ever expected. He wrote neither to his father nor to his wife. What was the point? His whereabouts must remain a secret especially now that his farm was running successfully. And when he took on the vivacious convict woman Kitty O'Brien as his housekeeper she was of course housekeeper in name only. Her many extra duties included her presence in his bed. And he had no complaints there.

Unfortunately Lord Clarendon was unaware that Kitty was playing along with his little game. She was a bitter woman for her husband Shamus had been killed in Ireland whilst rebelling against the English. And it was during the uprising that her home had been set alight. She had been captured and thrown into prison by the king's men. She remained there for more than a year until one day she was dragged from the prison, thrown aboard a ship and transported to the colony. But her campaign continued.

Lord Clarendon was a member of the English aristocracy, one of the king's men and as such he must eventually be punished.

But she knew she must bide her time before she sought retribution.

Jimmy stepped on board the *Marquis Cornwallis*. He had been told by one of the shipping masters at the Glasgow port that the ship would sail to New South Wales the following week after taking on board Irish convicts.

'I wish to speak with the master,' he said to an eager-faced cabin boy. 'Is he aboard?'

'Not today sir,' the lad said. 'But I have heard he will be here on the morrow.'

'I will be back,' Jimmy replied.

It had been well over two years since Jimmy had arrived in Glasgow and set about working at the docks to make enough money to return to the colony, and by that time his superior physical strength had been recognised by one of the bosses. Jimmy became his assistant, his duties being to allocate tasks to the other men for he knew their individual capabilities. But still he continued to involve himself in the lifting and carrying, for Jimmy was not a man to stand around idle whilst supervising others.

He turned down Henry's offer of half his savings

to pay for his ticket, for he was determined not to be in another's debt. But now he felt sure he would have sufficient to set up home with Emily and Lucy especially if, as Henry suggested, he could persuade a ship's master he was capable of working his passage. Best of all he had no fears about his mother now that she had re-married. Henry was a kind and gentle man. And his mother finally admitted to Henry she must let Jimmy go.

By the time Jimmy caught up with the master of the *Marquis Cornwallis* it seemed it was too late to secure work on board the ship.

'Had you come yesterday, I would have been able to set you on provided you had the right experience. But today you are too late. When I was at the Acorn Inn last evening I met up with some of my old crew members and I set them on again.'

'I am indeed disappointed, sir, for I came along yesterday to be told you would not be back at the ship until today.' Not to be put off, he continued to press the master on his plan for supervision of the convicts. 'I take it the felons you are taking on board will be accompanied by guards.'

'Aye, lad, they will. I am taking on board a small number of soldiers who are travelling to the colony to join the New South Wales Corps. They will be well capable of the task.'

The master pondered momentarily. 'But since there are only three dozen or so I have made other arrangements also. I have decided some of my crew members will assist in controlling the convicts.'

'If I might say, sir, from my experience aboard the *Lady Penrhyn* with the first fleet, I discovered that some of these felons are indeed scoundrels and they will try all manner of ways to outwit the captain and crew. I do declare that political prisoners are not exactly scoundrels for they are not true convicts but they will be more devious than those being sent down for ordinary crimes, for most are bright and intelligent. Their plots will be well thought out.'

'Indeed. I have taken that into account.'

'But the felons must be allowed to exercise. Since the disaster of 1790 when the second fleet arrived at the colony with a cargo of dead and dying convicts the government has insisted that once the ship has set sail the convicts be given freedom of the upper deck at least twice a day. It could present problems for you, especially if the guard is not capable of full control,' Jimmy pointed out. 'Remember how Captain Bligh was forcibly marched off the *Bounty* and pushed into a longboat by his own mutinous men.' He paused. 'And they were seamen not convicts. Goodness knows what the outcome would be if these felons outsmarted your crew members.'

'The guards will be the ones in charge. My men will merely assist them. If they are well trained they will be conversant with the cunning ways of the felons. Surely they would not allow such a thing to happen?'

Jimmy suspected he had raised doubts in the captain's mind.

'Have you someone to take charge of the guards for these men have not had the training the marines were given?'

'Maybe not but I gather they are young, strong lads. That is why they were chosen.'

'If I might be so bold, sir, they will need a leader, someone who can make the right decisions. I took the King's shilling back in 1786. I spent four years under the iron discipline as a corporal in the marines. Since that time I have worked at the docks with many of the men there in my charge. I have both the discipline and the experience you need. I would be well capable of organising the guard and of controlling the felons.'

'I cannot deny the fact that you are an imposing figure,' the master replied, an obvious look of interest now developing. 'Tell me why are you returning to the colony?'

'I am returning to marry. It is almost three years since I left New South Wales for I had personal matters to attend to in Glasgow. I do believe that at twenty-seven I am well qualified to control the guards.'

'You mentioned the plight of Bligh and the power of his crew. I recall the incident well. But I run a good ship and I am certain my men will be loyal,' he said, placing his hand on his heavily creased forehead and staring ahead of him, 'although it does seem that your presence would be useful for there are one hundred and sixty eight male and seventy three female prisoners in all to be collected from Cove in Scotland.'

He sighed. 'I shall peruse the information I have received regarding the New South Wales guard and discuss it with the first mate. Come back this afternoon and I will give you my final decision.'

'So many convicts sir?' Jimmy gasped, determined to have the last word. 'It would worry me greatly if I thought there might be an uprising by such a huge number of convicts. They could easily overpower the crew and the guard if they were not handled carefully. That is the point I am making. They need support and understanding for they are men and women who have fought for their rights and have not been given a fair hearing. There is bound to be a great deal of resentment. I would like you to bear that in mind sir.'

'You could be right. Indeed I will take cognisance of what you say,' the master stressed as he turned and took the ladder to the quarterdeck.

Jimmy was sure he had been convincing enough. His opinion was based on common sense for he had heard that political prisoners had already caused much trouble in the Irish prisons.

Later in the day he called upon the master again.

'Have you made a decision, sir?' Jimmy enquired.

'In view of what you told me I have decided to take you on Ballantyne. Report to me on the morrow before noon. We are to sail to Cove to collect the convicts. We shall set out for the colony next week.'

Jimmy, delighted at the captain's decision, was tentative about breaking the news to his mother. As he had expected she was tearful.

'Mother dear, I promise I will return to Scotland with my wife once we are settled and have the money to pay for a passage.'

His mother nodded but still the tears streamed down her cheeks. Henry slipped his arm around her.

'Let the boy go, Mary. He has promised to return with his new wife. We have that to look forward to.'

Jimmy's heart was heavy as he waved goodbye to her but once the ship left the estuary and his mother had disappeared from view he knew he would see her again and that had a calming effect on him.

His thoughts turned to his dear Emily and the voyage to the colony. His heart began to beat more rapidly. No longer would she live in poverty. He would be there to provide for her. Whether she had gained her freedom or not, he would now be allowed to marry her for he was no longer a soldier.

It was August 1795 when the *Marquis Cornwallis* left Cove and set out for New South Wales. By early 1796, he would see Emily again.

Dorothy clutched hold of Margaret's hand as Will Hopwood swung the flatcart through the open gateway. He stopped, helped her down and led her to the back door. 'We are back, Em,' he called out.

Dorothy stepped inside.

'Emily, I cannot believe we are here,' she said a beaming smile etching her face. 'It is very generous of you to help me. You can be sure I will try my best to carry out your every wish.'

'Dorothy,' Emily implored, 'there is no need for such gratitude. I require help and you are available. That is all there is to it. Come, follow me and I will show you to your room.'

Once Dorothy had set down her belongings she went back into the kitchen where Emily was busy making a pot of tea. 'Something smells good,' she said as Emily pointed to the kitchen chair.

'Do sit down, Dorothy, and rest your legs.'

Emily poured the boiling water into the pot.

'How long is it since you had a cup of real tea Dorothy? Sometime I'll be bound.'

'Real tea? It is many a year. Not since I left London. Is that real tea?'

'It is,' Emily said placing a cup before her. 'Enjoy it.' She smiled to herself for Dorothy's reaction to the tea was similar to her own when she had taken her first sip.

Now that Dorothy was at the homestead with her, Emily decided she must keep her on a tight rein for in a moment of guilt Dorothy may panic and decide to return to Sydney Cove and Frederick.

'I know it has been hard for you to wrench yourself away from the Cove but, believe me Dorothy, Frederick will never change even though he may promise to do so when he leaves the prison.'

'But I am afraid he may come after me.'

'I doubt it for if he causes more trouble he is sure to be thrown into prison again.'

As time passed it seemed that Dorothy had taken heed of Emily's words for there was no more mention of him. She settled at the farm and was willing to do whatever she was asked, and more besides, for when her indoor work was finished she would take herself outside and offer to help in the yard.

It was on one such day when Dorothy was sweeping the front of the property that a rather handsome carriage rattled its way up the drive towards the house. The carriage stopped at the front and the young man looked out and cast a derisory glance in Dorothy's direction.

'Your mistress,' he demanded. 'Is she available?'

'Indeed she is, sir. Who shall I say is calling?'

'Lord Clarendon,' was his reply.

The man might have been royalty the way Dorothy backed away and entered the house.

'Emily,' she called excitedly. 'You have a visitor.'

'Who is it, Dorothy?'

'Lord Clarendon,' she replied.

'Lord Clarendon? A member of the aristocracy here? We are honoured.'

Emily went to the front of the house. As she opened the door the man stepped from the carriage. He was of robust build and splendidly dressed. But her eyes were fixed on his face and she was hardly able to tear her gaze away. She held her breath. Lord Clarendon he said. Without the slightest trace of doubt Emily knew exactly who he was. Realising she was staring she pulled herself up sharply.

'Lord Clarendon. Good morning, sir.'

'Good day to you Mistress...'

'Spence,' she said her face a solemn mask and disguising the fact that she knew the man.

Neither her name nor her appearance seemed to trigger any recognition and Emily had no intention of telling him. Not yet. *He is still the lecherous beast*, she thought as she watched him cast his eyes along the lines of her. Although he was slightly overweight, no doubt resulting from the high life he led, Emily was sure he had changed very little.

'Can I be of assistance?' she asked.

'I hear you have a fair stock of horses,' he replied. 'I have a farm further up river and I am interested in buying stock.'

'Will,' she called. 'Take Lord Clarendon to the

stables and show him around. Do excuse me,' she said, turning to Clarendon. 'I will be with you shortly,' she added needing time to compose herself after this ordeal.

She went inside and took several deep breaths realising the shock of seeing him had struck inertia within her. But she must take control and generate the confidence of which she knew she was capable. The sooner she was rid of him the better. She must find out as much as she could and try to expose him for the sham he was.

When she entered the stables Clarendon was looking at the recently delivered foals.

'Ah here you are, Mistress Spence,' he said and he pointed to one of the foals. 'This is the one I am interested in at the present time. But I am so impressed with your stock I should like to purchase several fully grown horses.' He turned to face her. 'Now madam, what is your price?'

'That is a most unusual request Lord Clarendon. I would normally sell only the foals. I shall need time to think the matter through for I prefer to keep my stock for breeding.'

'Then we shall need time together to discuss arrangements and sort out details. At my place perhaps?' he said a trifle too hopefully for Emily's liking.

'I would prefer to deal with this matter here at my own farm,' came her reply.

'Then your farm it is. But I must return to my place for I have other business to attend to today. I would like to call and make our final arrangements on the morrow if that is convenient. I will return about seven.'

'I look forward to it.'

The *Marquis Cornwallis* sailed through the gap and into Sydney Harbour. At last Jimmy was back where he belonged and ready to be re-united with his darling Emily.

The master paid him off.

'You were well worth employing Ballantyne,' he said. 'Think on. Should you wish to sail with me again you will be most welcome.'

'As I told you I have business in Sydney. I will not return to England for a long time. When I do I shall reserve a cabin and travel with my wife.'

He smiled to himself at the mention of his wife and collected his bag. He left the quay and wandered up the road towards Emily's hut. But as he drew nearer he realised that things had changed dramatically. He barely recognised the place. Although he had sent a letter telling her of his feelings and advising her he would be returning to the colony within the year she would not be expecting him at this moment in time. It would be a surprise.

In the distance he saw two people working in the gardens. He knew the one with the black hair would be Tilly. But the other was a man. It was not Will; he could tell that by the colour of his hair. Things must be looking up if Emily had been able to employ more people. As he drew nearer he noticed both the house and the gardens had been well extended. And there were pigs to the side of the hut and cows in one of the fields. Could they be

Emily's? If so she had done better than he had ever expected.

He opened the little gate and stepped on to the path leading to the door of the house which had been re-built and more elaborately styled with a balcony surrounding it. Jimmy was most agreeably surprised. He knocked at the door and turned the handle, excitement building inside him.

'Emily. It's me, Jimmy,' he called and he stepped inside, his heart pounding.

An inner door opened and Jessie came through.

'Jimmy,' she said, her eyes wide with surprise. 'How wonderful to see you again! Does Emily know you are back?'

'Not until you tell her,' he said, laughing. 'Although I did write and let her know of my intentions.'

'Then she will be waiting for you. I take it you know the way to the farm.'

'The farm? Surely this is the farm?'

'Not Emily's farm, not any longer.'

'But I wrote to her here. Did she not receive my letter?'

'No letter arrived here. We would have taken it to her at Ambledon.'

'Ambledon?' Jimmy's heart turned over in his chest. It seemed he was too late. He knew he should have written more often but he had spent all his time working hard to save for his return. She had obviously not received his latest letter.

'That's right, Ambledon.'

'Let us get this straight, Jess. You are telling me that Emily no longer lives here, that this is no longer her farm. Does that mean she is now wed?' His stomach began to churn. In sheer dread he stood waiting for Jessie's answer. He supposed it was a long time for Emily to wait for him. But he had feelings for no-one else and he had thought she had felt the same way.

Jessie looked puzzled and that made him even more anxious. 'Wed? Not yet,' she said teasing him, a knowing smile tipping the corners of her mouth.

'Not yet? But why is she not living with you, Jess?'

'There have been many changes since you left Jimmy. Em now lives at Ambledon Farm. But I think it would be best if she told you herself. Perhaps you would like Alfred to saddle you a horse. You could ride there. The farm is close to the Hawkesbury River at the mouth of the estuary.'

'Maybe you are right,' Jimmy said, his voice losing all enthusiasm. There must be some reason why she had moved away. If it was not another man, what was the reason?

Jessie interrupted his thoughts. 'I do beg pardon, Jimmy. It is most remiss of me not to offer you tea. Do sit down and I will put the kettle on.'

'Thank you kindly but I would prefer to do as you suggest and take a horse to Ambledon Farm for there have been so many changes I need to know what is happening.'

'Of course but it is not every day a good friend returns from England.' She turned towards the door. 'I will ask Alfred to saddle a horse for you,' she said, a look of disappointment on her face.

Minutes later the lad called out, 'Ebony is ready!'

Jimmy was unable to isolate one emotion from another as he set off in the direction of Ambledon Farm. First he had felt elation that he would be reunited with Emily but then he had felt anger that the letter had not arrived. But Jessie had confirmed that Emily was not yet wed. And that was good enough for him.

Chapter 20

1796

Emily decided to play the game with Clarendon. Although she had not formulated a plan in her mind as to her next move, she was certain she now had the strength and the confidence to put him in his place once and for all.

It was almost seven o'clock when he arrived at the homestead, a huge bunch of flowers in his arm.

'Planted and nurtured with my very own hands,' he said handing them over and taking Emily's hand in his. 'I am indeed delighted to have made your acquaintance,' he continued and he kissed the back of her hand gently.

Emily shuddered and her body became rigid but, realising her folly and not wishing him to suspect, she relaxed. It was important to determine why he was here in New South Wales, why he called himself Lord Clarendon and exactly where his farm was. There was obviously something he was trying to hide. Perhaps the name change was an act of desperation. Whatever the reason she felt certain he was unaware of her identity or that she was living here in the colony.

'Where exactly is your farm, Lord Clarendon? Is it nearby?'

'It is a fair distance away at Rose Hill; Rochester Farm is the name. Much of my land is roamed by sheep. That is why I am here. The best way to keep a track on them is on horseback. I have twelve convict men working at the farm. They help keep a check on the sheep but without horses I am unable to send them very far. My philosophy is to keep them working.' He laughed.

Emily could feel the anger bubbling inside her. How dare he make such a statement? Many of those transported as convicts had been forced into crime because of people like him. Many were innocent and, of those who were not, many had reformed. She decided she must change the subject before she came out with something she would later regret.

'Do you have natives working at the farm?' she enquired.

He laughed again. 'You jest, Mistress Spence. My men would kill them on sight.'

Emily controlled her fury. There must be something she could do to rid the colony of this despicable character. It was regrettable that Governor Phillip had left. He would have clapped the fellow in irons.

Emily had heard that Governor Hunter was encountering huge problems with the New South Wales Corps who were interested in their own gains rather than the needs of the people.

Hunter had little power and it was muted that parts of the constitution would need to be reconsidered, like the appointment of magistrates for instance, before the governor could revert to his true mission of devoting more time to the needs of the convicts and the emancipists. It was a well-known fact that Hunter had inherited governorship of a colony riddled with corruption.

'But the country truly belongs to them Lord Clarendon. This land is theirs.'

He smirked 'Theirs? What progress have they made I ask you?'

She was on a dangerous footing again for she had strong views on this matter too. But it was not the time to air them, and if she failed to take heed the debate would flare into something that at the present time was unnecessary. She smiled.

'Perhaps we might discuss the issue some other time. I have little time to spare at present.'

'Then down to business, Mistress Spence. I would like to point out the horses I am interested in buying.'

'Then you will need to come along to the stables and discuss the stock, Lord Clarendon.'

He arranged to buy five more horses from Emily. And she deliberately quoted highly inflated prices. But he seemed not to care. Perhaps he had so much money he could afford to spread it around.

Once the business agreement was settled Emily began to move away. 'Now if you will excuse me, Lord Clarendon, I have important work to finish.'

'Not so fast my dear,' he said advancing towards her. 'That is hardly the way to seal a business arrangement. Have I not agreed to pay dearly for the stock?' He took hold of her hand. 'I take it there is no master living here.'

'You are right to make that assumption,' she said coldly, 'but what of it?'

He reached out and slid his arm around her waist, pressing her up against the door.

'A little taste that is all. You cannot deny me that,' he said and pressed his lips on hers.

Emily lifted her knee and thrust it to his groin.

'A little taste? You have had more than a little taste, Allenby. Do not dare touch me,' she cried, her face resolute. 'You will never have your way with me again,' she continued not fully realising what she was revealing.

By this time he was doubled up in pain and he groaned loudly. Then slowly he lifted his head.

'My God woman! What ails you?' he muttered white-faced with shock, his eyes cold with contempt. And then realisation dawned for his narrow eyes widened, revealing the venom within them. 'It is you,' he said pointing his finger. 'You little bitch. I should have known.'

Emily recalled the evidence collected by Sir William Brice. Governor Phillip had explained to her that shortly after her arrest, Allenby had seduced a close family friend and put her in the family way. She was apparently rather a plain woman of aristocratic birth who was obviously besotted by him.

At the insistence of his father, Lord Percy, Allenby married the woman hastily. But when he was accused of gambling and running up huge debts he was unable to repay and he secretly left Grantley to establish himself elsewhere, promising to send for his wife and son later. But the coward had disappeared off the face of the earth never to be seen again. He had fled the country, unfortunately unaware Emily had been sent here many years earlier. Now Emily understood why.

'The truth is out. Maybe you should have known! But now you do, Richard Allenby,' she said, attempting to push him away.

But his body was too heavy and she felt the pressure as he pressed her harder against the door.

'You should have been burnt at the stake for what you did.' He took hold of her wrists and threw her to the floor thrusting himself on top of her. 'I believed you to be under the sod, you devious wench.'

Emily struggled but she knew she had no chance of pulling herself free. And then he slid his hands around her neck pressing his thumbs in her throat.

Blackness descended.

Jimmy drew the horse to a halt at the front of the homestead beside the carriage standing there. He dismounted, tethered the horse and quickly approached the door. He knocked once and then again loudly. But there was no reply. Surely there would be someone at home. After all, it was a working farm. And who did the carriage belong to? It was rather an ostentatious affair.

He decided to look around the back of the house. The yard there was empty and he was surprised to see so many stables. He wandered over and he could hear voices inside, a man's and a woman's. His heart stirred within him. He stepped a little closer. The woman's voice was certainly Emily's. Could she be talking to her new man? Had someone else entered her life?

He dodged into one of the stables and peered through to where they were standing, his eyes now filled with admiration. Within his peripheral view he saw the rich mocha glow of her hair caught up in a neat chignon at the back of her neck and the smooth lines of her russet gown. There was nothing fancy or frivolous about her and she had all the airs of a businesswoman. He listened intently.

His heart began to beat faster. He stepped outside and looked around the yard. He felt sure it was certainly more extensive than any place Emily may have been able to afford. Perhaps she had some contract with another. Perhaps it was too late and she had already promised to marry the man.

It was when he heard a loud groan coming from inside the stable followed by the cries of a woman that he dashed inside. Emily was on the floor her face ashen her lips turning blue. The man was pressing down on her, his hands around her throat, a look of disdain mantling his face. He looked up, jumped to his feet and, swerving to avoid Jimmy, quickly shot outside and disappeared.

Jimmy bent over Emily and lifted her hand.

'Emmy my darling! It is me, Jimmy,' he said as Dorothy came in from outside, a look of horror in her eyes.

'Fetch the surgeon,' Jimmy called out, 'and bring smelling salts.' Dorothy dashed from the stable.

Jimmy was startled when he heard a shot. Through the opening he saw the man levelling his musket. He fired and the ball appeared to find its mark as smoke issued from the weapon in his hand. With a strangled groan one of the natives fell and blood poured from his arm.

A faint almost inaudible cry focused Jimmy's attention back to Emily who was now moving her head from side to side. He squeezed her hands and smoothed her brow.

'I am here, my darling.'

'I cannot believe it is you, Jimmy. I thought you were gone forever.'

'You are safe now.'

He called to the woman and when he looked up she was standing before him wringing her hands and whimpering softly.

'I have sent Will to fetch the surgeon and here are the smelling salts,' she said dashing the tears from her cheeks. 'Forgive me for I did not hear the commotion, sir.'

'It is no fault of yours. Do not worry, for Emily has regained consciousness. But I still need the surgeon to take a look at her. Stay with her whilst I go outside.'

'But sir, the man has a musket. He is a madman.'

'I promise I will take care,' Jimmy assured her.

To the front of the homestead the man was climbing into his carriage and shouting irately at his driver to make haste. Jimmy started to run beside it but the carriage gathered excessive speed. He stopped and watched it rumbling along unsteadily. But the driver pushed the horses to their limit and, before disappearing from view one of the horses stumbled.

The carriage was now enveloped in a huge cloud of dust. As the dust settled Jimmy realised the carriage had overturned and the horses lay on the ground making strange noises.

Not far away the second native boy was tending to his wounded friend and Jimmy, realising he was not urgently required, set off at a rapid pace towards the scene of the accident. The carriage was on its side, the driver's head trapped beneath it. Jimmy assumed him to be dead for when he lifted the man's arm to check for signs of life it was limp. The passenger was sprawled across the side of the carriage, his legs trapped in the door, the blood from his head dripping on to the dusty road. There was little sign of breathing but somehow Jimmy guessed the man still to be alive. The surgeon would be needed but not until he had taken a look at Emily and confirmed she would survive. The horses were in obvious agony and needed to be put out of their misery.

Surgeon Underwood, who lived only a short distance away in the opposite direction, was already at the homestead when Jimmy returned. He was taking a look at Emily.

'Her throat is very badly bruised. Someone has tried to strangle her but has obviously not succeeded. The bruises will disappear after a time but she may have problems with her voice.'

'Thank the Good Lord she is still alive. The culprit is out yonder,' he said pointing through the window. 'I believe the driver of the carriage is dead. The passenger appears still to be alive. But before you tend to them please take a look at the native boy. He has been shot in the arm with a musket at fairly close range.'

'He will be lucky to keep the arm if that is the case.'

Jimmy followed the surgeon outside.

'Fortunately the arm is not as bad as I expected,' the surgeon explained 'There is much blood but the shot has merely grazed the skin. It is lucky for the lad the musket was badly aimed.' He looked ahead at the overturned carriage. 'I will come back and dress the wound but I must see to the occupants of the carriage first.'

Jimmy followed the surgeon who after a quick examination gave his verdict.

'You are right. The driver is already dead, killed instantly I would say. But the passenger is still alive. My carriage is needed.'

He walked to the stable block where his driver was waiting with the carriage. Minutes later it drew up beside the overturned one.

'Help me lift this man,' the surgeon said, 'for we must take him to the hospital.'

They struggled to lift Allenby into the carriage.

'He truly is heavy,' the surgeon admitted. 'No doubt used to the excesses of life,' he added with an air of disgust.

He went back to the two native boys and dressed the wound before collecting the musket from the ground.

'The horses must be slaughtered immediately,' he said standing back, taking aim and firing. He shook his head. 'A waste of good animals,' he added, 'but I had no alternative.'

The governor offered the captain of the *Marquis Cornwallis* a glass of the very best Scotch whiskey, brought in earlier that year on the *Anne*.

'I am desirous of putting an end to the devious practices of the Rum Corps here in the colony, of wiping out the corruption that exists. God knows why such a vile and wretched lot were sent here, for they have no keener morals than some of the convicts.'

'It seems to me that you need to appoint an officer in charge of issuing documentation to cover all imports. Records need to be kept, records of the port of origin and the destination of the goods.' The captain raised the glass to his lips and savoured the golden liquid. 'I know exactly who you could trust to carry out such a task.'

'You do? But you have not long arrived here.' The governor was puzzled by the captain's comment. 'And who might that be Captain?'

'I had on board with me a James Ballantyne who took charge of the Irish convicts I brought over. He was one of the marines of the first fleet. I begged him to stay on board when we arrived here at the colony but he had other ideas. Apparently some woman took his fancy when he was first here and now that he has returned as a settler. He wishes to marry her.'

'Perhaps I know the fellow if he travelled with the first fleet.'

'I doubt it Governor for he was merely a lad at the time. But now he is a man in his twenties and he is tall of stature with a certain presence, a way of dealing with the men without causing further problems. The fellow is a diplomat for it appears he understood them completely. And they had a great respect for him.'

'Where is Ballantyne at the present time?'

'I directed him to the house of a woman close to the harbour. Perhaps he has moved now but I am sure one of my men will know his whereabouts.'

'Then would you be kind enough to send a member of your crew in search of him for there is no-one here who would recognise him?'

'You will realise why I recommend him for the post when you see him Governor. I will send someone I can trust to search him out.'

The governor was influenced by the reports given to him and when the man himself arrived he was impressed by his physical presence.

'The captain of the *Marquis Cornwallis* tells me you arrived on board his ship and, moreover, that you did an excellent job with the Irish mob.'

'Thank you for the compliment, sir. But all they need is to be treated with civility and to be listened to.' Jimmy was puzzled as to why the governor had sent for him.

'There is a new appointment I wish to make, for I am anxious to stop the scheming practices of the Rum Corps. I wish to break their monopoly on consumer goods arriving here on supply ships. You have been recommended to me as being the man to take up that position. If you are interested we will work out a strategy together, a means of preventing these fraudulent tendencies.'

'I shall be honoured to serve you, Governor. But on whose recommendation am I here?'

'The captain of the *Marquis Cornwallis* alerted me to your arrival at the colony.'

'I must show my gratitude when next I see him. When would you wish me to start, sir?'

'As soon as it is possible Ballantyne, although I am aware that you have matters to attend to first.' He took out a sketchily drawn map from his desk. 'I will grant you land at the Cove,' he said pointing to a spot to the west of his own mansion and some little distance away from the quay.' He slipped the map back into the drawer at the front of his desk. 'See me on the morrow and we will discuss the matter more fully.'

Jimmy returned from his visit to see the governor and he told Emily of the appointment he had been offered.

'That is wonderful Jimmy. I do hope you agreed to accept it.'

He slipped his arm around her shoulders and drew him to her.

'I did indeed Em. But there are matters I need to discuss with you before I commence. The governor has given me a week to sort out my private affairs and then he will expect me to start.'

Emily drew herself up and gazed into his face.

'But what is there to sort out Jimmy?'

'Us, you and me, Em. I thought I had lost you, not once but twice.' Jimmy took her hand in his. 'How are you feeling now that the bruising is fading?' He kissed her on the forehead.

'I am fine now Jimmy, absolutely fine. I know you thought Allenby had killed me but what do you mean not once but twice?'

'When I returned to the colony Jessie was reluctant to tell me your good news. She thought it would be better if you told me yourself, that it would be a surprise. Not knowing you had been pardoned I suspected you had married, for I could not believe that you would be rich enough to own your own farm unless that was so.'

'So you believe I am not capable of such a venture without a man at my side,' she said, her squeaky laugh infectious.

'My darling Emily, I know very well what you are capable of.' The light from the window caught the sparkle in his eyes. 'But I am sure you would be even more capable with a loving husband at your side.'

Her blood began to race, her body tingling now with excitement. She felt as though she had been re-born. At last Jimmy was here with her. At last they were to marry.

'You are right my darling. It would truly make a difference if we were to marry.'

But then his face took on a serious hue. 'It will not be for some time Em, for there is a slight problem.'

Emily's heart sank. 'A problem? I am free to marry you. There cannot be a problem. Tell me. What is it Jimmy?'

'I could not expect you to take my hand in marriage unless I could equal the sum you have put into the farm. Until then I shall continue to save and add to that I have already earned.'

'But Jimmy, the farm belongs to Lucy not to me. I have bought it on her behalf. Her name is on the deeds. I am working merely to make the farm a success for her.'

'That makes no difference Em. You are living here and making a good life both for yourself and for Lucy. I cannot match that.'

'Why do you have to match it? You are too proud Jimmy Ballantyne.' She took his hands in hers.

'Now I suggest whatever modest sum I take from the farm in payment of my work here be added to that you have so carefully saved. That will be ours. But I shall continue to work for my daughter's future.' She drew him close and planted a kiss on his lips. 'And when you have the new appointment at the Cove perhaps you could take up Governor Hunter's offer of land there. We could build a house from our own savings. What do you say to that, Jimmy?'

'How would you be in a position to continue your work at the farm if you lived at the Cove?'

'Will is quite capable of running the place now that he has been with me for more than two years. He received ticket-of-leave status over a year ago. I would spend my time between the two places.'

Jimmy laughed. 'It seems I am unable to escape from the plot you are hatching. But will you not be bored at the Cove?'

'Has it occurred to you Jimmy Ballantyne that I may need to have time to myself time to rest, especially if we are to extend our family.'

Jimmy's face reddened.

'Extend our family? Emily Spence, I am surprised that you should allow such thoughts to enter your mind.'

He pulled her close. 'But you will have your way as always.' He kissed her gently on the mouth. 'Now,' he continued, 'let us away to see the governor and secure the land. I cannot wait to put the plan into action. Perhaps whilst we are down there we could visit the Reverend Johnson and ask him to set a date to marry us.'

'Then that is settled. But before we do Jimmy there is something I must do.'

The perfectly still eyes glared coldly ahead and the red face, aflame with bitterness and resentment, was a tightly gnarled mass. The slack mouth issued spittle from its corners. Emily stared down at him. She would not have wished this upon anyone, but the fault was his and his alone.

'What is to become of him? Will he recover?'

'There is nothing more I can do other than amputate the legs. After being crushed in the carriage door they are in an extremely bad state. But I would prefer to leave them a little longer for perhaps they may heal. Maybe in a week or so we can send the man home to recover.'

'Can he hear what we are saying?' she asked.

'It is believed he can, despite the damage to his brain. Nobody knows for certain. But I am convinced that the brain damage is permanent. I have never known a patient recover from the likes.' He turned to the man lying there. 'I am still unsure of his identity.'

'He is Lord Clarendon,' she said. 'Apparently he lives at Rochester Farm further up the Hawkesbury River.' She saw no reason to complicate the issue by revealing his true identity, for the man was obviously now incapable of causing her more harm. 'I have no further information surgeon. Perhaps I should go there and find out if there is someone to care for him when he returns to the farm.'

'I would be most obliged if you would, for we have had a further outbreak of dysentery and beds here at the hospital are urgently needed.'

Emily left the hospital and when she arrived back at Ambledon Farm Jimmy had returned.

'I am surprised you visited that scoundrel, Em. Have you not had enough trouble from him?'

'He will never cause me trouble again, Jimmy, for he is severely brain-damaged. He does not know who I am anymore.'

'Then what is the point?'

'I must help the surgeon all I can for he has been exceedingly kind to us. I do hope you will accompany me to Rochester Farm. There is little more the surgeon can do. He is hoping to send Clarendon back to his home in a week or so.'

'Clarendon, Em? Have you not told the surgeon that is his alias?'

'I cannot see the point Jimmy.'

Jimmy did not argue with her. He knew once her decision had been made it would not be worth trying to influence her to change it.

He agreed to accompany her to Rochester Farm and when the carriage drew up outside they were met by a young woman.

'Can I be of help?' she asked in a lilting Irish brogue.

'I would hope you can,' Emily replied. 'My name is Emily Spence. I have come about your master, Lord Clarendon.'

'But he has disappeared. I have not seen him for days.'

'He has been caught up in an accident. Perhaps we could come inside and explain,' Emily insisted, realising that the woman had been taken aback by the news and forgotten her manners.

'I do beg your pardon, Mistress Spence. Do come in. Would you take tea?'

'Thank you for asking but we are anxious to return to our own place as soon as possible.' Emily took off her gloves and continued. 'I take it you are Lord Clarendon's housekeeper. Is there a Lady Clarendon may I ask?'

The woman gave a wry smile.

'Indeed no,' she said. 'Not yet. I am his housekeeper, Kitty O'Brien.'

'Then I gather you will care for him when he returns from the hospital. I am afraid his carriage overturned and he sustained severe damage to his legs. Unfortunately he is unable to speak for he has brain damage too. Are you willing to take up this task?'

The woman was a dark-haired beauty, and Emily suspected she had been chosen for her looks.

Kitty hesitated before she replied. 'I am indeed. When will he return?'

'The surgeon has not yet decided. We will call again when we know more.'

Kitty showed them to the door and stood there until their carriage disappeared down the drive.

He could smell the scent of her. He could see the huge blue eyes peering into his. He could see the curl of her lip and the sneer on her face. The pain inside his head intensified. Kitty was leaning over him now seductively revealing the curve of her breast. The damned woman! But there was nothing he could do. He tried to bring his fingers closer but there was no movement and the turmoil within his brain continued. He tried once more. If only he could get his hands around her throat. Hot blood rushed to his face and now he could feel the spittle oozing from his mouth. Why was the stupid wench doing this? She was deliberately taunting him. Had he not treated her well?

At least he still had his legs. He had heard the surgeon telling someone they may have to be amputated. But he had been lucky this time. He moved his toes. That was good. He knew he had some feeling there. One day he would walk again. And then he would show them who was master.

The woman straightened up, moved towards the door and locked it. He relaxed. But then she started to take off her clothes slowly and deliberately, all the while maintaining eye contact. She was sneering at him again as she stood there naked. She tiptoed towards him.

'Touch me Sammy. Like you always do.' She smiled invitingly.

Touch her? She knew damned well that was impossible. His eyes reflected the venom that once more started to build up inside him.

'Dearie me, Sammy! You seem to have lost your spark. It is not like you to refuse.' Her laugh was raucous. 'Maybe you will do as *I* wish in the future,' she said pushing her face close to his once more.

A scarlet flush mantled his forehead and spread. His mouth fell open and, try as he might, no sound was forthcoming.

She laughed again. 'How would you like that

Clarendon?' she added and she danced before him.

The seething inside him continued. No matter how long it took he would continue to move his toes until one day he would get out of bed and confront her. He would be the winner – as always. He had never been beaten and he did not intend things to change now.

She dressed and moved over to the beautifully crafted cartonnier. He glared. That was the desk where he kept his private papers and valuables.

Turning the tiny key in the lock she opened the drawer at the top and slipped out a document. Sparks of fury shot to his brain. What was she doing rifling through his private papers?

'The farm, Sammy darling. Thank you kindly for signing it over to me,' she said, a wicked glint in her eye, before adding softly, 'I managed both the signature and the seal.' She placed the document back in the drawer and locked it away.

'You remember Captain Callaghan, the magistrate you were so friendly with. He and I are to marry. And since you are in no state to continue with the farm, nor are you ever likely to be, the Judge Advocate signed over responsibility to me,' she said patting the drawer of the cartonnier.

Allenby's anger intensified. If this continued, his head would burst.

'I do believe the captain has come to visit,' Kitty purred, moving over to the door and unlocking it. 'Ah, do come in, Captain Callaghan. Lord Clarendon is anxious to speak with you. He will be eternally grateful you have agreed to take me on. Of course you too will assist me and be responsible for the running of the farm, Thomas darling.'

She leant forward and he embraced her, kissing her for a long moment on the lips and fondling her. He moved towards the bed.

'Lord Clarendon, I am delighted to see you once more. Do not worry for the farm will be in good hands. Unfortunately I cannot allow my wife-to-be to attend to your needs. Once we are married she will wish to attend to my needs,' he said, his eyes sparkling as he touched Kitty in a familiar way. 'Dearest one, you have made alternative arrangements I gather?'

Would this torture never end?

'Indeed I have, my love,' she said once more opening the door. 'Dorcas,' she called out, 'do come in my dear and I will introduce you to the master.'

The master? Dammit! He was anything but the master. But once he gained control things would change drastically. He kept on moving his toes. If he kept this up it would not be long before he was fit enough to take over. But he must keep it to himself. No-one should know his secret until he was ready to pounce.

When he heard the door swing open a great beast of a woman swept into the room, her grey hair parted down the centre and pulled severely over her ears into a tight bun at the nape of her neck, accentuating her round, sterile features. He could not bear the sight of her and he had to look away. He squeezed his eyes shut.

'Lord Clarendon,' she said as she bent over him, the familiar smell of carbolic soap penetrating his nostrils. She pulled the sheet tightly over his shoulders. 'Now be a good boy.'

A good boy? Nobody called him a good boy except Nanny Coates. Surely it was not her. He had been both glad and relieved when he had reached that age when she could bully him no longer. But now this! He prayed to God he had been mistaken. Tentatively he opened his eyes slightly and peered through the slits. She slapped a noisy wet kiss on his cheek.

'He is responding already. We shall be fine together,' she concluded.

The screaming inside his head confirmed it. He had no doubts. It was Nanny Coates. Had she come back to haunt him?

'My application for a land grant has been approved,' Jimmy announced when he returned to the farm. 'I, or should I say we, now have a fifty acre plot some distance away from the harbour where the governor indicated, but close enough to travel each day.' He took her hands in his.

'That is wonderful news, Jimmy and, since the Reverend Johnson has agreed to marry us, we shall plan a quiet family wedding and invite our closest friends.' Emily's eyes were filled with delight.

'At last we are to wed my darling Emily,' Jimmy stressed leading her towards the stables.

Emily looked into his handsome face and was filled with excitement at the thought of their togetherness at last.

And then the whole of her life seemed to flash before her. Her mind was filled with the happy times she had spent with her mother and father at the manor, and of cook who had reassured Jimmy on his visit to the manor that Jacob and Anna had been buried together. Cook had wept with joy when Jimmy told her of his love for Emily and of their plans to marry one day.

Fleetingly, Emily thought about Allenby's abuse and his visit to her farm at Ambledon. But these thoughts perturbed her no longer, for she remembered Jimmy's intervention. She reached out for his other hand, pulling him towards her.

'And not before time,' she replied, standing on tip-toe and kissing him. 'I love you with all my heart,' she confessed, suddenly feeling that familiar tingle knowing her body was filled with longing for him. One more week to wait and then they would be husband and wife. She smiled up at him.

It had been a tortuous journey, sometimes seemingly endless. But now she was ready to face their new life together away from the edge of poverty and disrespect. She had fought for her dreams, and now she was back to her roots and the happiness she deserved.

Jimmy pulled her closer and kissed her soundly on the lips. 'I am surely the luckiest man alive. I thought it would never happen, but now we shall be together for the rest of our lives.'

Made in the USA
Charleston, SC
11 December 2015